'The pa[...] [...]ere is an excellent climax . . . If you want thrills, Deaver is your man'
Guardian

'Confirms his status as one of the finest crime writers in the world . . . grabs the reader by the throat from the b[...]
S[...]'
Inde[...]

'[...] is not just an adrenaline-c[...] [...]me of d[...]ption and multiple double[...] [...]ps the reader g[...]sing right up to the final pag[...]'
The Times

'L[...]er has created a real page-turner from start to finish'
Daily Mirror

'A[...] pic cat-and-mouse chase . . . the number of twists and returns fi[...] the apparently dead is astonishing'
Sunday Telegraph

'[...] of his trademark misdirections, bluffs and double-bluffs . . . It'll be snapped up and devoured by Deaver's legions of lo[...] fans'
News of the World

'De[...]er cleverly keeps the surprises up his sleeve until the very end[...]'
Daily Mail

'A h[...]d-spinning, clever cat-and-mouse tale that hurtles along at 10C[...] ph . . . Full of twists, turns, bluffs and double bluffs, it's an edg[...] f-the-seat read from beginning to end'
Sunday Express

'The[...] lot twists are sudden, dazzling and unexpected, and climax in a[...] reathtaking finale'
Scotsman

'In t[...]e past few months I have read several of Jeffery Deaver's com[...] ex thrillers and am fast becoming his greatest fan . . . Apart from[...] he nuts and bolts of this relentless pursuit . . . he also makes the[...] aaracters live and breathe . . . There are whole shoals of red he[...] gs which are intriguing as any of the mantraps and decoys se[...] .t by the hunters and the hunted. Read this and no country walk will ever be the same again'
Daily Express

Also by Jeffery Deaver

Mistress of Justice
The Lesson of Her Death
Praying for Sleep
Speaking in Tongues
A Maiden's Grave
The Devil's Teardrop
The Blue Nowhere
Garden of Beasts

The Rune series
Manhattan is my Beat
Death of a Blue Movie Star
Hard News

The Location Scout series
Shallow Graves
Bloody River Blues
Hell's Kitchen

The Lincoln Rhyme thrillers
The Bone Collector
The Coffin Dancer
The Empty Chair
The Stone Monkey
The Vanished Man
The Twelfth Card
The Cold Moon
The Broken Window

The Kathryn Dance thrillers
The Sleeping Doll
Roadside Crosses

Short stories
Twisted
More Twisted

The
BODIES LEFT BEHIND

Jeffery
DEAVER

HODDER

First published in the United States of America in 2008 by Simon & Schuster, Inc.
First published in Great Britain in 2009 by Hodder & Stoughton
An Hachette UK company

This Hodder paperback edition 2009

1

A CIP catalogue record for this title is available from the British Library

A format paperback ISBN 978 0 340 97789 7
B format paperback ISBN 978 0 340 99403 0

Typeset in Fairfield Light by
Palimpsest Book Production Limited, Grangemouth, Stirlingshire

Printed and bound by
Clays Ltd, St Ives plc

Hodder & Stoughton policy is to use papers that are natural, renewable and
recyclable products and made from wood grown in sustainable forests. The logging
and manufacturing processes are expected to conform to the environmental
regulations of the country of origin.

Hodder & Stoughton Ltd
338 Euston Road
London NW1 3BH

www.hodder.co.uk

For Robby Burroughs

The clearest way into the Universe is through a forest wilderness

– John Muir

I
APRIL

Silence.

The woods around Lake Mondac were as quiet as could be, a world of difference from the churning, chaotic city where the couple spent their weekdays.

Silence, broken only by an occasional a-hoo-ah of a distant bird, the hollow siren of a frog.

And now: another sound.

A shuffle of leaves, two impatient snaps of branch or twig.

Footsteps?

No, that couldn't be. The other vacation houses beside the lake were deserted on this cool Friday afternoon in April.

Emma Feldman, in her early thirties, set down her martini on the kitchen table, where she sat across from her husband. She tucked a strand of curly black hair behind her ear and walked to one of the grimy kitchen windows. She saw nothing but dense clusters of cedar, juniper and black spruce rising up a steep hill, whose rocks resembled cracked yellow bone.

Her husband lifted an eyebrow. 'What was it?'

She shrugged and returned to her chair. 'I don't know. Didn't see anything.'

Outside, silence again.

Emma, lean as any stark, white birch outside one of the many windows of the vacation house, shook off her blue jacket. She was wearing the matching skirt and a white blouse. Lawyer clothes. Hair in a bun. Lawyer hair. Stockings but shoeless.

Steven, turning his attention to the bar, had abandoned his jacket as well, and a wrinkly striped tie. The thirty-six-year-old, with a full head of unruly hair, was in a blue shirt and his belly protruded inexorably over the belt of his navy slacks. Emma didn't care; she thought he was cute and always would.

'And look what I got,' he said, nodding toward the upstairs guest room and unbagging a large bottle of pulpy organic vegetable juice. Their friend, visiting from Chicago this weekend, had been flirting with liquid diets lately, drinking the most disgusting things.

Emma read the ingredients and wrinkled her nose. 'It's all hers. I'll stick with vodka.'

'Why I love you.'

The house creaked, as it often did. The place was seventy-six years old. It featured an abundance of wood and a scarcity of steel and stone. The kitchen, where they stood, was angular and paneled in glowing yellow pine. The floor was lumpy. The colonial structure was one of three houses on this private road, each squatting on ten acres. It could be called lakefront property but only because the lake lapped at a rocky shore two hundred yards from the front door.

The house was plopped down in a small clearing on the east side of a substantial elevation. Midwest reserve kept people from labeling these hills 'mountains' here in Wisconsin, though it rose easily 700 or 800 feet into the air. Presently the big house was bathed in blue late-afternoon.

Emma gazed out at rippling Lake Mondac, far enough from the hill to catch some descending sun. Now, in early spring, the surrounding area was scruffy, reminding her of wet hackles rising from a guard dog's back. The house was much nicer than they could otherwise afford – they'd bought it through foreclosure – and she knew from the moment she'd seen it that this was the perfect vacation house.

Silence. . . .

The colonial also had a pretty colorful history.

The owner of a big meatpacking company in Chicago had built the place before World War Two. It was discovered years later that much of his fortune had come from selling black-market meat, circumventing the rationing system that limited foods here at home to make sure the troops were nourished. In 1956 the man's body was found floating in the lake; he was possibly the victim of veterans who'd had learned of his scheme and killed him, then searched the house, looking for the illicit cash he'd hidden here.

No ghosts figured in any version of the death, though Emma and Steven couldn't keep from embellishing. When guests were staying here they'd gleefully take note of who kept the bathroom lights on and who braved the dark after hearing the tales.

Two more snaps outside. Then a third.

Emma frowned. 'You hear that? Again, that sound. Outside.'

Steven glanced out the window. The breeze kicked up now and then. He turned back and finished making the cocktails.

Her eyes strayed to her briefcase.

'Caught that,' he said, chiding.

'What?'

'Don't even think about opening it.'

She laughed, though without much humor.

'Work-free weekend,' he said. 'We agreed.'

'And what's in there?' she asked, nodding at the backpack he carried in lieu of an attaché case. Emma was wrestling the lid off a jar of cocktail olives.

'Only two things of relevance, Your Honor: my le Carré novel and that bottle of Merlot I had at work. Shall I introduce the latter into evid . . .' Voice fading. He looked to the window, through which they could see a tangle of weeds and trees and branches and rocks the color of dinosaur bones.

Emma too glanced outside.

'*That* I heard,' he said. He refreshed his wife's martini. She dropped olives into both drinks.

'What was it?'

'Remember that bear?'

'He didn't come up to the house.' They tinked glasses and sipped clear liquor.

Steven said, 'You seem preoccupied. What's up? The union case?'

Research for a corporate acquisition had revealed some possible shenanigans within the lakefront workers' union in Milwaukee. The government had become involved and the acquisition was temporarily tabled, which nobody was very happy about.

But she said, 'This's something else. One of our clients makes car parts.'

'Right. Kenosha Auto. See, I do listen.'

She looked at her husband with an astonished glance. 'Well, the CEO, turns out, is an absolute prick.' She explained about a wrongful death case involving components of a hybrid car engine: a freak accident, a passenger electrocuted. 'The head of their R&D department . . . why, he *demanded* I return all the technical files. Imagine that.'

Wrinkling his nose, Steven said, 'I liked your other case better – that state representative's last will and testament . . . the sex stuff.'

'Shhhh,' she said, alarmed. 'Remember, I never said a word about it.'

'My lips are sealed.'

Emma speared an olive and ate it. 'And how was *your* day?'

Steven laughed. 'Please . . . I don't make enough to talk

about business after hours.' The Feldmans were a shining example of a blind date gone right, despite the odds. Emma, a U of W law school valedictorian, daughter of Milwaukee/Chicago money; Steven, a city college B.A. from the Brewline, intent on helping society. Their friends gave them six months, top; the Door County wedding, to which all those friends were invited, was exactly eight months after their first date.

Steven pulled a triangle of brie out of a shopping bag. Found crackers and opened them.

'Oh, okay. Just a little.'

Snap, snap . . .

Her husband frowned. Emma said, 'Honey, it's freaking me a little. That *was* footsteps.'

The three vacation houses here were eight or nine miles from the nearest shop or gas station and a little over a mile from the county highway, which was accessed via a strip of dirt poorly impersonating a road. Marquette State Park, the biggest in the Wisconsin system, swallowed most of the land in the area; Lake Mondac and these houses made up an enclave of private property.

Very private.

And very deserted.

Steven walked into the utility room, pulled aside the limp beige curtain and gazed past a cut-back crepe myrtle into the side yard. 'Nothing. I'm thinking we—'

Emma screamed.

'Honey, honey, honey!' her husband cried.

The face studied them through the back window. The man's head was covered with a stocking, though you could see crew-cut, blondish hair, a colorful tattoo on his neck. The eyes were halfway surprised to see people so close. He wore an olive-drab combat jacket. He knocked on the glass with one hand. In the other he was holding a shotgun, muzzle up. He was smiling eerily.

'Oh, God,' Emma whispered.

Steven pulled out his cell phone, flipped it open and punched numbers, telling her, 'I'll deal with him. Go lock the front door.'

Emma ran to the entryway, dropping her glass. The olives spun amid the dancing shards, picking up dust. Crying out, she heard the kitchen door splinter inward. She looked back and saw the intruder with the shotgun rip the phone from her husband's hand and shove him against the wall. A print of an old sepia landscape photograph crashed to the floor.

The front door too swung open. A second man, his head also covered with mesh, pushed inside. He had long dark hair, pressed close by the nylon. Taller and stockier than the first, he held a pistol. The black gun was small in his outsized hand. He pushed Emma into the kitchen, where the other man tossed him the cell phone. The bigger one stiffened at the pitch, but caught the phone one-handed. He seemed to grimace in irritation, from the juvenile toss, and dropped the phone in his pocket.

Steven said, 'Please . . . What do you . . .?' Voice quavering.

Emma looked away quickly. The less she saw, she was thinking, the better their chances to survive.

'Please,' Steven said, 'Please. You can take whatever you want. Just leave us. Please.'

Emma stared at the dark pistol in the taller man's hand. He wore a black leather jacket and boots. His were like the other man's, the kind soldiers wear.

Both men grew oblivious to the couple. They looked around the house.

Emma's husband continued, 'Look, you can have whatever you want. We've got a Mercedes outside. I'll get the keys. You—'

'Just, don't talk,' the taller man said, gesturing with the pistol.

'We have money. And credit cards. Debit card too. I'll give you the PIN.'

'What do you want?' Emma asked, crying.

'Shhh.'

Somewhere, in its ancient heart, the house creaked once more.

'A what?'

'Kinda a hang-up.'

'To nine-one-one?'

'Right. Just, somebody called and said, "This — " and then hung up.'

'Said what?'

'"This".' The word "this."'

'T-H-I-S?' Sheriff Tom Dahl asked. He was fifty-three years old, his skin smooth and freckled as an adolescent's. Hair red. He wore a tan uniform shirt that had fit much better when his wife had bought it for him two years ago.

'Yessir,' Todd Jackson answered, scratching his eyelid. 'And then it was hung up.'

'*Was* hung up or he hung it up? There's a difference.'

'I don't know. Oh, I see what you mean.'

Five twenty-two p.m., Friday, April 17. This was one of the more peaceful hours of the day in Kennesha County, Wisconsin. People tended to kill themselves and their fellow citizens, intentionally or by accident, either earlier in the day or later. Dahl knew the schedule as if it'd been printed; if you can't recognize the habits of your jurisdiction after fourteen years running a law enforcement agency, you have no business at the job.

Eight deputies were on duty in the Sheriff's Department, which was next to the courthouse and the city hall. The department was in an old building attached to a new one. The old being from the 1870s, the new from exactly one century later. The area of the building where Dahl and the others worked was mostly open-plan and filled with cubicles and desks. This was the new part. The officers in attendance – six men and two women – wore uniforms that ranged from starched as wood to old bed sheet, reflecting the tour starting hours.

'We're checking,' Jackson said. He too had infant skin, though that was unremarkable, considering he was half the sheriff's age.

'"This,"' Dahl mused. 'You hear from the lab?'

'Oh, 'bout that Wilkins thing?' Jackson picked at his stiff collar. 'Wasn't meth. Wasn't nothing.'

Even here, in Kennesha, a county with the sparse population of 34,021, meth was a terrible scourge. The users, tweakers, were ruthless, crazed and absolutely desperate to get the product; cookers felt exactly the same about the huge profits they made. More murders were attributed to meth than coke, heroin, pot and alcohol combined. And there were as many accidental deaths by scalding, burning and overdoses as murders related to the drug. A family of four had just died when their trailer burned down after the mother passed out while cooking a batch in her kitchen. She'd overdosed, Dahl speculated, after sampling some product fresh off the stovetop.

The sheriff's jaw tightened. 'Well, damn. Just goddamn. He's cooking it. We all know he's cooking. He's playing with us is what he's doing. And I'd like to arrest him just for that. Well, where did it come from, that nine-one-one call? Landline?'

'No, somebody's cell. That's what's taking some time.'

The E911 system, which Kennesha County had had for years, gave the dispatcher the location of the caller in an emergency. The E was for 'enhanced', not 'emergency', It worked with cell calls too, though tracing them was a little more complicated and in the hilly country around this portion of Wisconsin sometimes didn't work at all.

This . . .

A woman's voice called across the cluttered space, 'Todd, Com Center for you.'

The deputy headed to his cubicle. Dahl turned back to the wad of arrest reports he was correcting for English as much as for criminal procedure.

Jackson returned. He didn't sit down in either of the two office chairs. He hovered, which he did a lot. 'Okay, Sheriff. The nine-one-one call? It was from someplace around Lake Mondac.'

Creepy, Dahl thought. Never liked it up there. The lake squatted in the middle of Marquette State Park, also creepy. He'd run two rapes and two homicides there and in the last murder investigation they'd recovered only a minority of the victim's body. He glanced at the map on his wall. Nearest town was Clausen, six, seven miles from the lake. He didn't know the town well but assumed it was like a thousand others in Wisconsin: a gas station, a grocery store that sold as much beer as milk and a restaurant that was harder to find than the local meth cooker. 'They have houses there?'

'Around the lake? Think so.'

Dahl stared at the blue pebble of Lake Mondac on the map. It was surrounded by a small amount of private land, which was in turn engulfed by huge Marquette Park.

This . . .

Jackson said, 'And the campgrounds're closed till May.'

'Whose phone?'

'That we're still waiting on.' The young deputy had spiky

blond hair. All the rage. Dahl had worn a crew cut for nine-tenths of his life.

The sheriff had lost interest in the routine reports and in a beer bash in honor of one of their senior deputies' birthdays, an event that was supposed to commence in an hour at the Eagleton Tap, and which he had been looking forward to. He was thinking of last year when some guy – a registered sex offender, and a stupid one – picked up Johnny Ralston from grade school and the boy had the presence of mind to hit LAST CALL on his cell phone and slip it in his pocket as they drove around, the sicko asking him what kind of movies he liked. It took all of eight minutes to find them.

The miracle of modern electronics. God bless Edison. Or Marconi. Or Sprint.

Dahl stretched and massaged his leg near the leathery spot where a bullet had come and gone, not stinging much at the time and probably fired by one of his own men in the county's only bank robbery shootout in recent memory. 'Whatta you think, Todd? I don't think you say, "This is the number I want", to four-one-one. I think you say, "This is an emergency". To *nine*-one-one.'

'And then you pass out.'

'Or get shot or stabbed. And the line just went dead?'

'And Peggy tried calling back. But it went to voice mail. Direct. No ring.'

'And the message said?'

'Just "This is Steven. I'm not available." No last name. Peggy left a message to call her.'

'Boater on the lake?' Dahl speculated. 'Had a problem?'

'In this weather?' April in Wisconsin could be frigid; the temperatures tonight were predicted to dip into the high thirties.

Dahl shrugged. 'My boys went into water that'd scare off polar bears. And boaters're like golfers.'

'I don't golf.'

Another deputy called, 'Got a name, Todd.'

The young man produced a pen and notebook. Dahl couldn't tell where they came from. 'Go on.'

'Steven Feldman. Billing address for the phone is two one nine three Melbourne, Milwaukee.'

'So, a vacation house on Lake Mondac. Lawyer, doctor, not a beggarman. Run him,' the sheriff ordered. 'And what's the number of the phone?'

Dahl got the numbers from Jackson, who then returned again to his cubicle, where he'd look up the particulars on the federal and state databases. All the important ones: NCIC, VICAP, Wisconsin criminal records, Google.

Out the window the April sky was a rich blue like a girl's party dress. Dahl loved the air in this part of Wisconsin. Humboldt, the biggest town in Kennesha, had no more than 7000 vehicles spread out over many miles. The cement plant put some crap into the air but it was the only big industry the county had, so nobody complained except some local Environmental Protection Agency people and they didn't complain very loudly. You could see for miles.

Quarter to six now.

'"This,"' Dahl mused.

Jackson came back yet again. 'Well, here we go, Sheriff. Feldman works for the city. He's thirty-six. His wife, Emma's a lawyer. Hartigan, Reed, Soames and Carson. She's thirty-four.'

'Ha. Lawyer. I win.'

'No warrants or anything on either of them. Have two cars. Mercedes and a Cherokee. No children. They have a house there.'

'Where?'

'I mean Lake Mondac. Found the deed, no mortgage.'

'Owning and not owing? Well.' Dahl hit Redial for the fifth time. Straight to voice mail again. '*Hi, this is Steven. I'm not available—*'

Dahl didn't leave another message. He disconnected, let his thumb linger on the cradle, then removed it. Directory assistance had no listing for a Feldman in Mondac. He called the phone company's local Legal Affairs man.

'Jerry. Caughtya 'fore you left. Tom Dahl.'

'On my way out the door. Got a warrant? We looking for terrorists?'

'Ha. Just, can you tell me there's a landline for a house up in Lake Mondac?'

'Where?'

'About twenty miles north of here, twenty-five. House is number three Lake View.'

'That's a town? Lake Mondac?'

'Probably just unincorporated county.'

A moment later. 'Nope, no line. Us or anybody. Everybody uses their mobiles nowadays.'

'What would Ma Bell say?'

'Who?'

After they disconnected, Dahl looked at the note Jackson had given him. He called Steven Feldman's office, the Milwaukee Department of Social Services, but got a recording. He hung up. 'I'll try the wife. Law firms don't ever sleep. At least not ones with four names.'

A young woman, an assistant or secretary, answered and Dahl identified himself. Then said, 'We're trying to reach Mrs Feldman.'

The pause you always got, then: 'Is something wrong?'

'No. Just routine. We understand that she's at her vacation house at Lake Mondac.'

'That's right. Emma and her husband and a friend of hers from Chicago were driving up there after work. They were going for the weekend. Please, is anything wrong? Has there been an accident?'

In a voice with which he'd delivered news of fatal accidents and successful births Tom Dahl said, 'Nothing's wrong that we know of. I'd just like to get in touch with her. Could you give me her cell phone number?'

A pause.

'Tell you what. You don't know me. Call back the Kennesha County Center's main number and ask to speak to the sheriff. If it'd make you feel any better.'

'It would.'

He hung up and the phone buzzed one minute later.

'Wasn't sure she'd call,' he said to Jackson as he was picking up the handset.

He got Emma Feldman's mobile number from the assistant. Then he asked for the name and number of the friend driving up with them.

'She's a woman Emma used to work with. I don't know her name.'

Dahl told the assistant if Emma called in to have her get in touch with the Sheriff's Department. They hung up.

Emma's mobile went straight to voice mail too.

Dahl exhaled, '"This"', the way he'd let smoke ease from his lips up until seven years and four months ago. He made a decision. 'I'll sleep better. . . . Anybody on duty up that way?'

'Eric's the closest. Was checking out a GTA in Hobart that turned into a mistake. Oops, should've called the wife first, that sort of thing.'

'Eric, hmm.'

'Called in five minutes ago. Went for dinner in Boswich Falls.'

'Eric.'

'Nobody else within twenty miles. Usually isn't, up there, with the park closed and all, this time of year.'

Dahl looked out the interior window, over the cubicles of his deputies. Jimmy Barnes, the deputy whose birthday was tomorrow, was standing beside two co-workers, all of them laughing hard. The joke must've been pretty funny and it'd surely be told again and again that night.

The sheriff's eyes settled on an empty desk. He winced as he massaged his damaged thigh.

'How'd it go?'

'Joey's fine,' she said. 'He's just fine.'

Graham was in the kitchen, two skills on display, Brynn observed of her husband. He was getting the pasta going and he'd progressed with the new tile. About twenty square feet of kitchen floor were sealed off with yellow police line tape.

'Hi, Graham,' the boy called.

'Hey, young man. How you feeling?'

The lanky twelve-year-old, in cargo pants, windbreaker and black knit hat, held up his arm. 'Excellent.' He was nearly his mother's five foot five inch height and his round face was dusted with freckles, which hadn't come from Brynn, though he and his mother shared identical straight chestnut brown hair. His now protruded from under the watch cap.

'No sling? How're you going to get any sympathy from the girls?'

'Ha, ha.' Graham's stepson crinkled his nose at the comment about the opposite sex. The lean boy got a juice box from the fridge, poked the straw in and emptied the drink.

'Spaghetti tonight.'

'All-*right!*' The boy instantly forgot skateboard injuries and female classmates. He ran to the stairs, dodging books that were stacked on the lower steps, intended for putting away at some point.

'Hat!' Graham shouted. 'In the house. . . .'

The boy yanked the hat off and continued bounding upward.

'Take it easy,' Graham called. 'Your arm—'

'He's fine,' Brynn repeated, hanging her dark green jacket in the front closet, then returning to the kitchen. Midwest pretty. Her high cheekbones made her look a bit Native-American, though she was exclusively Norwegian-Irish and in roughly the proportion her name suggested: Kristen Brynn McKenzie. People sometimes thought that, especially with her shoulder-length hair pulled back taut, she was a retired ballet dancer who'd settled into a size-eight life with few regrets, though Brynn had never danced outside of a school or club in her life.

Her one concession to vanity was to pluck and peroxide her eyebrows to draw somewhat less attention to them; more long-term tactics were in the planning but so far none had been put into practice. If there was any imperfection it was her jaw, which, seen from straight on, was a bit crooked. Graham said it was charming and sexy. Brynn hated the flaw.

He now asked, 'His arm – it's not broken?'

'Nope. Just lost some skin. They bounce back, that age.' She glanced at the kettle. He made good pasta.

'That's a relief.' The kitchen was hot and six-foot three-inch Graham Boyd rolled his sleeves up, showing strong arms, and two small scars of his own. He wore a watch with much of the gold plate worn off. His only jewelry was his wedding band, scratched and dull. Much like Brynn's, nestled beside the engagement ring she'd had on her finger for exactly one month longer than she'd worn the band.

Graham opened cans of tomatoes. The Oxo's sharp round

blade split the lids decisively under his big hands. He turned down the flame. Onion was sizzling. 'Tired?'

'Some.'

She'd left the house at five-thirty. That was well before the day tour started, but she'd wanted to follow up at a trailer park, the site of a domestic dispute the afternoon before. Nobody'd been arrested and the couple had ended up remorseful, tearful and hugging. But Brynn wanted to make sure the excessive make-up on the woman's face wasn't concealing a bruise she didn't want the police to see.

Nope, Brynn had learned at six a.m.; she just wore a lot of Max Factor.

After the pre-dawn start she was planning to be home early – well, for her, at five, but she'd gotten a call from an EMS medical tech, a friend of hers. The woman began: 'Brynn, he's all right.'

Ten minutes later she was in the hospital with Joey.

She now puffed out her tan Sheriff's Department uniform blouse. 'I'm stinky.'

Graham consulted the triple shelves of cookbooks, about four dozen of them altogether. They were mostly Anna's, who'd brought them with her when she moved in after her medical treatments, but Graham had been browsing through them recently, as he'd taken over that household duty. His mother-in-law hadn't been well enough to cook, and Brynn? Well, it wasn't exactly one of her skills.

'Ouch. I forgot the cheese,' Graham said, rummaging futilely in the pantry. 'Can't believe it.' He turned back to the pot, and his thumb and forefinger ground oregano into dust.

'How was your day?' she asked.

He told her about an irrigation system gone mad, turned on prematurely April first then cracking in a dozen places in the freeze that surprised nobody but the owner, who'd returned home to find his backyard had done a Katrina.

'You're making headway.' She nodded at the tile.

'It's coming along. So. The punishment fit the crime?'

She frowned.

'Joey. The skateboard.'

'Oh, I told him he's off it for three days.'

Graham said nothing, concentrated on the sauce. Did that mean he thought she was too lenient? She said, 'Well, maybe more. I said we'll see.'

'They oughta outlaw those things,' he said. 'Going down railings? Jumping in the air? It's crazy.'

'He was just in the schoolyard. Those stairs there. The three stairs going down to the parking lot. All the kids do it, he said.'

'He has to wear that helmet. I see it here all the time.'

'That's true. He's going to. I talked to him about that too.'

Graham's eyes followed the boy's route to his room. 'Maybe I should have a word with him. Guy-to-guy thing.'

'I wouldn't worry about it. I don't want to overwhelm him. He got the message.'

Brynn got her own beer, drank half. Ate a handful of Wheat Thins. 'So. You going to your poker game tonight?'

'Thought I might.'

She nodded as she watched him roll meatballs with his large hands.

'Honey,' a voice called. 'How's our boy?'

'Hey, Mom.'

Anna, seventy-four, stood in the doorway, dressed nice, as usual. Today the outfit was a black pantsuit and gold shell. Her short 'do had been put in place by the hairdresser just yesterday. Thursday was her day at Style Cuts.

'Just a few scrapes, a few bruises.'

Graham said, 'He was skateboarding down stairs.'

'Oh, my.'

'Just a step or two,' Brynn corrected quickly, sipped the

beer. 'Everything's fine. He won't do it again. Nothing serious, really. We've all done things like that.'

Graham asked Anna, 'What'd *she* do when she was a kid?' Nodding at his wife.

'Oh, I've got stories.' But she told none of them.

'I'll take him paintballing or something,' Graham suggested. 'Channel some of that energy.'

'That'd be a good idea.'

Graham ripped up lettuce with his hands. 'Spaghetti okay, Anna?'

'Whatever you make'll be lovely.' Anna took the glass of Chardonnay her son-in-law poured for her.

Brynn watched her husband take plates from the cupboard. 'Think there's some dust on them? From the tiling?'

'I sealed it off with plastic. Took it down after I was done.'

He hesitated then rinsed them anyway.

'Can somebody take me over to Rita's tonight?' Anna asked, 'Megan's got to pick up her son. Just for an hour and a half or so. I promised to take over bathroom duty.'

'How's she doing?' Brynn asked.

'Not good.' Anna and her dear friend had been diagnosed around the same time. Anna's treatment had gone well, Rita's not.

'I'll take you,' Brynn told her mother. 'Sure. What time?'

'Sevenish.' Anna turned back to the family room, the heart of Brynn's small house on the outskirts of Humboldt. The nightly news was on. 'Lookit. Another bomb. Those people.'

The phone rang. Graham answered. 'Hi, Tom. How's it going?'

Brynn set the beer down. Looked at her husband, holding the phone in his large hand. 'Yeah, I saw it. Good game. You're calling for Brynn, I'm guessing. . . . Hold on. She's here.'

'The boss,' he whispered, offering the handset then turning back to dinner.

'Tom?'

The sheriff asked about Joey. She thought he was going to lecture her about skateboards too but he didn't. He was explaining about a situation up in Lake Mondac. She listened carefully, nodding.

'Need somebody to check it out. You're closer than anybody else, Brynn.'

'Eric?'

Graham lit a burner on the Kenmore stove. Blue sparks ascended.

'I'd rather it wasn't him. You know how he gets.'

Graham stirred the pot. It was mostly the contents of cans but he still stirred like he was blending hand-diced ingredients. In the family room a man's voice was replaced by Katie Couric's. Anna announced, 'That's more like it. What the news should be about.'

Brynn debated. Then she said, 'You owe me a half day, Tom. Give me the address.'

Which turned Graham's head.

Dahl put on another deputy, Todd Jackson, who gave directions. Brynn wrote.

She hung up. 'Might be a problem up at Lake Mondac.' She looked at the beer. Didn't drink anymore.

'Aw, baby,' Graham said.

'I'm sorry. I feel obligated. I left work early because of Joey.'

'But Tom didn't say that.'

She hesitated. 'No, he didn't. The thing is I'm closest.'

'I heard you mention Eric.'

'He's a problem. I told you about him.'

Eric Munce read *Soldier of Fortune* magazine, wore a second gun on his ankle like he was in downtown Detroit and would go prowling around for meth labs when he should have been breathalyzing DUIs and encouraging kids to get home by ten p.m.

From the doorway, Anna said, 'Should I call Rita?'

'I guess I can take you,' Graham said.

Brynn put a stopper on her beer bottle. 'Your poker game?'

Her husband paused, smiled, then said, 'It'll keep. Anyway, with Joey being hurt, better to stay here, keep an eye on him.'

She said, 'You guys eat. And leave the dishes. I'll clean up when I get back. It'll be an hour and a half is all.'

'Okay,' Graham said. And everybody knew he'd clean up.

She pulled on her leather jacket, lighter-weight than her Sheriff's Department parka. 'I'll call when I get up there. Let you know when I'll be back. Sorry about your game, Graham.'

'Bye,' he said, not looking back, as he eased the jackstraws of spaghetti into the boiling pot.

North of Humboldt the landscape is broken into bumpy rectangles of pastures, separated by benign fences, a few stone walls and hedgerows. The sun was sitting on the tops of the hills to the west and shone down on the landscape, making the milk cows and sheep glow like bright, bulky lawn decorations. Every few hundred yards signs lured tourists this way or that with the promise of handmade cheeses, nut rolls and nougat, syrup, soft drinks and pine furniture. A vineyard offered a tour. Brynn McKenzie, who enjoyed her wine and had lived in Wisconsin all her life, had never sampled anything local.

Then, eight miles out of town, the storybook vanished, just like that. Pine and oak ganged beside the road, which shrank from four lanes to two. Hills sprouted and soon the landscape was nothing but forest. A few buds were out but the leaf-bearing trees were still largely gray and black. Most of the pines were richly green but some parcels were dead, killed by acid rain or maybe blight.

Brynn recognized balsam fir, juniper, yew, spruce, hickory, some gnarly black willows and central casting's oak, maple and birch. Beneath the trees were congregations of sedge, thistle, ragweed and blackberry. Day lilies and crocuses had been tricked into awakening by the thaw that had murdered the plants in the yard of Graham's client.

Although married to a landscaper, she hadn't learned about local flora from her husband. That education came from her job. The rampant growth of meth labs in out-of-the-way parts of rural America meant that police officers who'd never done anything more challenging than pulling over drunk drivers now had to make drug raids out in the boondocks.

Brynn was one of the few deputies in the department who took the State Police tactical training refresher course outside of Madison every year. It included assault and arrest techniques, part of which involved learning about plants, which ones were dangerous, which were good for cover and which might actually save your life (even young hardwoods could stop bullets fired from close range).

As she drove, the Glock 9mm pistol was high on her hip, and while the Sheriff's Department Crown Victoria cruiser had plenty of room for accessories the configuration of bucket seat and seatbelt in this Honda kept the gun's rectangular slide bridling against her hipbone. There'd be a mark come morning. She shifted again and put on the radio. NPR, then country, then talk, then weather. She shut it off.

Oncoming trucks, oncoming pickups. But fewer and fewer of them and soon she had the road to herself. It now angled upward and she saw the evening star ahead of her. Hilltops grew craggy and bald with rock and she could see evidence of the lakes nearby: cattails, bog bean and silver and reed canary grass. A heron stood in a marsh, immobile, his beak, and gaze, aimed directly at her.

She shivered. The outside temperature was in the mid fifties but the scene was bleak and chilly.

Brynn flicked the Honda's lights on. Her cell phone rang. 'Hi, Tom.'

'Thanks again for doing this, Brynn.'

'Sure.'

'Had Todd check things out.' Dahl explained that he still couldn't get through on either of the couple's mobiles. As far as he knew the only people at the house were the Feldmans, Steven and Emma, and a woman from Chicago Emma used to work with, who was driving up with them.'

'Just the three of them?'

'That's what I heard. Now, there's nothing odd about Feldman. He works for the city. But the wife, Emma . . . get this. She's a lawyer at a big firm in Milwaukee. Seems that she might've uncovered some big scam as part of a case or a deal she was working on.'

'What kind?'

'I don't know the details. Just what a friend in Milwaukee PD tells me.'

'So she's maybe a witness or whistle-blower or something?'

'Could be.'

'And the call, the nine-one-one call – what'd he say exactly?'

'Just "this".'

She waited. 'I missed it. What?'

A chuckle. 'Who's on first? I mean he said the word "this". T-H-I-S.'

'That's all?'

'Yep.' Dahl then told her, 'But it could be a big deal, this case. Todd's been talking to the FBI in Milwaukee.'

'The Bureau's involved? Well. Any threats against her?'

'None they heard of. But my father always said those that threaten usually don't do. Those that do usually don't threaten.'

Brynn's stomach flipped – with apprehension, sure, but also with excitement. The most serious non-vehicular crime she'd run in the past month was an emotionally disturbed teenager with a baseball bat taking out plate glass windows in Southland Mall and terrorizing customers. It was a potential disaster but she'd defused it with a brief face-to-face, smiling at his mad eyes while her heart thudded just a few beats above normal.

'You watch yourself, Brynn. Check the place out from a distance. Don't go stumbling in. Anything looks funny, call it in and wait.'

'Sure.' Thinking: as a last resort maybe. Brynn snapped her phone shut and set it in the cup holder.

This reminded her she was thirsty – and hungry too. But she pushed the thought aside; four of the roadside restaurants she'd passed in the last ten miles were closed. She'd check out whatever was happening at Lake Mondac, then get home to Graham's spaghetti.

For some reason she thought of dinners with Keith. Her first husband had cooked too. In fact, he did most of the cooking in the evening, unless he was working second-shift tour.

She eased the accelerator down a bit harder, deciding that the difference in response between the Crown Vic and the Honda was as noticeable as that between fresh Idahos and instant potato buds out of a box.

Thinking, as she had been, about food.

'Well, boy, you got yourself shot.'

In a downstairs bedroom of the Feldman house, shades drawn, Hart was looking at the left sleeve of his brown flannel shirt, dark to start with but darker now halfway between wrist and elbow from the blood. His leather coat was on the floor. He slouched on the guest bed.

'Yep, lookit that.' Tugging his green stud earring, skinny Lewis finished making obvious, and irritating, observations and began to roll up Hart's cuff carefully.

The men had taken off their stocking masks and gloves.

'Just be careful what you touch,' Hart said, nodding at the other man's bare hands.

Lewis pointedly ignored the comment. '*That* was a surprise, Hart. Bitch blindsided us. Never saw *that* coming. So who the hell is she?'

'I don't really know, Lewis,' Hart said patiently, looking at his arm as the curtain of sleeve went up. 'How would I know?'

'*It'll be a piece of cake, Hart. Hardly any risk at all. The other places'll be vacant. And only the two of them up there. No rangers in the park and no cops for miles.*'

'*They have weapons?*'

'Are you kidding? They're city people. She's a lawyer, he's a social worker.'

Hart was in his early forties. He had a lengthy face. With the mask off, his hair came well below the bottom of his ears, which were close to the side of his head. He swept the black strands back but they didn't stay put very well. He favored hats and had a collection. Hats also took attention away from you. His skin was rough, not from youthful eruptions but simply because it was that way. Had always been.

He gazed at his forearm, purple and yellow around the black hole, from which oozed a trickle of blood. The slug had gone through muscle. An inch to the left, it would have missed completely; to the right the bullet would have shattered bone. Did that make him lucky or unlucky?

Speaking to himself as much as to Lewis, Hart said of the blood, 'Not pulsing out. Means it's not a major vein.' Then: 'Can you get some alcohol, a bar of soap and cloth for a bandage?'

'I guess.'

As the man loped off slowly, Hart wondered again why on earth anybody would have a bright red and blue tattoo of a Celtic cross tattooed on your neck.

From the bathroom Lewis called, 'No alcohol. Whisky in the bar, I saw.'

'Get vodka. Whisky smells too much. Can give you away. Don't forget your gloves.'

Did the thin man give an exasperated sigh?

A few minutes later Lewis returned with a bottle of vodka. True, the clear liquor didn't smell as much as the whisky but Hart could tell that Lewis had had himself a hit. He took the bottle in his gloved hands and poured the liquid on the wound. The pain was astonishing. 'Well,' he gasped, slumping forward. His eyes focused on a picture on the wall. He stared at it. A jumping fish, a fly in its mouth. Who'd buy something like that?

'Phew . . .'

'You're not going to faint, are you, man?' Lewis asked as if he didn't need this inconvenience too.

'Okay, okay. . . .' Hart's head dropped and his vision crinkled to black but then he breathed in deeply and came back around. He rubbed the Ivory soap over the wound.

'Why're you doing that?'

'Cauterizes it. Stops the bleeding.'

'No shit.'

Hart tested the arm. He could raise and lower it with some control and not too much pain. When he closed his fist, the grip was weak but at least it was functioning.

'Fucking bitch,' Lewis muttered.

Hart didn't waste much anger; he was more relieved than anything. What ended up being a shot arm had almost been a shot head.

He remembered standing in the kitchen, scratching his face through the stocking, when he'd looked up to see movement in front of him. It turned out, though, to be a reflection of the young woman moving up silently from *behind*, lifting the gun.

Hart had leapt aside just as she'd fired – not even aware he'd been hit – and spun around. She'd fled out the door as he'd let go with a couple of rounds from his Glock. Lewis, who'd been standing next to him – and would have been the next to die – had spun around too, dropping a bag of snacks he'd pilfered from the refrigerator.

Then they'd heard a series of cracks from outside and Hart knew she was shooting out the tires of both the Ford and the Mercedes so they couldn't pursue her.

'Got careless there,' Hart now said ominously.

Lewis looked at him like he was being blamed, which he was – the skinny man was supposed to be in the living room, not the kitchen, at the time. But Hart let it go.

'Think you hit her?' Lewis now asked.

'No.' Hart felt dizzy. He pressed the side of the Glock pistol against his forehead. The cold calmed him.

'Who the hell is she?' Lewis repeated.

That was answered when they found her purse in the living room, a little thing with make-up, cash and credit cards inside.

'Michelle,' Hart said, glancing at a Visa credit card. He looked up. 'Her name's Michelle.'

He'd just got shot by a Michelle.

Wincing, Hart now walked across the worn rug, dark tan, and shut off the living-room lights. He peered carefully out the door and into the front yard. No sign of her. Lewis started into the kitchen. 'I'll get those lights.'

'No, not there. Leave 'em on. Too many windows, no curtains. She could see you easy.'

'What're you, some wuss? Bitch is long gone.'

Grim-faced, Hart glanced down at his arm, meaning, you want to take the chance? Lewis got the point. They looked outside again, through the front windows, and saw nothing but a tangle of woods. No lights, no shapes moving in the dusk. He heard frogs and saw a couple of bats flying obstacle courses in the clear sky.

Lewis was saying, 'Wish I'd knew that soap trick. That's pretty slick. Me and my brother were in Green Bay one time. We weren't doing shit, just hanging, you know. I went to pee by the railroad tracks and this asshole jumped me. Had a box cutter. Got me from behind. Homeless prick. . . . Cut me down to the bone. I bled like a stuck pig.'

Hart was wondering, What's his point? He tried to tune the man out.

'Oh, I whaled on that dude, Hart. Didn't matter I was bleeding. He felt pain that day. Come off the worst of it, I'll tell you.'

Hart squeezed the wound and then stopped paying attention to the pain. It was still there but was lost in the background of sensations. Gripping his black gun, he stepped outside, crouching. No shots. No rustles from the bushes. Lewis joined him. 'Bitch's gone, I'm telling you. Ass's halfway to the highway by now.'

Hart looked over the cars, grimaced. 'Look at that.' Both the Feldmans' Mercedes and the Ford that Hart had stolen earlier in the day had two flats each and the wheel sizes were different; the spares wouldn't be compatible.

Lewis said, 'Shit. Well, better start hiking, you think?'

Hart scanned the deep woods surrounding them, shadowy now. He couldn't imagine a better place in the world to hide. Good goddamn. 'See if you can plug one of those.' He nodded at the Ford's shot-out tires.

Lewis sneered. 'I'm not a fucking mechanic.'

'I'd do it,' Hart said, trying to be patient, 'but I'm a little disadvantaged here.' He nodded at his arm.

The skinny man tugged at his earring, a green stone, and loped off resentfully toward the car. 'What're you going to be doing?'

What the hell did he think? With his Glock at his side, he started in the direction he'd seen Michelle flee.

Eight miles from Lake Mondac the landscape ranged from indifferent to hostile. No farms here; the country was forested and hilly, with forbidding sheer cliffs of cracked rocks.

Brynn McKenzie drove through Clausen, which amounted to a few gas stations, two of the three unbranded, a few stores – convenience, package and auto parts – and a junkyard. A sign pointed to a Subway but it was 3.2 miles away. She noted another sign, for hot sausages, in the window of a Quik Mart. She was tempted. But it was closed. Across the highway was a Tudor-style building with all the windows broken out and roof collapsed. It bore a prize that had surely tempted many a local teenager but the *All Girl Staff* sign was just too high or too well bolted to the wall to steal.

Then this sneeze of civilization was gone and Brynn began a long sweep through tree- and rock-filled wilderness, broken only by scruffy clearings. The few residences were set well off the road, trailers or bungalows, from which gray smoke eased skyward. The windows, glowing dimly, were like sleepy eyes. The land was too harsh for farms and the sparse populace would drive their rusted pickups or Datsun-era imports to work elsewhere. If they went to work at all.

For miles the only oncoming traffic: three cars, one truck. Nobody in her lane, ahead or behind.

At 6:40 she passed a sign saying that Marquette State Park campground was ten miles up the road. *Open May 20.* Which meant that Lake Mondac had to be nearby.

Then she saw:

Lake View Drive – Private Road

NO TRESPASSING
NO PUBLIC LAKE ACCESS

Violators Will Be Prosecuted

And howdy-do to you too . . .

She turned, slowing as the Honda bumbled over the gravel and dirt, thinking she should've taken Graham's pickup. According to the directions that Todd Jackson had given her, the distance was 1.2 miles from the county route to 3 Lake View, the Feldmans' vacation house. Their driveway, he'd added, was 'a couple football fields long. Or that's what it looked like on Yahoo.'

Making slow progress, Brynn drove through a tunnel of trees and bushes and blankets of leaf refuse. Mostly the landscape was naked branch and bark.

Then the road widened slightly and the willow, jack pine and hemlock on her right grew sparse; she could see the lake clearly. She'd never spent much time on bodies of water, didn't care for them. She felt more in control on dry land, for some reason. She and Keith had had a tradition of going to the Gulf Coast in Mississippi, his choice pretty much. Brynn had divided her time there between reading and taking Joey to amusement parks and the beach. Keith spent most of the time in the casino. It wasn't her favorite locale but at least the beige water lapping at the shoreline was as easygoing and warm as the locals. Lakes around here seemed bottomless and chill and the abrupt meeting of rocky shore and black water made you feel helpless, easy prey for snakes and leeches.

She reflected on another course she'd taken through the State Police: a water safety rescue seminar. It had been held at a lake just like this and though she'd done the exercise – swimming underwater to rescue a 'drowning' dummy in a sunken boat – she'd hated the experience.

She now scanned the surroundings, looking for boaters in trouble, car accidents, fires.

For intruders too.

There was still enough light to navigate by and she shut the lights out so as not to announce her presence. And drove even more slowly to keep the crunch of the tires to a minimum.

She passed the first two houses on the private road. They were dark and set at the end of long driveways winding through the woods. Large structures – four, five bedrooms – they were old, impressive, somber. There was a bleakness about the properties. Like sets in the opening scene of a family drama: the homestead boarded up, the story to be told in flashbacks to happier days.

Brynn's own bungalow, which she'd bought after Keith bought her share of their marital house, would have fit inside either of these and still have left it half empty.

As the Honda crawled along, she passed a small bald patch between copses of fir, spruce and more hemlock, giving her a partial view of the house at number 3 – the Feldmans' – ahead and to her left. It was grander than the others, though of the same style. Smoke trailed from the chimney. The windows were mostly dark, though she could see a glow behind shades or curtains in the back and on the second floor.

She drove on toward the house and it was lost to sight

behind a large copse of pine. Her hand reached down and for reassurance tapped the grip of her Glock, not a superstitious gesture, but one she'd learned long ago: you had to know the exact position of your weapon in case you needed to draw it fast. Brynn recalled that she'd loaded the boxy black weapon with fresh ammo last week – thirteen rounds, which wasn't superstitious either but more than enough for whatever she'd run into in Kennesha County. Besides, it took all your thumb strength to jam the slick brass rounds into the clip.

Tom Dahl wanted his deputies on the range for a check-up once a month but Brynn went every two weeks. It was a rarely used but vital skill, she believed, and blew through a couple boxes of Remingtons every other Tuesday. She'd been in several firefights, usually against drunk or suicidal shooters, and had come away with the sense that the brief seconds of exchanging bullets with another human being were so chaotic and loud and terrifying that you needed any edge you could get. And a big part of that was making instinctive the process of drawing and firing a weapon.

She'd had to cancel her session last week because of another incident with Joey – a fight at school – but the next morning she'd made her range time of six a.m. and, upset about her son, had run through two boxes of fifty rounds. Her wrist had ached from the excess for the rest of the day.

Brynn slowed about fifty yards from the Feldmans' driveway and pulled onto the shoulder, sending a startling cluster of grouse into the air. She stopped, intending to walk the rest of the way.

She was reaching for her phone, in the cup holder, to shut the ringer off before approaching the crime scene, when it trilled. A glance at caller ID. 'Tom.'

'Look, Brynn. . .'

'Doesn't sound good. What? Tell me.'

He sighed. She was irritated he was delaying, though a lot more irritated at the news she knew was coming.

'I'm sorry, Brynn. Oh, brother. Wild goose chase.'

Oh, damn. . . . 'Tell me.'

'Feldman called back. The husband.'

'Called back?'

'Com Central called me. Feldman said he's got nine-one-one on speed dial. Hit it by mistake. Hung up as soon as he realized it. Didn't think it'd gone through.'

'Oh, Tom.' Grimacing, she stared at thrushes picking at the ground beside a wood lily.

'I know, I know.'

'I'm practically there. I can see the house.'

'You moved fast.'

'Well, it *was* a nine-one-one, remember.'

'I'm giving you a *whole* day off.'

And when would she have time for that? She exhaled long. 'At least you're buying me dinner out tonight. And not Burger King. I want Chili's or Bennigan's.'

'Not a single bit of problem. Enjoy it.'

'Night, Tom.'

Brynn called Graham but got his voice mail. It rang four times before it switched over. She left a message saying the call was a false alarm. She hung up. Tried again. This time it went right to voice mail. She didn't leave another message. Was he out?

Your poker game?

It'll keep. . . .

Thinking of the false alarm, though, Brynn wasn't wholly upset. She was going to take an advanced course next week in domestic violence negotiations and could use her dinner break tonight to make some headway in the course manual she'd just received. If she'd been home she wouldn't have been able to crack the book until bedtime.

She also had to admit that she wouldn't mind a bit of a break from evenings with Anna, especially if a run to Rita's was scheduled. It was odd having Anna back in the house after so many years of mutual independence. Emotions from years past surfaced. Like that night a few weeks ago when her mother had shot a cool look her way after Brynn returned late from a tour at the Sheriff's Department; the tension was identical to what she felt as a girl when she'd lost track of time while steeple-jumping and come home late. No fight, no lectures. Just a simple, burdened look, beneath an unflappable smile.

They'd never fought. Anna wasn't temperamental or moody. She was a perfect grandmother, which counted for a lot to Brynn. But mother and daughter had never been chummy, and during Brynn's first marriage Anna largely faded from her life, emerging only after Joey was born.

Now divorced and with a man whom Brynn believed Anna she approved of, they'd reconnected. At one point, a year ago, Brynn had wondered if mother and daughter would finally grow close. But that hadn't happened. They were, after all, the same people they'd been twenty years ago, and, unlike her siblings, Brynn had never had much in common with her mother. Brynn had always spent her life riding, pushing, looking for something outside Eau Claire. Anna's had been spent working unchallenging jobs – mostly four hours a day as a real estate office manager – and raising her three children. Evenings were invariably knitting, chatting and TV.

Perfectly fine for relations living apart. But when Anna moved in, after her surgery, it was like Brynn had been transported back to those days of her youth.

Oh, yes, she was looking forward to a few hours of evening time to herself.

And a free dinner at Bennigan's. Hell, she'd even order a glass of wine.

Brynn flipped the car lights on and put the car in reverse to turn around. Then she paused. The nearest gas station was back in Clausen, a good twenty minutes.

The Feldmans were behind this mix-up; the least they could do was let her use their bathroom. Brynn put the car in gear and headed for their driveway, curious to see just how far Yahoo thought two football fields was.

Squatting next to the stolen Ford they'd driven here from Milwaukee, Lewis sucked blood off the knuckle he'd gigged on the sheet metal trying to repair one or both of the flats. He examined the wound and spat.

Great, Hart thought. Fingerprints *and* DNA.

And here, *I'm* the one picked this guy to tag along tonight.

'Any sign of her?' the skinny man asked, crouched over one of the wheels.

Hart crunched over leaves, returning from making a circuit of the property. As he'd searched for Michelle, being as quiet as he could, he'd had the queasy sense of being targeted. Maybe she was gone. Maybe she wasn't.

'Ground's plenty muddy. I found some footprints, probably hers, going toward the county road at first but they seemed to turn that way.' He pointed to the dense woods and steep hillside behind the house. 'She's gotta be hiding there someplace. You hear anything?'

'No. But it's freaking me out. I keep looking over my shoulder. Man, she is going down. When we get back, I am tracking down that bitch. I don't care who she is, where she lives. She's going down. She fucked with the wrong man.'

I'm the one who got shot, Hart reminded Lewis silently. He examined the forest again. 'We almost had a problem.'

Lewis blurted sarcastically, 'You think?'

'I checked his phone.'

'The . . . ?'

'The husband's.' A nod toward the house. 'Remember? The one you took away from him.'

Lewis was looking defensive already. As well he should. 'Got through to nine-one-one. It was a connected call,' Hart said.

'Couldn't've been on it more than a second.'

'Three seconds. But it was enough.'

'Shit.' Lewis stood up and stretched.

'I think it's okay. I called back and told 'em I was him. I said I'd called by mistake. The sheriff said they'd sent a car to check it out. He was going to tell 'em to come on back.'

'That would've been fucking pretty. They believe you?'

'I think so.'

'Just *think*?' Going on the offensive now.

Hart ignored the question. He gestured at the Ford. 'Can you fix it?'

'Nope' was the glib response.

Hart studied the man, his sneering grin, his cocky stance. After Hart had agreed to do this job he'd gone out to find a partner. He'd checked around with some contacts in Milwaukee and gotten Lewis's name. They'd met. The younger man had seemed all right, and a criminal background check revealed nothing that raised alarms – a rap sheet for some minor drug arrests and larcenies, a few pleas. The skinny guy with the big earring and the red and blue neck decoration would've been fine for the routine job this was supposed to be. But now it had gone bad. Hart was wounded, they had no wheels and an armed enemy was out in the woods nearby. It suddenly became vital to know Compton Lewis's habits, nature and skills.

The assessment wasn't very encouraging.

Hart had to play things careful. He now tried some damage control and, keeping his voice as neutral as he could, said, 'Think your gloves're off.'

Lewis licked the blood again. 'Couldn't get a grip on the wrench. Detroit piece of crap.'

'Probably want to wipe everything.' A nod toward the tire iron.

Lewis laughed as if Hart had said, 'Wow, did you know grass is green?'

So that's how it was going to be.

What a night. . . .

'I'll tell you, my friend,' Lewis muttered, 'Fix-A-Flat does shit when there's a fucking bullet hole in the sidewall of a tire.'

Hart saw the can of tire sealant where Lewis had flung it in anger, he supposed. So that now the man's prints were on that too.

He blinked away tears of pain. Fourteen years in a business in which firearms figured prominently and Hart had never been shot – and he'd rarely fired a weapon himself, unless of course that was what he'd been hired to do.

'The other houses. Up the road? We could try them. Might have a car parked there.'

Hart replied 'Wouldn't make sense, leaving a car out here. Anyway, try hotwiring a car nowadays. You need a computer.'

'I've done it. I can do it easy.' Lewis scoffed. 'You never have?'

Hart said nothing, still scanning the brush.

'Any other ideas?'

'Call Triple A,' Hart said.

'Ha. Triple A. Well, guess that's it. We better start hiking. It's a couple miles to the county road. Let's empty out the Ford and get moving.'

Hart went into the garage and came back with a roll of paper towels and glass cleaner.

'The fuck's that for?' Lewis said. And gave one of those snide laughs again.

'Fingerprints're oil. You need something to cut it with. Wiping just distorts them. The cops can reconstruct them a lot of times.'

'That's bullshit. I never heard of that.'

'It's true, Lewis. I've studied it.'

'Studied?' Another sarcastic laugh.

Hart began spraying the cleaner on whatever Lewis had touched. Hart himself hadn't touched a single thing, except his own arm, with his bare hands since they'd been here.

'Heh. You do laundry too?'

As Hart scrubbed, he also was looking over the property three-sixty, listening. He said, 'We can't leave just yet.'

'What're you talking about?'

'We've got to find her.'

'But. . .' Lewis said, with a sour smile, as if the one word conveyed a whole argument about the futility of the task.

'No choice.' Hart finished wiping. He then took out his map, examined it. They were in the middle of a huge stew of green and brown. He looked around, studied the map some more, folded it up.

Another of those irritating snickers. 'Well, Hart, I know you want to fuck her up after what she did. But let's worry about that later.'

'It's not revenge. Revenge is pointless.'

'Beg to differ. Revenge is fun. That asshole I told you about with the box cutter. Fucking him up was more fun than watching the Brewers . . . depending on who's pitching.'

Hart reined in a sigh, hard though that was. 'It's not about revenge. It's just what we have to do.'

'Shit,' Lewis blurted.

'What?' Hart looked at him, alarmed.

Lewis tugged at his ear. 'I lost the back.' Started looking down at the ground.

'Back?'

'Of my earring.' He put the emerald, or whatever it was, carefully into the small front pocket of his jeans.

Jesus our Lord. . . .

Hart collected the flashlights and extra ammunition from the trunk of the Ford. Waiting until Lewis put his gloves back on, Hart handed him a box of 9mm ammo and one of 12-gauge shells for the shotgun.

'We've got a half hour before we lose the light completely. It'll be a bitch to track her in the dark. Let's get going.'

Lewis wasn't moving. He was looking past Hart and playing with the colorful boxes of bullets like they were Rubik's Cubes. Hart wondered if the head butting was going to start now in earnest. But it turned out that the younger man's attention was just elsewhere. Lewis put the cartons into his pocket, snagged the shotgun, clicking off the safety, and nodded down the driveway. 'We got company, Hart.'

As she approached the Feldman house Brynn McKenzie decided that even with the glow from behind ivory curtains the place was eerie as hell. The other two houses she'd passed might have been the sets for family dramas; this was just the place for a Stephen King movie, the kind she and her first husband, Keith, would devour like candy.

She looked up at the three-story home. You sure didn't see many houses of this style or size in Kennesha County. White siding, which had seen better days, and a wrap-around porch. She liked the porch. Her childhood house in Eau Claire had sported one. She'd loved sitting out in the chain swing at night, her brother singing and playing his battered guitar, her sister flirting with her latest boyfriend, their parents talking, talking, talking . . . And the home she and Keith owned had a real nice wrap-around. But as for her present house, she didn't even know where a porch would fit.

Approaching the Feldmans', she glanced at the yard, impressed. The landscaping was expensive. The place was surrounded by strategically placed dogwoods, ligustrum and crepe myrtles that had been cut way back. She recalled her husband's advice to his customers against this practice ('Don't rape your crepes').

Parking in the circular gravel drive, she caught movement inside, a shadow on the front curtain. She climbed out into the chill air, fresh and sweet with the perfume of blossoms and firewood smoke.

Hearing the comforting sound of frogs squeaking and croaking and the honk of geese or ducks, Brynn walked over gravel and up the three steps to the porch. Flashed on Joey, imagining him skateboarding off this height into the school parking lot.

Well, I *did* talk to him.

It'll be fine.. . .

Her issue black Oxfords, as comfy and unstylish as shoes could be, thunked on the wood as she approached the front door. Hit the bell.

It rang but there was no response.

She pressed the button once more. The door was solid but flanked by narrow windows curtained with lace, and Brynn could see into the living room. She noted no motion, no shadows. Only a pleasant storm of flames in the fireplace.

She knocked. Loud, reverberating on the glass.

Another shadow, like before. She realized that it was from the waving of the orange flames in the fireplace. There was light from a side room but most of the other rooms on this floor were dark, and a lamp from the top of the stairs cast bony shadows of the stair railings on the hallway floor.

Maybe everybody was out back, or in a dining room. Imagine that, she thought, a house so big you'd miss the doorbell.

A throaty honk above her. Brynn looked up. The light was dim and the sky was shared by birds and mammals: mallards on final approach to the lake, a few silver-haired bats in their erratic, purposeful hunt. She smiled at the sight. Then, looking back into the house, her eye noted something out of place: behind a massive brown armchair a briefcase and backpack lay open and the contents – files, books, pens – were dumped on the floor, as if they'd been searched for valuables.

Her gut clenched and in a snap came the thought: a 911 call cut short. An intruder realizes the victim dialed the police and then calls back to say it's a false alarm.

Brynn McKenzie drew her weapon.

She looked behind her fast. No voices, no footsteps. She was stepping back to the car to get her cell phone when she saw something curious inside.

What *is* that?

Brynn's eyes focused on the edge of a rug in the kitchen. But it was glistening. How can a rug be shiny?

Blood. She was looking at a pool of blood.

All right. Think. How to handle it?

Heart stuttering, she tested the knob. The lock had been kicked out.

Cell phone in the car? Or go inside?

The blood was fresh. Three people inside. No sign of the intruders. Somebody could be hurt but alive.

Phone later.

Brynn shoved the door open, glancing right and left. Said nothing, didn't announce her presence. Looking, looking everywhere, head dizzy.

She glanced into the lit bedroom to her left. A deep breath and she stepped inside, keeping her gun close to her side so it couldn't be grabbed, as Keith had lectured in his class on tactical operations, the class where she'd met him.

The room was empty but the bed was mussed and first aid materials were on the floor. Her misshapen jaw quivering, she moved back into the living room, where the fire crackled. Trying to be silent, she found the carpet and navigated carefully around the empty briefcase and backpack and file folders scattered on the floor, the labels giving clues about the woman's professional life: Haberstrom, Inc., Acquisition. *Gibbons v. Kenosha Automotive Technologies*. Pascoe Inc. Refinancing. Hearing – Country Redistricting.

She continued on to the kitchen.

And stopped fast. Staring down at the bodies of the young couple on the floor. They wore business clothes, the shirt and blouse dark with blood. Both had been shot in the head and the wife in the neck too – she was the source of the blood. The husband had run in panic, slipping and falling; a skid mark of red led from his shoe to the carpet of blood. The wife had turned away to die. She lay on her stomach with her right arm twisted behind her, a desperate angle, as if she were trying to touch an itch above her lower spine.

Where was the friend? Brynn wondered. Had she escaped? Or had the killer taken her upstairs? She recalled the light on the second floor.

Had the intruder left?

The answer to *that* question came a moment later.

A voice outside whispered, 'Hart? The keys aren't in the car. She's got 'em.'

It came from toward the front of the house, but she couldn't tell where exactly.

Brynn flattened herself against the wall. Wiped her right palm on her left shoulder, then gripped her gun firmly.

After a moment another voice – Hart's, she supposed – speaking firmly, not to his partner but to her: 'You, lady. In the house. Bring your keys out here. We just want your car is all. You'll be fine.'

She lifted the gun, muzzle up. Brynn McKenzie had fired a weapon at another human being four times in the decade and a half she'd been a public safety officer. Not a lot, but four times more than most deputies did in their whole careers. Like breathalyzing drivers and comforting beaten wives, this was a part of her job and she was filled with an odd blend of tension, terror and contentment.

'Really,' Hart called. 'Don't worry. Or, tell you what, just throw 'em out the front, you don't trust us. But otherwise we come in and get them. Believe me, we just want to be gone. Just want to be out of here.'

Brynn flicked the kitchen lights out. Now the only illumination was from the roaring fireplace and the bedroom she'd glanced into.

A whisper, its source uncertain. This meant they'd joined each other.

But where?

And were there just two? Or more? She found herself staring at the bodies of the couple.

And where was the friend?

Hart again, speaking so very calmly: 'You've seen those folks inside. You don't want that to happen to you. Throw the keys out here. I'm telling you not to be stupid. Please.'

Of course the moment she showed herself she'd be dead.

Should she say she was a deputy? And that more were on their way?

No, don't give yourself away.

Pressing back against the pantry door, Brynn scanned the back windows. They reflected the living room and she gasped softly as a man appeared in the front door, slipping inside. Cautious. He was tall, solid, wearing a dark jacket. Long hair, boots. He carried a pistol in his – the reverse image confused her momentarily – his *right* hand. The other arm hung at his side and she got the impression he'd been injured. He disappeared. Somewhere in the living room.

Brynn tensed, gripped the pistol in a shooting pose. She stared at the reflection at the front of the house.

Go for the shot, she told herself. Your only advantage is surprise. Use it. He's in the living room. It's only twenty feet.

Step into the doorway. Fire a burst of three, then back to cover. You can take him.

Do it.

Now.

Brynn swallowed and stepped away from the wall, turning toward the living room. She gasped as the voice from behind her, in the dining room, shouted, 'Listen, lady, you do what we're saying!' A skinny man in a combat jacket, with short, light hair, a tat on his neck and eyes mean, had come through the French doors. He was lifting a shotgun to his shoulder.

Brynn, spinning to face him.

They fired simultaneously. Her slug came closer than his buckshot – he ducked and she didn't – puncturing a stuffed dining room chair inches from him as the pellets from his shotgun crunched into the ceiling above her. The light fixture rained down.

He crawled out the French door. 'Hart! A gun! She's got a gun.'

She wasn't sure these were his exact words, though. The shots were thunderclap loud and had numbed her ears.

Brynn glanced into the living room. No sign of Hart. She started toward the back kitchen door. Then paused. She couldn't just leave if the Feldmans' friend was still here.

'I'm a sheriff's deputy,' she shouted. 'Hello! Is someone in the house? Are you upstairs?'

Silence.

Brynn desperately scanned the windows, shivered, sure somebody was aiming at her even as she crouched in the shadows. 'Hello?'

Nothing.

'Is anybody here?'

The longest twenty seconds of her life.

Leave, she told herself. Get help. You can't do anything for anybody if you're dead.

She raced out the back door, gasping in fear and from the effort. Her keys in her left hand, she made her way to the front yard. She saw no one.

The sun was down altogether and the darkness was growing fast. But there was still just enough light in the sky, barely, to make out one of the intruders running toward some bushes. His back was to her. It was the wounded man, Hart. She drew a target but he vanished in a thicket of bearberry and rhododendron.

Brynn scanned the front yard. The other man, with the shotgun and the narrow face, wasn't visible. She sprinted for her car. When she heard the rustle of bushes from behind her, she dropped instantly. The shotgun fired. Pellets hissed around her and clattered off the Ford. Brynn fired twice into the bush, breaking the number-one rule about never shooting, except at a clear target. She saw the slight man disappear behind the house, running in a crouch.

Then she stood and opened her car door. Rather than jump in, though, she remained standing, a clear target, pointing the black Glock at the bushes where Hart had fled. Struggling to steady her breathing. And her shooting grip.

Come on, come on . . . I can only wait a second or two . . .

Then Hart rose fast from the bushes. He was close enough for her to see him blink in surprise that she was waiting for him. Brynn too was surprised; she hadn't been expecting him so far to the right and by the time she corrected and fired three shots he'd dived to cover. She believed she might've hit him.

But now it was time to escape.

Jumping into the car, concentrating on getting the key in the ignition, not looking around. The engine roared and she slammed the shifter into reverse flooring the limp accelerator. The car skittered backward along the gravel, whipsawing – now rear-wheel drive. She glanced behind her to see the men converging in the driveway, sprinting flat-out after her. Answering one of her questions: She'd missed Hart, after all.

The skinny man stopped and fired the shotgun. The pellets missed.

'Our Loving Savior, look over us,' she whispered, an invocation they said at grace every night and that she'd never meant more than now.

Brynn had taken the State Police's pursuit and evasive driving course several times. She'd used the techniques often in the high-speed chases when after a speeder or a getaway car. This, though, was the opposite: evading an attacker, something she'd never imagined would happen. Yet her hours of practice came back to her: left hand on the wheel, right arm around the passenger seat, gripping the pistol. Two long football fields . . . She came to the end of the driveway and debated turning around to drive in forward or just stay in reverse and back down Lake View toward the county road. To pause even for five seconds to turn around could be disastrous.

The men continued to sprint.

Brynn decided: Stay in reverse and keep going. Put some distance between them.

As she approached Lake View Drive she realized it was the right decision. They were closer than she'd thought. She never heard the shotgun fire again but pellets snapped into the windshield, starring it. She took the turn onto the private road and accelerated as fast as she dared, staring out of the dirty rear window and struggling to keep the car under control. It whipped back and forth and threatened to slam into the rocks or trees to the right or tumble down the embankment to the lake on the opposite side of the road.

But she managed to keep control.

Brynn eased off the gas a little but kept the speed at thirty. The transmission was roaring in protest. She doubted she could make it to the county road before the gears tore apart.

She'd have to turn around soon. The private road was too narrow to do so but she could use the driveway at Number 2. It wasn't close – three, four hundred yards of the serpentine private road – but she had no choice.

Her neck stung from twisting to look backward. She glanced down at the cup holder. 'Goddamn.' The man who'd checked for keys had taken her cell phone. She realized she still gripped the gun in her right hand, finger around the trigger. Glocks have a very light pull. She set the weapon on the seat.

Brynn looked quickly behind her – out the front windshield. No sign of them. She turned back and steered the car through a curve to the left. The house at 2 Lake View was now about two hundred yards away.

The driveway was growing closer. She let up on the gas a bit; the raging whine of the gears diminished.

She was thinking: Pull in fast, get into drive and—

A solid load of buckshot crashed into the driver's side of the car, both windows vanishing into hundreds of pieces of ice, pelting her. A sphere of buckshot stabbed through her right cheek and knocked out a molar. She began choking on the tooth and the blood. Tears flowed and she couldn't see the road any longer.

Wiping her eyes, Brynn managed to hawk up the tooth and spit it out, coughing hard on the blood, which spattered the steering wheel, slippery as oil. She lost her grip and didn't make a curve. The car, going about thirty-five, dove off the edge and started down the steep rocky hill toward the lake.

She flew out of her seat, her feet nowhere near the brakes, as the Honda rolled backward down the cliff. It dropped about six feet and the trunk slammed onto a shelf of limestone, hood pointed straight up in the air. The gun hit her in the ear.

The car balanced for a moment, with Brynn sprawled across the backs of the two front seats. Then, with the utmost leisure, the Honda continued to topple, belly flopping upside down into the lake. The car filled instantly with dark water as it sank. Brynn, stunned, was snagged beneath the steering wheel.

She screamed as the frigid water embraced her body, swatting her hands in panic. She called out, 'Joey, Joey.'

And inhaled a breath that began as air and ended as water.

'Well, we're fucked,' Lewis said. 'Oh, man. She was a cop.'

'Don't panic.'

'The fuck you talking about? She was a cop, Hart. You get your head around that? There could be a dozen of 'em in the woods. We've gotta leave, my friend. *Leave!*'

Breathing hard from the run, the men had slowed and were walking through the dense woodland, toward where they'd seen the car go off the road after Lewis had sent a load of shot into the driver's side. They moved carefully, looking around like soldiers on patrol. They had no idea if the woman was out of commission from the crash or was in hiding, waiting for them.

And they couldn't forget about Michelle either, who might've been drawn out of hiding by the ruckus.

'She wasn't in a cruiser. And she wasn't in a uniform jacket.'

Lewis scrunched his face up skeptically. 'I didn't really get to see what she was wearing underneath. I was a little busy.' Again sarcastic. 'And I'm not panicking.'

'I'll bet she was probably off duty and came up here to check out that nine-one-one. Didn't get the message it was a false alarm.'

Lewis snickered. 'You *say* she wasn't on duty, my friend. But she was on enough duty to nearly blow your fucking head off.' He said this as if he'd won an argument.

Your head too, Hart corrected silently. He said, 'A lot of cops have to carry their pieces. All the time. Regulation.'

'I know that.' Lewis gazed at the lake. 'I heard the bang, you know. Like a crash. But I wasn't sure if there was a splash.'

'I couldn't hear it go in the water.' Hart nodded toward the Winchester and tapped his ear. 'Loud. I don't usually use shotguns.'

'You oughta learn 'em, boy. *The* weapon of choice. Nothing like a scattergun. Scares the shit out of folks.'

Weapon of choice.

Crouching, they continued walking slowly. In this morass of trees and tangled brush Hart grew disoriented. They could see the road but he now had no idea where the car had gone over the side. With every step, it seemed, the vista changed.

Lewis paused, rubbed his neck.

Hart looked him over. 'You hit?'

'Nope. Right as rain. I dodged in time. I can sense when bullets're coming. Like in *The Matrix*. Now, that was a good flick. I have the whole set. You see it?'

Hart had no idea what he was talking about. 'No.'

'Jesus. You don't get out much, do you?'

A crinkle in the bushes nearby.

Lewis swung the shotgun toward the sound.

Something low was in the grass nearby, moving fast. Badger or coyote. Maybe a dog. Lewis aimed for it, clicked the safety off.

'No, no, no . . . Give ourselves away.'

And you *never* shoot anything you don't have to . . . human or animal. Who the hell was this boy?

Lewis muttered, 'We take it out, whatever the fuck it is, it won't spook us anymore.'

You're spooked; I'm not. Hart picked up a rock and flung it nearby. The animal, an indistinct shadow, moved off.

But it moved off slowly. As if the men weren't worth bothering about. Crouching, Hart saw a few paw prints in the mud. Not normally superstitious, he couldn't help thinking that the indentations were a warning sign of sorts. Telling them that they'd strolled casually into a very different universe from what they were used to. This is my world, the creature who'd left the prints was saying. You don't belong here. You'll see things that aren't there and miss things that're coming up right behind you.

For the first time that night, including the gunshot at the house, Hart felt a trickle of real fear.

'Fucking werewolf,' Lewis said, then looked back to the lakeshore. 'So she's gone. Gotta be. I'm saying, we gotta keep going, get out of here. After that—' He nodded back to the Feldmans' house. '— all bets are off. This thing is very fucked up. We'll get a car on the county road. Take care of the driver. And we're back in the city in a couple hours.' He snapped his fingers theatrically.

Hart didn't respond. He gestured down the road. 'I want to see if she went for a swim or not.'

Lewis sighed, exasperated, like a teenager. But he followed Hart. They walked stealthily toward the rocky shore in silence, pausing every so often.

The younger man was looking over the lake. It was completely shaded by dusk shadow now, the water rippling in the breeze like black snake scales. He announced, 'That lake, I don't like it. It's freaky.'

Talking too loud, walking too loud, Hart thought angrily. He decided he had to get some control of the situation. It'd be a fine line but he had to. He whispered, 'You know, Lewis, you shouldn't've said anything back there. About the keys. I could've gotten up behind her.'

'So *I* gave it away, huh? It's all *my* fault.'

'I'm saying we've gotta be more careful. And when you were in the dining room you started talking to her. You should've just shot.'

Lewis's eyes were good at being defensive and surly at the same time. 'I didn't know she was a cop. How the fuck could I know that? I stood my ground and nearly took lead there, my friend.'

Took lead? Hart thought. Nobody ever said 'took lead'.

'I hate this fucking place,' Lewis muttered. He rubbed the bristle on his head, poked the lobe where his earring had been. Frowned, then remembered he'd put it away. 'Got a thought, Hart. It's what, a mile or so back to the county road?'

'About that.'

'Let's get the spare on the Ford, the front, and drive her to the county road, drag the bad wheel behind us. You see what I'm saying? It's front-wheel drive. Won't be a problem. Get to the county road. Somebody'll stop to help. I'll flag 'em down, then they'll open the window and, bang, that's it. Fucker won't know what hit 'em. Take their car. Back home in no time. We'll go to Jake's. You go there ever?'

Eyes on the lake, Hart said absently, 'Don't know it.'

Lewis scowled. 'And you call yourself a Milwaukee boy. Best bar in town.'

Peering along the shore, he said, 'I think it was there.' He pointed at a spot about fifty yards to the south.

'Hart, I hit her in the fucking head. And her car's in the water. She's dead, either way, from buckshot or drowning.'

Maybe, Hart thought.

But he couldn't shake the image back at the Feldmans' house, standing in the driveway. She hadn't scurried away, she hadn't panicked. She'd just stood tall, brownish hair pulled back off her forehead. The car keys – keys to safety, you could say – in one hand, her weapon in the other. Waiting, waiting. For him to present a target.

None of that meant she wasn't drowned, trapped in a two-ton automobile, of course, at the bottom of the *spooky* lake But it did mean she wouldn't drown without one hell of a fight.

Hart said, 'Before we go anywhere let's just make sure.'

Another scowl.

Hart was patient. 'A few minutes won't hurt. Let's split up. You take the right side of the road, I'll do the left. If you see anybody, it's got to be either one of 'em so just draw a target and shoot.'

He was going to remind Lewis not to say anything, just shoot. But the skinny man was already bunching his mouth up into a little pout.

So Hart just said, 'Okay?'

A nod. 'I'll just draw my target and shoot. Yes, sir, captain.' And gave a snide salute.

Her cheek rested against a rock, slimy with algae. Her body was submerged in breathtakingly cold water, up to the neck.

Teeth clicking, breath staccato, cheek swollen. It seemed to push her eye out of the socket. Tears and sour lake water covering her face.

Brynn McKenzie spat blood and oil and gasoline. She shook her head to get the water out of her ears. Had no effect. She felt deaf. Wondered if a piece of buckshot or glass had pierced her eardrum. Then her left ear popped and tickling water flowed out. She heard the lapping of the lake.

After muscling her way out of the car, nestled in 20 feet of opaque water, she'd tried to swim to the surface but couldn't – too much weight from her clothes and shoes. So she'd clawed her way to the rocks at the shore and scrabbled upward, desperate hands gripping whatever they could find, feet kicking. She'd hit the surface and sucked in air.

Now, she told herself, get out. Move.

Brynn pulled up hard. But got only a few inches. No part of her body was working the way it should and her wet clothes must've boosted her weight by fifty pounds. Her hands slipped on the slime and she went under again. Grabbed another rock. Pulled herself up to the surface.

Her vision blurred and she started to lose her grip on a rock. Then forced her muscles to attention. 'I'm not dying here.' She believed she actually growled the words aloud. Brynn finally managed to swing her legs up and found a ledge with her left foot. The right one joined in and finally she eased herself onto the shore. She rolled through debris – metal and glass and red and clear plastic – into a pile of rotting leaves and branches, surrounded by cattails and tall, rustling grasses. The cold air hurt worse than the water.

They'll be coming. Of course, those two men'll be coming after her. They wouldn't know exactly where the car went in but they could find out easily enough.

You have to move.

Brynn climbed to her knees and tried crawling. Too slow. Move! She stood and immediately fell over. Her legs wouldn't cooperate. In panic she wondered if she'd broken a bone and couldn't feel the injury because of the cold. She frisked herself. Nothing seemed shattered. She rose again, steadied herself and staggered in the direction of Lake View Drive.

Her face throbbed. She touched the hole in her cheek, and with her tongue probed the gap where the molar had been. Winced. Spat more blood.

And my jaw. My poor jaw. Thinking of the impact that had cracked it years ago, and later the terrible wire, the liquid meals, the plastic surgery.

Was all that cosmetic work ruined?

Brynn wanted to cry.

The ground here was steep, rocky. Narrow stalks – willow, maple and oak – grew out of the angular ground horizontally but obeying nature turned immediately skyward. Using them as grips, she pulled herself up the hill, toward Lake View Drive. The moon, neatly sliced in half, was casting some light now and she looked behind her for the Glock. But if it had flown from the car before the dive, the weapon, perfectly camouflaged for a dark night, was nowhere to be seen.

She picked up a rock shaped a bit like an ax head. Gazed at the weapon manically.

Then Brynn recalled finding Joey bloody and gasping after eighth-grader Carl Bedermier had challenged him after school. Acting by rote, from her medical training, she'd examined the wounds, pronounced him fine and then said, 'Honey, there are times to fight and times to run. Mostly, you run.'

So what the hell are you doing? she now snapped to herself, staring at the chunk of granite in her hand.

Run.

She dropped the rock and continued up the incline to the private road. As she neared the top her foot slipped, dislodging an avalanche of shale and gravel. It fell in a huge clatter. Brynn dropped to her belly, smelling compost and wet rock.

But no one came running. She wondered if the men were deafened themselves from the shooting.

Probably. Guns are much louder than people think.

Move fast while you can still take advantage of it.

Another few feet. Then ten. Twenty. The ground leveled some and she could move faster. Eventually she was at Lake View Drive. She saw no one on it and crossed fast, then rolled into a ditch on the far side, hugging herself and gasping.

No. Don't stop.

She thought of a high-speed chase last year. Bart Pinchett in his Mustang GT, yellow as yolk.

'Why didn't you pull over?' she'd muttered, ratcheting the cuffs on. 'You knew we'd get you sooner or later.'

He'd lifted a surprised eyebrow. 'Well, long as I was moving, I was still a free man.'

Brynn rolled to her knees and stood. She slogged up the

hill away from the road and into the trees, plunging into a field of tall yellow and brown grass.

Ahead of her, two or three hundred yards or so, she saw the silhouette of the house at 2 Lake View. As she'd seen earlier, it was dark. Would the telephone be on? Did they even have a telephone?

Brynn gave a brief prayer that they would. Then she looked around her. No sign of the attackers. She shook her head again, swiveling it from side to side until the second water bead burst.

Which made the sudden sound – footfalls charging through the grass directly toward her – all the more vivid.

Brynn gasped and started to sprint away from Hart or his partner, maybe both, when a forsythia branch caught her foot and she went down hard, breathlessly hard, in a tangle of branches, which were covered with yellow buds bright as you'd see on wallpaper in a baby's bedroom.

They were driving back from Rita's, a mile away. It seemed to Graham that every place in Humboldt was a mile away from every other place.

He'd brought Joey along – didn't want to leave him alone, because of the skateboard injury, even if he was 'fine', and because he'd ditch homework for video games, instant messaging and MySpace or Facebook on the computer and texting and emailing from his iPhone. The boy wasn't crazy about picking up his grandmother but was in pretty good humor, as he sat in the back seat and text-messaged a friend – or half the school, to judge from the volume of his keyboarding.

They collected Anna and headed back home. There, Joey charged upstairs, taking the steps several at a time.

'Homework,' Graham called.

'I will.'

The phone rang.

Brynn? he wondered. No. A name he didn't recognize on caller ID.

'Hello?'

'Hi. This's Mr Raditzky, Joey's central section advisor.'

Middle school was a lot different nowadays, Graham

reflected. He'd never had advisors. And 'central section' sounded like a communist spy organization.

'Graham Boyd. I'm Brynn's husband.'

'Sure. How you doing?'

'Good, thanks.'

'Is Ms. McKenzie there?'

'She's out, I'm afraid. Can I take a message? Or can I help you?'

Graham had always wanted children. He made his living with plants but he had an innate desire to nurture more than that. His first wife had decided against motherhood, suddenly and emphatically – and well into the marriage. Which was a big disappointment to Graham. He believed he had instinctive skills for parenting and his radar was picking up early warning signals from Mr. Raditzky's tone.

'Well, I want to talk to you about something . . . Did you know Joey cut school today? And that he was 'phalting.' Something faintly accusatory in the tone.

'Cut school? No, he was there. I dropped him off myself. Brynn had to be at work early.'

'Well, he did cut, Mr. Boyd.'

Graham fought the urge to deny. 'Go on, please.'

'Joey came to central section this morning, gave me a note that he had a doctor's appointment. And left at ten. It was signed by Ms. McKenzie. But after we heard he hurt himself, I checked in the office. It wasn't her signature. He forged it.'

Graham now experienced the same unexpected alarm he'd felt last summer while wheeling a plant across a customer's yard, not realizing he'd rolled it over a yellow jackets' nest. Blithe and happy, enjoying the day, unaware that the threat had already been unleashed and dozens of attackers were on their way.

'Oh.' He looked up in the direction of the boy's bedroom. From it came the muted sounds of a video game.

Homework . . .

'And what else did you say? "Defaulting"?'

'The word is apostrophe P-H, 'phalting. As in asphalt. It's when kids run up behind a truck at a stoplight with their skateboards and hold on. *That*'s how Joey hurt himself.'

'He wasn't in your school lot?'

'No, Mr. Boyd. One of our substitutes was on her way home. She saw him on Elden Street.'

'The *highway*?'

In downtown Humboldt, Elden was a broad commercial strip but once past the town line it returned to its true nature, a truck route between Eau Claire and Green Bay, where the posted limit meant nothing.

'She said the truck was doing probably forty when he fell. He's only alive because there weren't any cars close behind him and he veered into a patch of grass. Could've been a telephone pole or a building.'

'Jesus.'

'This needs some attention.'

I talked to him . . .

'It sure does, Mr. Raditzky. I'll tell Brynn. I know she'll want to talk to you.'

'Thanks, Mr. Boyd. How's he doing?'

'Okay. Scraped up a little.'

He's fine . . .

'He's one lucky young man.' Though there was an undercurrent of criticism in the man's tone. And Graham didn't blame him.

He was about to say goodbye when something else popped into his head.

'Mr. Raditzky.' Graham crafted a credible lie. 'We were just talking about something yesterday. Was there any fallout from that scuffle Joey was in?'

A pause. 'Well, which one?'

Lord, how many were there? Graham hedged. 'I was thinking about the one last fall.'

'Oh, the bad one. In October. The suspension.'

Treading again blithely over a yellow jackets' nest . . . Brynn'd told him there was a pushing match at the school's Halloween party, nothing serious. Graham recalled Joey had stayed home afterward for a few days – because he hadn't felt well, Brynn explained. But that was a lie, it seemed. So he'd been suspended.

The teacher said, 'Ms. McKenzie told you the parents decided not to sue, didn't she?'

Lawsuit? . . . What exactly had Joey done? He said, 'Sure. But I was mostly wondering about the other student.'

'Oh, he transferred out. He was a problem, ED.'

'What?'

'Emotionally disturbed. He'd been taunting Joey. But that's no excuse for nearly breaking his nose.'

'Of course not. I was just curious.'

'You folks dodged a bullet on that one. It could have cost you big.'

More criticism now.

'We were lucky.' Graham felt his gut chill. What else didn't he know about his family?

A little pushing match. It's nothing. Joey went to the Halloween party as a Green Bay Packer and this other boy was a Bears fan . . . Something silly like that. A little rivalry. I'll keep him out of school for a bit. He's got the flu anyway.

'Well, thanks again for the heads-up. We'll have a talk with him.'

When they'd hung up, Graham got another beer. He sipped a bit. Went into the kitchen to do the dishes. He found the task comforting. He hated to vacuum, hated to dust. Set him on edge. He couldn't say why. But he loved doing the dishes. Water, maybe. The life blood of a landscaper.

As he washed and dried he rehearsed a half-dozen speeches to Joey about cutting school and dangerous skateboard practices. He kept refining them. But as he put the dishes away he decided the words were stilted, artificial. They were just that – speeches. It seemed to Graham that you needed conversation, not lectures. He knew instinctively that they'd have no effect on a twelve-year-old boy. He tried to imagine the two of them sitting down and speaking seriously. He couldn't. He gave up crafting a talk.

Hell, he'd let Brynn handle it. She'd insist on that anyway.

'Phalting . . .

Graham dried his hands and went into the family room and sat down on the green couch, near Anna's rocker. She asked, 'Was that Brynn?'

'No. The school.'

'Everything okay?'

'Fine.'

'Sorry you missed poker tonight, Graham.'

'No problem.'

Returning to her knitting, Anna said, 'Glad I went to Rita's. She doesn't have long.' A tsk of her tongue. 'And that daughter of hers. Well, you saw, didn't you?'

Occasionally his soft-spoken mother-in-law surprised him by letting go with a steely judgment like this one. He had no idea what the daughter's crime was but he knew Anna had considered the offense carefully and come back with a reasonable verdict. 'Sure did.'

He flipped a coin for the channel, lost and they put on a sitcom, which was fine with him. His team was toast this season.

The frantic young woman was in her mid-twenties, face gaunt and eyes red from tears, her stylishly short, pixie-ish hair, dark red, now disheveled and flecked with leaves. Her forehead was scratched and her hands shook uncontrollably, but only partly from the cold.

It had been her panicked footsteps Brynn had heard, not those of an intruder, moving toward her through the brush.

'You're their friend,' Brynn had whispered, feeling huge relief that the woman hadn't met the Feldmans' fate. 'From Chicago?'

She had nodded and then gazed out into the deepening dusk as if the men were hot on her trail. 'I don't know what to do,' she said in a manic voice. She seemed childlike. Her fear was heartrending.

'We stay here for the time being,' Brynn said.

Times to fight and times to run . . .

Times to hide too.

Brynn looked over at the couple's houseguest. She wore chic clothes, city clothes – expensive jeans and a designer jacket with a beautiful fur collar. The leather was supple as silk. Three gold hoops were in one ear, two in the other, a stud atop both. A sparkling diamond tennis bracelet was on her left wrist and a bejeweled Rolex on her other. She was about as out of place in this muddy forest as she could possibly be.

Scanning the forest around them, Brynn could see no movement other than swaying branches and herds of leaves migrating in the breeze. The wind was pure torment on her soaked skin. 'Over there,' she finally said, pointing to cover. The women crawled a dozen feet away – to a cavity beside a fallen chinquapin oak in a snarled area of the forest, fifty yards from Lake View Drive and about a hundred and fifty from the house at Number 2. When they'd settled into a nest of forsythia, ragweed and sedge Brynn looked back toward the road and the Feldmans'. No sign of the killers.

As if awakening, the young woman suddenly focused on Brynn's uniform blouse. 'You're a policewoman.' She turned her gaze to the road. 'Are there others?'

'No. I'm alone.'

She took this news without emotion and then looked at Brynn's cheek. 'Your face . . . I heard gunshots. They shot you too. Like Steve and Emma.' Her voice choked. 'Did you call for help?'

Brynn shook her head. 'You have a phone?'

'It's back there. In the house.'

Brynn wrapped her arms around herself. It did nothing to warm her. She looked at the woman's supple designer jacket – enviously, though not for the garment's obvious luxury, but for the warmth. Her face was pretty, heart-shaped. Her nails were long and perfectly sculpted. She could have been on the cover of a grocery store checkout magazine, illustrating an article on ten ways to stay fit and sexy. The woman dug into her pocket and pulled out tight, stylish gloves whose price Brynn couldn't even guess at.

Brynn shivered again and was thinking if she didn't get dry

and warm soon, she might pass out. She'd never been this cold.

'That house.' The young woman nodded toward 2 Lake View. 'I was going to call for help. Let's go there, let's call the police. We can get warm. I'm so damn cold.'

'Don't want to yet,' Brynn said. It seemed less painful to speak in abbreviation. 'Don't know where they are. Wait until we know. They could be headed there too.'

The young woman winced.

'You hurt?' Brynn asked.

'My ankle. I fell.'

Brynn had run plenty of trauma calls. She unzipped the woman's boots – made in Italy, she noticed – and examined the joint through her black knee-highs. It didn't look badly hurt. A sprain probably; thank God it wasn't broken. She saw a gold anklet. Brynn didn't think that anybody over twelve wore ankle bracelets.

The young woman stared toward the Feldman's house. Chewing her lip.

'What's your name?'

'Michelle.'

'I'm Brynn McKenzie.'

'Brynn?'

A nod. She usually didn't explain its derivation. 'I'm a deputy with the county sheriff's office.' She explained about the 911 call. 'You know who they are, those men?'

'No.'

Brynn whispered, her voice growing more distorted, 'Need to figure out what to do. Tell me what happened.'

'I met Emma after work and we picked up Steve and all drove up together. Got here about five, five-thirty. I went upstairs – I was going to take a shower – and I heard these bangs. I thought the stove exploded or something. Or some-body dropped something. I didn't know. I ran downstairs and saw two men. They didn't see me. One of them'd put down his gun. It was on the table near the stairs. I just picked it up. They were in the kitchen, standing over the . . . over the bodies, talking. Just looking down and they had this expression on their faces.' She shut her eyes. Whispered, 'I can't even describe it. They were, like, "We shot them. Okay, no big deal. What's next?"' Her voice cracked. 'One of them, he was going through the refrigerator.'

As Brynn scanned the woods the young woman continued, forcing back tears, 'I started to walk toward them. I wasn't even thinking. I was, like, numb. And one of them – one had long hair and one had a crew cut – the one with the long hair started to turn and I guess I just pulled the trigger. It just happened. There was this bang . . . I don't think I hit them.'

'No,' Brynn said. 'One of them's hurt, I think. One you just mentioned. With long hair.'

'Hurt bad?' she asked.

'His arm.'

'I should've . . . I should've told them to stop, or put their hands up. I don't know. They started shooting at me. And I panicked. I just lost it completely. I ran outside. I didn't have the car keys.' A disgusted look on her face. 'I did something so stupid . . . I was afraid they'd come after me so I shot out the tires. They would've just left if I hadn't done that. Got in the car and left . . . I was so stupid!'

'That's all right. You did fine. Nobody'd think straight at a time like that. You have the gun still?'

Please, Brynn thought. I want a weapon so badly.

But the woman shook her head. 'I used up all the bullets. I threw it into a creek by the house so they couldn't find it. And I ran.' She squinted. 'You're a deputy. Do *you* have a gun?'

'I did. But lost it in the lake.'

Suddenly Michelle became animated. Almost giddy. 'You know, like, I saw this show one time, it was on A&E or

Discovery, and somebody'd been in a car wreck, a bad one, and they lost a lot of blood and they were in the wilderness for days. They should've died. But something happened, like the body stopped the bleeding itself. The doctors saved them and . . .'

Brynn had experienced this mania before, at car wrecks and heart attack scenes, and knew the implicit question was best answered simply and honestly. 'I'm sorry. I was there, in the kitchen. I saw them. I'm afraid they're gone.'

Michelle held on to a fragment of hope for a moment longer. Then let it go. She nodded and lowered her head.

Brynn asked, 'You have any idea what they want? Ow!' She flinched as she bit her tongue, and her eyes lensed with tears. 'Was it robbery?'

'I don't know.'

The shivering grew worse, consuming Brynn. Michelle's perfect fingernails, she had noticed, were dark from plum-colored polish; Brynn's, unpolished, were the same shade.

'I understand you and Emma worked together. Are you a lawyer too?'

A shake of her pretty head. 'No, I was a paralegal in Milwaukee for a while before I moved to Chicago. That's how we met. It was just a way to make some money. I'm really an actress.'

'Did she ever talk to you about her cases?'

'Not too much, no.'

'Could be – a case at her law firm. She might've found out about a scam or crime of some kind.'

Michelle gasped. 'You mean they came up here to kill her on purpose?'

Brynn shrugged.

A snap nearby. Brynn gasped and turned fast. About twenty feet away a badger, elegant in its round, clumsy way, nosed past warily.

Wisconsin, the Badger State.

Brynn asked Michelle, 'Will somebody start to wonder if they don't hear from you?'

'My husband. Except he's traveling. We said we'd talk in the morning. That's why I came up here with Steve and Emma. I had the weekend free.'

'Look.' Brynn was pointing toward the Feldman house. Two flashlight beams were scanning the side yard, a quarter mile away. 'They're back there. Hurry. The other house. Let's go.' Brynn rose to a crouch, both of them staggering forward.

So the cop *had* gone into the water.

Hart and Lewis had found debris and an oil slick.

'Dead, gotta be,' Lewis'd said, looking distastefully at the lake, as if he were expecting monsters to slither out. 'I'm outa here. Come on, Hart. Jake's. I need a fucking beer. First round's on you, my friend.'

They'd returned to the Feldman house. The fire in the hearth had burned itself out and Hart had shut off all the lights. He'd put into his pocket all the used medical supplies stained with his blood. He didn't bother with the spent shells that littered the house and front yard; he'd worn gloves when loading the Glocks and had watched to make sure Lewis had too.

Then he sprayed and wiped everything Lewis had come near with his bare hands.

Lewis couldn't resist a snicker at this.

'Keep that,' an irritated Hart said, pointing to Michelle's purse.

Lewis slipped it into his combat jacket pocket and took a bottle of vodka from the bar. Chopin. 'Shit. This is good stuff.' He uncorked it and took a drink. He lifted the bottle to Hart, who shook his head because he didn't want any booze just now, though Lewis took it as a criticism about drinking on the job, which was true too. At least he wore gloves when handling the bottle.

'You worry too much, Hart,' Lewis said, laughing. 'I know the score, my friend. I know how they operate in places like this. I wouldn't do that in Milwaukee or St.Paul. But here . . . these cops're like Andy in Mayberry. Not *CSI*. They don't have all that fancy equipment. I know how to play it and how not to.'

Still, Hart noted that he wiped the lip of the bottle with his shirtsleeve before replacing it.

And he saw in that tiny gesture – so fast you'd miss it easily – a clue. A telling clue about Mr Compton Lewis. He recognized the careless, aggressive attitude that he'd seen in other men – in his brother, for instance. The source was simple insecurity, which can control you the way a pinch collar controls a dog.

They returned outside. Lewis went to work on the Ford once more, getting the spare on the front, in place of one of those that'd been shot out – so they could drag the other flat on the rear, like he'd suggested.

Hart reflected on how much the disaster at the house was eating at him.

Blindsided . . .

Looking for clues he should've seen but hadn't. He hated incompetence but hated it most when he was the guilty party. Hart had once cancelled a hit in St. Louis, when it turned out that the 'park' his victim used to walk home from work – a perfect shooting zone – was a neighborhood playground, filled with dozens of energetic little witnesses. Angrily, he'd realized that the two times he'd surveyed the place in preparation for the kill had been in mid-morning, while the kids were still in school.

He now looked around the house and yard. There was a

possibility that somewhere he'd left damning trace evidence. But probably Lewis was right; the cops here weren't out of that famous show, *CSI – Crime Scene International* or whatever it was called. Hart didn't watch TV, though he knew the idea: all that expensive scientific equipment.

No, something more fundamental was bothering him. He was thinking back to the paw print and the creature who'd left it, its disregard for the men who'd invaded its territory. Any challenges here weren't about microscopes and computers. They were more primitive.

He felt that tickle of fear again.

Lewis was moving along with the jack and the lug wrench, swapping the wheels on the Ford. He looked at his watch. 'We'll be back to civilization by ten thirty. Man, I can taste that beer and burger now.'

And returned to the task, working fast with his small but clever fingers.

'No alarm,' Brynn whispered, grimacing.

'What?' Michelle asked, not understanding the mumpy voice.

She repeated slowly, 'No. Alarm.' Brynn was looking over the spacious mountain house, 2 Lake View. The owners clearly had money; why no security?

She broke a window in the back door with her elbow, unlatched the lock. The women hurried into the kitchen. Brynn walked immediately to the stove and turned on a burner to warm herself, risking the light. Nothing. The propane was shut off outside. No time to find the valve and turn it on. Please, she thought, just have some dry clothes. It was cold inside but at least they were protected from the wind, and the bones of the house retained a bit of heat from the day's sun.

She touched her face – not the bullet wound but her jaw. When the weather was cold or she was tired the reconstructed spot throbbed, though she often wondered if the sensation was imaginary.

'We've gotta move fast. First, look for a phone or a computer. We could email or instant-message.' Joey was always online. She was sure she could get a message to him but she'd have to phrase it so that he'd get the urgency but not be upset.

There'd be no vehicular escape; they'd already peered into the garage and found it empty. Brynn continued, 'And look for weapons. Not much hunting here, with the state park and most of the land posted. But they still might have a gun. Maybe a bow.'

'And arrow?' Michelle asked, her eyes panicked at the thought of shooting one at a human being. 'I can't do that. I wouldn't know how.'

Brynn had played with one of the weapons at summer camp, once or twice, years ago. But she'd learn to handle it fast if she had to.

She was considering this fantasy when she noted that Michelle had walked away. She heard a click and a rumble.

A furnace!

Brynn ran into the living room and found the young woman at the thermostat.

'No,' Brynn said, her teeth chattering.

'I'm freezing,' Michelle said. 'Why not?'

Brynn shut the unit off.

Michelle protested, 'I'm so cold, it hurts.'

Tell me about it, Brynn thought. But she said, 'There'll be smoke. The men could see it.'

'It's dark out. They won't see anything.'

'We can't take the chance.'

The woman shrugged resentfully.

The furnace hadn't been on for more than a few seconds and from the distance the men wouldn't've have been able to see anything.

'We don't have much time.' Brynn glanced at a clock radio, which glowed blue. 8:21. 'They might decide to come here. Let's look fast. Phone, computer, weapons.'

The darkness outside was now almost complete and the frustration intense: Maybe their salvation was two feet away, a phone or gun. But it was impossible to tell. They had to search mostly by touch. Michelle was cautious, moving slowly.

'Faster,' Brynn urged.

'They have black widow spiders up here. I found one in my room when I came to visit Steve and Emma last year.'

The least of our worries.

They continued to search frantically for ten minutes, through drawers, closets, baskets of papers and personal junk. Brynn smiled as she found a Nokia, but it was an old one, no battery and a broken antenna. She dumped out all the contents on the rug and felt for a charger.

Nothing.

'Damn,' Brynn muttered, standing stiffly, her face throbbing. 'I'll check upstairs. Keep on looking down here.'

Michelle nodded uncertainly, not happy about being left alone.

Spiders . . .

Brynn climbed the stairs. Her search of the second floor revealed no weapons or phones or computers. She didn't bother with the attic. A glance out the window revealed flashlights in the yard around the Feldman house but the men couldn't be counted on to stay there much longer.

She longed to turn on a light but didn't dare and continued feeling her way through the bedrooms, concentrating on the largest. She began ripping open drawers and closet doors and finally found some clothing. She stripped off her jacket and the leathery, wet uniform and dressed in the darkest clothing she could find: two pairs of navy blue sweat pants, two men's T-shirts and a thick sweatshirt. She pulled on dry socks – her heels were already blistering from the waterlogged footgear – but had to put on her Sheriff's Department Oxfords again; there were no spare shoes. She found a thick black ski parka and pulled it on, and finally began to feel warmer. She wanted to cry, the sensation was so comforting.

In the bathroom she opened the medicine cabinet and felt her way through the bottles until she found a rectangular one. She sniffed the contents to make sure it was rubbing alcohol, then soaked a wad of toilet paper with it and bathed her wounded cheek. She gasped at the pain and her legs buckled. Swabbed the inside of her mouth too, which hurt ten times more. She dropped her head before she fainted. Inhaled deeply. 'Okay,' she whispered as the pain slowly dissolved to tolerable. Then pocketed the alcohol, ran downstairs.

'Any phones or guns, anything?' Michelle asked.

'No.'

'I looked . . . but it's so spooky. I couldn't go into the basement. I was afraid.'

Brynn herself took a fast look down there. She risked the light but since she'd seen no windows she figured it was safe. She found nothing helpful, though, either for communications or defense in what seemed like an endless series of small rooms and passages. Several small doorways led to what would probably be pretty good hiding places.

As Brynn returned to the kitchen Michelle whispered, 'I found those.' She nodded at a block of kitchen knives. Chicago Cutlery. Brynn took one, about eight inches long. She tested the factory honed blade with her thumb.

The deputy looked back at the Feldmans', saw the flashlight beams still scanning the yard. She had a thought, gazed around the house. 'Didn't we see a pool table somewhere down here?'

Michelle gestured toward the dining room. 'Through there, I think.'

As they walked quickly in that direction Brynn said, 'The way I drove up, Six Eighty-two, was from the east. After Clausen, I didn't see anything but some trailers and a few shacks in the distance. Nothing for miles. If I'd kept going west, would I have come to some stores or a gas station? A place with a phone?'

'I don't know. I never went that way.'

The women entered the recreation room, a spacious place with a bar, pool table and thousands of books on built-in shelves. Beneath the big-screen TV the cable box showed the time: 8:42.

Brynn was now warm again; curious, she reflected, she had no direct memory of the cold. She recalled how terrible she'd *felt* but couldn't summon up the sensation, as intense as it had been.

She studied the room, the sports memorabilia, the liquor bottles, the family pictures, the rack of pool cues, the balls aligned in their triangular nest on the table, then began rummaging through drawers at the bottom of the bookshelves.

No weapons, no phones.

'Let's see if we can find a map.'

They began to scour the shelves and stacks of papers. Brynn was looking through a bookcase when Michelle gave a cry.

Brynn gasped and spun around.

'Look! Somebody's coming!'

The women dropped to their knees by the window. Brynn could see, several hundred yards away, headlights moving slowly down Lake View Drive toward the county highway.

'Are there any other houses past the Feldmans'?' Brynn asked. She seemed to recall that there were only three residences here.

'I don't know. Maybe it's a neighbor. Or the police! Maybe a police car came to look for you and we missed them. If we run we can stop them! Let's go!' Michelle rose and in a frantic, limping rush started for the door.

'Wait,' Brynn said in a harsh whisper.

'But they'll be gone in a few minutes!' Her voice was angry. 'We can't wait! Don't be crazy!'

Brynn held up a hand. 'Michelle, no. Look.'

The moon was higher now, bright enough for them to make out the car. It was the killers' Ford.

'Oh, no,' the young woman said through set teeth. 'How can they drive it with the flat tires?'

'You shot out two, they put the spare on the front and they'll let the other one rim. It's front-wheel drive; they'll just drag the rear. Look, see the dust.'

'Can they get very far?'

'Miles, yeah, if they don't go fast.'

The taillights cast a ghostly red aura in the dust kicked up by the dragging wheel. The Ford eased around the snaky road and toward the county highway. The lights were soon obscured by a tangle of jack pine, yew and elegant willow. The car vanished.

Michelle hugged herself. She sighed with relief. 'So they're gone . . . It'll be okay, right? We can just wait here. We can put the heat on now, can't we? Please.'

'Sure,' Brynn said, staring after the car. 'Let's put the heat on.'

Lewis piloted the limping Ford along Lake View Drive, past the house at Number 2 and then turned and continued along the winding road toward the county highway.

Hart said, 'Was a good shot you made with that scattergun, hitting her car all that distance.'

Lewis offered a dismissive sneer but Hart saw that the words hit home; the punk was pleased. 'I wanted to take *her* out. That's why I was aiming high. Compensated for the wind too. Didn't want to hit the tires. I didn't hit 'em, you see?'

'I did.'

'But I led her just right, didn't I? About four feet. And high. Didn't think she'd go out of control.'

'Who'd guess that?'

A moment or two passed. Lewis said, 'Hey, Hart?'

Looking at the woods around him. 'Yeah?'

'Okay, what it is . . . I shouldn't've said anything. About the keys.'

'Keys?'

'In the house. With the woman cop. I gave it away . . . You were right. I got excited. My brother always said I do things or say something before I think. I gotta watch that.'

'Who'd've thought, a cop?' Hart nodded at him. 'Can't stay on top of everything. But you did some fine shooting.'

The car was filled with the smell of hot rubber and metal from the self-destructing tire.

It was then that Hart glanced back. 'Shit!' he whispered.

'What? Whatta you see?'

'I think it's her. Yeah, it is! The cop.'

'What? She got out of the water? Fuck. Where is she?'

'In that other house. The one we just passed. Number Two. The cop.'

'No shit. You're sure?'

'In the window. Yeah. I saw her plain as day.'

'I can't even see the house.'

'Was a break in the trees. She probably saw us go past and stood up. Thinking we were gone. Man, that was stupid of her.'

'They both there?'

'I don't know. All I saw was the cop.' Hart was silent a moment. Lewis kept driving. Hart continued, 'I don't know what to do. We're doing pretty good with the tire.'

'She's holding up,' Lewis agreed.

'And we'll be at the highway in ten minutes. I'd love to get the fuck out of here.'

'Amen.'

'Course, then we miss the chance for some payback. Jesus, that woman's slugs came six inches away from my head. I don't dodge lead the way you do.'

'True too,' Lewis said, thinking things over and laughing about the bullet dodging.

'And wouldn't be a bad idea to get things finished up now so we don't have to worry. Especially since she knows my name.' Hart shrugged. 'But I don't know. Whatever you're up for. Get her or not.'

A pause. Then Lewis lifted his foot off the accelerator,

considering this. 'Sure. And Michelle, maybe she's there too
. . . Fuck *her* up bad is what I really want, my friend.'

'Okay, I say let's do it,' Hart said. He looked around again
and then pointed ahead to the driveway at 1 Lake View. 'Shut
the lights off and head up there. We'll move around behind.
She'll never guess.'

Lewis grinned. 'Payback. You son of a bitch, Hart. I knew
you'd be up for it.'

Hart gave a short laugh and pulled his pistol from his belt.

In fact, Hart hadn't seen anything in the window at Number
2. Like Lewis, he couldn't even *see* the place. But instinct had
told him that the cop was there. He knew she'd survived the
crash; he'd seen footprints leading from the lake. She'd have
gone toward the closest shelter she could find: the second
house on Lake View, he'd concluded. None of this he'd shared
with Lewis, though. Hart had been taking soundings for the
past couple of hours and knew his partner definitely didn't
want to stay here. He wanted to head back to Milwaukee. He
talked big about tracking down the two women later taking
care of them. But Hart knew it was just that: talk. The man'd
get lazy and forget about it – until somebody came for him
in the middle of the night. But if Hart had insisted they remain
here to hunt the women down, Lewis'd dig his heels in and
there'd be a fight.

Hart did *not* need any more enemies tonight.

But seeing Lewis wipe the lip of the bottle, back at the
Feldmans' house, Hart had sized up the younger man and
decided he could get Lewis to stay here if he played on the
man's insecurities: complimenting his shooting and making it
seem like staying to get the cop was Lewis's idea.

Hart was sometimes called 'the craftsman', a reference to
his hobby of furniture making and woodworking, though the
term was usually used by people in his profession, the one that
had brought him here to Lake Mondac tonight. And the

number-one rule of craftsmanship is knowing your tools: the animate ones, like Lewis, in addition to those made from steel.

No, Hart never intended to return to the city without killing these two women, even if it took all night. Or all the next day, for that matter, even if the place was swarming with cops and rescue workers.

Yes, he wanted to kill Michelle, though that was a lower priority than getting the policewoman. *She* was the one he absolutely had to kill. She was the threat. Hart couldn't forget her. Standing by her car. Just standing tall and waiting for him. The look on her face, a flash of Gotcha, which might've been his imagination, though he didn't think so. Like a hunter, waiting for just the right moment to take the shot. Like Hart himself.

Only his instant reflex, diving to the ground, had saved him. That, and the fact that she'd fired one-handed, wisely not letting go of her car keys. He actually heard a bullet near his ear, a pop, not a *phushhhh*, like in the movies. Hart knew he was closer to death at that moment than when Michelle had snuck up behind him and taken her shot.

Lewis now continued up the drive of 1 Lake View. At Hart's direction, he beached the Ford in a stand of brush behind the house. It was well hidden in the tall grass and shrubs. They climbed out and moved west, into the woods about thirty feet, and then started going north, parallel to the private road, moving as quickly as they could toward Number 2.

Hart led Lewis around a pile of noisy leaves and they picked up the pace, staying in the thick of the forest for as long as they could.

A snap of branches behind them. Both men spun around. Lewis readied the shotgun nervously. The visitor wasn't human, though. It was that animal again, the one nosing in the grass earlier, or a similar one. A dog or coyote, he supposed. Or maybe a wolf. Did they have wolves in Wisconsin?

It kept its distance. Hart sensed no threat other than the risk of noise that might alert someone in the house. This time Lewis paid it no mind.

The creature vanished.

Hart and Lewis paused and studied the house for a long moment. There was no motion from inside. Hart thought he heard someone talking but decided it was the wind, which brushed over leaves and made the sound of a mournful human voice.

No light, no movement inside.

Had he been wrong in his guess that the cop had come here?

Then he squinted and tapped Lewis on the arm. A thin trail rose from the heating system exhaust duct next to the chimney. Lewis smiled. They eased closer to the house, under cover of thorny berry bushes that stretched from the woods nearly to the back porch. Hart carried his pistol with his trigger finger pointed forward, outside the guard. He held the gun casually, at his side. Lewis's grip on the shotgun was tense.

At the back door, they stopped, noting the broken glass in the window. Hart pointed to the porch, at their feet. Two fragments of differing footprints, both women's sizes.

Lewis gave a thumbs-up. He hooked the gun through his left arm and reached in through the broken pane, unlatched the lock. He swung the door open.

Hart held up a hand, whispered as low as he could, 'Assume one of 'em has a weapon. And they're waiting for us.'

Lewis gave another of his patented sneers, evidencing his low opinion of their enemy. But Hart lifted an impatient eyebrow and the man mouthed, 'Okay.'

'And no flashlights.'

Another nod.

Then, their gun muzzles pointed forward, they moved into the house.

Moonlight slanted through the large windows and gave some illumination throughout the first floor. They searched quickly. In the kitchen, Hart pointed to the drawers. A half dozen were open. He tapped the knife block. Several slots were empty.

Hart heard something. He held up a hand, frowning. Tilted his head.

Yes, it was voices. Women's voices, very faint.

Hart pointed up the stairs, noting that his pulse, which had been a little elevated by the trek through the forest, was now back to normal.

Stanley Mankewitz was eating dinner with his wife in an Italian restaurant in Milwaukee, a place that claimed to serve the best veal in the city. That was a meat that troubled both Mankewitz and his wife but they were guests of the businessman making up the threesome and so they'd agreed to come here.

The waiter recommended the veal saltimbocca, the veal Marsala and the fettuccini with veal Bolognese.

Mankewitz ordered a steak. His wife picked the salmon. Their host had the chopped-up calf.

As they waited for their appetizers they toasted with glasses poured from a bottle of Barbaresco, a spicy wine from the Piedmont region of Italy. The bruschetta and salads came. The host tucked his napkin into his collar, which seemed tacky but was efficient and Mankewitz never put down whatever was efficient.

Mankewitz was hungry, but he was tired too. He was head of a local union – maybe the most important on the western shore of Lake Michigan. It was made up of tough, demanding workers, employed at companies owned by men who were also tough and demanding.

Which words also described Mankewitz's life pretty well.

Their host, one of the heads of the national union, had flown in from New Jersey to talk to Mankewitz. He'd offered Mankewitz a cigar as they sat in a conference room in the union headquarters – where no-smoking ordinances weren't taken seriously – and proceeded to tell him that the joint federal and state investigation had better be concluded, favorably, pretty soon.

'It will be,' Mankewitz had assured. 'Guaranteed.'

'Guaranteed,' the man from New Jersey had said, in the same abrupt way he'd bitten the tip off his cigar.

Hiding his fury that this prick had flown from Newark to deliver his warning like a prissy schoolteacher, Mankewitz had smiled, conveying a confidence he absolutely didn't feel.

He began spearing his romaine lettuce from the Caesar salad, dressing on the side but anchovies present and accounted for.

The dinner was purely social and the conversation meandered as they ate. The men talked about the Packers and the Bears and the Giants but delivered merely sound bites, aware that a lady was at the table, and everyone found the subject of vacationing in Door County or the Caribbean a more palatable topic. The New Jersey man offered his anchovies to Mankewitz, who declined but with a smile, as a wave of absolute fury passed through him. Hatred too. He'd decided that if their host ever ran for head of the national union Mankewitz would make sure his campaign sank like the *Edmund Fitzgerald*.

As the salad plates were noisily whisked away, Mankewitz noticed a man enter the restaurant by himself and shake his head curtly to the hostess. He was in his late thirties, with short, curly hair and an easy face and looked like a good-natured Hobbit. The man oriented himself, looking around the underlit and over-Italianized place, which was owned by Ukrainians and staffed by Eastern Europeans and Arabs. He finally spotted Mankewitz, who was hard to miss, being 230 pounds, with an enviable shock of silver hair.

They made eye contact. The man stepped back, into the corridor. Mankewitz took a slug of wine and wiped his mouth. He stood up. 'Be right back.'

The labor boss joined the Hobbit and they walked toward the banquet rooms, tonight empty, down a long corridor, where the only other presences were effigies: pictures of people like Dean Martin and Frank Sinatra and James Gandolfino, all of whose signatures and endorsements of the restaurant in bold marker looked suspiciously similar.

Eventually Mankewitz got tired of walking and stopped. He said, 'What is it, Detective?'

The man hesitated, as if he didn't want his job title used under these circumstances. And Mankewitz decided that of course he didn't.

'There's a situation.'

'What does that mean? "Situation"? That's a Washington word, a corporate word.' Mankewitz had been in a bad mood lately, unsurprisingly, which prompted the retort but there wasn't much edge to it.

The Hobbit said, without a fleck of emotion, 'Up in Kennesha County.'

'The hell is that?'

'About two hours northwest of here.' The cop lowered his voice even more. 'It's where the lawyer in the case has a summer house.'

The Case. Capital C.

'The lawyer from—'

'Got it.' Now Mankewitz was concerned about indiscretion and cut the cop off with a wave before he mentioned Hartigan, Reed, Soames & Carson. 'What's the story?' Mankewitz had dropped the irritated act, which was replaced by a concern that was no act at all.

'Apparently what happened was there was a nine-one-one call from her husband's phone. Went to the county. We're monitoring all communication involving the players.'

The Players. In the Case . . .

'You told me that. I didn't know they were checking all the way out there.'

'The systems're all consolidated.'

How did they do that? Mankewitz wondered. Computers, of course. Privacy was fucked. As well he knew. 'A call. A nine-one-one call. Go on.' Mankewitz looked at a smiling Dean Martin.

'Nobody seems to know what was said. It was really brief. And then it seemed to get rescinded.'

That's a word cops don't use very often. 'Whatta you mean?'

'The husband, he called back and said it was a mistake.'

Mankewitz looked along the dark corridor to where his wife was chatting happily with a tall, balding man standing at the table. He wondered if the man only stopped by because he'd seen Mankewitz wasn't at the table.

Determined, slick, tough pricks . . .

He focused on the Hobbit. 'So it was an emergency and then it wasn't.'

'Right. That's why it didn't go to anybody on the taskforce. I'm the only one who knows. The record's there but it's buried . . . I have to ask, Stan, what should I know about?'

Mankewitz held his eyes. 'There's nothing you should know about, Pat. Maybe it was a fire. Nine-one-one – who knows? A fender-bender. A break-in. A raccoon in the basement.'

'I'll go out on a limb for you but not walk the plank.'

For what he was slipping into the cop's anonymous account, the man should've been willing to jump *off* the fucking plank and kill sharks with his bare hands.

Mankewitz happened to notice his wife glancing his way. The entrees had arrived. He looked back at the cop and said,

'I told you from the beginning there's nothing you have to worry about. That was our deal. You're completely protected.'

'Don't do anything stupid, Stan.'

'Like what, eat here?'

The detective gave a halfhearted grin. He nodded at a photo next to them. 'Can't be that bad. It was Sinatra's favorite restaurant.'

Mankewitz grunted and left the man in the corridor, heading for the men's room and fishing a prepaid cell phone out of his pocket.

On the second floor of the house at 2 Lake View were five doors, all closed. The carpet was Home Depot Oriental and on the walls were posters from an art gallery that was thirty feet of aisle in Target or Wal-Mart.

Hart and Lewis moved with infinite care, slowly, pausing at each door. They finally found the one the women's voices were coming from. Lewis was staying focused. And, thank God, quiet.

The words the women were speaking were impossible to make out but it was clear that they didn't seem at all suspicious the men were nearby.

What the hell were those gals talking about?

Strange allies on a strange night.

Hart wasn't thinking much about that, though. He was feeling keen satisfaction in the success of the car trick. That he was about to kill two human beings meant nothing to him, nor did the fact there'd be some pleasure in the death of Michelle, who'd shot him, or of the policewoman, who'd tried to. No, this nearly sexual pleasure he felt was due only to the approaching conclusion of a job he'd begun. The bloody deaths of two women happened to be that resolution but, to him, it was no different from that glow he felt when he gave the last fine-steel-wool buff to the lacquer on a cabinet he'd built or dusted herbs on an omelet he'd fixed for a woman who'd spent the night.

Of course, there'd be consequences from the deaths. His life was about to change and he understood that. For instance, the cop's colleagues would go all out to find her killer. He even wondered whether her kin – husband, brother or father – might take the law into their own hands, if the local investigators didn't do a very good job finding Hart, which he suspected they wouldn't.

But if and when the cop's husband, say, came after him, Hart would create a plan to deal with that. He'd execute it and eliminate the problem. And feel just as satisfied with the symmetry of conclusion as he was about to now, when he fired the fatal bullet into her body.

Hart gingerly tried the knob. Locked. The voices continued, unalarmed.

Hart pointed to himself and his good shoulder.

Lewis lowered his mouth to Hart's ear and whispered, 'Your arm?'

'I'll live with it. When I'm through I'll drop down on the floor and give covering fire. You come in over me and take them out.'

'They have guns, you think?' Glancing toward the door.

'Why take knives if you've got guns? But we oughta count on one of them having a piece.'

Lewis nodded and gripped the shotgun, eyed the safety. The red button showed.

Inside, the talking continued, casual as could be.

Hart stepped back, glanced at Lewis, who held the muzzle of the Winchester skyward and nodded. Then, hunched down like a tackle, Hart sped forward and flinched as his right shoulder connected with wood. With a loud crack the lock popped and the door flew inward, but stopped only a few inches inside. Hart gasped as his head slammed into the oak and he stumbled back, stunned.

The door had hit some barricade.

Inside the bedroom the voices stopped instantly.

Hart shoved the door again – it moved no farther – and then snapped to Lewis, 'Push, help me. Push! It's blocked.'

The younger man dug his feet into the carpet but the door wouldn't budge. 'No way. It's blocked solid.'

Hart looked around the hall. He ran to the bedroom next door, to the right, and pushed his way inside. He searched the room fast. It had a French door leading to a deck outside. He kicked this open and looked out, to the left. The deck was thirty feet long and the bedroom where the women hid opened onto it as well, via a similar French door. There were no stairs off the deck. They hadn't escaped this way; they were still inside.

Hart called for Lewis to join him. Together they stepped out onto the deck. They moved to the first bedroom, stopping just short of the windows, which were closed, shades pulled or curtains drawn, and it seemed that other pieces of furniture had been pushed against the windows as barricades. The French door, beyond the end of the windows, was curtained as well.

Considering how best to approach the assault, whether the woman would be holding her Glock toward the hall or toward the window, other weapons, barricades, escape routes – for the women and for Hart and Lewis . . .

Lewis was eager to move but Hart took his time. Finally he decided. 'You go down to that door. I'll stay here and kick this window out and try to push that dresser or table, whatever it is, out of the way. I'll fire. They'll focus on that. Then you let go with a couple rounds.'

'Crossfire.'

Hart nodded. 'We got ammo. We can afford to use it. Then we'll go in through the door. Okay?'

Lewis, crouching, covered the distance to the door, staying low. He took a deep breath and glanced back. Hart nodded, kicked in the window, with a huge crash, and pushed over a small dresser. He dodged back as Lewis broke out a pane in the door and fired three shotgun rounds into the room, shaking the curtains and rattling the glass, while Hart fired his Glock four times in a random pattern. He didn't expect to hit anything but he knew it would keep their prey down, give him and Lewis time to get inside.

'Go!'

The men ran through the doorway, guns ready.

They found a room filled with mismatched antiques, rustic prints, last fall's magazines and books stacked on dressers and in baskets. But no human beings.

Hart thought for a moment that the women had used the delay to escape by the door to the hallway but it was still blocked – by a big dresser, it turned out. He gestured to the closet. Lewis pulled the door open and fired a shotgun round inside.

The noise was deafening. Hart wished the man had held back. The sudden deafness was freaking Hart out; he couldn't have heard anybody sneaking up behind him.

Looking around again. Where? The bathroom, Hart supposed. Had to be.

The door was closed.

Lewis stood in front of it. Hart pointed at Lewis's fatigue-jacket pocket. The man nodded and set down the shotgun and pulled out his silver SIG-Sauer pistol, still loud but less deafening than the Winchester scattergun. He chambered a round and flicked off the safety.

Hart started forward. Just as he was about to kick in the bathroom door, though, he paused, cocking his head. He gestured Lewis back. 'Wait,' he mouthed. He pulled a drawer out of a dresser and tossed it into the door, which snapped open.

Fumes poured from it. Their eyes stung fiercely and both men began to cough.

'Jesus, what is that?'

'Ammonia,' Hart answered.

'Like fucking teargas.'

Holding his breath, Hart flicked on the bathroom light.

Well, look at this.

The women had propped a bucket of ammonia on the top of the door so that whoever walked through would get drenched – and possibly blinded. Luckily the door eased shut by itself and tipped the bucket to the floor before the men arrived.

'A fucking trap.'

He imagined what it would've been like to get soaked with the chemical. The pain, unbearable.

Wiping his eyes, Hart slammed the door shut and scanned the bedroom. 'Look.' He sighed. 'It wasn't them at all talking. *That*'s what we heard.' He pointed to a TV. The electric cord of the Sony was tied around the leg of the dresser and then plugged into the wall outlet. When Hart had tried to break in the door, he'd pushed the dresser inward about three inches, which had unplugged the TV – making it seem that the women had stopped talking and presumably were hiding in the room.

He plugged the cord in again. The Shopping Channel came on. 'Women talking,' Hart whispered, shaking his head. 'No music. Just voices. They set it up and went out the patio door and through the other bedroom. To keep us busy and give 'em time to get away.'

'So they waited in the woods, saw us go past and're halfway to the county road.'

'Maybe.' But Hart wondered too if they'd made it *seem* like they were escaping to the highway when in fact they were hiding somewhere else in the house. He'd glanced downstairs earlier; the place seemed to have a large basement.

Yes or no? He finally decided: 'I think we'll have to search.'

Lewis replaced his pistol in his jacket and picked up the shotgun. 'Okay. But let's get the fuck out of *here*.' He was coughing. They pulled the dresser away from the door. But Hart paused, noticed something stuffed under a table. It was a pile of wet clothes. Of course, the cop would have changed after her swim in the freezing lake. Hart looked through the clothes. The pockets were empty. He examined the front of the shirt, the name tag, black and etched with white lettering. *Dep. Brynn McKenzie*.

She'd tricked him, sure, but Hart was pleased. For some reason he always found knowing the name of his enemy comforting.

Muted gunshots from inside 2 Lake View Drive snapped like impatient fingers. There was a pause and then more shots followed.

Brynn and Michelle were approaching the Feldmans' house, which was now completely dark. The air was thick with the smell of fireplace flames and loam and rotting leaves. The young woman had shut down again, sullen and resentful. She limped along more slowly, using a pool cue as a cane.

Brynn squeezed her arm.

No response.

'Come on, Michelle, we have to move faster.'

The young woman complied but was obviously distraught. She seemed put out. As if she were the only victim here. It reminded her of Joey's attitude when Brynn insisted he do homework before playing computer games or text-messaging his friends.

As they neared the house Brynn was reflecting on the dispute she'd had with Michelle back at 2 Lake View after agreeing to put the furnace on.

But she'd done that simply to trick the men into believing

they were hiding out in the house. She'd said to the young woman, 'Come on. We're going back to the Feldmans' place.'

'What?'

'Hurry.'

Michelle, with her injured ankle and in shock from losing her friends, had begged to stay in the house at Number 2, hiding, even in the spider-filled basement, and waiting for the police. Acting like a bit of a princess, she'd resisted heading outside. She couldn't understand why Brynn felt certain the men would circle back, rather than go on to Route 682.

But Brynn was convinced they would do just that. The drive to the highway was just a trick.

'But why?' the young woman had argued adamantly. 'It doesn't make sense.'

Brynn explained her logic. 'From what you told me, I don't think this was just a random break-in. They're professional killers. That means they're going to come after us. They have to. We can identify them. And *that* means we're a link to whoever hired them. So they're doubly desperate to find us. If they don't, their boss is going to come after them.'

Brynn didn't, however, tell her that there was another basis for her conclusion: the man named Hart. He wasn't going away. She'd recalled how confident he'd sounded talking to her in the house. Unemotional and fully prepared to kill her without a second's hesitation when she showed herself.

Hart reminded her of the surgeon who, in a perfectly even voice, explained how her father had died during exploratory surgery.

More chillingly, though, he reminded Brynn of her ex-husband. Hart's look was the same as in Keith's face once when she found him slipping a pistol she didn't recognize into the lock-box in the bedroom. She'd asked about it and the state trooper had hesitated but confessed to her that fellow officers would sometimes pocket a weapon found at crime scenes, if it wasn't necessary evidence. They'd collect them. 'Just to have,' Keith had explained.

'You mean . . . you mean, to plant them on a perp – so you can say you shot him in self defense?'

Her husband hadn't answered. But he'd glanced at her with a look that was identical to Hart's in that instant he rose from the foliage, holding his pistol and looking for a target.

There was something else in the glance too, Brynn decided. Admiration?

Maybe.

And a challenge too.

May the best person win . . .

Assuming the men would return to the house where she and Michelle were hiding, Brynn had set the TV to a shopping network, blocked the door with a dresser and rigged the power cord around the leg. Then she'd found a bottle of ammonia and poured it on the floor, alongside a bucket, to make it look as though she'd set a trap. That would make Hart and his partner wary, thinking she was willing to blind her pursuers – though in reality she would not risk hurting the homeowners or rescue workers later.

They'd grabbed a few other things, which they now carried: weapons. Each woman had a sock containing a billiard ball – like a South American bolo throwing weapon, which Brynn had learned about helping Joey with a project on Argentina for school. They also had Chicago Cutlery knives in their pockets, wrapped in sock scabbards, and Brynn carried a pool cue at the end of which was taped a 10-inch-long Chicago Cutlery carving knife.

Michelle had taken the weapons reluctantly. But Brynn had insisted.

And the young woman had grudgingly agreed.

Then they'd slipped into the woods behind the house and turned north, back toward the Feldmans' place, picking their way carefully through the boggy ground and using logs and rocks as stepping-stones to climb over the streams that ran to the lake.

Now, keeping under cover in the yard of her friends' house, Michelle was staring south toward the gunshots. She muttered to Brynn, 'Why did you want to come back here? We should've gone the other way. To the county road. Now we've got to go past them to get there.'

'We're not going that way.'

'What do you mean? It's the only way to the county road.'

Brynn shook her head. 'I was on Six Eighty-two for nearly a half hour and I saw three cars. And that was at rush hour. We'd have to risk walking on the shoulder in the open for who knows how long. They'd find us there for sure.'

'But weren't there some houses on the highway? We'll go there. Call nine-one-one.'

'We can't go to any of them,' Brynn said. 'I won't lead those men to somebody else's place. I don't want anybody else hurt.'

Michelle was silent, staring at the Feldmans' house. 'That's crazy. We have to get out of here.'

'We're going to get out. Just not the way we came in.'

'Well, why aren't there more police here?' she snapped. 'Why'd you just come here by yourself? The police wouldn't do it that way in Chicago.' The young woman's voice was positively surly. Brynn tamped down her irritation. She squinted as she looked past her and pointed.

In the house at 2 Lake View, she could make out two flash-light beams, one upstairs, one on the ground floor. Scanning eerily. The men were both in the house, searching for them.

'Keep an eye on the flashlights. I'm going to look inside. Did Steven have a gun?'

'I have no idea,' Michelle scoffed. 'They really weren't the gun type.'

'Where's your cell phone?' Brynn asked.

'In my purse, in the kitchen.'

As Brynn sprinted for the porch she glanced back and could see the young woman's eyes, just visible in the moonlight. Yes, there was a measure of sorrow – that her friends had died. But it was the put-upon expression Brynn sometimes recognized in her son during one of his irritated moments. The expression that asked, Why me? Life just isn't fair.

'Nothing.'

Spoken in a whisper.

In the basement of the house at 2 Lake View Drive, Hart nodded, acknowledging the comment by Lewis, who was sweeping his flashlight around a dark storage area, which would have been perfect for hiding in.

And had been pretty much their last hope of finding the women in the house.

Hart was feeling more confident. It was likely that the women were no longer armed, a conclusion he'd come to by default: Otherwise they would have lain in wait and shot the men. Still, he'd insisted they use flashlights and not put on the overhead lights.

Once, Hart had seen a movement, spun around and fired. But the target turned out to be just the shadow of a fleeing rat, its shadow magnified a dozen times. The creature scurried away slowly. Hart was angry with himself for the panicked shot. He'd hurt his injured arm in the maneuver and they'd been temporarily deafened again. Angry too for the loss of control. Sure, it was logical. The sudden motion, jumping toward him, it seemed . . . Naturally he'd fired.

But excuses always tasted bad in Hart's mouth. You had nobody to blame but yourself if you cut the plank wrong or planed a bow into a chair leg meant to be straight, or split a dovetail joint.

'Measure twice, cut once,' his father used to say.

They trooped upstairs into the dark kitchen. Hart was looking out the back windows and into the forest, wondering if he was staring right at the women. 'Wasted some good minutes searching. That's why they set up that little scene in the bedroom. Buy time.'

And to blind us. He could smell the ammonia all the way down here, even with the upstairs bedroom door closed.

Then Hart mused, 'But where are they? Where would I go, if I was them?'

'The woods? Snuck past us and're making for the highway?'

Hart agreed. 'Yep. That's what I'd guess. There's no other way out. They'll be thinking they can hail a car but there won't be much traffic this time of night. Hell, there wasn't much on the way up here. And they'll have to stick close to the shoulder, out in the open. And that blood on Brynn's uniform? She's hurt. Be moving slowly. We'll spot 'em easy.'

Brynn McKenzie was making a fast sweep through the Feldmans' house. She left the lights out, of course, and searched by feel for weapons and cell phones. She found none.

Michelle's purse was gone, which meant the killers had it – and that they'd now know her name and where she lived.

Brynn walked into the kitchen, where the bodies lay in their death poses, the blood making a paisley pattern next to the husband and a near-perfect circle around the wife. Brynn hesitated briefly and then knelt and searched their pockets for cell phones. None. She tried the jackets. Similarly empty. She then stood and looked down at them. Wished there were time to say some words, though she had no idea what.

Did the couple have laptop computers? She looked at the briefcase on the floor – it was the woman's – and at the pile of file folders all stamped with the word *CONFIDENTIAL*. But no electronics. The husband apparently used a backpack for his briefcase but that had contained only a few magazines, a paperback novel and a bottle of wine.

Brynn's feet were beginning to sting again from chafing; the lake water had soaked through the dry socks. She looked in the laundry room and found two pairs of hiking boots. She pulled on dry socks and the larger of the boots. She took the second pair for Michelle. She also found a candle lighter and slipped that in her pocket.

Was there anything—?

She gasped in shock. Outside, the croak of frogs and the whisper of wind vanished in the insistent blare of a car alarm.

Then Michelle's desperate voice calling, 'Brynn! Come here! Help me!'

Brynn ran outside, gripping her makeshift spear, blade forward.

Michelle was standing beside the Mercedes, the window shattered. The young woman was frantic, wide-eyed. And paralyzed.

Brynn ran to the car, glancing at the house at Number 2. The flashlights went out.

They're on their way. Great.

'I'm sorry!' Michelle cried. 'I didn't think, I didn't think . . .'

Brynn ripped the passenger door open, popped the hood and ran to the front of the car. She'd made a point to learn all she could about cars and trucks – vehicles make up the majority of police work in a county like Kennesha – and her studies included mechanics as well as driving. Brynn struggled to work the cable off the positive terminal of the battery with the Chicago Cutlery knife. Finally the piercing sound stopped.

'What happened?'

'I just . . .' Michelle moaned angrily. 'It's not my fault!'

No? Whose was it?

She continued, 'I have low blood sugar. I was feeling funny. I brought some crackers with me.' She pointed to a bag of Whole Foods-brand snacks in the backseat. She said defensively, 'If I don't eat, sometimes I faint.'

'Okay,' said Brynn, who'd avoided breaking into and searching the Mercedes specifically because she'd known it would be alarmed. She now climbed in fast, grabbed the crackers and handed them to Michelle, then rifled through the glove compartment. 'Nothing helpful,' she muttered.

'You're mad,' she said, her voice an irritating whine. 'I'm sorry. I said I was sorry.'

'It's okay. But we have to move. Fast. They're on their way.' She handed Michelle the boots she'd found inside, the smaller pair, which should fit fine. Michelle's own boots were chic and stylish, with spiky three-inch heels – just the sort for a young professional. But useless footgear for fleeing from killers.

Michelle stared at the fleece boots. She didn't move.

'Hurry.'

'Mine are fine.'

'No, they're not. You can't wear those.' A nod at the designer footwear.

Michelle said, 'I don't like to wear other people's clothes. It's . . . gross.' Her voice was a hollow whisper.

Maybe she meant dead people's clothes.

A glance toward Number 2. No sign of the men. Not yet.

'I'm sorry, Michelle. I know it's upsetting. But you have to. And now.'

'I'm fine with these.'

'No. You can't. Especially with a hurt ankle.'

Another hesitation. It was as if the woman were a pouty eight-year-old. Brynn took her firmly by the shoulders. 'Michelle. They could be here any minute. We don't have any choice.' Her voice was harsh. 'Put the goddamn boots on. Now!'

A long moment. Michelle's jaw trembling, eyes red, she snatched away the hiking boots and leaned against the Mercedes to put them on. Brynn jogged to the garage and found beside it what she'd seen when she'd arrived: a canoe under a tarp. She hefted it. The fiberglass boat wasn't more than forty or fifty pounds.

Although Yahoo's estimate was accurate and two hundred yards separated them from the shoreline, a stream was only about thirty feet from the house and it ran pretty much straight to the lake.

In the garage she found life preservers and paddles.

Michelle was staring down at her friend's boots, grimacing. She looked like a rich customer who'd been sold inferior footwear and was about to complain to the store manager.

Brynn snapped, 'Come on. Help me.'

Michelle glanced back toward the house at 2 Lake View and, her face troubled, shoved the crackers in her pocket, then hurried to the canoe. The two women dragged it to the stream. Michelle climbed in with her pool cue walking stick and Brynn handed her the spear, paddles and life vests.

With a look back at the morass of forest, through which the killers were surely sprinting right now, the deputy climbed in and shoved off into the stream, a dark artery seeping toward a dark heart.

The men ran through the night, sucking in cold, damp air rich with the smell of rotting leaves.

At the sound of the horn, Hart had realized that rather than head for the county road, like he'd thought, the women had snuck back to the Feldman house. They'd probably broken into the Mercedes hoping to fix the tire, not thinking the car was alarmed. He and Lewis had started running directly for the place but immediately encountered bogs and some wide streams. Hart started to ford one but Lewis said, 'No, your feet'll chafe bad. Gotta keep 'em dry.'

Hart, never an outdoorsman, hadn't thought about that. The men returned to the driveway and jogged to Lake View Drive and then north toward Number 2.

'We go . . . up careful,' Hart said, out of breath, when they were halfway to the Feldmans' driveway. 'Still . . . could be a trap.' The jogging was hell on his wounded arm. He winced and tried moving it into different positions. Nothing helped.

'A trap?'

'Still . . . worried about a gun.'

Lewis seemed a lot less obnoxious now.

They slowed at the mailbox, then started up the drive, Hart first, both of them sticking to the shadows. Lewis was silent, thank God. The kid was catching on, if you could call a thirty-five-year-old a kid. Hart thought again of his brother.

About fifty feet up the driveway they paused.

Hart scanned what they could see, which wasn't much because of the dusk. Bats swooped nearby. And some other creature zipped past his head, floating down to a scampering landing.

Hell, a flying squirrel. Hart'd never seen one.

He was squinting at the Mercedes, noting the broken window. He saw no signs of the women.

It was Lewis who spotted them. He happened to look back down the driveway toward the private road. 'Hart. Look. What's that?'

He turned, half expecting to see Brynn rising from the bushes about to fire that black service piece of hers. But he saw nothing.

'What?'

'There they are! On the lake.'

Hart turned to look. About two hundred feet into the lake was a low boat, a skiff or canoe. It was moving toward the opposite shore but very slowly. It was hard to see for certain but he thought there were two people in it. Brynn and Michelle had seen the men, stopped paddling and hunched down, keeping a low profile. The momentum was carrying them toward the opposite shore.

Lewis said, 'That alarm, it wasn't a mistake. It was to distract us. So they could get away in the fucking boat.'

The man had made a good catch. Hart hadn't even been looking at the lake. He bridled once again at being outguessed – and he decided it was probably Brynn who'd tried to trick them.

The men ran down to the shore.

'Too far for the scattergun,' Lewis said, grimacing, disappointed. 'And I'm not much of a pistol shot.'

But Hart was. He went to a range at least once a week. Now, holding his gun in one hand, he began firing slowly, adjusting the elevation of the barrel as he did so. The sharp detonation rolled across the lake with each shot and returned as a pale echo. The first and second kicked up water in front of the boat; the rest did not. They were right on target. One shot every few seconds, the bullets pelted the canoe, sending fragments of wood or fiberglass into the air. He must've hit at least one of them – he saw her slump forward and heard a woman's panicked scream filling the damp air.

More shots. The wailing stopped abruptly. The canoe capsized and sank.

Hart reloaded.

'Nothing's moving,' Lewis said, shouting because of their numb ears. 'You got 'em, Hart.'

'Well, we gotta make sure.' Hart nodded at a small skiff nearby. 'Can you row?'

'Sure,' Lewis answered.

'Bring some rocks. To weigh the bodies down.'

'That was some fine shooting, Hart. I mean, really.' Lewis muscled the small boat upright.

But Hart wasn't thinking about marksmanship. Shooting was just a skill and in this business you had to be good at it, just like you couldn't be a carpenter without knowing how to plane or lathe. No, he was recalling his earlier thoughts. Now that the evening's mission was finished he had to turn his attention to what came next: how to anticipate and prepare for the hard consequences that would flow from these women's deaths.

Because, Hart knew, they surely would.

Graham Boyd sat forward on the green couch, frowning, looking not at the TV screen but at an antiqued table nearby, splotched in white and gold, under which sat a box containing the only knitting project he'd ever known Brynn to tackle – a sweater for a niece. She'd given it up years ago, after six inches of uneven sleeve.

Anna looked up from her own knitting. 'I let it go for a while.'

Her son-in-law lifted an eyebrow.

She swapped the big blue needles for a remote control, turned down the volume. Once again, Graham caught a glimpse of a tougher core within her than the spun hair and faint smile in her powdered face suggested.

'You might as well tell me. I'll get it out of you sooner or later.'

What the hell was she talking about? He looked away, at some nonsense on the flat screen.

Her eyes didn't leave him. 'That call, right? The one from the school?'

He started to say something, then paused. But he went ahead finally. 'Was a little worse than I let on.'

'Thought so.'

He explained what Joey's section advisor had said – about the boy's cutting school, the forgery, the 'phalting and even the suspension last fall. 'And there were some other fights he got into, too. I didn't have the heart to ask his advisor about it.'

Well, which one? . . .

'Ah.' Anna nodded. 'I had a feeling.'

'You did?'

She retrieved the knitting project. 'What're you going to do about it?'

Graham shrugged. He sat back. 'Had an idea to talk to him. But I'll leave that for Brynn. Let her handle it.'

'Been eating at you, I could see. You didn't laugh once at Drew Carey.'

'If this's happened once, it's happened before. Cutting class? Don't you think?'

'Most likely. My experience with children.' Anna was speaking from knowledge. Brynn had an older brother and a younger sister, a teacher and computer salesperson respectively. Pleasant, kind people, fun people. Conventional. Brynn tended to swim upstream more than her siblings.

Anna McKenzie now dropped the Hallmark-Channel demeanor, which she donned like camouflage when needed. The tone in her voice changed, day to night. 'What I want to say: You *never* discipline him, Graham.'

'After Keith, I never knew whether to do this or that.'

'You're not Keith. Thank God. Don't worry.'

'Brynn doesn't let me. Or that's the message I get. And I never pushed. I don't want to undermine her. He's her son.'

'Not just,' she reminded quickly. 'He's your boy too now. You get the whole package – even came with an ornery old lady you hadn't bargained for.'

He gave a laugh. 'But I want to be careful. Joey . . . I know he had a tough time with the divorce.'

'Who doesn't? That's life. No reason for you to be a shrinking violet when it comes to him.'

'Maybe you're right.'

'I am. Go up and see him. Now.' She added, 'Maybe it's the best thing in the world Brynn went out on that call tonight. Give you two a chance to talk.'

'What do I say? I tried coming up with something. It was stupid.'

'Go with your instincts. If it feels right it probably is. That's what I did with my children. Got some things right. And some things wrong. Obviously.'

The last word was heavily seasoned.

'You think?'

'I think. Somebody's got to be in charge. He can't be. And Brynn . . .' The woman said nothing more.

'Any advice?'

Anna laughed. 'He's the child. You're the adult.'

Graham supposed that was a brilliant insight but it didn't seem to help.

Evidently she could see he was confused. 'Play it by ear.'

Graham exhaled and walked upstairs, the steps creaking under his big frame. He knocked on the boy's door and entered without waiting for a response, which he'd never done before.

Joey's round, freckled face looked up from his desk, dominated by a large flat-screen monitor. He'd put his knit hat back on, like a rapper. Or gangsta. He was apparently instant-messaging with a friend. A webcam was involved. Graham didn't like it that the friend could see him, see the room.

'How's the homework coming?'

'Finished.' He typed away, not looking at the keyboard. Or at Graham.

On the wall was a series of still pictures from the Gus Van Sant movie *Paranoid Park*, about skateboarders in Portland. Joey must have printed them out. It was a good movie – for adults.

Graham had protested about their taking the boy. But he'd become obsessed with the movie and sulked until Brynn had acquiesced. As it turned out, though, they'd fled the theater after one particularly horrific scene. Graham had dodged the incident that a told-you-so would have bought, though he came real close to telling his wife that next time she should listen to him.

'Who's that?' Graham asked, glancing at the screen.

'Who?'

'You're IMing?'

'Just some guy.'

'Joey.'

'Tony.' The boy continued to stare at the screen. Graham's secretary could type 120 words a minute. Joey seemed to be going faster.

Worried it might be an adult, Graham asked, 'Tony who?'

'In my, you know, class. Tony Metzer.' His tone suggested that Graham had met him, though he knew he hadn't. 'We're, like, into Turbo Planet. He can't get past level six. I can get to eight. I'm helping him.'

'Well, it's late. That's enough IMing for tonight.'

Joey continued typing and Graham wondered if he was being defiant or just saying goodbye. Would this become a fight? The man's palms sweated. He'd fired employees for theft, he'd faced down a burglar who'd broken into the office, he'd stopped knife fights among his workers. None of those incidents had made him as nervous as this.

After some fast keystrokes the computer screen went back to the desktop. The boy looked up pleasantly. Asking, What now?

'How's the arm?'

'Good.'

The boy picked up his game controller. Pushed buttons so fast his fingers were a blur. Joey had dozens of electronic gadgets, MP3 players, iPod, cell phone, computer. He seemed to have plenty of friends but he communicated more with his fingers than with words spoken face to face.

'You want some aspirin?'

'Naw, it's okay.'

The boy concentrated on the game but his stepfather could see he'd grown wary.

Graham's first thought was to trick the boy into confessing about the 'phalting but that seemed to go against the instinct that Anna had told him to rely on. He thought back to his dishpan reflections: dialogue, not confrontation.

The boy was silent. The only noise was the click of the controller and the electronic bass beat of the soundtrack of the game, as a cartoon character strolled along a fantastical road.

Okay, get to it.

'Joey, can I ask you why you skip school?'

'Skip school?'

'Why? Are there problems with teachers? Maybe with some other students?'

'I don't skip.'

'I heard from the school. You skipped today.'

'No, I didn't.' He kept playing on the computer.

'I think you did.'

'No,' the boy said credibly. 'I didn't.'

Graham saw a major flaw with the dialogue approach. 'You've never skipped?'

'I don't know. Like, once I got sick on the way to school and I came home. Mom was at work and I couldn't get her.'

'You can always call me. My company's five minutes from here and fifteen minutes from school. I can be there in no time.'

'But you can't sign me out.'

'Yes, I can. I'm on the list. Your mother put me on the

list.' Didn't the boy know that? 'Tell you what, Joey, shut that off.'

'Shut it off?'

'Yeah. Shut it off.'

'I'm nearly to—'

'No. Come on. Shut it off.'

He continued to play.

'Or I'll unplug it.' Graham rose and reached for the cord.

Joey stared at him. 'No! That'll dump the memory. Don't. I'll save it.'

He continued to play for a moment – a dense twenty seconds – and then hit some buttons, and with a deflating computer-generated sound the screen froze.

Graham sat down on the bed, near the boy.

'I know you and your mother talked about your accident today. Did you tell her you skipped school?' Graham was wondering if Brynn knew and hadn't told him.

'I didn't skip school.'

'I talked to Mr. Raditzky. He says you forged the note from your mother.'

'He's lying.' Eyes evasive.

'Why would he lie?'

'He doesn't like me.'

'He sounded pretty concerned about you.'

'You just don't get it.' Apparently thinking that this was irrefutable proof of his innocence, he turned back to the frozen screen. A creature of some sort bounced up and down. Running in place. The boy eyed the game controller. He didn't go for it.

'Joey, somebody from school saw you 'phalting on Elden Street.'

The boy's eyes flickered. 'They're lying too. It was Rad, right? He's making that up.'

'I don't think they were, Joey. I think they saw you on your board, going forty miles an hour down Elden Street when you wiped out.'

He bounced onto his bed, past Graham, and pulled a book off the shelf.

'So you didn't tell your mother you cut and you didn't tell her you were 'phalting, did you?'

'I wasn't 'phalting. I was just boarding. I went off the parking lot steps.'

'Is that where you had the accident today?'

A pause. 'Not really. But I don't 'phalt.'

'Have you ever?'

'No.'

Graham was at a complete loss. This was going nowhere. Instinct . . .

'Where's your board?'

Joey glanced at Graham and said nothing. Turned back to the book.

'Where?' his stepfather asked adamantly.

'I don't know.'

Graham opened the closet, where the boy's skateboard was sitting on a pile of athletic shoes.

'No more boarding this month.'

'Mom said two days!'

Graham thought Brynn had said three. 'One month. And you have to promise that you're never going to 'phalt again.'

'I don't 'phalt!'

'Joey.'

'This's such bullshit!'

'Don't say that to me.'

'Mom doesn't mind.'

Was that true? 'Well, I do.'

'You can't stop me. You're not my father!'

Graham felt an urge to argue. To explain about authority and hierarchy and family units, his and the boy's respective roles in the household. An argument on the merits, though, seemed like an automatic loss.

Instinct, he reminded himself.

Okay. Let's see what happens.

'Are you going to tell me the truth?'

'I *am* telling the truth,' the boy raged and started to cry.

Graham's heart was pounding furiously. Was he being honest? This was so hard. He tried to keep his voice steady. 'Joey, your mother and I love you very much. We were both worried sick about you when we heard you'd been hurt.'

'You don't love me. Nobody does.' The tears stopped as quickly as they'd started and he slouched back, reading his book.

'Joey . . .' Graham leaned forward. 'I'm doing this because I care about you.' He smiled. 'Come on. Brush your teeth, put on your PJs. Time for bed.'

The boy didn't move. His eyes were frantically scanning words he wasn't even seeing.

Graham rose and left the room, carrying the skateboard. He headed downstairs, fighting the urge with every step to go back and apologize and beg the boy to be happy and forgive him.

But instinct won. Graham continued to the ground floor, put the skateboard on the top shelf of the closet.

Anna watched him. She seemed amused. Graham didn't think anything was funny.

'When'll Brynn be home?' his mother-in-law asked.

He looked at his watch. 'Soon, I'd guess. She'll probably stop for dinner. But she'll eat in the car.'

'She shouldn't do that. Not on those roads at night. You look down for one minute, pick up your sandwich and there's a deer in front of you. Or a bear. Jamie Henderson nearly hit one. It was just there.'

'I heard that, I think. Big one?'

'Big enough.' A nod toward the ceiling. 'How'd it go?'

'Not good.'

She continued to give him a half smile.

'What?' he asked, irritated.

'It's a start.'

Graham rolled his eyes. 'I don't think so.'

'Trust me. Sometimes just delivering a message's the important thing. Whatever that message is. Remember that.'

He picked up the phone and dialed Brynn again. It went right to voice mail. He tossed the phone on the table and stared absently at the TV screen. Thinking again about the yellow jackets. How he'd been going about his business, wheeling a big shaggy plant, enjoying the day, never realizing that he'd trod on the nest ten feet back.

Never realizing it until the hard little dots, with their fiery stingers, were all over him.

He thought now: And why does it even matter?

Just let it go.

Graham reached for the remote control. Upstairs, a door slammed.

Brynn and Michelle were making their way through scruffy tangled forest about three hundred yards north of the Feldmans' house. Here the trees were denser, mostly lush pine, spruce and fir. The view of the lake was cut off.

The car alarm had been an unfortunate mistake. But, since it had happened, Brynn hoped that she'd turned it around to work to their advantage, making the men think that it was an intentional distraction and that the women were escaping by canoe to the far shore of the lake. In fact, though, they'd used the boat only to paddle downstream a short distance and cross to the opposite shore of the creek. They'd propped up life preservers to look like two huddling passengers and then shoved the canoe into the speedy current, which propelled the vessel into the lake.

They'd then hurried as best they could, given Michelle's ankle, away from the lake house enclave, north toward Marquette State Park.

When the gunfire came, as Brynn expected, she was ready and let go a fierce, harrowing scream. Then abruptly stopped as if shot. She'd known the men would be half deafened and, with the confusing echoes from the hills, couldn't tell the scream had come from someplace else entirely. The trick might not fool them for long but she was sure she'd bought some time.

'Can we stop now?' Michelle asked.

'Why, does your ankle hurt?'

'Well, sure it does. But, I mean, let's just wait here. They'll be gone soon.' She was eating her snack crackers. Brynn looked at them. Michelle, reluctantly, it seemed, offered her some. She ate a handful hungrily.

'We can't stop. We have to keep going.'

'Where?'

'North.'

'What does "north" mean? Is there a cabin that way or something, or a phone?'

'We're getting as far away from them as we can. Into the park.'

Michelle slowed. 'Look at this place. It's all a mess, it's tangled and . . . well, a mess. There aren't any paths. It's freezing.'

And you in that two-thousand-dollar coat . . . complaining, Brynn reflected.

'There's a ranger station maybe four, five miles from here.'

'Five miles!'

'Shhh.'

'That's bullshit. We can't walk five miles through this.'

'You're in good shape. You run, right?'

'On a treadmill at my health club. Not in places like this. And which way do we go? I'm already lost.'

'I know the general direction.'

'The woods? I can't!'

'We don't have any choice.'

'You don't understand . . . I'm afraid of snakes.'

'They're more afraid of you, believe me.'

Michelle displayed the crackers. 'This isn't going to be

enough food. Do you know about hypoglycemia? Everyone thinks it's nothing. But I could faint.'

Brynn said firmly, 'Michelle, there are men out there who want to kill us. Snakes and your blood sugar really come pretty low on the scale of problems here.'

'I can't do it.' The woman reminded Brynn of Joey's first day at elementary school: he'd planted his feet and refused to go. It took two days for her to persuade him to attend. In fact, Brynn now recognized similar signs of hysteria in Michelle's face. The young woman stopped walking altogether. Her eyes were wide and she gestured broadly with twitchy hands. 'I shop at Whole Foods. I buy coffee at Starbucks. This isn't me, this isn't my world. I can't do it!'

'Michelle,' Brynn said gently, 'it'll be okay. It's only a state park. Thousands of people come through here every summer.'

'On the paths, the trails.'

'And we're going to find one.'

'But people get lost there. I saw this thing on TV. This couple got lost and they froze to death and the animals ate their bodies.'

'Michelle—'

'No, I don't want to go! Let's hide here. We'll find a place. Please.' She looked as if she was going to cry. Brynn remembered that the poor woman had seen her friends shot down – and had nearly been killed herself. She tried to be patient. 'No. That one man, at least, Hart, he'll come after us as soon as he finds we tricked 'em with the boat. He won't know for sure we came this way but he might guess.'

Michelle looked back, her eyes zipping around in panic, her breath fast.

'Okay?'

Michelle ate another handful of crackers, not offering any to Brynn, and then shoved them back into her pocket. She gave a disgusted grimace. 'All right. You win.'

With one more glance back, the women started their trek, moving as fast as they could, picking their way around the tangles, many of which would be impossible to get through even with machetes. There were plenty of conifer woods, though, and it was possible to find flat routes unobstructed by steel-wool underbrush.

They continued on, away from the houses, Michelle doing a fair job of keeping up the pace despite the limp. Brynn gripped her spear firmly, feeling both confident and ridiculous because of the weapon.

Soon they'd covered another quarter mile, then a half.

Brynn started and spun around. She'd heard a voice.

But it was only Michelle, muttering to herself, her face ghostly in the blue moonlight. Brynn also had the habit of engaging in self-dialogue. She'd lost her father to disease and a dear friend in the Department to a drunk driver. And she'd lost a husband too. She had talked to herself during those times of sorrow, praying for strength or just plain rambling. For some reason, she'd found, words made pain less painful. She'd done the same just that afternoon, with Joey in the X-ray unit at the hospital. She couldn't remember what she'd said then.

They skirted scummy ponds choked with bog bean and cranberry. She was surprised to see, in a swath of moonlight, a cluster of pitcher plants – a carnivore Brynn had learned about when helping Joey with a report for school. Frogs screeched urgently and birds gave mournful calls. It was too early in the season for mosquitoes, thank the Lord. Brynn was a magnet and in the summer wore citronella like perfume.

Reassuring herself now as much as Michelle, Brynn whispered, 'I've been to the park on two search-and-rescues here.' She'd volunteered for the assignments to put to use some of the expertise she'd picked up at the State Police tactical training seminars, which included an optional – and extremely exhausting and painful – mini-survival course.

One of the two search-and-rescues in Marquette State Park had become a very unpleasant body-recovery operation. But Brynn didn't mention that.

'I don't know the place real well but I have a rough idea of the layout. The Joliet Trail's near here someplace, no more than a mile or two. You know it?'

Michelle shook her head, eyes on the bed of pine needles in front of her feet. She wiped her nose on her sleeve.

'The trail'll take us to that ranger station. It'll be closed now but we could find a phone or a gun there.'

The station was Brynn's first choice. But, she went on to explain, if they missed the building or couldn't break into it they could continue on the Joliet, which angled northeast till it crossed the Snake River. 'We can follow the river east to Point of Rocks. That's a good-sized town on the other side of the park. They'll have stores – for phones – and a public safety office of some kind. Probably part-time but we can wake 'em up. It's a ways, six or seven miles, but we can follow the river and it's pretty flat walking. The other option when we hit the Snake is to turn west . And climb the rocks along the Snake River Gorge. That'll take us to the interstate by the bridge. There's traffic all the time there. A trucker or somebody'll stop for us.'

'Climb the rocks,' Michelle muttered. 'I'm afraid of heights.'

So was Brynn (though that hadn't stopped her rappelling down a sheer cliff face to a waiting keg of Old Milwaukee – the traditional graduation exercise in the State Police course). And the climb at the gorge would be steep and dangerous. The bridge was nearly 100 feet above the river and the rocks were often nearly vertical faces. It was in that part of the park where the body the law officers had been searching for had been recovered. A young man had lost his footing. The fall was only twenty feet but he'd been impaled on a sharp tree limb. The coroner said it probably took him twenty minutes to die.

To this day Brynn McKenzie was haunted by the image.

As they moved from the pine into ancient forest – denser and slathered in darkness – Brynn tried to pick out the route that would be easiest on Michelle's ankle. But the way was often impacted with rooty brush, tangles of saplings and vines, forcing them around. Some they just had to fight their way through.

And some routes were so dim they avoided them completely for fear of missing a steep drop-off or deep bog.

And always, reminders that they weren't really alone. Bats zipped by, owls hooted. Brynn gasped when she trod on the end of a deer rib rack, which swung up and clapped her in the knee. She danced away from the bleached, chewed bone. The scarred skull of the animal was nearby.

Michelle stared at the skeletal remains, eyes wide, without response.

'Let's go. It's just bones.'

They pushed through the tangled wilderness for another hundred yards. Suddenly Michelle stumbled, grabbed a branch to support herself and winced.

'What's the matter?'

She ripped off her thin glove, staring at her hand. Two thorns from the branch had punctured her palm and broken off into her skin. Her eyes flashed with horror.

'No, no, it's just blackberry. You're fine. Here. Let me look.'

'Don't touch it.'

But Brynn took the woman's hand and flicked the candle lighter over the skin, examining the tiny wounds. 'We just want to get them out so it doesn't get infected. In five minutes you won't feel a thing.'

Brynn eased the thorns out of her skin and the woman

winced, wimpering and staring at the growing dots of blood. Brynn pulled out the bottle of alcohol, dampened the edge of a sock with it and started to bathe the wounds. She couldn't help noticing the woman's dark, artistic nails.

'Let me do it,' Michelle said and dabbed at the skin. She handed back the sock and found a tissue in her pocket, pressed it onto the wound. By the time she lifted it away the bleeding had almost stopped.

'How is it?'

'It's okay,' Michelle said. 'You're right. It doesn't hurt anymore.'

They continued on their route, heading in the direction that Brynn pointed.

Sure, she thought, Hart would pursue them and they'd have to remain vigilant. But he'd have no idea where they were headed. The women could have gone in any direction except south to the county road – since they'd have to sneak around the killers to get there.

With every passing yard, Brynn grew more confident. At least she knew something about the forest and where the trail ahead of them lay. The men did not. And even if Hart and his partner happened to choose this direction, the men would surely find themselves lost in ten minutes.

Back on the shore near the Feldman house Hart was looking over the GPS function on his BlackBerry. Then he consulted the map of the area they'd brought with them.

'The Joliet Trail,' he announced.

'What's that?'

'Where they're headed.'

'Ah,' Lewis said. 'You think.'

'Yep.' He held up the map. 'We're here.' He tapped a spot then moved his finger north. 'That brown line's the trail. It'll take 'em right to that ranger station there.'

Lewis was distracted. He was looking over the lake. 'That was smart, I gotta say. What they did.'

Hart didn't disagree. Their short row into the lake had revealed that the women had propped up life vests to resemble bodies hunched down in the canoe and then shoved the boat into the water. The scream – at the sound of the shots – was ingenious. Had Brynn or Michelle uttered the sound? Brynn, he bet.

Hart wasn't used to having to out-think his opponents. Part of him liked the challenge but a bigger part liked being in control. The contests he preferred were those in which he had a pretty good idea that the outcome would be in his favor.

Like working with ebony: The wood was temperamental – hard and brittle – and could split easily, wasting hundreds of dollars. But if you took your time, you were careful, you foresaw any potential problems, the end result was beautiful.

What kind of challenge was Brynn McKenzie?

Smelling the ammonia.

Hearing the *crack, crack, crack* of her gun.

Ebony, of course.

His aching arm prodded him to think, too: And what kind was Michelle?

That would remain to be seen.

'So you're thinking of going after them?' Lewis asked. He opened his mouth and puffed out a bit of steam.

'Yep.'

'I gotta say, Hart. This isn't what I planned on.'

Putting it mildly.

Lewis continued, 'Everything's changed. That bitch shooting you, trying to shoot me. The cop . . . You or me, in that bathroom, the ammonia trap. If it'd worked, one of us'd be blinded. And that shot in the house, the cop? Missed me by inches.'

I can dodge bullets . . .

Hart said nothing. He wasn't riled up the way Lewis was. The women were just being true to their nature. Like that animal he'd seen. Of course they'd fight back.

'So that's what I'm thinking,' Lewis said. 'I just want to get the hell out of here. She's a cop, Hart. Lives 'round here. She knows this place. She's halfway to that ranger station or something right now. They'll have phones in the park . . . So we've gotta get outa here now. Back to Milwaukee. Whoever that girl is, Michelle, she's sure as hell not going to ID us. She's not stupid.' He tapped his pocket, where her purse, containing her name and address, rested. 'And the cop didn't really get a good look at us. So, back to Plan A. Get to the highway, 'jack a car. Whatta you say?'

Hart grimaced. 'Well, Lewis, I am tempted. Yes, I am. But we can't.'

'Hmm. Well, I'm inclined to think otherwise.' Lewis was speaking softly now, more reasonable, less surly.

'We have to get them.'

'"Have to"? Why? Where's that written down? Look, you're thinking I'm scared. Well, I'm not. Tonight, against two women? This's nothing. Let me tell you a story. I did a bank job in Madison? Last year?'

'Banks? Never done a bank.'

'We got fifty thousand.'

'That's pretty good.' The average bank robbery take nation-wide was $3800. Another stat Hart knew: 97 per cent of the perps were arrested within one week.

'Yep, was. So. This guard wanted to be a hero. Had a backup gun on his ankle.'

'He'd been a cop.'

'What I figured. Exactly. Came out shooting. I covered the other guys. Right out in the open. Kept him down. I didn't even crouch.' He laughed, shaking his head. 'One of my crew, the driver, was so freaked he dropped the keys in the snow, took a couple minutes to find them. But I held that guard off. Even stayed upright while I reloaded, and we could hear sirens in the distance. But we got away.' He fell silent to let Hart digest this. Then: 'I'm talking about what makes sense . . . You stand your ground when you need to. You get the hell out when you need to. And then take care of 'em later.' Another tap of Michelle's purse. 'Nothing good's going to come of this.' He repeated, 'Everything's changed.'

A mournful call filled the moist air, a bird of some sort, Hart guessed. Waterfowl or owl or hawk, he couldn't tell them apart. He squatted down, pushed his hair off his forehead. 'Lewis, I'm thinking that nothing *has* changed, not really.'

'Sure it has. The minute she tried to cap you, it all went

to shit in there.' A nod back at the house and a skeptical glance.

'But it's shit we could've foreseen. We *should've* foreseen. Look, when you make a choice – signing on for this job, for instance – there's a whole slew of consequences that can follow. Things could go left, they could go right. Or, what happened tonight, they could turn around and slug you in the gut . . .'

Or shoot you in the arm.

'Nobody forced me to live this kind of life. Or you either. But we chose it and that makes it our job to think everything through, figure out what could happen and plan for it. Every time I do a job I plan everything out, I mean *every* detail. I'm never surprised. Doing the job itself's usually boring, I've been through it so often in my mind.'

Measure twice, cut once.

'Tonight? I figured out ninety-five percent of what could happen and planned for that. But what I didn't bother to think about was the last five percent – that that Michelle was going to use me for target practice. But I should've.'

The slim man, rocking on his haunches, said, 'The Trickster.'

'The what?' Hart asked.

'My grandmother said when something went wrong, something you didn't think could happen, it was the Trickster's fault. She got it out of a kid's book or something. I don't remember. The Trickster was always hanging around looking for ways to make things go wrong. Like Fate or God or whatever. Except Fate could do you good things too. Like give you a winning lotto ticket. Or could make you stop for a yellow light, even if you would've gone though, and save you from getting T-boned by a garbage truck. And God would do things that were right, so you'd get what you deserved. But the Trickster? He was just there to mess you up.' He nodded again at the house. 'Trickster paid us a visit in there.'

'Trickster.' Hart liked that.

'But that's life sometimes, ain't it, Hart? You miss that five percent. But so what? Best thing still might be to get the hell out of here, put it all behind us.'

Hart rose. He winced as he accidentally reached his shot arm out to steady himself. He looked out at the lake. 'Let me tell *you* a story, Lewis. My brother . . . younger'n me.'

'You have a brother?' Lewis's attention had turned from the house. 'I've got two.'

'Our parents both died about the same time. When I was twenty-five, my brother was twenty-two. I was kind of like a father figure. Well, even back then we were into this kind of stuff, you know. And my brother got this job one time, easy, just numbers. He was a runner mostly. He had to pick up some money and deliver it. Typical job. I mean, thousands of people do that shit every day, right? All over the world.'

'They do.' Lewis was listening.

'So I didn't have anything going on at the moment and was helping him out. We picked up the money—'

'This was Milwaukee?'

'No. We grew up in Boston. We pick up the money and're about to deliver it. But turns out we were going to be set up. The guy ran the numbers operation was going to clip us and let the cops find the bodies and some of the books and some of the money. The detectives'd think they closed up the operation.'

'You two were fall guys.'

'Yep. I had this sense something was wrong and we went around back of the pick-up location and saw the muscle there. My brother and me, we took off. A few days later I found the guys hired to do the clip and took care of them. But the main guy just vanished. Word was he'd moved to Mexico.'

Lewis grinned. 'Scared of your bad ass.'

'After six months or so I stopped looking for him. But it

turns out he never went to Mexico at all. He'd been tracking us whole time. One day he walks up to my brother and blows his head off.'

'Oh, shit.'

Hart didn't speak for a moment. 'But see, Lewis. He didn't kill my brother. I did. My *laziness* killed my brother.'

'Your laziness?'

'Yep. Because I stopped looking for that son of a bitch.'

'But six months, Hart. That's a long time.'

'Didn't matter if it was six years. Either you're in all the way, a hundred and ten percent. Or don't bother.' Hart shook his head. 'Hell, Lewis, forget it. This's my problem. I was the one hired on. It's not your issue. Now, I'd consider it a privilege if you came with me. But if you want to head back to Milwaukee, you go right ahead. No hard feelings at all.'

Lewis rocked. Back and forth, back and forth. 'Ask you a question?'

'Sure.'

'What happened to that prick killed your brother?'

'He enjoyed life for three more days.'

Lewis debated a long time. Then he gave a what-the-fuck laugh. 'Call me crazy, Hart. But I'm with you.'

'Yeah?'

'You bet I am.'

'Thanks, man. Means a lot to me.' They shook hands. Then Hart turned back to his BlackBerry, moved the bull's-eye to the closest part of the Joliet Trail and hit the Start Guidance command. The instructions came up almost immediately.

'Let's go hunting.'

A slight man in his thirties, James Jasons sat in his Lexus, the gray car slightly nicked, a few years old. He was parked in the lot of Great Lakes Intermodal Container Services, Inc., on the Milwaukee lakefront. Jasons was watching the cranes offload the containers from ships. Incredible. The operators lifted the big metal boxes as if they were toys, swung them from the ships and set them down perfectly, every time, on the flatbed of a truck. The containers must've weighed twenty tons, maybe more.

Jasons was always impressed by anybody with skill, whatever their profession.

A rumble filled the night. A horn blared and a Canadian Pacific freight train ambled past.

The door of the old brick building opened. A brawny man in wrinkled gray slacks, a sports coat, blue shirt, no tie, climbed down the stairs and crossed the parking lot. Jasons had learned that the head of the legal department of the company – Paul Morgan – regularly worked late.

Morgan continued through the lot to his Mercedes. Jasons got out of his car, which was parked two slots down. He approached the man, arms at his side.

'Mr Morgan?'

The man turned and looked over Jasons, who was nearly a foot shorter and a hundred pounds lighter than the lawyer. 'Yeah?'

'We've never met, sir. I work with Stanley Mankewitz. My name's James Jasons.' He offered a card, which Morgan glanced at and put into a pocket, where it could be easily retrieved when Morgan found himself near a trash can. 'I know it's late. I'd just like a minute of your time.'

Morgan's eyes swept around the parking lot. Meaning, here, now? Friday night? He hit the key fob and with a click the Mercedes unlocked.

'Stanley Mankewitz didn't have the balls to come himself? Doesn't surprise me.' Morgan sat down in the front seat, the car sagging, but he left the door open. He looked Jasons up and down, from the delicate shoes to the size-36 suit to the rock-hard knot in the striped tie. 'You're a lawyer?'

'I'm in the legal department.'

'Ah. There's a distinction for you,' Morgan said. 'You go to law school?'

'Yes.'

'Where?'

'Yale.'

Morgan grimaced. He wore a pinky ring that probably had a DePaul crest on it. Well, Jasons hadn't brought up the alma mater issue. 'Tell me what your noble leader wants and then scoot off.'

'Sure,' Jasons said agreeably. 'We're aware that your company hasn't been particularly supportive of Mr Mankewitz and the union during this difficult time.'

'It's a federal investigation, for Christ's sake. Why the fuck would I want to support him?'

'Your employees are members of his union.'

'That's their choice.'

'About the investigation – you know that no charges have been filed.' A good-natured smile on Jasons's face. 'There are a few officials looking into some allegations.'

'Officials? It's the fucking FBI. Look, I don't know what you're after here. But we're a legitimate business. Look out there.' He waved toward the brilliantly lit cranes. 'Our customers know we're a union shop and that the head of that union, Stanley Mankewitz, is under investigation. They're worried that *we're* involved in something illegal.'

'You can tell them the truth. That Mr Mankewitz hasn't been indicted for anything. Every union in the history of the country has been investigated at one point or another.'

'Which tells you something about unions,' Morgan muttered.

'Or about people who don't like the common folk standing up for their right to fair pay for hard work,' Jasons replied evenly, remaining close to the man despite the odor of garlic rising on Morgan's breath. 'Besides, even if Mr Mankewitz was found guilty of something, which is highly unlikely, I'm sure your customers would be able to draw the distinction between a man and his organization. Enron, after all, was ninety-nine percent hardworking people and a few bad apples.'

'Again, "Hardworking". Mr Jason . . . Jasons? With an *s*? Mr Jasons, you don't understand. You ever hear of Homeland Security? . . . We're in the business of moving shipping containers. Any hint of something wrong with the people we're connected with and everybody goes right to anthrax in our warehouses or a nuclear bomb or something. Customers're going to go elsewhere. And your *hardworking common* folk'll lose their fucking jobs. I repeat my question. What the hell do you want?'

'Just some information. Nothing illegal, nothing classified, nothing sensitive. A few technical things. I've written them down.' A slip of paper appeared in Jasons' gloved hand and he gave it to Morgan.

'If it's nothing classified or sensitive look it up yourself.' Morgan let the slip float to the damp asphalt.

. 'Ah.'

Morgan studied the thin, smiling face closely. He laughed hard and ran his hand through his thinning black hair. 'So, what's this, like, *The Sopranos*? Only, instead of sending Paulie or Chris to extort me, Mankewitz picks a scrawny little asshole like you. That the plan? You whine at me until I cave?' He leaned forward and laughed. 'I could fuck you up with one hand. I've got half a mind to do it. Send you back to your boss with a broken nose.'

Again, a good-natured grimace. 'You look like you could, Mr Morgan. I haven't been in a fight in probably twenty years. Schoolyard. And I got whipped pretty bad.'

'You're not worth the sweat,' the man snapped. 'So what's next? The big boys come back with lead pipes? You think that scares me?'

'No, no, there's nobody else coming. It's only me here and now, this one time. Asking if you'll help us out. Just this once. Nobody'll bother you again.'

'Well, I'm not helping you out. Now get the fuck off our property.'

'Thanks for your time, Mr Morgan.' Jasons started to walk away. Then he frowned, as if he'd remembered something, and lifted an index finger just as the lawyer was about to close the car door. 'Oh, one thing. Just to be helpful. You hear about tomorrow morning?'

Paul Morgan gave an exaggerated grimace and said, 'What *about* tomorrow morning?'

'Public Works is starting some construction on Hanover Street. On Saturday, can you believe it? And at eight-thirty. You might want to check out a different route if you want to get to the school by ten.'

'What?' Hand on the half-open door, Morgan was frozen, staring at Jasons. The word was a whisper.

'For the concert.' The slim man nodded pleasantly. 'I think it's great when parents take an interest in their children's activities. A lot of them don't. And I'm sure Paul Junior and Alicia appreciate it too. I know they've been practicing hard. Alicia especially. Every day after school in that rehearsal room, three to four-thirty . . . Impressive. Just thought you might want to know about the road work. Okay, you have a good evening, Mr Morgan.'

Jasons turned and walked to his Lexus, thinking that the odds of getting rushed were about ten percent. But he got inside safely and started the car.

When he looked out the rear-view mirror, there was no sign of Morgan's Mercedes.

The slip of paper was gone too.

The first of this evening's tasks was finished. Now for the second. His stomach rumbled again but he decided he'd better get on the road right away. The directions told him it would take more than two hours to get to Lake Mondac.

The ground around Brynn and Michelle was swampy and they had to be careful not to step on what seemed to be solid leaves but which were only a thin façade covering a deep bog. The frogs' calls were insistent, piercing, and they irritated Brynn because the *creek-crack* could obscure the sound of anyone approaching.

They walked for twenty minutes in tense silence – following the least choked route they could, sucked further into the forest's discouraging labyrinth. Brynn and Michelle descended into a gully that was matted with blackberry, trillium, wood leek and a dozen plants she didn't recognize. With considerable effort they climbed to the top of the other side.

Where Brynn realized suddenly that she was lost. Completely lost.

On higher ground they'd had more of a sense of the correct direction: due north to the Joliet Trail. Brynn had used certain landmarks to guide them: peaks, a stream, unusual patterns of tall oak trees. But they'd been forced farther and farther downward into the low ground by rocky cliffs and the compacted mass of brush and thorny bushes. All of her navigation beacons had vanished. She recalled the instructor at the State Police tactical procedures course saying that if you put somebody in unfamiliar territory without recognizable landmarks, they'd be completely disoriented within thirty-five minutes. Brynn had certainly believed him but hadn't realized that too many landmarks could be as much of a problem as too few.

'Did you and your friends ever hike this way?'

'I don't hike,' Michelle said petulantly. 'And I've only been to their place once or twice.'

Brynn looked around slowly.

'I thought you knew where we were,' Michelle muttered.

'I thought so too,' she said with more than a little exasperation.

'Well, find some moss. It grows on the north side of trees. We learned that in grade school.'

'Not really,' Brynn replied, looking around. 'It grows where there's the most moisture, which is *usually* on the north side of trees and rocks. But only if there's enough sun to dry out the south side. In deep forest it'll grow everywhere.' Brynn pointed. 'Let's try that way.' Wondering if she was taking that route simply because it seemed less daunting, the vegetation less tangled. Michelle followed numbly, limping along with her polished rosewood crutch.

A short time later Brynn stopped again. If it was possible she was even more lost than ten minutes earlier.

Can't keep going on like this.

She had a thought, asked Michelle, 'Do you have a needle?'

'A what?'

'A needle, or a pin, maybe a safety pin.'

'Why would I have a needle?'

'Just, do you have one?' The woman patted her jacket. 'No. What for?'

Her badge! Brynn pulled it out of her pocket. Kennesha County Sheriff's Department. Chrome. Ridges radiating like sun rays out of the county seal.

She turned it over and looked at the clasp pin on the back.

Could this actually work?

'Come on.' She led Michelle to a nearby stream and dropped to her knees. She began to clear away a thick pelt of leaves, saying, 'Find me some rocks. About the size of a grapefruit.'

'Rocks?'

'Hurry.'

The young woman grimaced but began walking up and down the bank, picking over stones, while Brynn cleared a space on the bank. The ground was cold; she could feel the chill through her knees. They began to ache. From her pocket she took the bottle of rubbing alcohol, the Chicago Cutlery knife and the candle lighter. Set them on the ground in front of her, next to her badge.

Michelle returned, limping along with five large rocks. Brynn needed only two. Forgot to mention that.

'What are you doing?'

'Making a compass.' This had been in the survival manual issued by the State Police, though the team Brynn was on had not actually made one. But she'd read the material and thought she remembered enough to craft the instrument.

'How can you do that?'

'I'm not sure I can. But I know the theory.'

The idea was simple. You pounded a needle or pin with a hammer, which magnetized it. Then you rested it on a piece of cork floating in a dish of water. The needle aligned itself north and south. Simple. No hammer now. She'd have to use the back of the knife blade, the only metal object they had.

On her knees, Brynn set a rock in front of her. She tried to break the pin off her badge by bending it. The metal would not fatigue, though. It was too thick.

'Shit.'

'Try to cut through it with the knife,' Michelle suggested. 'Hit it with a rock.'

Brynn opened the pin as far as she could, laid it on the rock and set the blade against the base of the needle. Holding the Chicago Cutlery in her left hand, she tapped the back with another rock. It didn't even make a mark.

'You'll have to hit it hard,' Michelle said, now intrigued with the project.

She slammed the rock into the pin once more. The blade made a slight scratch on the needle but danced along the chrome metal. She couldn't hold both blade and badge down on the rock in one hand.

Handing the rock to Michelle, she said, 'Here. You do it. Use both hands.'

The younger woman took the second rock, the 'hammer,' which weighed about fifteen pounds.

In her left hand Brynn continued to hold the wooden knife handle. She cupped her palm around the badge and, with her fingers, gripped the end of the blade, near the point.

Michelle looked at her. 'I can't. Not with your hands there.' Michelle had about an eight-inch target on the back edge of the knife. A miss could crush one of Brynn's hands. Or flip the blade sideways and slice the pads off her fingers.

'We don't have any choice.'

'I could break your fingers.'

'Go ahead. Don't tap. Hit hard. Come on, do it!'

The young woman took a deep breath. She lifted the rock. Then grimaced, exhaled and swung the stone in a blur.

Whether it was headed for Brynn's fingers or for the knife was impossible to tell but Brynn didn't move a muscle.

Snap.

Michelle hit the blade clean, driving it through the metal and cutting off a two-inch bit of needle.

Which spiraled through the air and disappeared in a shadowy sea of leaves near the stream.

'No!' Michelle cried, starting forward.

'Don't move,' Brynn whispered. Presumably their prize had landed on top of the pile, though it wouldn't take more than a footstep to send it slipping into the leaves, lost forever. 'It couldn't have gone very far.'

'It's too dark. I can't see anything. Damnit.'

'Shhhh,' Brynn reminded. They had to assume that Hart and his friend were still after them.

'We need the lighter.'

Brynn leaned toward the leaves. The young woman was right. In this dense grove, with the light of a half moon, sliced to pieces by a thousand branches and stubborn leaves still clinging to them, it was impossible to see the metal. But the candle lighter would shine like a warning beacon atop a skyscraper for Hart to see.

Again, the bywords for the evening came to mind: no choice.

'Here.' Brynn gave her the lighter. 'Go around there.' She pointed to the far side of the pile. 'Keep it low and wave it over the ground.'

Michelle hobbled off. 'Ready?' she whispered.

'Go.'

A click and the flame blossomed. It was far brighter than she'd expected. Anybody within a hundred yards could have seen.

Brynn leaned forward and scanned the ground, crawling forward carefully.

There! Something was shiny. Was that it? Brynn reached out carefully and picked up a tiny twig covered in bird shit.

A second possibility turned out to be a streak of mica in a rock. But finally Brynn spotted a silver flare in the night, sitting on top of a curl of oak leaf. She picked up the needle carefully. 'Shut it out,' she said to Michelle, nodding at the candle lighter.

The area went soot black – even darker now because the light had numbed their eyes. Brynn's sense of vulnerability soared. The two men could be walking directly toward them and she'd never see them. Only a cracking branch or crunch of leaves would give away their approach.

Michelle crouched. 'Can I help?'

'Not yet.'

The young woman sat down, crossed her legs and fished the crackers out. She offered them to Brynn, who ate several. Then she began tapping the needle with the back of the knife. Twice she struck a finger hard and winced. But she never let go and never paused in the pounding – like the flare of the lighter, the sound of the *tink tink tink* seemed to broadcast their position for miles.

After an eternal five minutes she said, 'Let's try it. I need some thread. Something thin.' They unraveled a strand from Brynn's ski jacket and used it to tie the needle to a bit of twig.

Brynn dumped out the alcohol from the bottle and refilled it halfway with water, slipped the twig and pin inside and set the bottle on its side. Brynn hit the candle lighter trigger. Heads close, they stared through the clear plastic bottle. The bit of wood slowly revolved to the left and stopped.

'It works!' Michelle blurted, giving her first true smile of the night.

Brynn glanced at her and smiled back. Damn, she thought, it does. It surely does.

'But which end's north and which's south?'

'Around here the high ground's generally west. That'd be to the left.' They shut the lighter out and after their eyes were accustomed to the dark Brynn pointed out a distant hilltop. 'That's north. Let's head for it.'

Brynn screwed the lid on the bottle and slipped it into her pocket, picked up her spear. They started walking again. They'd pause every so often to take another reading. As long as they continued north they would have to cross the Joliet Trail sooner or later.

Curious, she thought, how much reassurance she'd gotten by making this little toy. Kristen Brynn McKenzie was a woman whose worst enemy, worst fear, was the lack of control. She'd begun this night without any – no phone or weapon – crawling cold, drenched and helpless out of a black lake. But now, with a crude spear in hand and a compass in her pocket she felt as confident as that character out of one of Joey's comic books.

Queen of the Jungle.

The Dance.

What Hart called it.

This was a part of the business and Hart was not only used to dancing; he was good at it. Being a craftsman, after all.

A month ago, sitting in a coffee shop – never a bar; keep your head about you – he'd looked up at the voice.

'So, Hart. How you doing?'

A firm handshake.

'Good. You?'

'I'm okay. Listen, I'm interested in hiring somebody. You interested in some work?'

'I don't know. Maybe. So how do you know Gordon Potts? You go back a long ways?'

'Not so long.'

'How'd you meet him?'

'A mutual friend.'

'Who'd that be?'

'Freddy Lancaster.'

'Freddy, sure. How's his wife doing?'

'That'd be tough to find out, Hart. She died two years ago.'

'Oh, that's right. Bad memory. How does Freddy like St. Paul?'

'St Paul? He lives in Milwaukee.'

'This memory of mine.'

The Dance. It went on and on. As it has to.

Then two meetings later, credentials finally established, the risk of entrapment minimal, the dancing was over and they got down to details.

'That's a lot of money.'

'Yeah, it is, Hart. So you're interested?'

'Keep going.'

'Here's a map of the area. That's a private road. Lake View Drive. And there? That's a state park, all of it. Hardly any people around. Here's a diagram of the house.'

'Okay . . . This a dirt road or paved?'

'Dirt . . . Hart, they tell me you're good. Are you good? I hear you're a craftsman. That's what they say.'

'Who's they?'

'People.'

'Well, yeah, I'm a craftsman.'

'Can I ask you a question?'

'Yeah.'

'I'm curious. Why're you in this line of work?'

'It suits me.'

'It looks like it does.'

'Okay. What's the threat situation?'

'The what?'

'How risky's the job going to be? How many people up there, weapons, police nearby? It's a lake house – are the other houses on Lake View occupied?'

'It'll be a piece of cake, Hart. Hardly any risk at all. The other places'll be vacant. And only the two of them up there, the Feldmans. And no rangers in the park or cops around for miles.'

'They have weapons?'

'Are you kidding? They're city people. She's a lawyer, he's a social worker.'

'Just the Feldmans, nobody else? It'll make a big difference.'

'That's my information. And it's solid. Just the two of them.'

Now, in the middle of Marquette State Park, Hart and Lewis circled around a dangerous stand of thorny brush. Like a plant out of a science fiction movie.

Hart reflected sourly, Yeah, right, just the two of them. Feeling the ache in his arm.

Angry with himself.

He'd done ninety-five percent.

It should've been a hundred and ten.

At least they knew they were on the right path. A half mile back they'd found a scrap of tissue with blood on it. The Kleenex couldn't've been there for more than a half hour.

Hart now paused and gazed around them, noted some peaks and a small creek. 'We're doing fine. Be a lot tougher without the moonlight. But we've caught a break. Somebody's looking out for us.'

The Trickster . . .

'Somebody . . . You believe that?' Lewis said this as if he did.

Hart didn't. But no time for theology now. 'I'd like to move a little faster. When they hit the trail they might start running. We'll have to too.'

'Run?'

'Right. Smooth ground'll give us the advantage. We can move faster.'

'Them being women, you mean?'

'Yep. Well, and one of them being hurt. Pain slows people down.' He paused and stared to their right. Then hunched over the map and examined it closely with flashlight, the lens muted by his undershirt.

He pointed. 'That a smoke tower?'

'What's that?'

'Rangers look for forest fires from them. It's one of the places I thought she might go for.'

'Where?'

'On that ridge.'

They were looking at a structure about a half mile away. It was a tower of some sort but through the trees they couldn't tell if it was a radio or microwave antenna or a structure with a small enclosure on top.

'Maybe,' Lewis said.

'You see any sign of them?'

Now that their eyes were used to the dark, the half moon provided fair illumination but the ravine separating the men from the ranger tower was shadowy, and in the bottom a canopy of trees provided perfect cover.

The women heading for the tower made some sense, rather than the Joliet Trail or the ranger station. The place might have a radio, or even a weapon. He debated for a moment and risked scanning the ground with the flashlight. If the women were near, at least they'd be moving away and might not see the light.

Then they heard a rustle of leaves, and turned fast toward the sound.

Six glowing red eyes were staring at them.

Lewis laughed. 'Raccoons.'

Three big ones were pawing at something on the ground. It glistened and crackled.

'What's that?'

Lewis found a rock and pitched it toward them.

With a mean-sounding hiss, they ran off.

Hart and Lewis approached and found what they'd been doing – fighting over some food. It looked like bits of crackers.

'Theirs?'

Hart picked one up, broke it in half with a snap. Fresh. He studied the ground. The women had stopped here apparently – he could make out prints of knees and feet. And then they had continued north.

'Women. Stopping for a fucking picnic.'

Hart doubted, though, it was to rest. That wasn't Brynn. Maybe somebody needed first aid; he believed he smelled rubbing alcohol. But, whatever the reason, the important thing to Hart was that they hadn't made for the fire tower; they were headed right for the trail.

He consulted the GPS and pointed ahead. 'That way.'

'Mind that patch there,' Lewis said.

Hart squinted. When the moon was obscured by branches or a wisp of cloud, the forest around them turned black as a cave. He finally saw what Lewis was pointing at. 'What's that?'

'Poison ivy. Bad stuff. Not everybody's allergic. Indians aren't.'

'Doesn't affect them?'

'Nope. Not a bit. You might not be allergic but you don't want to take a chance.'

Hart hadn't known that. 'What were you, a Boy Scout?'

Lewis laughed. 'Funny, hadn't thought about that for years. But, yeah, I was. Well, not really *in* them. I went on a couple camping trips then kind of dropped out. But I know that's poison ivy 'cause my brother threw me in a patch once. And that fucked me up good. I never forgot what it looked like.'

'You were saying you have two? Brothers?'

'He was the older one, what else? I'm in the middle.'

'He know it was poison ivy?'

'I don't think so. But something I always wondered about.'

'Must've sucked, Lewis,' Hart said.

'Yup . . . Oh, 'bout that. My friends call me Comp. You can use that.'

'Okay, Comp. Where's that come from?'

'Town where my parents lived when I was born. Compton. Minnesota. My parents thought it sounded, you know, distinguished.' He snickered. 'Like *anybody* in our family was ever distinguished. What a joke. But Daddy tried. Give him that. And yours're both dead? Your folks?'

'That's right.'

'Sorry about that.'

'Was a while ago.'

'Still.'

They continued on through the tangled brush in silence for what seemed like two miles though it was probably a quarter of that. Hart checked his watch. Okay, he decided. It's time.

He reached into his pocket and pulled out the phone he'd been carrying. He pushed the On button, and it went through that electronic ritual they all did nowadays. He figured out the settings and put the ringer on vibrate. Then scrolled through recent calls. The one on top was 'Home'. He noted that the call had lasted eighteen seconds. Long enough for a message was all.

He wondered how long it would take before—

A light flashed and the phone buzzed.

Hart touched Lewis's arm and motioned for him to wait, then lifted his fingers to his lips.

Lewis nodded.

Hart answered the call.

Graham felt his scalp crawl when Brynn's mobile actually began to ring, rather than go right to voice mail.

It clicked. He heard the rustle of wind and his scalp stopped tensing but his heart took over, thumping hard. 'Brynn?'

'This's Officer Billings,' said the low voice.

Graham frowned and glanced at Anna.

The voice asked, 'Hello?'

'Well, this is Graham Boyd, Brynn McKenzie's husband.'

'Oh, sure, sir. Deputy McKenzie.'

'Is she all right?' Graham asked fast, chest throbbing.

'Yessir. She's fine. She gave me her phone to hold.'

Relief flooded through him. 'I've been trying all night.'

'Reception's terrible up here. Comes and goes. Surprised when it rang just now, to be honest.'

'She was due home a while ago.'

'Oh.' The man sounded confused. 'She said she called you.'

'She did. But her message said she was coming right home. It was a false alarm or something.'

'Oh, she was going to call again. Probably couldn't get through. About the case, turned out it wasn't a false alarm, after all. Was a domestic dispute, pretty ugly. Husband tried to downplay it. Lot of times that happens. Deputy McKenzie's talking to the wife right now, getting the facts sorted out.'

The relief was so thick Graham could taste it. He smiled and nodded to Anna.

Billings continued, 'She left her phone with me, didn't want any distractions. She's calming the situation down. She's good at that. That's why the captain wanted her to stay. Oh, hold on a minute, sir . . . Hey, sergeant? . . . Where's Ralph? . . . Oh, okay . . .' The trooper came back on the line. 'Sorry, sir.'

'Do you know how long she'll be?'

'We've got to get Child Protective Services up here.'

'Lake Mondac?'

'Near there. Could be a few hours. Bad situation with the kid. Husband's going to spend the night in jail. At *least* the night.'

'Few hours?'

'Yessir. I'll have her call you when she's free.'

'Okay. Well, thanks.'

'You bet.'

''Night.' Graham hung up.

'What?' Anna asked and he explained what was going on.

'Domestic situation?'

'Sounded pretty bad. Husband's going to jail.' Graham sat on the couch, staring at the TV screen. 'Why'd *she* have to handle it, though?'

Not expecting an answer. But he was aware that the knitting needles had stopped and Anna was looking up from the scarf she was knitting. The colors were three shades of blue. It was pretty.

'Graham, you know Brynn had some trouble with her face.'

'Her jaw? Sure, the car accident.'

He had no idea where she was going with this.

The woman's gray eyes were on his. That was one thing about Anna McKenzie. As demure as she could be, as polite and proper, she always looked you right in the eye.

'Accident,' she repeated slowly. 'So you don't know.'

More yellow jackets, Graham was beginning to sense.

'Go on.'

'I just assumed she'd told you.'

He was alarmed and hurt at the lie, whatever it might be. Yet he wasn't very surprised. 'Go on.'

'Keith hit her, broke her jaw.'

'*What?*'

'Wired shut for three weeks.'

'God, it was that serious?'

'He was a big man . . . Don't feel too bad she kept it from you, Graham. She was embarrassed, ashamed. She didn't tell hardly anybody.'

'She said he was moody. I didn't know he hurt her.'

'Moody? True. But mostly it was his temper problem. Like some people drink and some people gamble. He'd lose control. It was scary. I saw it happen a few times.'

'Rage-aholic. What happened?'

'The night he hit her? I'm sure it wasn't anything big that set him off. It never was. That was the scariest. It could be the power went out before a game, the store was out of his brand of beer, Brynn telling him she was going back to work part-time when Joey got a little older. Whatever it was, he'd just snap.'

'I never knew.'

'So domestic problems – they mean a lot to her.'

'She does run those a lot,' Graham agreed. 'I always thought it was Tom Dahl. You know, wanting a woman there.'

'No. She'd volunteer.'

'What did she do? After Keith hit her?'

'She didn't have him arrested if that's what you mean. I think she was worried about Joey.'

'He ever do it again?'

'No. Not that she ever told me.'

Hitting someone you were married to. He couldn't imagine it. Hell, hitting anyone, unless it was self-defense, was almost impossible to picture.

Graham was matching this information against other incidents in their past, against his wife's words, her behavior. Dozens of times she'd touch her jaw in the morning. Even her waking, sweaty and groaning, from dreams. Her moodiness, her defensiveness.

Her control . . .

He pictured her hand, coasting along the uneven line of her jaw as they sat at the dinner table or watching TV on the green couch.

Still, sitting back, he said, 'She didn't know what was going on at Lake Mondac until she got there. Domestic may've been why she stayed tonight. It's not why she volunteered in the first place. *That*'s what I want to know.'

'I think the answers're pretty much the same, Graham.' The needle clicks resumed as Anna cranked up the assembly line of yarn once again.

They paused to take a compass reading, as they'd been doing every quarter mile or so.

The routine was that Brynn and Michelle would kneel down, rest the alcohol bottle on its side and tease their magnetic vessel into the center of its tiny ocean, where it would nose out north for them. The compass was a lifesaver. Brynn was astonished at how easily they would start to veer in the wrong direction, though she'd been absolutely convinced they were on course.

Michelle asked, 'How did you know how to make that?' Nodding at the device as Brynn slipped it back into her pocket. 'You have children? A school project?'

'A course I took through the State Police. But I do have a son.' She tried to imagine skateboarding fiend Joey sitting still long enough for a science fair project. The idea was amusing.

'How old is he?' Michelle was suddenly animated.

'Twelve.'

'I love children,' she said. Then she smiled. 'What's his name?'

'Joseph.'

'Biblical.'

'I guess so. We named him after his father's uncle.'

'Is he a good boy?'

'He sure is.' Hesitated. And didn't tell her about the incident today. Or the others – the many others. 'You and your husband have kids?'

Michelle glanced at her. 'Not yet. We lead pretty busy lifestyles.'

'And you're an actress, you were saying?'

A shy smile. 'Just little things now. TV commercials, community theater. But I'm going to get into Second City. The improv comedy troupe. I've had a couple of callbacks. And I'm auditioning for the touring company of *Wicked*.'

Brynn listened attentively as the young woman told her about some parts she was pursuing. Brynn's opinion, though, was that she was a dilettante. It sounded like she jumped from medium to medium, hoping to find one she was talented at. Or one that was easier than others. She wasn't surprised to learn that Michelle also tried her hand at writing plays, but had recently decided that independent films were the way to go. And was thinking of getting a job in LA to meet people in the movie industry.

They were walking uphill now and, breathless, fell silent as they slogged their way over another quarter mile.

She'd thought they'd have come across the Joliet Trail by now. It couldn't be that far away. But with all this dense brush, she had no realistic sense of how fast they were traveling. Like treading through water; a lot of effort didn't lead to a long distance covered.

After fifteen minutes they paused in a clearing surrounded by briars to take another compass reading. The lighter flared and Brynn saw they were on track. 'Okay, shut it out.'

According to the routine they'd fallen into, they now sat for a moment or two, eyes squeezed shut to help them adjust to the dark.

A snap sounded behind them.

Loud.

Michelle gasped.

Both women tensed, rising to a crouch from their knees. Brynn slipped the compass away and grabbed the spear.

Another snap and a rustle of footsteps.

Brynn squinted until her cheek screamed in pain. But she couldn't see anything.

Was it the killers?

'What? Do you—?'

'Shhh.'

Something was moving, circling them. Then stopped. Moved again.

Snap . . .

Then it vanished.

A moment later, from their right, came another snap, a shuffle of leaves. They spun suddenly in that direction. Brynn could vaguely make out a shadowy form, rocking back and forth.

It wasn't the men. In fact it wasn't a human. Brynn observed that it was an animal, about the size of a German shepherd.

Brynn believed it was staring at them with shoulders tensed and hackles high.

Michelle gasped and gripped Brynn's arm.

Was it a mountain lion? The last one in Wisconsin had reportedly been shot a hundred years ago. But every year there were supposed sightings. You'd see coyotes from time to time. They were timid, but rabid ones, their minds melting, had strolled right into tents and attacked campers. Lynx weren't unheard of either.

But this seemed too big for that. She decided it was a gray wolf, which were being reintroduced into the state. She didn't know if they'd attack humans but the eerie, probing face – almost human – was unsettling.

Had Michelle and Brynn come close to the creature's lair? Were there pups to be protected? A crazed mother was the worst of enemies, Keith, an avid hunter, had told her.

A flash of anger burned within her. They didn't need another enemy tonight. She gripped the spear firmly and stood up. She strode forward, between Michelle and the creature.

'What're you doing? Don't leave me.'

Brynn thought: Don't hesitate. Keep going.

The animal's head cocked and its eyes caught light from the lopped-off moon.

Brynn kept walking, moving faster, hunched over.

Still staring their way, the animal backed up then turned and receded into the night. Brynn stopped and returned to the young woman, who was staring at her. 'Jesus,' Michelle said.

'It's okay.'

But it wasn't the animal she was referring to. 'Are you all right?' she asked uncertainly.

'Me?' the deputy asked. 'Sure. Why?'

'You were . . . you were making this noise. I thought you couldn't breathe or something.'

'Noise?'

'Like, growling. It was scary.'

'Growling?' Brynn was aware of breathing hard, teeth set tightly together. She wasn't aware that she'd made a noise.

Queen of the Jungle . . .

She gave an awkward laugh and they continued on. Their route led them into a ravine, the rocks and trees along the side ensnared with vines, and the floor covered with patches of poison ivy and vinca. Boggy pools too, surrounded by mushrooms and fungus. They pushed through it all, exhausted, and struggled up the other side, using saplings and sandstone outcroppings for hand- and footholds.

At the top they stumbled onto a trail.

It wasn't wide – about four feet – and was overgrown from disuse during the winter months but it was heaven compared with what they'd been slogging through since fleeing the Feldman's house.

'Is this it?' Michelle asked.

They found their answer only thirty feet away, a large wooden sign:

> **Perkinstown 64 miles**
> **Duluth, MN 187 miles**
>
> **Camp Responsibly on the Joliet Trail**
> **Only YOU can prevent forest fires**

'How much time do you think it bought us?' Lewis asked.

He was referring to the conversation with Graham Boyd, Brynn's husband.

'Hard to say.'

They'd come miles through the underbrush, adjusting their course occasionally after consulting the GPS, Google Earth and the paper map as they made their way north.

'So that was why you turned it on, her phone?'

'Right.' Though just after the conversation he'd removed the battery so the police couldn't trace it. 'I've been waiting for that. Wanted to hold out for as long as we could. Now we put him at ease. He'll go to sleep and won't worry until three or four when he wakes up in an empty bed. By then they'll both be dead and buried.'

'He believed you?'

'Pretty sure.'

As they walked on, Hart was wondering about her husband, somebody married to a woman like Brynn . . . what would *he* be like? Low voice, seemed smart, well spoken, wasn't drunk. He wondered if the man's words had contained clues that might help him find and kill her more efficiently.

Not really.

Still, he kept replaying the conversation. It fascinated him.

Two different last names. Didn't surprise him that Brynn had kept her maiden name.

Graham . . . The man she slept with, the man she shared a life with. Unusual name. Where did it come from? Was he conservative, liberal? Religious? What did he do for a living? Hart was interested in the relief that had filled his voice. Something seemed a bit off about it. Hart didn't know what to make of that. Yeah, relieved . . . but another emotion too.

He wished he'd gotten a better look at her in the Feldmans' driveway. Pretty enough, he recalled. Brownish hair, pulled back. A nice figure. Hadn't let herself go. Picturing her eyes. Brows furrowed as she registered his presence when he rose from the bushes.

Hart had killed six people. Three had looked at him as he did it. Seeing their eyes meant nothing to him. He didn't prefer that they look away. He didn't look away either. The only one who hadn't cried was the one woman he'd killed, a drug dealer.

'Yo, you gonna do this?'

He hadn't answered.

'You and me, we work something out?'

She'd stolen money, or hadn't, skimmed the drugs, or hadn't. Wasn't Hart's issue. He'd made an agreement with the man who wanted her dead. And so he, a craftsman, made her dead, staring into her face as he did so to make sure she wasn't going to leap aside or pull a hidden weapon.

Brynn had looked *him* in the eye too as she fired.

A craftswoman.

'Hart?'

Lewis's voice shook him out of his reflection. He tensed, looking around. 'Yeah?'

'You're a Milwaukee boy, I'm one too. How come we never worked together before?'

'Don't know.'

'You work in the city much?'

'Not much, no. Safer that way.'

'Where you live?'

'South of town.'

'Toward Kenosha.'

'Not that far.'

'Lotta building going on in those parts.'

Lewis stopped suddenly. 'Look up there, a post or something. A sign.'

'Where?'

'See it? On the right.'

They moved forward carefully, Hart putting aside his thoughts about Brynn with some reluctance, and stopped at the sign.

In the summer of 1673, Louis Joliet, a twenty-seven-year-old philosopher, and Fr. Jacques Marquette, a thirty-five-year-old Jesuit priest, crossed Wisconsin on their way to the Mississippi River. Although the trail you are standing on is named for him, Joliet never hiked this 458 mile route. He and Marquette made their voyage mostly by waterway. The Joliet Trail was created by fur traders and people just like you, outdoor-lovers, some years later.

Hart consulted the GPS on his BlackBerry and the paper map.

'Which way'd those girls get?'

'Has to be to the right. That's the ranger station, few miles away.'

Lewis looked up and down the trail, which, little traveled this time of year, was overgrown and tangled with branches and dotted with stubborn saplings rising through the sludge of leaves.

'What's wrong?'

'You ask me, this ain't no trail at all. It's just less forest.'

Hart smiled at that. Which made Lewis smile too.

Here they were, two women moving relentlessly forward on a tourists' trail. One with an inlaid rosewood cane, one with a matching spear. Bolos and knives in their pockets and grim faces both.

The trail reminded Brynn of the last time she'd been horseback riding – one spring several years ago. She'd loved cantering along the bridle path in some woods near Humboldt. Years ago, before she'd become a deputy, she'd been an amateur competitive jumper and loved the sport. In fact, it was at a competition that she'd seen an exhibition by some mounted police from Milwaukee. The eighteen-year-old had spent time talking to an officer, which had ignited a fascination, ironically, not in the art of dressage riding but in police work.

Which, a few years later, provided the same thrill she'd experienced hurtling over jumps atop a half ton of animal.

Now, she realized how much she missed riding and wondered if she'd ever have the chance to get back into the saddle.

As they continued along the trail they'd see poignant evidence that the park was usually a far more innocent place than tonight, signs dispensing bits of history and information. The most troubling dangers had to do with fires, steep drop-offs and ecological risks.

Emerald Ash Borer WARNING

Fire wood purchased from Clausen may be infested with Emerald Ash Borer. If you have purchased any Henderson brand fire wood, please burn any such wood immediately to avoid endangering our hardwood trees with the Emerald Ash Borer!

One tree – a massive oak – earned a sign all its own. Maybe the biggest or oldest (tourists loved their superlatives). Brynn, though, thought of it simply as a source of cover. Around here the trail wound through patches of bare fields, exposing them to pursuers. To move off the trail, into the lowland brush, though, would slow them down way too much.

The flying squirrels were plentiful and bats flitted by silently, owls noisier. Several times they'd hear a beat of wing and a final squeak from a predator's successful strike.

Michelle kept up pretty well but Brynn was growing concerned about her. Her ankle wasn't bad – from the job and from Joey's many mishaps she knew about serious injuries; when to dole out sympathy and when to call medics. Rather, it was the young woman's resignation. She was lagging behind. Once, she paused and looked up a steep incline, grimaced.

'Let's go,' Brynn urged.

'I need to rest.'

'Let's cover a little more ground.' She smiled. 'Let's earn a break.'

'I'm tired *now*. I'm so tired. My blood sugar, I told you.' Then she gasped and jerked back as a small animal scampered past. 'What was that?'

A vole or mouse, Brynn told her. 'Harmless.'

'It could crawl up your pants.'

Not yours, Brynn thought, considering Michelle's tight jeans.

The younger woman's good mood from earlier had faded. She was like a child who'd missed her afternoon nap. Patiently Brynn said, 'Come on, Michelle. The more we walk, the closer to getting back home. And we can't stop here.' They were in a clearing, very visible in the moonlight.

Her lips tight, almost in a pout, she complied and they climbed the steep hill. At the top Brynn suddenly smelled rosemary and wanted to cry, thinking back to the Easter lamb she'd made just weeks ago.

They slipped through a copse of wiry trees, eerie, something out of *Lord of the Rings*.

Her face was now throbbing with every step. She touched her cheek and inhaled as the ache flowed through her head and neck. The swelling was worse. She wondered if the wound would get infected. Would there be terrible scarring? The thought of plastic surgery came to mind, and she actually smiled, thinking, You vain girl. Maybe you should concentrate on staying alive before you worry about making yourself presentable for the multiplex on Saturday night.

Graham had caught her once in the habit of stroking the dip in her crooked chin. She'd blushed and he'd smiled, then whispered, 'It's sexy. Don't fret.'

She grew irritated at how persistently thoughts of her past kept intruding tonight. She hadn't thought about Keith so much in years. And Graham and Joey kept making regular appearances – while her only goal was getting to safety.

Like that old cliché, memories flashing through her thoughts at the end of her life.

Dammit, concentrate.

They followed the trail around a bend to the left. Brynn looked back. A clear panorama was behind them and she could see, a hundred yards away, the crest of a rolling hill.

There was movement along it, going from tree to tree.

She gripped Michelle's arm. 'What's that?'

It was as if a sniper were crawling into position to take a shot.

'Get down,' Brynn ordered. They both crouched. She surveyed the ridge and the trail. No clouds now and the half moon cast light bright enough to shoot by. At this distance they were probably safe from a shotgun but Hart had fired at her with a Glock. A 9mm slug could easily make it here, and he obviously was skilled.

She squinted at the ridge.

Then she laughed. 'It's just our friend.' She pointed, standing up. 'Or maybe one of *his* friends.'

The pursuer was of the four-legged variety, loping from tree to tree. The gray wolf, she assumed. They usually hung in packs, Brynn believed. But this one was clearly solo. Was he following them? Maybe her growl hadn't scared him off completely.

Then the creature stiffened, looked back. Was gone in a fraction of a second.

'You see that? Like he disappeared . . .' Brynn's smile faded. 'No . . . Oh, no!'

In the distance two men were moving quickly along the Joliet Trail, headed in their direction. A half mile away, moving doggedly. No doubt that they were Hart and his partner; one carried a shotgun. The men vanished where the trail dipped beneath the cover of trees.

'No!'

'It's them,' Michelle whispered. 'How did they find us?'

'Bad luck. There were a dozen ways we could've gone. They

gambled and won. Come on. Move!' The women began jogging, and hobbling, as quickly as they could, their breath coming fast.

Go, go, go . . .

'I didn't think they'd really follow us,' Michelle's rasping voice whimpered. It was a pathetic sound. 'Why?'

Hart, Brynn thought. The answer is Hart.

The trail turned to the right, due east, and when they broke from the trees the ground opened up with a moonlit view of rocky terrain: tall hills rising above the path and deep ravines falling away below. Gashes in the trees revealed rugged sandstone bluffs.

'Look. There.'

They saw an intersection. Another path, narrower than the Joliet, branched off to the left and rose up a hillside, skirting a steep cliff descending into a dim valley. Brynn motioned her companion along. Michelle followed, glancing back from time to time, her hand in her jacket, where the Chicago Cutlery knife rested in her waistband. She seemed to find solace in making sure the weapon hadn't vanished.

At the juncture they paused. There was an open shelter with a bench – no phone, Brynn noted immediately. A trash can, which was empty. The area was trampled down, courtesy of a hard Wisconsin winter. The Joliet Trail continued on into the inky night, descending to the right – northeast. The small path was marked with a sign.

> *Apex Lake 1.1 miles.*
> *Trapper Grove 1.9 miles.*
> *Umstead Ranger station 2.2 miles.*

Brynn walked to the fence marking the edge of the cliff and looked into the valley. She pointed to the left. 'Down there. Can you see it? That building? It's the ranger station.'

'Oh. Way over there. I don't see any lights.'

'No, I'm sure it's closed.'

The place was less than a mile away – as the crow flew – through a deep valley, though hiking via this path would take them on a much longer trip: more than two miles, according to the sign. The path would meander, leading to Apex Lake, the grove and finally to the station.

Brynn had a vague memory of the station, which had served as a staging area for one of the searches she'd been on. It had been closed then too – the time of year was winter – but she could picture it clearly.

'I remember phones there. But I don't know if they're working now. And a gun cabinet, I think. But we can't take the path.' Nodding toward the sign. 'It's too long. We'd never make it in time.'

'They might not go that way. Just keep going on the Joliet Trail.'

Brynn considered. 'I think they'd be inclined to figure that we headed for the station.' She was staring at the dark void beyond the cliff and stepped even closer to the edge. She paused by a *Danger* sign. Looked down.

Climb it, or not?

Whatever they did they'd have to choose soon. The men could be here in ten or fifteen minutes.

'Is it straight down?' Michelle asked.

Still gazing down into the murkiness, Brynn saw a narrow ledge maybe twenty feet below them; below that the cliff face descended for another fifty or sixty feet.

Brynn whispered, 'I think it's climbable. Tough, but it can be done.'

If they could make it to the forest floor they'd have an easy direct walk to the ranger station.

The odds of a working phone and gun and ammunition?

Brynn couldn't say. A roll of the dice.

She decided that breaking in wouldn't be a problem. If they could get to the building, even the strongest lock in the world wouldn't keep her out.

'I hate heights,' Michelle whispered.

I'm with you there, baby . . .

'Are we going to try it?' the young woman asked in a shaky voice.

Brynn grabbed a birch sapling and leaned out into space, studying the rocks below.

They'd managed a fast walk, breaking into a jog occasionally.

Lewis pulled up, gripping his side. He leaned against a tree.

'You all right?'

'Yeah. I quit smoking last week.' He inhaled deeply. 'Well, pretty much a month ago but I had one last week. Then stopped for good. But it catches up with you. You smoke?'

Wincing at a pang from his shot arm, Hart kept looking from side to side. 'Nope.' He'd grown convinced that the women weren't armed but he didn't like that damn dog or wolf or whatever it was nosing around. People were predictable. He'd made a study of human nature in the extremes and he was comfortable taking them on, however dangerous they were. Animals, though, operated with a different mind-set. He recalled the paw print near the Feldman house.

This is my world. You don't belong here. You'll see things that aren't there and miss things that're coming up right behind you.

But then he inhaled hard and leaned against another tree. The men's eyes met and they shared a smile. Hart said, 'I haven't run like this in years. I thought I was in shape. Man.'

'You work out?'

He did, regularly – his line of work required strength and stamina – but it was mostly weight-lifting, not aerobic. That wouldn't've been helpful; Hart rarely chased anyone; and he didn't think he'd ever run from anybody, not once in his life. He told Lewis, 'I don't do much jogging.'

'Nope. Health clubs don't figure much in the Lewis family. But I work construction some. Was working for Gaston on that tower near the lake.'

'For who?'

'Gaston Construction? The big tower? Other side of the expressway. The glass is up now. I hired out with the concrete sub. That'll keep you in shape. You handy?'

Hart said, 'Some. I've done plumbing. No patience for painting. And electricity I stay away from.'

'I hear that.'

'Carpentry's my favorite.'

'Framing?'

'More furniture,' Hart explained.

'You make furniture?'

'Simple things.'

Measure twice, cut once . . .

'Like tables and chairs?'

'Yeah. Cabinets. It's relaxing.'

Lewis said, 'I built my grandmother a bed once.'

'A bed? Come on, let's keep going.' They started walking again. 'How'd you happen to build her a bed?'

Lewis explained, 'She started going crazy, getting older. Maybe that Alzheimer's thing, I don't know. Or maybe she just got old. She'd walk around the house singing Christmas carols all year 'round. All the time. And she'd start putting up decorations and my mother'd take them down and then she'd be putting them up again.'

Hart picked up the pace.

'So she's pretty flaky. And she starts looking for her bed. The bed she had with my grandfather. It musta got thrown out years ago. But she thought it was somewhere in the house. Walking all over the place trying to find it. I felt bad for her. So I found some pictures of it and made her one. Wasn't all that good but it looked close enough. I think it gave her a good couple of months. I don't know.'

Hart said, 'Like "making" a bed. Only you really did make one, not with sheets and blankets.'

'Yeah, I guess I did.' He gave a laugh.

'Why're you in this line, Comp? You could be making union scale.'

'Oh, I'm in it for the money. How can you score big at sweat labor?'

'You score big doing this?'

'I score *bigger*. Now my mother's in a home too. And my brothers, they contribute. I can't do less than them.'

Hart felt Lewis's eyes on him, like he wanted to ask about his family but remembered the story about the brother and the parents being dead.

'Anyway, I'm good at this. What I do. Hell, you heard my rep. You checked, right? People vouched for me.'

'They did. That's why I called you.'

'Banks, payroll offices. Collection work, protection . . . I've got a talent for it. I got contacts all over the lakefront. How 'bout you, Hart? Why're you in this fucked-up business?'

He shrugged. 'I don't do well working for other people. And I don't do well sitting. I do well doing. Got that itchy gene.'

It suits me . . .

Lewis looked around. 'You think they're hiding?'

Hart wasn't sure. But he didn't think so. He had a feeling that Brynn was somehow like him. And he would rather move any day, keep moving, however dangerous it was. Anything rather than hiding. But he didn't tell Lewis this. 'No, I don't.

They'll keep going. Besides, I saw some patches of mud back there. Prints in them.'

Lewis gave a crisp laugh. The sound had irritated Hart at first. Now he didn't mind so much. The man said, 'You're the last of the Mohicans. That movie rocked . . . You hunt, I'll bet.'

Hart said, 'Nope. Never been.'

'Bullshit. Really?'

'Truth. You?'

Lewis said he hadn't for a while but he used to. A lot. He liked it. 'I think you would too. You seem like you know your way around here.'

'This isn't the North Woods. That'd be different. We're in Wisconsin. A state park. Just using logic.'

'Naw, I think you're a natural.'

Hart was about to ask, 'Natural what?' But froze. A shout, a woman's voice, came to them on the wind. A shout for help. She was trying to keep it quiet, he got the impression, but he heard alarm, if not desperation. It was in the distance but not too far, maybe a quarter, a half mile up the Joliet Trail, the direction they were headed.

Another call, the words ambiguous.

'Same person calling?' Hart asked.

'I don't know.'

'Let's go.'

Staying low, they moved forward as quickly as they dared.

'Keep a lookout. I don't trust her. One of 'em screamed fake before, at the lake, don't forget. Maybe they're trying to sucker us in, wanting a fight. Maybe no guns. But they've got knives.'

Ten minutes later the men, keeping low and scanning the greenery around them, paused. Ahead of them the trail broadened and a smaller trail branched off to the left. The intersection was marked by a wooden sign, visible in the moonlight. An arrow pointed out a path that Hart had seen on GPS. It went west and north and, after circling a small lake, ended at a ranger station. From there a two-lane road led to the highway.

Hart gestured Lewis down into the bushes beside him. Scanning the surroundings. 'You see anything?'

'Nope.'

Hart listened carefully. No more cries, no voices. Just the breeze, which hissed through the branches and made the leaves scuttle along like crabs.

Then Lewis touched his arm, pointed. Fifteen feet past the intersection was a dark wood fence with a sign that said, *Danger*. Black space behind it, where cliff dropped into ravine. 'That tree there, Hart.'

'Where?'

Finally he spotted it: A branch had broken off the tree beside the cliff. You could see the white wood below the bark.

'I don't know if it's a trick or not,' Hart whispered. 'You go round there to the right. That bunch of bushes.'

'Got it.'

'I'm going to the edge and look around. I'll be making some noise to give 'em a chance to make a move.'

'If I see anybody I'll take her out. Shoot high, then low.' Lewis grinned. 'And I'll keep my mouth shut.'

For the first time that night Lewis looked confident. Hart, finally at ease with his partner on this difficult night, decided the man would do fine. 'Go on. Stay clear of the leaves.'

Silently Lewis, crouching, crossed the path and slipped behind a stand of brush. When Hart saw he was in a good position to cover the area, he started forward, also low. Head swiveling back and forth.

He noticed in the distance, at the bottom of the ravine, what appeared to be the ranger station.

Holding his own weapon pointed forward, he moved to

the sign. He examined the broken branch. Then peered over the edge of the cliff. He couldn't see anyone. Took out his flashlight and shone it down into the night.

Jesus.

He stood, put the gun away. Called Lewis over.

'What is it?'

'Look . . . They tried to climb down. But it didn't work.'

Peering over the edge of the cliff, they could see in the faint moonlight a ledge twenty feet below, at the bottom of a steep, rocky wall. One of the women, or maybe both, had fallen. On the ledge was a four-foot-long branch – the one that had broken off of the tree beside them. And around it was a large smear of bright red blood, glistening under the flashlight.

'Man,' Lewis said, 'she hit hard.' He tried to peer further into the ravine. 'Broke her leg, I'll bet. Bleeding plenty.'

'They had to've kept going down. They couldn't get back up, not hurt like that. Or maybe there's a cave. Behind the ledge. They're trying to hide in.'

'Well, we gotta go after 'em,' Lewis announced. 'Like hunting. You follow a wounded animal till you find it. No matter what. You want, I'll go down first.'

Hart lifted an eyebrow. 'Bit of a climb.'

'I told you – construction on the lakefront. Thirty stories up and I'm strolling around on the ironwork like it's a sidewalk.'

No. Something's wrong.

Graham Boyd rose from the couch, walked past Anna, who had switched from knitting to a large needlepoint sampler – the woman found peace and pleasure in transforming cloth of all kinds – and walked into the kitchen. His eyes glanced at a picture of his wife as a teenager, sitting atop the horse she'd later ride to win the Mid-Wisconsin Junior Horse Jumping Competition years ago. She was leaning down, her cheek against the horse's neck, patting him, though her eyes were focused elsewhere, presumably on one of her competitors.

He found the county phone book and looked at the map. The nearest towns to Lake Mondac were Clausen and Point of Rocks. Clausen had a town magistrate's office, Point of Rocks a public safety office. He tried the magistrate first. No answer, and the message referred callers to City Hall, which turned out to be just a voice mail. The office in Point of Rocks was closed, and the outgoing message said that anyone with an emergency should call either the county Sheriff's Office or the State Police.

'*And thank you for calling,*' it concluded politely. '*Have a nice day.*'

How can a fucking police department be closed?

He heard Joey's bedroom door open and close. The toilet flushed.

A moment later: 'When's Mom coming home?' The boy, still not in his pajamas, was at the top of the stairs.

'Soon.'

'You called her?'

'She's busy. She can't be disturbed. Put your pajamas on and go to bed. Lights out.'

The boy turned around. The bedroom door closed.

Graham thought that he heard the video game again. He wasn't sure.

Anna asked, 'Where is she? I'm worried, Graham.'

'I don't know. That deputy I talked to said it was just routine. But it didn't feel right.'

'How do you mean?'

'Her phone. Giving it to somebody else? No way.' He could talk to Anna without worrying that she'd become defensive. When it came to serious topics, he had trouble talking to Brynn and to her son – hell, that was tonight's theme, apparently – but he could talk to his mother-in-law. 'She's too much of a control person for that.'

He had, however, pulled back from 'control freak.'

Anna's frown morphed into a smile, as if she'd caught on. 'That's my daughter. You're right.'

Graham picked up the landline. Made a call.

'Deputy Munce.'

'Eric, it's Graham.'

'Hey. What's up?'

'The sheriff in?'

'Now? Nope. He goes home about six, seven most nights.'

'Look, Brynn went out on something tonight. Up at Lake Mondac.'

'Right. Heard about that.'

'Well, she's not back yet.'

Silence. 'Not back? Forty minutes from there to your place. You're north of town. Forty minutes *tops*. I've drove it in a half hour.'

'I called and got some other deputy. Said there was a domestic. And that Brynn was handling it. Child Services or something.'

A pause. 'That doesn't sound familiar, Graham. Who were you talking to?'

'I don't remember. Maybe Billings.'

'Well, that's nobody from our office. Hold on . . .' Muted sounds of conversation.

Graham rubbed his eyes. Brynn had been up at five. He'd been up at five-thirty.

The deputy came back on. 'All right, Graham. Story is the guy who made that nine-one-one call called back and said it was a mistake. Brynn was going to turn around. That was close to seven, seven-thirty.'

'I know. But this deputy said it wasn't a mistake. It was some domestic dispute, and they wanted Brynn to handle it. Could she have run into some State Police up there, town cops?'

'Could happen but that's not the sort of things the troopers'd handle.'

Graham's skin chilled at this. 'Eric, something's wrong.'

'Let me call the sheriff. He'll get back to you.'

Graham hung up. He paced the kitchen. Surveyed the new tiles on the floor. Organized a stack of bills. Drew a line in the dust on top of the small, rabbit-ear TV. Listened to the computer game upstairs.

Goddamnit. Why wasn't the boy listening to him? He decided to ban Joey from skateboards for the rest of the school year.

Anger or instinct?

The phone rang.

"Lo?"

'Graham, it's Tom Dahl. Eric just called. We checked with the State Police. Nobody got any calls up at Lake Mondac. Clausen, Point of Rocks, even as far as Henderson.'

Graham explained what he'd told Eric Munce, irritated that the man hadn't filled the sheriff in. 'The deputy was named Billings.'

Silence for a moment. 'Billings's the name of a road between Clausen and the state park.'

So it might've been fresh in the mind of somebody trying to make up a name. Graham's hands were sweating.

'Her phone keeps going to voice mail again, Tom. I'm plenty worried.'

'What's wrong?' a voice called. Joey's.

Graham looked up. The boy was standing halfway down the stairs. He'd been listening. 'What's wrong with Mom?'

'Nothing. Go back to bed. Everything'll be fine.'

'No. Something's wrong.'

'Joey,' Graham snapped. 'Now.'

Joey held his eye for a moment, the chill look sending a shiver through Graham's back, then turned and stomped up the stairs.

Anna appeared in the door, glanced at Graham's grimacing face. 'What?' she whispered.

He shook his head, said, 'I'm talking to the sheriff.' Then: 'Tom, whatta we do?'

'I'll send some people up there. Look, relax. Her car probably broke down and she hasn't got cell phone reception.'

'Then who was Billings?'

Another pause. 'We'll get up there right away, Graham.'

Gasping, face dotted with cold sweat, Michelle crouched, leaning against her pool cue cane, Brynn beside her. They were still on the Joliet Trail, hiding in a tangle of juniper and boxwood, which smelled to Brynn of urine.

They'd come a half mile from the cliff top intersection with the *Danger* sign and shelter, running as best they could the entire distance.

They now watched the beam from a flashlight, pointed downward, slowly sweeping the ledge and cliff face as Hart and his partner climbed down. They continued walking along the trail, moving quickly.

The men had bought the sham Brynn had orchestrated: the shouting, the broken branch, the blood – her own – spattered on the ledge. The men would continue to the bottom now, either on the cliff or the path around Apex Lake, and make for the ranger station. Which would give Brynn and Michelle an extra hour to get to safety before Hart and his partner realized that they'd been tricked.

In the end it hadn't been Michelle's fear of heights – or Brynn's – that decided the matter. Brynn had concluded that even climbing down the cliff and hiking through the tangled brush in the ravine would take too much time. The men would have caught up with them before they were halfway to the ranger station. But the cliff was a good chance to mislead their pursuers. Brynn had broken the branch to make it look like an accident, then carefully climbed down the cliff to the ledge. There she'd taken a deep breath, and cut her scalp with the kitchen knife. As a deputy she knew a lot about head injuries, and that lacerations on the head didn't hurt badly but bled copious amounts. (She knew this from Joey as much as from auto accident calls.) After smearing the blood on the stone, she'd climbed back up to the cliff top and they'd fled down the Joliet Trail.

She now looked back. The sweeping flashlight beam was still visible through the bones of trees. Then the path turned and the women lost sight of the killers.

'How does it feel?' Michelle nodded at Brynn's head. She apparently thought Brynn had made her decision not to climb down the cliff face because of the young woman's fear of heights. She glowed with gratitude.

Brynn said she was fine.

Michelle began rambling, telling a story about how she'd been hit on the head by a schoolgirl on the playground, and had bled all over a new dress, which had upset her more than the fight. 'Girls're worse than boys.'

Brynn didn't disagree. She did anti-gang campaigns at the high schools. Gangs . . . even in modest Humboldt.

Though an image of Joey, panting and bloody, after one of his fights at school also came to mind. She pushed it away.

Michelle kept up the manic banter and Brynn tuned her out. She paused and looked around. 'I think we should go off the trail now, find the river.'

'We have to? We're making good time.'

But the trail, Brynn told her, didn't lead them anywhere except deeper into the woods. The closest town that way was fifteen miles.

'I need to use the compass.' She knelt to the side of the trail and set the alcohol bottle on the ground. With some prodding the needle finally swung north. 'We go that way. It's not far. A couple of miles, I'd guess. Probably less.' She put the bottle in her pocket.

They were on higher ground here and, looking back, they could still see a flashlight slowly probing for the pathway down the cliff face that would lead the killers into the valley and to the ranger station. They'd eventually learn that the women weren't going that way but every minute they delayed on the cliff was a minute more Brynn and Michelle had to escape.

Brynn found a section of the woods that was less ensnarled than others and she moved off the trail. Michelle, somber again, gazed at the rocky, boggy ground and started forward with a look of distaste, like a girl reluctantly climbing into her date's filthy car.

They were doing eighty, without the light bar going or the throaty siren. Didn't need them. There was hardly any traffic out here, this time of night. And none of the retrofit accessories in the Dodge would have any inhibiting effect on suicidal wildlife. Sheriff Tom Dahl's feeling was that deer were born without brains.

He was sitting in the passenger seat and a young deputy, Peter Gibbs, was driving. Behind them was another car, Eric Munce at the wheel and, beside him, Howie Prescott, a massive, shaven-headed deputy who got good respect at traffic stops.

Dahl had called his deputies and found no shortage of volunteers to help find out what had happened to their colleague Brynn McKenzie. They all stood ready to go, but four, he figured, was plenty.

The sheriff was on the phone with an FBI agent in Milwaukee. His name was Brindle, which Dahl thought was a coloring of a horse or dog. The agent had been getting ready for bed but didn't hesitate to help out. He sounded genuinely concerned.

The subject of the conversation was the woman lawyer, Emma Feldman.

'Well, Sheriff, started out as a little thing. She's handling this corporate deal. She's doing her homework and finds out that a lot of the companies on the lakefront have more than their fair share of documented aliens. Next thing a CI . . . that's a—'

'Confidential informant?' Dahl asked, but Brindle missed the irony.

'Right. He says that Stanley Mankewitz, head of some local, is selling forged green cards to illegals.'

'How much could he make doing that?'

'No, that's not what it's about. He doesn't even charge 'em. What he does is gets them to guarantee that they'll get jobs in open shops then unionize the workers. The union gets bigger, Mankewitz gets richer.'

Hmm, Dahl thought. Clever idea.

'That's what we're investigating right now.'

'And this Mankewitz? He done it?'

'Up in the air so far. He's smart, he's old school and he only hires people who keep their mouths shut. He's a prick too, pardon my French, so, yeah, he did it. But the case's weak. It takes just one witness having an accident or getting killed in a, quote, random house invasion and the whole case could fall apart.'

'And here she is, out in the wilderness, this lawyer. A lot of accidents could happen there.'

'Exactly. Milwaukee PD should've had somebody on her. They dropped the ball there.'

This was offered a little too fast, Dahl thought. The finger-pointing'd already started up, it seemed. Policing wasn't much different in Milwaukee, Washington, D.C., or Kennesha County.

Dahl said, 'Go faster.'

'What?' the FBI agent asked.

'I'm talking to the driver . . . When my deputy's husband

called her phone, some man answered, claiming to be a deputy. Near as we can tell, there're no troopers or neighboring law out there. None at all.'

'I see why you're worried. Where is this happening?'

'Lake Mondac.'

'I don't know it.'

'Next to Marquette State Park.'

'I'll give my man a call who runs CI's, see if there's any word about somebody talking to a pro – hired killer, I saying.'

So *that's* what he means by pro. Dahl was getting irritated. 'That'd be much appreciated, Agent Brindle.'

'You want one of our people there, on the ground?'

'Not yet, I don't think. Let's see what's going on first.'

'Okay. Well, call if you need to. We'll be totally on board, Sheriff. This Mankewitz, he's fucking around with illegals and Homeland Security and terrorist issues.'

Not to mention putting a poor family at risk, Dahl thought. Something else he refrained from saying. He thanked the agent and they hung up.

'How soon?' he muttered to the young deputy beside him.

'Half hour . . .'

'Well,' Dahl began impatiently, rubbing his scarred leg.

'I know, Sheriff,' Gibbs said. 'But we're doing eighty. Any faster and all it takes is one deer. And if it doesn't kill us coming through the windshield, Eric'll get us from behind. That boy really oughta back off a bit.'

They'd left the Joliet Trail twenty minutes before, with Brynn deviating only when necessary – around thickets and brambles and beds of leaves that might cover trip holes and bogs. They headed up into the hills, steep ones, and already the incline was dramatic in some places. A slip could turn into a tumble down a hillside for many yards, over sharp rocks and through thorn bushes.

The men would be at the bottom of the cliff by now. She hoped that, finding no bodies, they'd continue through the ravine to the ranger station. It could be forty minutes, an hour before they realized they'd been tricked and returned to the Joliet Trail to resume the hunt.

A brief pause for another compass reading. They'd remained largely on course, due north.

For the first time tonight Brynn was beginning to feel that she and Michelle might survive.

They'd be at the river soon. And then either a trek south along the bank to Point of Rocks or the shorter but arduous – and dangerous – climb up the gorge. She couldn't get that image out of her head: the hiker who'd fallen and been impaled on the tree limb.

The recovery team had needed a chain saw to cut the body free. They'd had to stand around waiting for an hour for an officer to arrive with the tool.

Brynn squinted at a silver flash in the distance ahead of them. Was that the river?

No, just a narrow band of grass shining in the moonlight. Otherworldly. She wondered what kind it was. Graham could have told her in a heartbeat.

But she didn't want to think about Graham.

Then she shivered at the sound of a howl behind them. A creature baying. Was it the wolf that seemed to be following them as persistently as the men?

Michelle looked back at the sound. She froze. And then she screamed.

'Michelle, no!' Brynn whispered harshly. 'It's just the—'

'Them, it's them!' The young woman was pointing into the darkness.

What? What did she see? All Brynn was looking at were layers of shadow, some moving, some still. Smooth or textured.

'Where?'

'There! Him!'

Finally Brynn could see: A hundred feet away a man stood behind a bush.

No! They hadn't believed the trick at the junction. Brynn gripped her spear.

'Get down!'

But whatever'd been building within the young woman now exploded in rage and madness. 'You fuckers!' she screamed. 'I hate you!'

'No, Michelle. Please, be quiet. We have to run. Now!'

But the younger woman seemed transfixed, as if Brynn weren't even present. She flung aside the pool cue steadying her and pulled out a pool ball bolo.

Brynn stepped forward, gripping Michelle's leather jacket.

But, her face a mask of fury, the woman shoved Brynn away, sending her slipping down an incline of slick leaves.

The bolo in one hand, the knife in the other, Michelle charged the man, moving fast despite her limp. 'I hate you, I hate you!' she screamed.

'No, Michelle, no! They have guns!'

But she seemed deaf to the pleas. When she was thirty feet away from the man she flung the bolo, which flew in a fierce arc and nearly struck his head. He stood his ground – just as Brynn herself had, back in the Feldman's driveway.

Undaunted, Michelle continued her charge.

Brynn debated. Should she follow? It'd be suicide . . .

Then decided: Oh, hell. She grimaced, rose to her feet and charged after the woman, trying to keep low. 'Michelle, stop!' Any minute the man would fire. It must've been Hart; he remained motionless, waiting for the perfect shot.

Michelle sprinted directly toward him.

The man couldn't miss.

But no shots came.

Slowing to a stop, Brynn could see why. It wasn't a person at all. What the crazed young woman had been attacking was just a weird configuration of tree trunk, broken about six feet up, the branches and leaves giving the impression of a human. It was like a scarecrow.

'I hate you!' the young woman's shrill voice echoed.

'Michelle!'

Then, when she was ten feet away, Michelle apparently realized her mistake. She stopped, gasping for breath, staring at the trunk. She dropped to her knees, lowering her head, hands over her face, sobbing. An eerie keening came from her throat, both mournful and hopeless.

The horror of the evening finally poured out; the tears up until now had been tears of confusion and pain. This was a rupture of pure sorrow.

Brynn approached and then stopped. 'Michelle, it's okay. Let's—'

Michelle's voice rose to another wail. 'Leave me alone!'

'Please. Shhhh, Michelle. Please be quiet . . . It's okay.'

'No, it's not okay! It's not okay at all.'

'Let's keep at it. We don't have much farther to go.'

'I don't care. You go on . . .'

A faint smile. 'I'm not leaving you here.'

Michelle hugged herself, rocking back and forth.

Brynn crouched next to her. She understood that something else was going on within the young woman. 'What is it?'

Michelle looked absently at the knife, slipped it back in the sock scabbard.

'There's something I have to tell you.'

'What?' Brynn persisted.

'It's my fault they're dead,' she whispered, her face miserable. 'Steve and Emma. It's my fault!'

'You, why?'

She snapped, 'Because I'm a spoiled little brat. Oh, God . . .'

Brynn looked behind them. A few minutes. This was important, she sensed. They could afford a few minutes. The men were miles away. 'Tell me.'

'My husband . . .' She cleared her throat. 'My husband's seeing somebody else.'

'What?'

A faint, pained smile and she managed to say, 'He's cheating on me. I said he's on a business trip. He is, but he's not going alone.'

'I'm sorry.'

'A girlfriend of mine works for the travel agency his company uses. I made her tell me. He's going with somebody else.'

'Maybe it's just somebody he works with.'

'No, it's not. And they got one hotel room.'

Oh.

'I was so mad and so hurt. I couldn't be alone this weekend! I just couldn't be. I talked Emma and Steve into coming up here and bringing me along. I wanted to cry on their shoulders. I wanted them to tell me it's not my fault. That he's a bastard, that they be *my* friends after the divorce and they'd dump *him* . . . And now they're dead beçause I couldn't act like a grown-up.'

'That's hardly your fault.' Brynn looked back and saw no pursuers. Nor any sign of their mascot, the wolf. She put her arm around the young woman and helped her to her feet. 'Let's walk. Tell me while we walk.'

Michelle complied. They collected her pool cue and continued toward the river.

'How long've you been married?'

'Six years.' Her voice caught. 'Ryan was like my best friend. Everything seemed so fine. He was so laid back, generous. He took really good care of me . . . And you know what's so messed up? *That's* why I lost him – being a spoiled little girl.' She gave a sour laugh. 'He's a banker. He makes all this money. When we got married I quit my job. It's not like he wanted me to or anything. It was my idea. It was, like, my chance to go to acting school.'

Michelle winced, stepping hard and apparently jarring her ankle. But she ignored the pain and continued, 'I told you I was an actress . . . Bullshit. I'm a twenty-nine-year-old acting student. And not a very good one. I was an extra in two local commercials. And Second City told me no. My life is lunch with my girlfriends, tennis, my health club, my spa. The only thing I'm good at is spending money, shopping and keeping myself in shape.'

To the tune of a svelte size 4, Brynn couldn't help but observe.

'And I became . . . a nobody. Ryan'd come home and I couldn't even talk about the housework – because the maids had done it all. I got boring. He fell out of love with me.'

Part of a law enforcer's job is to recognize the psychological issues at work within the people she meets professionally – the bystanders, witnesses and victims, in addition to the criminals. Brynn didn't know that she had any particular insights but she told Michelle her honest assessment: 'It's not all your fault. It never is.'

'I'm such a loser . . .'

'No, you're not.'

Brynn believed this. A little spoiled, true, a little too pampered, a little too much in love with money and the good life. In a curious way maybe this night was teaching her there was more within her than a rich-girl dilettante.

As for the other issue, the more important one, Brynn now put her arm around Michelle's shoulders. 'There's one thing you have to understand. Whether you asked them here or not made no difference. Whoever killed Emma and Steve was a professional, hired to murder her. If it wasn't tonight it would've been next week. You had nothing to do with that.'

'You think?'

'I do, yes.'

The girl wasn't completely convinced. Brynn knew that guilt has a complex DNA; it doesn't need to be purebred to be virulent. But Michelle seemed to take some comfort in Brynn's words. 'I just wish I could turn back the clock.'

Isn't that a prayer for every day? Brynn thought.

Michelle sighed. 'I'm sorry I lost it. I shouldn't've screamed.'

'I don't think we have to worry. They're miles away, in the bottom of the ravine. They couldn't hear a thing.'

Graham Boyd was pulled from his stew of thoughts about his wife when he heard the distinctive sound of the engine in his F150 start up.

'Somebody's stealing the truck.' He stared at his mother-in-law and instinctively slapped his pants pocket, felt his set of keys.

How? he wondered. In the shows Anna watched, *Matlock* and *Magnum, P.I.,* everybody was hot-wiring cars. He didn't think you could anymore.

But when he saw the deadbolt on the kitchen door open and that the spare keys on the hook were gone, he knew. 'Jesus, not this. Not now.'

'I'll call the sheriff,' Anna said.

'No,' Graham called. 'It's okay.'

He ran outside.

The truck was backing up against the gardening shed to turn around so the driver could head out, hood first, down the narrow driveway. It tapped into the corrugated metal with a loud bang. Not much damage, none to the truck. The driver shoved the transmission into drive.

Waving his hands like a traffic cop stopping an approaching

driver, Graham walked to the passenger window, which was open. Joey looked straight at him with a fierce expression.

Graham said, 'Shut off the engine. Get out of the truck.'

'No.'

'Joey. Do it now. This minute.'

'You can't make me. I'm going to look for Mom.'

'Out of the car. Now.'

'No.'

'There are people doing that. Tom Dahl, some deputies. She'll be fine.'

'You keep saying that!' he shouted. 'But how do you know?'

True, Graham thought.

He saw the boy's edgy eyes, his firm grip on the wheel. He wasn't short – his father was well over six feet – but he was skinny and looked tiny in the big seat.

'I'm going.' He still couldn't make the turn down the driveway so he eased forward, tapped a trash can and backed up again, this time judging correctly; he stopped before he hit the shed. He straightened the wheels toward the road and put the truck in forward once more.

'Joey. No. We don't even know where she is.' Saying this seemed like a retreat. He shouldn't be arguing from logic. He was commander-in-chief.

Instinct, remember.

'Lake Mondac.'

'Shut the engine off. Get out of the truck.' Should he reach in for the keys? What if the boy's foot slipped off the brake? One of Graham's workers had been badly injured reaching into a moving truck, just like this, trying to grab the shifter when the driver forgot to engage it. Our bodies are no match for two tons of steel and detonating gasoline.

He glanced at the seat. Jesus. The boy had a pellet gun – Graham recognized the powerful break-action model. At close range it was as accurate as a .22, and as deadly to squirrels and river rats. Brynn had forbidden him to have weapons. Where had he gotten it? Stolen, Graham wondered.

'Joey! Now!' Graham snapped. 'You can't do anything. Your mother'll be home soon. And she'd be furious if you weren't here.'

Another retreat in the be-the-parent-in-control game.

'No, she won't. Something's wrong. I know something's wrong.' The boy let up on the brake and the truck began to roll forward.

And, not even thinking, Graham ran in front of the vehicle and stood there, hands on the hood.

'Graham!' Anna called from the porch. 'No. Don't make a war out of it.'

And he thought, no, it's time somebody *did* make it a war.

'Get out of that truck!'

'I'm going to find Mom!'

The only thing keeping him alive was a twelve-year-old's untied running shoe on the pedal of brakes that had needed servicing for a year. 'No, you're not. Shut the engine off, Joey. I'm not going to tell you again.' When Graham was a child, that was all his father had needed to say to get him to comply, though the offenses back then were things like failure to take out the trash or neglecting his homework.

'I'm going!'

The truck lurched forward a foot.

Graham gasped but didn't move.

If you move, he told himself, you lose.

Though his mind was also running through the places he could leap if the boy floored the accelerator. He didn't think he'd make it in time.

'*You're* not going!' the boy raged. 'Are you?'

He was inclined to say, It's not our job to go. Let the police do their thing. They're the experts. But instead he said calmly, 'Get out of the truck.'

Aware that his instincts might be about to kill him.

'Are you going to go find her?' He muttered something else. Graham thought one word may be 'coward.'

'Joey.'

'Get out of the way!' the boy screamed. His eyes were wild.

For a moment – an eternal moment – Graham believed the boy was going to hit the gas.

Then Joey grimaced, looked down at the shifter and jammed it into park. He climbed out, reaching for the gun.

'No. Leave it.'

Graham walked up to the boy and put his arm around his shoulders. 'Come on, Joey,' he said kindly. 'Let's get some—' The boy, who seemed furious at this defeat, shrugged the gesture off and stormed into the house, past his grandmother. Saying not a word.

After a compass reading, the women continued through a portion of the park less entangled with shrubbery and ground cover than the area they'd left behind, around Lake Mondac. There were patches of clearing – grass and meadow. And, increasingly, imposing rock formations pushed up by glaciers millions of years ago.

They walked in silence now.

A quarter mile from the last compass check Brynn was about to ask Michelle how her ankle was feeling. Instead, she said, 'My husband is too.'

Shocking herself.

Did I really say that? she wondered. My God, did I really?

Michelle glanced at her, frowning. 'Your husband?'

'Just like yours.' Brynn inhaled the cold, fragrant air. 'Graham's having an affair.'

'Oh, God. I'm sorry. Are you separated? Getting a divorce?'

After a pause she said, 'No. He doesn't know I found out.'

Then she regretted speaking. This was absurd, Brynn thought. Just shut up and keep walking. But she wanted to tell the story. Desperately wanted to. Which was curious because she hadn't shared it with anyone else. Not her mother, not her best friend Katie from the Fire Department or Kim from the parent–teacher organization.

In fact, she supposed it was significant that only here, in these extreme circumstances, with a complete stranger, could she talk about what had been tormenting her for months. Part of her hoped Michelle would respond with a few words of sympathy, that the subject would dwindle and they could get back to completing their trek. But the young woman responded with genuine interest: 'Tell me. Please. What's the story?'

Brynn arranged her thoughts. Finally she said, 'I was married to a state trooper. Keith Marshall.' She glanced at Michelle to see if the name had registered.

It didn't seem to. Brynn continued, 'We met at a State Police training seminar in Madison.' She remembered seeing the tall, broad-shouldered man standing in front of the table that served as their desk.

Keith had glanced her way with a lingering gaze that confessed he certainly liked her looks; but she hadn't really caught his interest until her turn at running the mock hostage negotiation, which the psychologist in charge of the exercise said was perfect. What really got his attention, though, seemed to be the Glock field-stripping and reassembly test. She had her slide mounted and clip loaded while the runner-up was still struggling to get the locking block pin back into the frame.

'That's pretty romantic,' Michelle offered.

What Brynn had thought too.

After the seminar they'd had coffee and discussed small-town policing, and small-town dating. He'd winced once and she'd asked if he was all right. Then he explained that he'd just gotten back from a medical; he'd been shot in a real-life hostage rescue, which nonetheless ended happily – for everybody but the hostage takers.

'The HTs didn't quite make it.'

Oh, *that* incident? she'd thought, recalling the bank robbery gone bad, two armed tweakers – meth heads – inside a branch of Piney Grove Savings with customers and employees. The windows were too thick for a safe sniper shot, so Keith had walked around the barricade and through the front door, holding his weapon at his side. Not even crouching to present a smaller target, he'd shot one in the head, took a round in the side and in the vest from the other one, then killed him too, through the kiosk he tried to hide behind.

The HTs didn't quite make it.

Keith had recovered quickly from his minor injuries. He was reprimanded – it had to be done – for the Bruce Willis/Clint Eastwood procedure. But nobody had treated his disobedience very seriously and, of course, the media lapped it up like a kitten gorging on milk.

Brynn made him tell her the story in depth. She was fascinated. Too fascinated, she'd decided later, utterly won over by the tough, quiet man.

Their first date involved a horror movie, Mexican food and lengthy discussions of calibers, body armor and high speed chases.

They were married eleven months after that.

'So you married a cowboy?'

Brynn nodded.

Michelle added with a grimace, 'I married my father, my therapist says . . . Anyway, what happened?'

'Ah, what happened? Brynn reflected.

She managed to refrain from stroking her deformed jaw but couldn't stop a compulsive memory: Keith, his face flipping instantly from rage to shock, stumbling back under the impact of the bullet, gripping his chest, as their brightly lit kitchen filled with pungent smell of gun smoke from her service Glock.

'Brynn?' Michelle persisted softly. 'What happened?'

Finally she whispered, 'Things just didn't work out . . . So, there I was, single again. I had Joey and my job – my mother was living with us then, so there was a built-in babysitter. I loved work. Had no plans to get married again. But a couple years ago I met Graham. Bought some plants from his land-scaping company. They didn't grow very well and I came back for more. He told me what I was doing wrong and then asked me out. I said yes. He was funny, he was nice. He wanted children but his first wife hadn't. We went out for a while. And I found it was really comfortable. He proposed. I accepted.'

'Comfortable's nice.'

'Oh, real nice. No fights. Home every night.'

'But . . . ?'

Now she *was* touching her jaw. She lowered her hand.

Brynn grimaced. 'A little time goes by and suddenly I'm working more assignments, longer hours, tougher jobs. Lot of domestics. And when I wasn't doing that I'd spend time with Joey . . . He'd had some problems at school. That's an issue, I don't know if you heard? Children of law enforcers?'

Michelle shook her head.

'Statistically more behavior problems, psychological issues. Joey keeps getting into scrapes at school. And he can be a little reckless . . . I wasn't completely forthcoming earlier when I told you about him. He gets into things sometimes. I mean, gets into trouble.' She told Michelle about the skateboarding incident today, some of his scrapes at school. The woman listened with interest – and sympathy. Brynn continued speaking about the past. 'I was focusing on my job and on Joey, and next thing I know Graham's started going out to regular poker games.'

'But they weren't really poker games.'

'Sometimes they were. But sometimes he wouldn't go for the whole game. Sometimes he didn't show up at all.'

One thing she didn't share with Michelle was that when Tom Dahl asked her to drive to Lake Mondac earlier her first thought was: If I go, Graham can't leave tonight, can't see *her*.

Thinking too: He didn't answer his phone when she'd called from the car; had he gone anyway?

'You're sure?' Michelle asked.

'Oh, there was an eyewitness. Saw them together.'

'Do you trust 'em?'

'Pretty much. It was me.' Brynn could picture the scene now. Outside of Humboldt. Driving in a detective's car to a briefing on a meth lab situation. She'd seen Graham standing next to a blonde, tall, outside the Albemarle Motel. She was nodding, smiling. Brynn remembered it seemed like a nice smile. He was talking to her, head down, outside the motel, when he'd told Brynn that he was going to be twenty miles away on a job in Lancaster. At dinner that night he'd looked her in the eye and told her about the drive up to that idyllic vacation town, how the job had gone – offering a liar's saturation bombing of too many details. Brynn knew all about that; she'd run plenty of traffic stops.

Seeing them at the motel, she'd wondered: Was it after or before they'd been to the room?

'What'd you say to him?'

'Nothing.'

'No?'

'I don't know why exactly. Didn't want to rock the boat for Joey. Splitting with Keith. Then another divorce. Couldn't do that to him. And he's such a good person, Graham is.'

'Aside from cheating,' Michelle said darkly.

Brynn smiled wanly. And echoed her earlier comment. 'It's not all his fault. Really . . . I'm pretty good at being a deputy. I'm not so good at this family stuff.'

'I think people ought to take more than a blood test when they get married. There ought to be a two-day exam. Like the bar.'

Brynn felt like she was in a movie, a comedy in which two sisters separated young are reunited: one who'd gone to live the high life in the city, one off to the country. And then they find themselves going on some trip together and learning that at heart they're virtually the same.

Michelle paused. Then pointed ahead and to the left. 'Careful. There's a steep drop-off that way.'

They steered the safer route. Brynn realized that for the first time that night Michelle was walking in the lead . . . and she was content to let her.

'There they are.'

Compton Lewis touched Hart's good arm and pointed through a gap in the trees.

Two, three hundred yards away they could just make out in the moonlight the backs of two figures dressed in dark clothes. One limping along, using what looked like a pool cue for a walking stick.

Hart nodded. His heart tapped faster, seeing their quarry in clear view at last, not quite in range but close. And completely unsuspecting.

The men began to move toward their targets.

The Trickster had been at work again.

As they'd stood at the top of the cliff, the bloody ledge below, Hart had been debating fiercely with himself: Had the women really tried to climb down the rock face and make for the ranger station?

Or had they continued along the Joliet Trail?

Finally he'd decided that Brynn was faking. If either one of them had actually fallen and been hurt she would've done whatever she could to hide the bloodstain with dirt or mud.

Leaving it exposed was an attempt to fool them, get them to head to the station.

Hart had turned the trick against them, though. He wanted Brynn to think she'd been successful, lull them into slowing down and growing careless. He didn't know for sure if they'd have any view of the cliff face, but in case they did, he'd decided to sacrifice one of the flashlights. He'd tied it to a rope made out of Lewis's cut-up undershirt and dangled it from a branch. The wind eased it back and forth close to the ledge, giving the impression they were searching for a way to climb down to the forest floor and pursue the women.

The craftsman had surveyed his handiwork and he was pleased.

Then he and Lewis had continued fast over the trail.

But as to where the women had actually gone – that was up for speculation. It was likely they'd continued on the trail, which according to the GPS kept northeast for a ways – through nearly fifteen miles of woods. They wouldn't have gone that way. Somewhere north of here they'd have to make a decision: They could go left off the trail, west, bypass the ranger station and find the road that led eventually to the county highway. Or they might go north, aiming for the Snake River, which would lead them either west to the interstate or east to the town of Point of Rocks.

But thanks to the scream – the wailing voice a few minutes before, he knew that they were making for the river. The earlier shout – from the intersection by the shelter – had been faked, of course, like the screams when the men were shooting at the canoe. But the second howling was real, Hart knew, since the women believed the men had climbed down the cliff and were miles away.

Hart and Lewis had left the trail too and moved in the

general direction of the sound, picking their way slowly to avoid noisy leaves and branches, as well as the knife-sharp thorns and the steep drop-offs.

As for where the women actually were in this mess of woods north of the trail, they couldn't say – until they found a clue. Lewis stopped, pointing to something white, lying on the ground. Small but very bright in the sea of blacks.

They approached it very slowly. Hart didn't *think* it was a trap – couldn't imagine what it would be – but he didn't trust anything about Brynn now.

The Trickster . . .

'Cover me. I'll check it out. Don't shoot unless I'm about to get shot or stuck. I don't want to give us away.'

A nod.

Hart, crouching, moved in close until he was about three feet away from the object. It was a white tube about eighteen inches long and three inches wide. One end bulged out. He prodded the object with a branch. When nothing happened he looked around. Lewis was scanning the nearby scenery. He gave a thumbs-up to Hart.

The man bent down and picked it up. Lewis joined him.

'A sock with a billiard ball inside.'

'That was theirs?'

'Has to be. It's clean and dry.'

'Shit. One of 'em was going to use that to clobber us. Man, that'd break some bone.'

Brynn, Hart thought.

'What's that?' Lewis asked.

Hart looked at him, eyebrow raised.

'What'd you say? I missed it.'

'Nothing. Didn't say a thing.' Hart, wondering if he'd said Brynn's name aloud. Couldn't have.

They'd continued straight, going almost due north, and just now their prey had come into view.

They were directly behind the women on a relatively flat stretch of forest, mostly oak and maple and birch, that seemed to end in a clearing about a quarter mile ahead. To the right the ground dropped sharply toward a small, rocky trough – a streambed feeding what seemed to be a small lake, surrounded by dense pine forest. On their left the ground rose to a series of ridges, some covered with trees, some dotted with brush and rock, some bald.

Hart crouched, motioning Lewis to join him. The man complied instantly.

'We're going to split up here. You go way round to the left. That ridge, see it?'

A nod.

'You'll be in grass, so you can move faster. Then come in and get close to them on their left flank. I'll keep going straight, come up behind them. When they hit that place there – see that sweet little clearing?'

'Yeah, got it.'

'I'll wave the sock.' He tapped his pocket where he'd stuffed the billiard ball cudgel. 'You shoot. That'll keep 'em down. I'll come up behind and finish them.'

'Bodies?' Lewis asked. 'We can't leave 'em. The animals'll carry the parts off all over the park. That'll be a lot of evidence.'

'No, we'll bury them.'

'Been cold this April. Ground's pretty hard still. And what'll we dig with?' Lewis looked around. He pointed at a small lake to their right. 'There. We could weigh 'em down with rocks. Probably nobody comes there. It's a pretty shitty little lake.'

Hart glanced at it. 'Good.'

'Now, I'll set the choke wide but if I don't hit both of 'em with the first shot the other'll go to cover right away. We'll have to track her down. Who'd I ought to target first? Michelle or the cop?'

Hart was watching the women make their way through the

forest, casual as oblivious tourists. 'You get Michelle. I'll take Brynn.'

'My pleasure.' Lewis nodded. This was clearly his preference anyway.

The white F150 sped out of Humboldt and onto the highway.

The pickup truck was doing close to fifty, the gassy engine accelerating hard.

Graham Boyd was driving and his only passengers were three azaleas in the truck bed, which he hadn't bothered to untether. He'd locked away the pellet gun in the same closet that contained Joey's skateboard.

After the confrontation Graham had stepped into Joey's room to talk to him but the boy was clearly pretending to sleep, his back to the door. Graham called, 'Joey', twice, in a whisper. Part of him had been relieved that the boy didn't respond; he'd had no clue what he was going to say. He just hated that all this tension was unresolved.

He'd thought about taking the game cartridges, the computer and the whole Xbox itself and locking them in the toolshed. But he didn't. It seemed to him that when it came to children, decisions about punishments shouldn't be made in anger.

You're the adult, he's the child.

Chalk that one up to instinct.

He'd checked five minutes later and the light under the boy's door was still out.

'I'm pretty worried, Graham,' Anna had said.

He'd stared again at the picture of his wife in her riding outfit and velvet helmet and then walked out the back door, with a full beer bottle in his hand, so cold it stung his fingers. He'd stood on the small deck, which he'd built himself, and looked up at the half moon.

He'd fished his phone from his pocket, intending to try to reach Brynn.

But then paused. What if the man answered again? Graham knew he wouldn't be able to stay calm. If he gave away that they were suspicious and the police were on their way then the man might hurt Brynn and flee. He'd dropped the phone into his pocket and poured the beer onto a mulch bed surrounding a Christmas azalea behind the deck.

When he'd returned to the living room he'd blinked in surprise. Joey had come downstairs, in his pajamas. He was curled up on the couch beside his grandmother, his head in her lap.

Anna was whisper-singing Joey a song.

Graham's eyes had met his mother-in-law's. He'd pointed to himself and then the door.

'You sure you want to do that, Graham?' she'd asked softly.

No, he'd thought. But nodded.

'I'll hold down the fort here. Be careful. Please be careful.'

He'd fired up the temperamental engine and sped out of his driveway, tires skidding and scattering gravel.

Now he gripped his phone again, started to type in a number – Sandra, of course, wasn't on speed-dial. But he hesitated and decided not to call her. He slipped the device back into his pocket. The protocol was off; the hour was late and he'd already talked to her earlier, briefly, sneaking a call when Anna was in the bathroom, to tell her he couldn't make it tonight. And even if she answered now, which she probably would not, what would he tell her?

He wasn't sure.

Besides, he reasoned, it was better to concentrate on his driving. He was going just over seventy in a forty zone, defying any trooper to stop him.

What exactly he would do when he got to Lake Mondac, he had no idea.

Why he was doing this was even more of a mystery.

For his part, he longed to be lying in bed, end-of-day groggy, with his arm around his wife's tummy and lips against her shoulder. Talk about his day at work and hers, a dinner party coming up on Friday, their child's braces and report card, a re-financing offer on the mortgage, until they dozed off, one after the other. But that wasn't apparently to be his fate. Would it ever be? And when? Tomorrow? Next year? Defying the troopers further, he edged the boxy truck up to eighty, as the kidnapped azaleas shivered in the back.

'There!' Brynn whispered excitedly. 'See that?'

'What?' Michelle was following Brynn's extended arm as they crouched behind a still-bare dogwood, the ground beneath them thick with crocus shoots and fragrant decay.

In the distance, a thin sparkling ribbon.

'The river. The Snake.' Their lifeline.

They walked for five minutes without another glimpse of the water. Brynn was looking around to orient herself and make sure they were traveling in the right direction when she froze.

'Jesus.' She crouched, a hum of fear in her chest.

It was one of the men: the one with the shotgun, Hart's partner. He was no more than two hundred yards away, on a ridge to their left.

'It's my fault . . .' Michelle's face was grim. 'I had that fucking outburst!' Her face revealed the self-disgust of earlier. 'They heard me!'

Spoiled little girl . . .

'No,' Brynn whispered. 'They couldn't be here this fast if they'd bought our trick at the cliff. They rigged something with the flashlight. Hart did. To fool us.'

Same way I tried to fool him. Except *his* trick worked.

And where was he, Hart? She remembered a recent tactical training course. The instructor had lectured about pie-wedge crossfire. Never directly opposite, of course – risk of friendly fire injuries. Hart would be coming up behind them, not from the right flank.

She couldn't see him but she knew he was back there someplace.

Which meant the men had spotted them and were moving in for the kill.

They were on flat ground here, headed for a clearing, which Brynn had been looking forward to – no dense tangles to fight through, just planes of low grass, flat. But now she steered Michelle to the right toward a steep, rocky hill, several hundred feet long, descending to a creek bed. At the bottom there was no moonlight and they'd have good cover. 'There, down into the ravine. Do the best you can. Come on. Fast.'

They started down the hill, sticking to the thicker clumps of oak and dense brush, where they'd be less of a target. They half slid, half ran, scrabbling down the steep slope, Michelle in front, Brynn behind her.

They were doing well until halfway down, Brynn tripped, her foot catching on a vine or branch. She landed hard on her butt and slid on the slick leaves right into Michelle, taking her legs out from under her. They began a long, unstoppable tumble down the hillside, Brynn desperately trying to keep a grip on the spear so it didn't slash either of them to death.

They ended up in a shallow ravine.

The knife in Brynn's pocket had poked through the ski parka but the blade hadn't cut her. Michelle lay on her back, frantically patting her belly. Brynn was terrified that the younger woman's knife had cut her deeply.

Gasping for breath, Brynn whispered, 'You all right?'

Michelle's hand found the knife inside her jacket. It hadn't apparently done any damage. A nod.

Brynn slowly sat up, gripping the spear. She looked around and saw a depression in the dry creek bed. They headed into it. Brush and a natural line of three- and four-foot boulders gave them some cover.

'Look,' Michelle whispered and pointed.

Brynn watched Hart's partner, holding the shotgun ready to shoot, moving east – toward them – in a jog. The breeze was busily stirring leaves but he must've heard something. He was looking directly at the spot where they'd fallen. Then he gazed around him and vanished into a thick copse of trees to the north.

Brynn gripped the spear handle, staring toward him. 'How's your ankle?'

'Okay. I fell on my other leg.'

Scanning the hill. Neither of the men was visible.

Brynn was estimating distances and speculating where the partner might've gone. Michelle whispered something. Brynn didn't hear. She was lost in consideration. She made a decision. Then surveyed the ground. 'Okay. We're going to split up. I want you to move that way, stay in the ravine and keep your head down. Over there, see that dip? Get down into it and cover yourself up with leaves.'

'What are you going to do?' Michelle asked, her eyes wide.

'See it?' Brynn repeated firmly.

'You're going after him, aren't you?'

Times to run, times to fight . . .

Brynn nodded.

'I want to come with you. I can help.'

'It'll be a bigger help to me if you just stay hid.'

Michelle looked somber for a moment. Then smiled. 'I won't worry about breaking a nail, if that's what you mean.'

Brynn smiled too. 'This is my job. Let me do it. Now go

on down there, cover yourself up. If they get close and you have to run.' She looked along the dry streambed and pointed to the lake, which was really no more than a pond. 'That'll be our rallying point. The near shore, by those rocks.'

'Rallying point. What's that?'

'Where soldiers meet when they get split up. It's not a cop thing. I got it from *Saving Private Ryan*.'

Drawing another smile from Michelle.

Charles Gandy, a lean, bearded man in his early thirties, wearing a North Face insulated windbreaker, stood beside a Winnebago camper parked in the woods of Marquette State Park, next to a ramshackle ranger station that had been abandoned years ago. The camper was nicked and dented and the butt end sported a half-dozen bumper stickers extolling the importance of green energy and listing such accomplishments as mountain biking Snoqualmie Pass and hiking the Appalachian Trail.

'You hear anything else, honey?' asked Susan, a round woman with straight, light brown hair. A few years older than Gandy. She wore a necklace in the shape of an Egyptian ankh, two braided friendship bracelets and a wedding ring.

'Nope.'

'What was it?'

'Voices, I'm pretty sure. Well, sounded like a shout almost.'

'The park's closed. And this time of night?'

'I know. When's Rudy due back?'

'Any time.'

Her husband squinted into the night.

'Daddy?'

He turned to see his nine-year-old stepdaughter standing in the doorway, T-shirt, denim skirt and old running shoes.

'Amy, it's time for bed.'

'I'm helping Mommy. She wanted me to.'

Gandy was distracted. 'All right. Whatever your mom says. But go on inside. It's freezing out here.'

The girl disappeared with a swirl of long blond hair.

The camper had two doors, front and back. Gandy walked to the back one, stepped inside and found a battered deer rifle. He loaded the clip.

'What're you doing, honey?'

'I've got to go see.'

'But the rangers—'

'Not around here and not now. You lock up tight, pull the curtains and don't open the door for anybody 'cept me or Rudy.'

'Sure, honey. Be careful.'

Susan climbed the steps inside and closed and locked the door. Shutters closed and the camper went dark. The faint sound of the generator was pretty much covered up by the wind. Good.

Zipping up his jacket and pulling on a gray knit hat that Susan had bought him for his birthday, Gandy started down the small path that led eventually to the Joliet Trail, the rifle held in the crook of his arm.

He made his way south and east. They'd been here for four days and he'd spent much of that time hiking nearby. He knew the place well, had found impromptu paths and trails, made by deer – trampled leaves, broken branches and pellets – and people (ditto, minus the shit).

He moved slowly, cautiously. Not afraid of getting lost, afraid of whom he might run into out here.

Had that sound been a scream or not? he wondered.

If so, human or animal?

Gandy now walked two or three hundred yards in the

direction he thought he'd heard the sounds, and then knelt down, surveying the moonlit forest. He heard snaps and a crack or too, not far away, maybe branches falling, maybe deer, maybe bear.

'Or maybe my damn imagination.'

But then he tensed.

There, yes . . . No doubt about it. He was looking at a person – a woman, he was sure – moving from tree to tree, keeping low. She was carrying something in her hand. It seemed thin. A rifle? He gripped his own, a Savage .308, tightly.

What was this all about? Shouting and howling in a deserted, and officially closed, state park so late at night? His heart was slamming. His instinct was to get back to the camper and get the hell out of here. But the rattling diesel could attract unwanted attention.

As he hunkered low, spying on her, he wondered why she was acting like a soldier. Cautious, creeping from cover to cover. She was clearly no ranger. She didn't have on a distinctive Smokey the Bear hat or a typical ranger uniform jacket. It seemed she was in a ski parka.

His instincts told him she was a threat.

The woman disappeared behind a large clump of blackberry and he didn't see her emerge. Gandy rose and, holding the gun muzzle up, moved in her direction.

Just get the hell out of here, part of his mind shouted.

But then: No. You've got too much at stake. Keep going.

He stopped at a steep decline that led down to the forest floor, steadying himself with his left hand on thin birch and oak saplings and then, when the ground flattened, he moved toward the bush where the woman had disappeared.

He studied the area. No sign of her.

Then there she was, thirty or so feet away. She was in a shadow but he could just make her out, lying half-hidden beside the bush, her head down, like a lioness waiting for an antelope.

Very quietly he worked the bolt on the Savage, chambering a round, and started forward, picking his steps around branches and leaves, as if he were treading through a mine field.

Playing at being a soldier himself. A role he wasn't very comfortable with at all.

Kristen Brynn McKenzie crouched behind a gnarled but stately black oak, gripping the pool cue spear hard and taking deep breaths, her mouth open wide for silence. She'd climbed back up the hill toward the spot where the man had disappeared.

Her palms were damp, though she was cold again, having slipped out of her parka and one set of sweatpants. The clothes, stuffed with leaves, now sat like a fallen scarecrow under a blackberry bush, bait to attract Hart's partner.

The trick seemed to be working. He was now approaching cautiously.

Still no sign of Hart.

Good, she'd thought.

One on one, I can take you.

She'd risked his shooting at her from a distance and stepped into the moonlight to give him a brief view of her, then disappeared fast behind the blackberry bush, where she'd stripped off the clothes, and left them on the ground like someone hurt or hiding.

She'd slipped down the hill, circled back to this tree.

Praying that Hart's partner would take the bait.

Which he had. Gun pointed up, the shadowy form started down the hill toward the effigy.

Brynn now huddled behind the tree, tracking his progress by his footsteps. Her hearing was sharply attuned. All her senses were, in fact. The blade of the spear, the Chicago Cutlery knife, was close to her face, deep in the shadow of the tree, so that it wouldn't flash in the moonlight and give her position away. She reflected that it was curious that this unused kitchen tool's first task wouldn't be to trim a beef tenderloin or chicken cutlet but to kill a human being.

And she reflected too that this thought troubled her very little.

A faint snap, a rustle.

Then the breeze came up and blew hard. She momentarily lost track of his footfalls in the scampering of leaves and the hiss through branches.

Where? she thought in panic.

Then she could hear him again. The partner was still headed directly for the bait. His route would take him just past the tree where she was hiding.

Twenty feet.

Ten feet. The faint crunch of his steps.

She examined as much of the area as she could from her hunting blind, looking for Hart. Nothing.

Six feet, five . . .

Then he was even with the tree.

Finally, he walked past it.

Brynn looked out at his back. He'd swapped the combat jacket she remembered from the Feldmans' for a North Face ski parka, which he'd probably stolen from their house or from 2 Lake View. He'd put on a cap too, covering his blond crew cut.

Okay, now's the time, she told herself.

Her body filled with a calm, almost euphoric sensation.

This had happened on other occasions but usually at the most unexpected times. A triple-combination jump with her atop a speeding chestnut mare in a horse competition. A frantic pursuit of a weapons dealer down a county road, hitting 140 mph. When she and Keith, on vacation, defused a potentially fatal fight by two teenagers in Biloxi.

Times to fight . . .

She now thought: Stun him with the bolo and charge in fast. Jam the spear into his back as hard as you can. Grab the shotgun.

And get ready for Hart to come. Because come he would; at the first sound of his partner's screams.

Brynn stepped from the tree, sized up her target, then swung the bolo and let it fly.

The ball arced toward him and clipped his ear. He cried out and dropped the gun.

Brynn ignored the pain in her body and leapt forward.

She wasn't a deputy now. Not a wife or mother.

She was the wolf, a primitive creature, survival its only thought. Running, running, toes of her boots digging into the hard earth, in her hands the spear, now gleaming bright in the cold light, and aimed directly for him. She managed to resist a fierce urge to let go a man howl.

Now they were gone.

Hell. For ten minutes Hart had closed the distance between himself and the women, heading straight toward the clearing – the shooting zone, he thought of it – while he'd kept tabs on Lewis.

The other man had seen or heard something to the right, the east, and hurried down the hill into the flatter ground. He'd looked around but apparently it had been a false alarm. He'd returned to the woody ridge on Hart's left. Both men had continued forward, scanning the landscape for the prey that had disappeared.

Where were they?

Had they spotted him or Lewis?

And if they had, what were their options for escape? The clearing was in front – to the north – and they obviously weren't there. Lewis was now on a ridge to the west and Hart himself was facing due south. There was a band of trees around the clearing, which the women might be hiding in. Or they might've fled down a steep drop-off to the right and were making their way east into the thick of the park. That direction would take them back eventually to the Joliet but according to the GPS the trail was a long way off now, and they'd have to cover miles of dense woods to get there.

What would Brynn do?

He decided she'd gone down the incline that led to the streambed and then continued north toward the Snake River – only avoiding the exposure of the clearing. A longer route and harder, but safer.

She was like an animal with finely tuned instincts of survival, anticipating him.

He glanced to the ridge, where Lewis had now paused and was looking around. Then he turned toward him and lifted his arms. Meaning: They've vanished.

Hart pointed to himself and then to Lewis, who nodded. Hart began the climb to the high ground to join his partner.

Where?

Where was Michelle?

Carrying the Savage rifle in one hand, the spear in the other, Brynn McKenzie paused and looked around her. She was disoriented. She'd been so focused on Hart's partner that she hadn't paid enough attention to her route after she'd left the other woman to hide under the blanket of leaves.

Had she gone to the rallying point?

Brynn hoped not. The lake was farther than she'd thought and she didn't want to have to make any detours. She was flagging as it was.

Then she spotted a configuration of trees that looked familiar. She paused, glancing around for the pursuers. None in sight. She jogged down a short hill.

Turning the corner behind a large rock, Brynn stopped suddenly.

Startled, Michelle was reaching into her pocket to grab her knife. Her eyes were fierce, feral. Brynn stopped and blinked. The young woman sighed in relief. 'Jesus, Brynn. You scared me.'

'Shhh. They're still around here someplace.'

'What happened?' the young woman whispered. 'Where'd you get that?' Looking at the rifle.

'Come on. Quick. I hurt somebody.'

'One of them?' Michelle's eyes glowed.

Brynn grimaced. 'No.'

'*What*?'

'Somebody else. This way.'

They climbed the hill back to the blackberry tangle, where the bearded man was sitting on the ground, head low between his legs, nursing his torn ear. He looked up at Michelle, blinked. Then nodded, wincing.

Brynn explained that she'd beaned him with the billiard ball and was charging forward to spear him when he'd glanced back, having heard her footsteps.

She'd stopped just before she stabbed him, seeing his bearded face, realizing her mistake. Not expecting to find anyone else out here, armed and stoked by adrenaline, Brynn had missed that he was carrying a deer rifle, not a shotgun, and that his build seemed different from Hart's partner's.

Brynn had apologized profusely. Still, she was a law officer and, after showing her ID and badge, took control of the weapon and asked to see his driver's license.

His name was Charles Gandy, and he, his wife and some friends were camping in a Winnebago not far away.

'Are you okay to walk?' she asked him. Brynn wanted to get to the camper as soon as they could.

'Sure. It's not bad.' He was holding the sock, from the bolo, against his injured ear. It seemed most of the bleeding had stopped.

Which didn't mean he wasn't going to sue the department. But that was fine with Brynn. She'd insist that the county pay whatever he wanted. She couldn't describe the reassurance she felt having found a way to escape from the park – and with a rifle in her hands.

Control . . .

While Brynn kept guard, Michelle helped Gandy up.

'You're hurt too?' he asked, nodding at the pool cue.

'It's okay,' Michelle said absently, looking warily over the overwhelming tangle of branches, brush and trees.

'We should get moving,' Brynn said. 'Lead the way.'

Charles Gandy knew the woods well, it seemed. He directed them past the dry streambed and along paths that Brynn hadn't even seen. This was good, since they avoided entirely the noisy leaves and branches that could have given them away. They moved up an incline then he led them around a clearing, going steadily higher. The general direction was north. Michelle limped along as quickly as she could, now using the spear for her cane.

Brynn, gripping the rifle, followed, looking behind more often than she looked forward.

They paused, hiding behind a seven- or eight-foot outcropping of granite. Gandy touched Brynn's arm and pointed.

Her heart jumped.

Across a long ravine was a bare ridge. Hart and his partner, holding the shotgun, stood there, scanning the ground. Frustration seemed evident in their posture.

'Is that the ones you were telling me about?' Gandy asked softly, alarm in his voice.

'Yep.'

It was then that Michelle whispered, 'Shoot them.'

Brynn turned toward her.

Wide eyed, the young woman said, 'Go ahead and shoot them.'

Brynn looked down at the rifle in her hands. She said nothing, didn't move.

Michelle's head turned toward Gandy. He said, 'Hey, don't look at me. I work in an organic grocery store for a living.'

'I'll do it,' Michelle said. 'Give me the gun.'

'No. You're a civilian. If you killed one of them it'd be murder. You'd get off probably but you don't want to go there.'

Then Brynn leaned over a large rock. Set the rifle on it, the muzzle in the men's direction.

They were about 100 yards away, and Gandy's rifle didn't have a telescopic sight. But Brynn was familiar with rifles – from the training courses mostly. She'd also been hunting a few times though she gave it up years ago on a trip to Minnesota; Keith had been reloading his rifle when they'd been charged by a wild boar. Brynn had killed the crazed animal with two fast shots. She'd quit the sport after that, not out of fear – she'd secretly enjoyed the rush – but because she'd killed an animal whose only crime was defending its invaded home.

She'd been prepared to kill the partner with her spear a few minutes ago. But this seemed different, shooting somebody like a sniper.

Well, are you going to do it or not? Brynn coolly asked herself. If so, now. They're not going to be standing still forever.

Brynn decided to aim about two inches high to compensate for the arcing of the bullet over that distance. The breeze? Well, that was anybody's guess; it whipsawed back and forth.

Have to hope for luck here.

Brynn gazed along the rifle's sights, set the front blade on her target.

Both eyes open. Focus. Don't squint. Breathe slowly.

Focus . . .

She flicked the safety off. She started to squeeze the trigger. The trick was to keep the sights aligned on the target and apply pressure until the gun went off; you never actually pull the trigger.

But just then the men separated. What had been a cluster of target became two distinct ones. Hart had apparently seen something and had moved forward. He was pointing.

'Are you sure you want to do that?' Gandy asked. 'Are you sure it's them?'

'Yes,' Michelle snapped in a whisper. 'It's them. Shoot!'

But which one? Brynn asked herself. Assuming the one I don't hit gets under cover, who should I target?

Choose. Now!

She aimed at the partner, the man with the shotgun. She lifted the muzzle high. Began to squeeze the trigger again.

But at that moment the men started down into the ravine. In an instant they were simply dark forms moving through the brush.

'No!' Michelle cried. 'Shoot anyway!'

Then there was no target at all. They'd disappeared.

Brynn lowered her head. Why had she hesitated? she wondered. Why?

Gandy said, 'We better go. They're headed in this direction.'

Brynn didn't look at Michelle. It was as if the young woman, the spoiled princess, the dilettante, had been more in control than she.

Why didn't I take the shot?

She clicked on the safety and stared at the pool of gloom where Hart and his partner had disappeared. Then turned away to follow the others.

'The camper's not far,' Gandy said. 'A quarter mile. My friend's got a van and he should be back now. He was getting some food and beer. We'll all jump in it and get out of here.'

'Who's there?' Michelle asked.

'My wife and stepdaughter, a couple of our friends.'

'Stepdaughter?'

'Amy. She's nine.' Gandy touched his ear and examined his fingers. The bleeding had stopped.

'She's with you tonight?' Brynn asked, frowning.

'It's spring break.' He noted her troubled expression. 'What's wrong?'

'I didn't know you had a child,' she said softly.

'You're not bringing us trouble if that's what you're thinking. Imagine what'd happen if I hadn't found you. Those guys might've stumbled onto our camper and who knows what they would've done.'

'You have a phone?' Michelle asked.

Brynn's first question, after she'd made sure Gandy wasn't badly hurt.

'I was telling your friend,' he replied, 'I'm not a big fan of microwaves in the brain. But we've got one back at the camper.' He asked Brynn, 'Say, you have a helicopter? You could get officers here pretty fast with one of them.'

Brynn said, 'Just medevac. Not tactical.' She was thinking about the daughter and the man's family. Here, she'd tried all night not to bring this horror to innocent local residents . . . and now she'd endangered a family with a child.

Walking fast, breathless from the largely uphill route, they'd put the ravine far behind them. Brynn shamefully thought of it as 'the place where I balked'. She was furious with herself for the lapse.

Gandy said to Brynn, 'You just said they were after you. You didn't say why.'

Michelle, wincing as she limped, said, 'They killed my friends. I'm a witness.'

'No! Oh, my God.'

Brynn added, 'House break-in by Lake Mondac.'

'Just . . . you mean, tonight?'

Michelle nodded.

'I'm so sorry. I—' Gandy could think of nothing to say. He asked Brynn, 'And you tried to arrest them?'

'There was a nine-one-one call. We weren't sure what it was about. I got there afterward, lost the car and my weapon. We had to run.'

'Lake Mondac? Where's that?'

'About five, six miles south. We were making for the Snake when they found us. We had to detour. How much farther to your camper?'

'Not far.' He paused as a sheet of high cloud slipped between earth and moon and complete darkness enveloped them. A thin wash of illumination returned and he gestured to their right. Gandy led them farther through the woods. Then pointed out the start of a smaller trail. After they began down it, he stopped and gathered some brush, using it to obscure the path.

Brynn helped him add more camouflage. Michelle pitched in too, looking over their handiwork and announcing, 'Perfect. They'll never find it.'

Brynn shivered. The adrenaline from her abortive assault – and the sniper shot – had worn off. She'd dressed once more in the parka and the second set of sweats but the chill was back in her bones. 'Are you in a campground?' The search-and-rescue mission here had been limited to the Joliet Trail and the Snake River Gorge.

'No, there's an old ranger station and a parking lot. Deserted. All overgrown. Nobody's been there for years, looks like. Kind of spooky. Stephen King ought to write a book about it. *Ghost Rangers*, he could call it.'

Brynn asked, 'How far to the access road from there?'

Gandy considered this for a moment. 'There's a dirt road that goes for about a mile. It takes you to the main road in the park. Then it's about four miles to the entrance on Six Eighty-two. That's the closest.' He looked their way. 'You can relax. We'll be on the highway in twenty minutes.'

'Where?' Hart muttered.

The men were moving through the dry streambed where they'd seen their prey disappear.

'Look,' Lewis called softly. He was staring at a muddy patch of ground.

'What? I can't see anything.'

Lewis pulled off his jacket and made a tent with it. He took a cigarette lighter out of his pocket and, inside the garment, flicked it. Kneeling, Hart could see a series of footprints in the mud. They came from three people. 'How old you think those are?'

'Look fresh to me. Who the hell's with them? Shit, if it's a cop he's got a cell phone or radio.'

The lighter clicked off. The men stood up and looked around, as Lewis tugged his jacket on. Hefted the shotgun. He shook his head. 'You wouldn't think a cop'd be around this time of night.'

'True.'

'But who else'd be here?'

'No campers this time of year. Ranger maybe. We gotta find 'em fast.' Hart walked a little farther up the streambed.

He crouched and ran his hand over another patch of mud. 'They're going that way.' He pointed up the hill. 'That a path?'

'Looks like it.'

Hart grabbed a fallen tree trunk to push himself to his feet. The wood was rotten and a portion of it crumbled under his grip.

In less than a second the rattlesnake nesting inside, about two and a half feet long, had launched itself silently into the back of Hart's hand – on his good arm. Before he could even shout in horror, the dark, glistening stripe of muscle had vanished.

'Lewis!' Hart gasped. He pulled off his glove and saw two puncture wounds in the back of his hand, near the wrist. Shit. Was he going to die? One of the fangs had pierced a vein. Feeling faint, he sat down.

Lewis, who'd seen the strike, flicked his lighter and examined the wound.

Hart asked, 'Should I suck it out? I saw that on TV, a movie.'

'You're going to be okay. You don't want to suck it out. Venom gets to your heart faster under your tongue than through a vein.'

Hart noted that his breathing was suddenly coming fast.

'Stay calm. The calmer the better. Let me look.' Lewis studied the wound carefully.

'You going to burn it?' Hart's eyes danced as he gazed at the Bic flame.

'No. Relax.'

Lewis let the lighter go dark. He took a shotgun shell out of his pocket and, with his Buck knife, carefully cut it open. He tossed aside the pellets and the plastic wad. 'Hold your other hand out.'

Hart did and the man poured the gunpowder, fine little black cylinders, into his cupped palm.

Lewis told him, 'Spit in it. Go ahead.'

'Spit?'

'I know what I'm doing. Go ahead.'

Hart did this.

'Again. Get it wet.'

'Okay.'

Then Lewis reached into his inner pocket and took out a pack of Camels. He smiled like a cookie-stealing schoolboy. 'I *meant* to give up smoking last week.' Then he ripped open three of the cigarettes and sprinkled the tobacco into Hart's palm. 'Mix it all up.'

Hart thought this was crazy but he was feeling even more light-headed. He did what he was told. With the knife Lewis cut the tail off his shirt. 'Put that mess on the wound and I'll tie it.'

Hart pressed the black-brown wad onto the punctures and Lewis tied the cloth around them and helped him put his glove back on.

'It'll sting. But you'll be fine.'

'Fine? I just got bit by a rattler.'

'It was pretty much a dry bite.'

'A what?'

'Snake was a rattler, yeah, but a massasauga. They control how much venom they let go. They're small and don't have a lot, so they conserve it, use it on prey so they can eat. For defense they don't use much. Just enough to scare off a threat.'

'Well, scared the shit out of me. I didn't hear it rattle.'

'That's only if they sense you coming. You surprised him as much as he surprised you.'

'No, not quite,' Hart muttered. 'I feel faint.'

'You got a little venom and you'll feel funny some. But if that was a wet bite your hand'd be twice its size and you'd be screaming already. Or out like a light. I know we've gotta move but it's better you just sit still for five, ten minutes.'

Hart had been in fist fights, he'd faced down people with weapons when he'd had none and he'd exchanged bullets from time to time. But nothing had shocked him like that snake.

This is my world. You'll see things that aren't there and miss things that're coming up right behind you . . .

Hart took a deep breath, exhaling slowly. 'That's a rush for you.' He was almost enjoying the giddy sensation. He looked down at his hand, which had stopped stinging now. 'How come you know all this, Comp?'

'My dad and me'd go hunting. Same thing happened to you happened to him. He explained it all what to do. Then he switched my bare behind for not looking where I was going and stepping on the nest.'

They sat in silence for a moment. Hart wished that Lewis had pocketed one of the vodka bottles. He wouldn't have minded a jolt right about now.

Hart remembered that Lewis's mother was in a home. 'Your father still alive?'

'Yep.'

'You see him much?'

'Not really. You know, things happen.' Lewis grinned, looked away and said nothing more for a moment. He started to say something. But didn't. They looked around at the wilderness, the wind shuffling leaves, the faint lapping of the lake.

'I was thinking, Hart.'

'Yeah?'

'When we take care of them and get back home? You and me, we could do a job together. I was thinking with my contacts, guys in my crew, and your, you know, the way you plan things and think, we'd be a good team. This thing tonight, we just fell into it. It happened fast.'

'Too fast,' Hart muttered. To put it mildly.

'I know some people in Kenosha. There's money there. Illinois money, Chicago money. So how 'bout it? You and me.'

'Go on.'

'I was thinking of this place outside of town, Benton Plastics. You know it?'

'No.'

'It's on Haversham Road? Big fucking place. Sell shit all over the world. On payday they have this big-ass check-cashing truck. The guard's this lazy asshole. We could walk up and clear twenty, thirty thousand. If it was early on Friday morning. How 'bout that?'

Hart was nodding.

Lewis continued, 'I'd get all the information. You know, like reconnaissance.' He patted his shirt, felt the cigarettes but it was like he was doing it from habit. He wasn't about to light up out here. 'I'm a good listener. Everybody talks to me, tells me all kinds of shit. One time this guy and I were bullshitting and he mentions the name of his dog, along with a bunch of other stuff. So, guess what? I boost his ATM card and the dog's name is his PIN. I cleaned him out. I got that just by talking.'

'That was pretty slick.'

Another bashful grin. 'So, whatta you say?'

'You know what, Comp? I like the idea.'

'Yeah?'

'We'll look at the details. And put together a plan. Do it right this time.'

'A hundred ten percent.'

'One ten. Now, I've rested enough. We've got unfinished business. And our girlfriends could be calling in the cavalry right now.'

'You feeling okay?' Lewis asked.

'No, sir,' Hart whispered, laughing. 'I just got shot. I just got snake bit. And let's not leave out I nearly took a shower in ammonia. No, I'm not feeling okay at all. But what's a man going to do?'

Lewis picked up the shotgun and they started to walk in the direction the tracks seemed to lead.

Hart flexed his snake-bit hand. It felt fine. He asked, 'That tobacco and gunpowder – what exactly does it do?'

'You ask me, it doesn't do shit. Excepting, it calms you down.'

Hart inhaled deeply. 'Nothing like the smell of country air. Our luck's changing, Comp. Let's go that way. I think I see a path. Looks like the Trickster's on our side now.'

'Right down there, in that hollow.'

Charles Gandy led them along the dim path toward the camper. It was a big one. Their escape vehicle, a long panel van, like an Econoline, sat nearby.

Gandy's friend was back.

'I'm freezing,' Michelle muttered.

Gandy smiled. 'You can sit right in front of the heater in the van if you want.'

'I want. The coldest I've ever been was skiing in Colorado. And you can head back to the lodge anytime. This's a little different.'

They plunged along another path, steeply downhill. The camper was in a crumbling parking lot. An old building being reclaimed by the forest was nearby.

They were fifty feet from the lot when Brynn, inhaling the cool night air, stopped suddenly. She turned back, played her eyes up the path they'd just descended. She lifted the gun. The others stopped too.

'What is it, Brynn?' Michelle asked.

Gandy took a step forward, paused, scanning the forest. 'What?' he whispered.

Brynn said to Gandy, 'Get down. I heard something over there to the right. See anything?'

The man crouched and studied the trees.

Brynn pulled Michelle into a crouch on the other side of the path. She leaned close to the woman's diamond-studded ear. Smelled sweat and very expensive perfume. She said in a barely audible voice, 'We're in trouble here, Michelle. Don't ask questions and don't say a word. You remember the rallying point?'

The young woman froze. Then nodded.

'When I tell you, run for it. Run like hell. Keep that with you.' Glancing at the spear.

'But—'

Brynn waved her hand, dismissing the young woman's perplexed frown. Brynn turned to Gandy and in a normal voice asked, 'See anything?'

'No.'

Brynn clicked the safety off on the Savage, pointed the weapon at Gandy, who blinked in shock.

'What're you doing?'

'Now, Michelle, run!'

The man stepped back but stopped fast as Brynn tensed and lifted the gun higher.

'Run!' she cried. 'I'll meet you where I said.'

Michelle hesitated only a moment, then fled back up the path. She melted into the night.

'What the hell's going on here?' Gandy snapped, eyes wide in confusion.

'Get down on your knees, hands on your head.'

'This is bullshit.'

'Now, who's in—' Her words were cut off as a hand grabbed her collar from behind and tugged hard. Off balance, she stumbled backward. A large woman with straight hair and fury in her eyes, stepped in front of her and swung a fish-killing club into her belly. Brynn dropped to her knees and vomited. The gun fell to the ground and the woman snatched it up.

'The fuck is she?' the woman muttered.

Gandy strode forward and pulled Brynn to her feet. He searched her and pulled the knife out of her pocket. He hit her in the face with a hard fist; the shotgun pellet wound opened. She cried out and shoved Gandy away hard, making a grab for the rifle in the heavy woman's hand. But the man twisted the deputy around and got her in a neck lock. 'Don't fucking move.'

Brynn slumped, defeated. When he relaxed his grip she stomped on his foot, high and hard, and he let go a fast scream. 'You fucking cunt.'

The woman aimed the rifle at her and growled, 'That's it, honey.'

'All right, all right . . .' Brynn at her pinprick eyes.

'You okay?' the woman asked Gandy.

'Do I look okay?' he spat out. He jerked his head up the path. 'Was another one. She got away.'

'Who is she? They with Fletcher?'

He grabbed Brynn by the collar and hair. 'How'd you know? Goddamn it, how'd you know?'

She didn't tell him that the distinctive smells from cooking methamphetamine – propane, chlorine and ammonia – had wafted to her on the damp night air.

The camper was a portable lab.

'Let's get inside,' the woman said, looking around. 'We've gotta tell Rudy. He's not gonna be happy.'

Gandy dragged Brynn along the path. He snarled, 'You scream, you say a word, you're dead.'

'You're the one screamed,' she couldn't resist saying. And was rewarded with another fist in her face.

The camper was filthy, filled with plates of old food and discarded beer cans and clothing and other trash.

And it was hot. A half-dozen metal pots sat on two propane stoves. Canisters of anhydrous ammonia lined one wall, and a workstation for cutting apart lithium batteries was in the corner. There were also huge piles of matches.

Gandy pushed Brynn inside and tossed her knife on a table.

'Who's that?' asked a scrawny, twitchy young man in an Aerosmith T-shirt and filthy jeans. He hadn't shaved in some time or washed his hair. His fingernails were black crescents. A heavier man in overalls, with curly red hair, looked Brynn over.

The overweight woman who'd slugged her with the club said to a little girl, about nine or ten, in a shabby T-shirt and stained denim skirt, 'Keep going. You're not through yet.' The girl – Amy, the stepdaughter, Brynn assumed – blinked at the visitor and returned to filling larger plastic bags with smaller ones containing the finished product.

The skinny man said, 'Lookit her face. It's all swole up. What's going—'

'Shhh,' the heavy one snapped. 'What's the story?'

Gandy grimaced. 'She's a deputy, Rudy.'

'Bullshit. Dressed like that? And she's a fucking mess. Look at her . . . She's from Fletcher's crew.'

'I saw her ID.'

Rudy was looking Brynn over carefully with a disgusted visage. 'Well, fuck me. Police? I don't want to burn this place too. Fuck, I don't want to do that. After all this work.'

Brynn muttered, 'There are troopers on the way—'

'Shut up,' Gandy said, though lethargically, as if it would take too much effort to hit her again.

The skinny one, obsessed with her face, picked at the speed bumps on his forearm. Gandy, the woman and Rudy didn't seem to have been slamming their own product. Which didn't put her at ease; it meant they'd make rational decisions about protecting their operation. And that meant killing her and finding Michelle and doing the same. She remembered how casually Gandy had offered his ID; because the man had known she'd be dead soon.

'Mommy . . .'

The woman slapped her own thigh twice. Apparently a command meaning: Be quiet. Amy instantly stopped speaking. This infuriated Brynn – and broke her heart.

The woman's fingers were stained yellow. Though she probably wasn't a tweaker herself, she clearly wanted a cigarette. But lighting up in a meth lab would be like using a match to find a gas pocket in a coal mine.

Rudy asked, 'Was she alone?'

'No. Somebody was with her. She got away. They claim a couple of guys're after them. I saw 'em. But I don't know what's going on. Something about a break-in in Lake Mondac. It's about five miles—'

'I know where it is.' Rudy walked close. Examined Brynn's wound. He announced, "S'a setup. Fletcher called them, had that ho of his do it, I'll bet. The skanky redhead. Said we were here. Didn't have the balls to come up against us himself.'

Gandy said, 'I don't know. How the hell could he find us here? We covered all the tracks.'

Rudy's eyes went mad for a moment and he leaned into Brynn's face, raging, 'Talk to me, bitch. Talk to me! What's going on? Who the fuck are you?'

Brynn had dealt with the emotionally disturbed. Rudy was out of control, running on pure anger. Her heart beat fast, from both present fear and past memory of Keith's fist strafing her jaw.

When she said nothing he screamed, 'Who are you?' He pulled a pistol from his taut waistband and pushed it against her neck.

'No,' Brynn whispered and turned away, as if avoiding the challenging eyes of a mad dog. She managed to say evenly, 'There'll be state troopers and county deputies and tactical backup in the area anytime now.'

The woman dropped the club on the counter. 'Oh, no . . .'

But Gandy was laughing. 'No way. She had a fucking spear. She was on the run from some assholes broke into a house around here. What she told *me's* the truth. No police, no troopers. Oh, and no choppers in the county. She told me they don't use them around here for tactical work. Only medical. That answers one of our questions.' He smiled at Brynn. 'Thanks for the info, by the way.'

'That's true,' she said, speaking evenly, though still struggling to breathe after the blow to her belly. The pain was making her jaw quiver. 'We weren't part of a drug operation. But the protocol is if a deputy doesn't report in a certain amount of time they'll send backup.' She glared at Gandy. 'Tactical backup.'

Rudy considered this, chewing his wet bottom lip. He put the gun away.

She continued, 'If they're not on their way by now, they will be soon. Don't make this worse on yourselves. I'm way overdue.'

'This is a state park,' the woman said. 'They won't search here.'

Rudy sneered. 'Well, Susan, why *wouldn't* they search? Can you give me a reason? Of course not. Jesus. Don't be stupid . . . We had a good deal going and now it's fucked up. You understand that? You understand how fucked we are?'

'Sure, Rudy. I understand.' Susan looked down. And angrily gestured to the child to fill the bags faster.

Gandy said, 'That leaves those other two. The men after them. At least one had a gun, I could see. *They* could be with Fletcher.'

Rudy asked Brynn, 'These men . . . either of them Hispanic? One of 'em black?'

She didn't answer. Rudy looked at Gandy, who said, 'Was night. They were a couple hundred yards away. I couldn't tell.'

Brynn said, 'You're in enough trouble. We can—'

'Shut up. Do you believe her, these guys just broke in?'

Gandy replied, 'I don't know. If she was lying she was really good at it.'

'You see anybody actually shooting at her?'

'No. She tried to shoot them, with the Savage. . . .' Then Gandy frowned. 'But she didn't take the shot. She could've. That seemed off to me. Maybe she was trying to trick me. I don't know.'

'You gave her your gun?'

'What was I going to do? Say no because my family's back in the camper cooking crystal? I could've taken it away from her anytime I wanted.'

'But she didn't shoot?'

'Nope. Balked.'

'Why?' Rudy asked, moving close to Brynn.

I don't know, she thought, and stared into the fat man's watery eyes.

In the corner, little blond Amy was sealing up bags of

meth. She was working real hard for a kid who was up at this hour.

Rudy grabbed the duct tape the little girl was using, taped Brynn's wrists behind her back and shoved her toward Gandy. 'I can't worry about her now. We'll bring her with us. Get her out of here.' He pointed a pudgy finger at the kettles. 'Cool it down. Everything, pack it up to travel. Fuck, what a waste.'

The woman and the skinny young man were shutting down the cooker and filling bags with the finished product. 'Amy,' the mother whined. 'Faster. What's your problem?'

'I'm sleepy.'

'You can sleep when we're on the road. No excuses.'

'Where's Chester?' the child asked.

'He's *your* doll. It's *your* job to remember where you put him.'

Rudy took the deer rifle and handed it to the scabby young guy. 'Henry, get outside, up the path. Don't shoot unless you can take everybody out. We don't want any calls for backup. If fact, don't shoot at all unless you have to. You see anybody, get your ass back here.'

'Sure, Rudy. You're not . . . you're not going to leave with me out there, are you?'

Rudy gave a guttural sound, registering his disgust. 'Move.'

Gandy roughly took Brynn's arm. Limping, he pulled her outside and dragged her to the van, pushed her inside. It was filled with clothes, suitcases, junk, magazines, toys, bottles of chemicals. He looped a rope through her bound arms, knotted it to a tie-down.

Brynn said, 'There'll be roadblocks. And the State Police *does* have helicopters. You're not going to get through. And don't think about using me as a hostage. That never works. They'll shoot you before you shoot me, or after. They'd prefer the first but they'll do the second. It's the way we train.'

He laughed. 'Even now you're balls out.'

'But I will cut a deal with you. You personally. Call my office. We'll get it worked out.'

'Me personally?'

'You.'

'Why me? Because I'm the one who washes his hands? Who doesn't say "him and me are going to do this"? Because I have green bumper stickers on the camper so I may actually care about the environment? Which means I'll be reasonable?'

Yep. Exactly.

'You've got that little girl in there. Do it for her, at least.'

'I just fuck her momma. The kid's not mine.' He slid the door closed with a hollow bang.

James Jasons was still some distance from Lake Mondac but figured he'd better cut off the GPS (not as easy as you'd think but he'd had a special switch installed). Those satellites and those servers . . . who knew what incriminating information they retained?

Good for security but bad to find restaurants. Still, he'd spotted a golden arches and went for it. He did the drive-through, going for two plain hamburgers, sliced apples and a diet cola.

He was back on the road, driving fast but not too far over the limit. He looked to all appearances like a slim, agreeable businessman. But if you got stopped, even for nothing other than an unplanned DUI roadblock – at which they'd let nondrinkers like him go immediately – your name and tag might still go into the system.

But tonight he had to make good time and was pushing the limit. He was prepared for a speed stop, of course. Presently listening to jazz, he would flip the preset selector on the steering wheel if stopped by a trooper, and a Christian inspirational sermon would come on. He also would slip a sponge-backed Jesus effigy and pro-life sticker onto the dash.

Might not save him from a ticket but it would probably prevent a car search.

And James Jasons definitely didn't want his car searched tonight.

Eating his food, he wondered how things were going at Great Lakes Intermodal Container Services.

In 99 percent of the cases, all you have to do is find a sensitive spot and you touch it. That's all. You don't need to hit, you don't need to stab.

A touch.

Only instead of sending Paulie or Chris to extort me, Mankewitz picks a scrawny little asshole like you. That the plan? You whine at me until I cave?

Jasons chuckled. His satellite phone chirped. It was an Iridium model and customized; the signal was scrambled both through a camouflage system and a multiline shifting program, impervious to any snooping, probably even to the government's infamous Echelon, because of the dual-mode scrambling.

He swallowed the burger he was fastidiously chewing. 'Yes?'

The voice said, 'Your meeting seemed to go well.' Mankewitz didn't identify himself. The key word about Echelon was 'probably.'

'Good.'

'There've already been certain overtures of cooperation.'

So Morgan had read the note and decided to be smart. Jasons wondered if the information he was going to deliver to Mankewitz would be helpful. There was always the chance it wouldn't and the risk had been wasted. But isn't that the truth about life?

The union boss said, 'On that other matter, your personal trip now?'

'Yes?'

'I've heard from a relative.'

He'd mean the round, fuzzy-haired detective in the

Milwaukee PD – whom Jasons thought was cute. The cop was more than on the take; he was basically on the payroll. 'And?'

'It seems there's going to be a party up there.'

This was troubling. 'Really? Did he know who'd be attending?'

'No close relatives. Mostly local but I think some folks from the East Coast might be. They're debating coming.'

Meaning no Milwaukee police, just local officers, probably county, though the FBI – the East Coast family – was a possibility. That was very troubling.

'So it could be pretty crowded?'

'Could be.'

'Anything more about what they'll be celebrating?'

'Nope.'

Jasons wondered what the hell was going on up there. 'Still think I should go?'

He said 'think,' but the real verb was 'want'.

'Sure, have some fun. You've had a busy day. A party'll do you good.'

Meaning: hell, yes. Get your ass up there.

And fix whatever's broken, whatever it takes.

Without hesitating, Jasons said, 'I think I'll go, then. Like to see who shows up. Besides, I'm not that far away.'

'Have fun,' Mankewitz said, the weight of the world on his shoulders.

They disconnected.

Jasons sipped the soda, then ate some of the green apple. It was sour. They gave some yogurt dip for it but he didn't like the flavor. He was reflecting on Mankewitz's deferential tone. The man always sounded like he didn't know what planet Jasons came from, was almost afraid of him.

Stan Mankewitz, one of the most powerful men on the lakefront, from Minnesota to Michigan and yet he was uncomfortable around the slim young man who weighed probably half what the union boss did and who walked around with a pleasant smile most of the time. Some of this might have been because Jasons, although he did have a law degree from Yale and an office in the union's legal department, didn't technically work for Mankewitz. A 'labor relations specialist,' he was an independent contractor, powerful in his own right. He had his autonomous fiefdom – with the authority, and budget, to hire whomever he wanted. Jasons could also use money in ways that were beneficial to the union and Mankewitz but that avoided various inconvenient reporting regulations.

Then there was a lifestyle difference too. Mankewitz was not a stupid man. Nobody was going to do what Jasons did without his complete dossier – verbal at least – being delivered to the union boss. He'd know that Jasons lived alone in a nice detached house near the lakefront. That his mother lived in a nice apartment connected to her son's house. That his boyfriend of several years, Robert, lived in an *amazing* town house near the lakefront. And he probably knew that Robert, a successful engineer and one hunky bodybuilder, shared Jasons's interest in hockey, wine and music and that the partners had planned a civil union next year, with a honeymoon in Mexico.

But Jasons appreciated that Mankewitz did his homework. Because it was exactly how he himself worked his magic.

Alicia especially. Every day after school in that rehearsal room, three to four-thirty. . . . Impressive.

Mankewitz didn't care about Jasons's lifestyle, of course. Which was ironic, considering that the membership of Local 408 was made up of blue-collar folk, men mostly, some of whom would beat the crap out of James Jasons and Robert, given no excuse, some opportunity and a few too many beers.

Welcome to the new millennium.

A last bite of apple, sweetened by the diet soda.

He put the second hamburger back in the bag, which he twisted closed.

He passed a sign that announced it was 49 miles to Clausen, which he knew was 7.2 miles before the turnoff for Lake Mondac. Since he hadn't seen any traffic, let alone a patrol car, on the road for miles, he edged the speed up to 75.

And clicked the selector to the Christian CD, just for the fun of it.

Holding the heavy Savage rifle, Henry headed down the path toward where Rudy had directed him. He took a foil pack out of his pocket, a pipe and lighter too. Then he hesitated and put them away. He blew into his hands and continued along the path, scratching at the scars on his arm.

He stopped where the small path met the bigger one, the one that led down to the lake they got their water from. He stood there for five minutes, squinting, looking from right to left. Didn't see a soul. He leaned the rifle against a tree. As he was reaching into his pocket again for the pack of meth and the lighter a man stepped out of the shadows and hit him in the forehead with the butt of a shotgun, which was rubber padded but still hard enough to knock Henry off his feet. His head lolled back, eyes unfocused. A gurgling rose from his throat and his hands flailed and knees jerked.

When the butt of the deer rifle, which wasn't padded, crushed his windpipe Henry stopped thrashing quite so violently. After a minute he stopped moving altogether.

Cradling the deer rifle in his arm, Hart tensed as someone approached. But it was just Lewis, who glanced at the body on the ground, grunted and picked up the shotgun.

Hart bent down and felt the skinny man's neck with the backs of his fingers. 'Dead. You know they can lift prints from skin.'

'No. I didn't. They can?'

'Yep.' Hart pulled his gloves back on. 'What's the story?'

Lewis said, 'That girl deputy, Brynn's in the van. I saw some guy put her there. Looked like she was taped, her hands behind her, I mean.'

'So they walked right into the helpful arms of meth cookers.' Hart gave a faint laugh. 'Everybody's having a reversal of fortune tonight. We end up with a cop coming to visit in Lake Mondac, and they end up with a trailer full of slammers. Was she alone in the van?'

'I didn't see anybody else. I wasn't that close.'

'So where's Michelle?'

'No idea.'

Hart pressed the catch on the bolt of the deer rifle, slipped it out of the gun, flung it away. Threw the gun itself in the opposite direction. He was a much better shot with a pistol than rifle. Besides, a bolt action let you fire off a round only every few seconds. In that time he could have emptied the Glock's fifteen-round clip and been halfway through reloading.

They eased silently toward the camper.

'How many people inside?' Hart whispered.

'Couldn't see too good. Definitely one other man – and the guy who put Brynn in the van. A woman too.'

Hart was looking over Lewis carefully. The man was staring at the camper and kneading the shotgun stock. His eyes were troubled.

'Comp?'

'Yeah?' He looked up.

'We've gotta do it.'

'Sure.'

'I know what you're thinking – they haven't exactly done us harm. But they're tweakers, Comp. They cook meth. They'll be dead anyway in a year. OD'd or burned to death or clipped by somebody upset they're peeing on his turf. This'll be faster. This'll be better for them. We'll get Brynn, find Michelle, finish with them and that's it.'

Lewis was looking at the van.

'How we handle it's this: They're pros and that means they're going to have guns. Now, we bought some time when I talked to Brynn's husband, but that's not to say he believed me, or that they aren't going to send a car around to the park, just for what the hell. I think we have to assume there're cops at the house already and on a quiet night like this, sound'll carry. They could hear the gunshots. We've got to finish it up fast, once the shooting starts. Real fast.'

'Sure.'

'You have that lighter of yours?'

'Always carry one. In case I meet a lady in a bar needs a light.' The crack in his voice belied the joke.

'Courteous of you, non-smoker that you are.' Hart smiled and Lewis exhaled a brief laugh. 'Okay, you go around to the right side of the camper, the one without the doors. Get some dirty leaves and see if you can find something plastic or rubber. Start a fire under the camper. Just small. We don't want it to spread and call attention to us. I just want smoke. With all that ammonia and propane in there, they'll freak and get the hell out, head for the van. When they come out . . . okay?'

He nodded.

'I'll take the front door, you take the back. You locked and loaded?'

'Yes, I am.'

Hart checked his Glock and made sure one of the full clips was upside down in his waistband, to the right, so he could grab it easily in his left hand to reload.

'Keep your SIG handy too.'

Lewis fished his chrome-plated pistol out of his jacket pocket. And slipped the automatic into his waistband.

Hart noticed that the suggestion was greeted with none of the sarcasm or resistance of earlier.

Lewis gave an uneasy laugh. 'Well, aren't we a couple of gunslingers.'

'Move in slow, move in quiet. Get the fire going. Then come back around. Let 'em all get out before you start shooting. Last thing we want is to have to go in and get anybody. You counted three, right?'

'Yeah, but now I think about it, the woman turned her head and said something. She wasn't looking at the two men. Maybe there's somebody else.'

'Okay, we'll plan on four.'

The rope Gandy had used to hook her to the tie-down in the back of the fourteen-foot van was thick and made of nylon – strong but slippery. Brynn finally managed to untie it. The tape on her hands, behind her, wouldn't yield but she managed to climb to her feet. The buttons in the back doors were flush and she couldn't lift them. She stumbled to the front of the van, tripped over the transmission shifter and hit her head on the dash. She lay stunned for a moment. Then managed to right herself and, turning her back to the glove box, got it open. Empty, except for papers.

She collapsed into the front passenger seat of the van, catching her breath. Her stomach muscles were in agony from the navigation to the front and from the smack of the club Gandy's wife had used on her. Brynn tried for the unlock button on the armrest but it was just out of reach of her bound hands. She surveyed the rest of the van, the junk, the boxes, the shopping bags. No knives or tools. No phones. She sat back in the seat, despairing eyes closing.

Then behind her a woman screamed.

'Michelle,' she whispered. Had she returned, had they found her at the lake and dragged her back here? Brynn spun around.

But there were only two windows in the van aside from those in the front: in the rear doors. They were opaque with dirt.

Brynn looked in the side-view mirror. Smoke filled the night. Was the camper burning? Meth labs were notorious for incinerating the cookers.

The little girl was inside! she thought, panicked.

The voice called again, 'No, no! Please!' The woman's voice wasn't Michelle's. It was Amy's mother's.

Then the crack of pistol fire.

The boom of a shotgun.

Four or five more rounds. A pause, for reloading maybe. More shots.

Silence. Then a voice, high pitched in fear or desperation. A man or woman or child? . . . Brynn couldn't tell.

Another shot.

More silence.

Please, let her be all right. Please . . . Picturing the tiny girl's face.

Motion flickered in the side-view mirror. A figure, carrying a pistol, was walking around the camper, studying it carefully and bushes nearby.

He then turned toward the van Brynn sat in.

She looked around for anything that would free her hands. She slipped them around the gear shift lever between the seats and began to saw against the gluey tape. The gesture was futile.

She glanced outside. The figure was now looking directly at the van.

Sheriff Tom Dahl stood over the two bodies in the kitchen: a businesswoman in her thirties, looking like she'd kicked off her shoes after work, happily anticipating a weekend of relaxation; the other corpse was a solid man about her age, with a mop of post-college hair. He was the sort of guy you'd have a beer with at The Corner Place in Humboldt. The blood made huge stains on the floor.

Although Dahl had the edge most law enforcers develop from the job, this particular crime shook him. The majority of deaths in Kennesha County were accidental and occurred outside. Homeless people frozen, car accident victims, workers betrayed by their equipment and sportsmen by the forces of nature. Seeing these poor young folks inside their own home, gangland-killed like this, was hard.

He was staring at their pale hands; those of the typical dead around here were ruddy and calloused.

And on top of it all, his own deputy – his secret favorite in the department, the daughter he would've liked to have – was missing from a house tattooed with small-arms fire.

He exhaled slowly.

Footsteps came downstairs. 'The friend?' Dahl asked Eric

Munce, the man he'd chosen not to send here, picking instead Kristen Brynn McKenzie. And the man whose future presence in the department would be a constant reminder of that decision, however things turned out.

'No sign of her.'

One relief. He'd been sure that they were going to find her body upstairs in the bedroom. Murdered and maybe not right away.

Munce said, 'They might have her with them. Or she's with Brynn, hiding somewhere.'

Let's pray for that, Dahl thought, and he did, though very briefly.

A call came in for him. The FBI, Special Agent Brindle explained, was sending several agents – now that Emma Feldman, a witness in the case against Mankewitz was dead. A State Police commander was headed here too and wouldn't like the Feebies – he tended to squeeze hard in pissing contests – but Dahl was all for the more the merrier. No criminals ever escaped because too many talented cops were on his trail. Well, most of the time.

A crime scene unit from the State Police was en route as well, so Dahl ordered his boys to leave the evidence for collection but to look everywhere they needed in order to figure out what had happened and where Brynn and the Feldmans' friend might be.

It didn't take long to find significant pieces of the puzzle: Gunshots through windows, gunshots inside, gunshots outside, footprints that suggested two males were probably the perps. Brynn's uniform shoes were inside, and the friend had abandoned her chic city boots by the Feldmans' Mercedes – both in favor of practical hiking footgear. One was injured; she was using a cane or crutch and appeared to be dragging one foot.

The Mercedes sat in front of the garage with gunshots in two tires, window smashed and hood up, a battery cable dangling. Another car had burned rubber — well, scattered gravel — as it fled. Another had limped out, dragging a flat.

But the jigsaw pieces didn't give any sense of the big picture. Now, standing in front of the fragrant fireplace in the living room, Dahl summarized to himself: a mess. We got a mess on our hands.

And where the hell is Brynn?

'Eric?'

'I'd rather it wasn't him. You know how he gets.'

Dahl noticed something in the woodwork. 'Anybody trying to play *CSI*?' he asked sourly, eyes on Munce.

The deputy looked where he was pointing. It seemed like someone had dug a bullet out of the molding. 'Not me,' he said defensively.

Why would somebody take the trouble to dig out one but not the other bullets? Why? Because it had his DNA on it?

Most likely, and that meant he was wounded.

It also meant that he was a pro. Most crimes in Kennesha County involved people who didn't even know what DNA was, much less worried about leaving any.

A hit man.

Okay, think. The two men had been hired to kill Emma Feldman. They'd surely succeeded — and killed her husband too. Then, maybe, they'd been surprised by the friend who'd driven up with them. Maybe she'd been out for a walk or upstairs in the shower when the killers arrived.

Or maybe it was Brynn who'd surprised them.

Somebody, Brynn probably, had shot one of the men, wounding him, and he'd dug the DNA-coated bullet out of the wall.

But what had happened after that?

Had they ditched their car somewhere and taken Brynn's? Were the friend and Brynn with them, captives? Had the women put on those hiking boots to run off into the woods?

Were they dead?

He called deputy Howie Prescott on his radio. The big man was near the lake in the yard between 2 and 3 Lake View, where they'd found some footprints. He was looking for any sign of a trail anybody'd left. Prescott was the best hunter in the office, though how the 280-pound man snuck up on his prey was a mystery to them all.

'Anything, Howie?'

'No, sir. But it's dark as night here.'

Dark as night, Dahl thought. It *is* goddamn night.

'Keep looking.'

Dahl said to Eric Munce, who was rubbing the grip of his pistol the way a child plays with its sippy cup, 'I want to get some bodies . . .' Dahl hesitated at the inappropriate word. 'I want to get some searchers up here fast. As many as we can. But armed only. No volunteers.'

Munce hurried to his squad car to call in a search party.

Dahl stepped outside and gazed toward the lake. The moon was low, withholding most of its illumination from the surface.

Dahl's radio crackled. 'This's Pete.'

'Go ahead.'

'I'm in the driveway of Number One. Haven't checked it out yet but wanted to tell you.' He was breathless. 'There's a truck just passed me. White pickup. Headed your way.'

A truck.

'Who's inside?'

'Couldn't see.'

'Okay. Check out the house. I want to know what you find.'

'Will do.'

'Got company,' the sheriff said to Munce, then called Prescott and told him to keep an eye out for the vehicle.

They saw it approach slowly and turn up the drive.

Both Dahl's and Munce's hands were near their weapons.

But it turned out not to be a threat.

Though it was certainly a complication.

Graham Boyd climbed out of the cab, leaving his passengers, three fuzzy bushes, in the back and walked straight up to Dahl.

'She's not here, Graham. We don't know where she is.'

'Let me see,' the big man said in an unsteady voice, heading for the house.

'No, I can't let you in. There's some bodies. People've been killed, shot. It's a crime scene.'

'Where *is* she?' Graham's voice was urgent and ragged.

The sheriff put his arm around the man's solid shoulders and led him away. 'Brynn and those folks' friend got away, we think.'

'They did? Where?'

'We don't know anything for sure. We're getting a search team up here now.'

'Jesus Christ.'

'Look, let us do our job here. I know it's hard. But I'm going to ask you to help us out and go on home. Please.'

The radio crackled once more. 'Sheriff, it's Howie. I was looking around the shore and found something.'

'Go ahead.'

'A car off the road. Went into the lake, looks like.'

'*Looks* like?' he snapped. 'Or *did*?'

A pause. 'Yeah, it did.'

'Where?'

'Can you see the flashlight? I'm signaling.'

Two or three hundred yards away a small yellow dot waved through the darkness.

Graham shouted, 'What's the debris, what color?'

A hesitation. Dahl repeated the question.

Prescott said, 'There's a bumper here. It's dark red.'

'Oh, shit,' Graham said and started running.

'Goddamn,' Dahl spat out. He and Munce climbed into the

sheriff's car, Munce driving. They stopped and Graham got in the back, then they sped to the shore.

Skid marks, airbag dust, scrapes on the rocks and auto detritus – hunks of red plastic from lights, bits of glass – and an oil slick near the shore left no doubt. The car had sailed off the road, hit a rocky ledge then tumbled into the water.

'Jesus,' Graham muttered.

What did this do to the scenario? Who was in the car?

Or who *is* in the car still?

'Doesn't mean it's hers for sure, Graham. Or that she was even in it.'

'Brynn!' her husband shouted. The voice echoed across the lake. Graham scrabbled down the rocks.

'No!' Dahl said. 'We don't know where the shooters are.' Then to Munce: 'Call back the State Police. We need a diver and a truck with a winch. Tell 'em Lake Mondac. Western shore. They can check the depth . . . Graham, no. That's a crime scene too. We can't have you fucking it up.'

Graham scooped something out of the water and dropped to his knees. His head was down. Dahl was about to shout at him again. But held back.

'I get him up here?' Munce asked.

'No. Let him be.' Dahl made his way to the water's edge, moving carefully down the rocks, his game leg in agony.

Graham stood slowly and handed the sheriff a Hagstrom map of the county. On the soggy cover was written in marker. *Dep. K. B. McKenzie.*

For a moment Dahl thought Graham was going to dive in after her. He was tensing to restrain him. But the big man did nothing. His shoulders were lifted with tension as he scanned the black water.

A hiss and a crackle. 'Sheriff, Pete. I'm at Number One Lake View. Nobody's home and it's sealed up. But there's a car abandoned behind the house.'

'Abandoned?'

'I mean recent. I called it in. Stolen in Milwaukee a few days ago. According to the VIN. The plates match the same year and model but not this ID number. And there're two bullet holes in the side and a rear tire's shot out.'

So that's the car that rimmed its way out of the Feldmans' drive.

He thought of Graham and wished with all his heart Brynn's husband was elsewhere. But he couldn't waste any time. 'Pop the trunk. Tell me what's inside.'

'I did, Sheriff. Empty.'

Thank you, Lord.

'And nobody broke into the house?'

'No, I've been around it. They might've picked the lock and locked back up.'

'Forget it. Get to the closer house. Number Two.'

'Yessir.'

'You get over there too,' Dahl said to Prescott.

The big deputy nodded and he started up the dirt road.

A lengthy silence. Graham rubbed his eyes, then peered into the lake. 'Don't imagine it's that deep. She could've got out.'

'I'm sure of it.'

'You don't believe that, do you? You think she's dead. Well, she isn't.'

'I'm not saying that at all, Graham. She's real tough. One of the toughest.'

'You have to search the area.'

'We will.'

'I mean now! Get state troopers here.'

'They're on their way. I've already called.'

'The FBI. They'll get involved for something like this, won't they?'

'Yep. They'll be here too.'

Graham turned and looked at 2 Lake View. Gibbs's squad car was pulling up now.

Dahl had a lot on his mind but not so much that he couldn't offer a silent prayer that his deputy and the houseguest weren't in that house, dead as the Feldmans. 'Go on home. Be with Joey. He'll need you now.'

Then an excited clatter through the tinny speaker: 'Got something here, Sheriff,' Pete Gibbs radioed.

'Go ahead.'

'Been broken into. And I think I see bullet holes in some windows upstairs.'

'Stay put till Eric gets there.' He nodded at the young hotshot of a deputy, who took off at an earnest run.

'Looks empty to me,' Gibbs said.

'Hold your position.'

'Yessir.'

'When Eric gets there, move in. But assume they're inside. And we know they're armed.'

Graham was examining the shore, his back to Dahl, who was staring at the house. The minutes passed, slow as could be, and Dahl found himself holding his breath, waiting for a gunshot.

Finally, the radio crackled teasingly.

No transmission.

Dahl didn't want to call back, and have their radios squawk, giving away their position.

Nothing.

Damnation.

Finally Eric Munce called in. 'House is cleared, Tom. They *were* here. Been a firefight. But no bodies. But we've got something weird.'

'Weird, Eric. I can't use weird. Just tell me.'

'Upstairs bedroom. There's ammonia all over the bathroom floor. Stinks like a baby's diaper bin.'

'Ammonia.'

'And we found Brynn's uniform. All her clothes.'

Graham tensed.

'They were soaking wet and full of mud. And the closet and dresser were open. I think she changed clothes and then took off.'

Dahl glanced at Graham, who closed his eyes in relief.

'Sheriff, it's Howie. I'm outside. I see two sets of footprints, women's, I'd guess, they're smaller, running to the woods behind the house. They go to a stream heading back to the Feldmans'. Then I lose them.'

'Roger that.' Dahl put his arm around Graham's massive shoulders, walked the man back to his squad car. 'Listen, we know your wife got outa the car okay. If anybody knows how to stay alive, it's her. I mean, I know that for a fact, Graham; I signed the payment request for her to go to all those training courses of hers. Hell, she takes so many of 'em, the boys call her Schoolmarm behind her back. Only don't tell her I said that. Come on, I'll drive you back to get your truck. You and me, we're too old to be out jogging.'

The van's automatic lock clicked.

Brynn turned toward the passenger door as it opened.

Hart stood there, his gun forward, scanning carefully for threats. He saw her hands were taped and that the van was otherwise unoccupied. He climbed in.

The door slammed behind him.

He put his gun away and began searching through the mounds of junk on the floor and directly behind the front seats.

Brynn said, 'The girl back there, in the camper? The little girl?'

'No. She's all right.'

'The fire?'

'Diversion. The camper wasn't burning.'

Brynn looked. The smoke had cleared. He was telling the truth.

Hart found some bleach, opened it and drenched his gloves and the keys, which were bloody. Then poured more in a tear in his leather jacket – the bullet hole from Michelle's shot, it seemed. He exhaled slowly from the pain.

The chlorine stench rose and stung her eyes. His too. They both blinked.

'Druggies ... Needles and blood. Can't be too safe nowadays.' It was like he was apologizing for the fumes. Hart looked her over, focusing on her vastly swollen cheek. He frowned.

'Are you telling me the truth? Is she alive?' Her eyes bored into his. He gazed back.

'The girl? Yes, I told you. The mother, if she was the mother, she's not. The others aren't either ... You're interested, they left the kid in the camper when they thought it was burning. And ran outside. Maybe they just meant to fight. Or maybe they just meant to leave her to burn.'

Brynn looked him over. A solid face, gray eyes, long hair, dark and dry. Skin rough. She'd had a bout of acne as a girl; it had tormented her. But the condition had cleared up as soon as she hit college. He wasn't handsome, not really, but he had confidence in spades, an attraction all its own.

'Brynn,' he mused.

How'd he know her name? Had Gandy told him before he died? No, of course: The men had been in the second house along Lake View Drive, the bedroom. He would have seen the name badge on her blouse.

'Hart.'

He nodded with a weary smile. 'My friend was talking a bit much. Giving that away.'

'What's *his* name again?'

The smile lingered.

Brynn said, 'Tell me where the girl is.'

'In her room in the camper.' Hart continued. 'She's in bed with some doll named Chester. I found it for her. Or a rabbit. I don't know.'

'You left her there?' Brynn asked angrily. 'She could look outside and see her mother's body?'

'No, my friend's moving them all into the woods. I told the girl to stay put. Come morning soon this park'll have more cops per square foot than the police academy. They'll find her.'

'She's dead, isn't she? You killed her too.'

His face tightened. He was upset that she doubted him. 'No, I didn't kill her. She's in bed with Chester. I told you.'

Brynn decided she believed him.

'So what happened?' he asked. 'You met that fellow in the woods and he was going to let you use his phone here. And you walked into a meth lab.'

'I figured it out before. But not before enough.'

'Smelled it, right? The ammonia?'

'Yep. And the chlorine too. And burning propane.'

'That's how I found it,' Hart said. 'I was down by that lake and could smell it down there.'

'Wind must've shifted,' she said. 'I didn't smell it till we were almost here.'

Hart stretched. 'Phew. Quite a night. Bet you don't see many of 'em like this in . . . what's this county again?'

'Kennesha.'

He looked again at the wound on her face. He'd be noting how infected it was, how painful. She supposed he'd be considering how long she could hold out before she told him where Michelle was.

Forever.

Wondering if that was true.

And as if he were reading her thoughts: 'Where is your friend Michelle?' he said evenly.

'I don't know.' Recalling that they'd found her purse. They knew who she was and where she lived.

Hart moved in the seat slightly and grimaced, apparently at the pain in his shot arm. 'What's that name – Brynn?'

'Norwegian.'

He nodded as he took this in. 'Well, about Michelle, you're lying to me. You *do* know where she is.' He actually seemed offended. Or hurt. After a moment Hart said, 'I talked to somebody tonight, you know. On the phone.'

'Talked to somebody?'

'Your husband.'

She said nothing, thinking at first that he was bluffing. But then remembered that they'd taken her phone. Graham might have called and Hart might have answered.

'I pretended I was another trooper. I told him you'd been delayed. He bought it. I could tell. There's nobody coming to save you. And before you get your hopes up I took the battery out. Can't be traced. Now, where is she? Michelle?'

They held each other's eyes. She was surprised at how easy it was.

'You killed her friends. Why would I tell you where she is, so you can kill her too?'

'So,' he said, nodding, 'Michelle was a friend of the family? Is that how she got mixed up in this whole thing?' A laugh. 'Wrong time and wrong place, you might say. A lot of that going around tonight.'

'We need to talk about making arrangements here.'

'I'll bet this's a first for you. Has been for me.'

'What?'

'The game we've been playing tonight. Like poker. Bluffing. You fool me, I fool you.'

Poker . . .

'My friend was telling me about this character. His mama or grandma, I forget, was talking about the Trickster. Some mythology thing, a fairy tale. He causes all kind of grief. That's what I've been calling you all night, Brynn.'

Trickster, she reflected.

Hart continued, 'That TV in the house at Number Two Lake View – finding a channel with women talking. That was smart. And the ammonia above the door. But now I think about it, you didn't rig it to fall, did you? You'd worry about rescue workers or your cop friends getting blinded. Funny – knowing you didn't come up with a cowardly trap . . . makes me feel better about you.'

Brynn McKenzie repressed a smile and didn't give him the satisfaction of a response.

'Then the canoe. And the blood on the ledge.'

'And you in the three-wheeled car,' she replied.

'Didn't fool you, though, did it?'

'I can say the same. After all, here you are. You found me.'

He looked her over. 'The blood at the ledge. You cut yourself extra for that?'

'Didn't bring any ketchup with me.' She tilted her head so he could see the coagulated blood in her hair.' Then she added, 'The flashlight tricked me, on the ledge. What'd you do, make a rope out of a T-shirt?'

'Yep. My friend's. Got to see more of his tattooed body than I wanted. I used a branch too so it'd hang out a ways and dangle in the wind.'

'But how'd you find us?'

'BlackBerry.'

She shook her head, smiling ruefully. He has satellite. I have a homemade toy compass . . . though one worked as good as the other, Brynn thought. 'The Sheriff's Department won't pay for those.'

'I figured you'd make for that trail, the Joliet, and north from there. And go to the interstate or Point of Rocks.'

'I'd decided on the interstate. The climb'd be a bitch but it's closer and by the time we got to the highway there'd be plenty of trucks on the road.'

'How come you didn't get lost?'

'Good sense of direction.' She looked him over closely. 'Why are you doing this, Hart?' she asked. 'It's hopeless.'

'Ah, Brynn, we're both too smart for hostage negotiation one oh one.'

She continued nonetheless, 'Less than two percent of perps get away with murder – and those're usually drug clips where nobody cares about the victim or there're so many suspects it's not even worth investigating. But tonight . . . They won't stop until they get you . . . You're not stupid, Hart.'

Again he seemed hurt. 'That was condescending . . . And what you're trying's cheap. I've been treating you with respect.'

He was right. She felt like apologizing.

He stretched and massaged his shot arm. The bullet hole was near the edge of the jacket. It had apparently missed bone and vital vessel. He mused, 'Crazy line of work we're in, don't you think, Brynn?'

'We're not in the same line of work.' She couldn't help but scoff.

'Sure, we are . . . Take tonight: We came up here to do jobs we'd agreed to do. And now we've still got the same goals. To stop each other and get out of this damn forest alive. Who writes your paycheck and who writes mine, that's just a technicality. Doesn't matter much *why* we're here. The important thing is that we are.'

She had to laugh.

But he continued, as if she'd conceded his point. And looked into her eyes as he said, animated, 'But don't you think it's what makes everything worthwhile? Even what's gone down tonight, all this crap. I do. I wouldn't trade the life I lead for anything. Look at most of the rest of the world – the walking dead. They're nothing but dead bodies, Brynn. Sitting around, upset, angry about something they saw on TV doesn't mean a single thing to them personally. Going to their jobs, coming home, talking stuff they don't know or care about . . . God, doesn't the boredom just kill them? It would me. I need more, Brynn. Don't you?' He massaged his neck with his uninjured arm. 'Tell me where she is. Please. It's going to get bad.'

'I tell you and you let me live?'

A pause. Then: 'No, I can't hardly do that. But I have your phone number. I know you have a husband and you might have children, probably do. If you tell me, they'll be fine.'

'What's your full name?'

He shook his head, giving her a frown.

'Well, okay, Hart first or last name, listen: You're under arrest. You have the right to remain silent.' She continued with the *Miranda* warning. She never used those laminated cards that bail bondsmen handed out. She'd memorized the language years ago.

'You're arresting me?'

'Do you understand your rights?'

Amused, he said, 'I know you know where she is. You had a meeting point somewhere, didn't you? I know that. Because that's what I would have done.'

Breaking the silence that followed he continued, 'Life's funny, isn't it? Everything seems perfect. The plan, the background, the research, the details. You even nail that fishy human factor. Clear road, easy escape, you've distracted everybody who needs distracting. And then something small happens. Too many red lights, tire goes flat, an accident ties up traffic. And the psycho security guard, who just got a new forty-four Desert Eagle he's itching to use, comes to work ten minutes early because he woke up before the alarm because a dog started barking two blocks away because a squirrel . . .'

His voice faded. He tented his gloved fingers, wincing slightly when he moved his left arm. 'And all your plans go up in smoke. The plans that couldn't go wrong go wrong. That's what happened to us tonight, Brynn. You and me both.'

'Undo my hands, give me your weapon.'

'You really think you're going to arrest me? Just like that?'

'You weren't paying attention. I already did.'

He stretched again. 'Not as young as I used to be.' He massaged his left arm. 'How long have you been married?'

She didn't answer but involuntarily glanced at his gloved hand.

'Marriage doesn't suit me. Does it suit you, Brynn? . . . Come on, what's Michelle to you?'

'My job. That's what she is.'

'How important can a job be?'

Brynn was wrinkling her brow cynically – and in pain. 'You know the answer to that.'

He began to speak then stopped. Tipped his head in concession.

'You might've talked to my husband but you don't know him. He'll've put things in motion by now. He's not the sort to fall asleep during the ten o'clock news.'

Again, disappointment in his face. 'That's a lie, Brynn.'

She inhaled slowly. 'Maybe it is,' she found herself saying. 'So. Okay. No more lies, Hart. Graham might've gone to sleep. But he'll wake up about four a.m. for the bathroom. Which he does like clockwork. And when I'm not there he'll call my boss, and *his* first call'll be to mobilize the State Police. You have some time but not a lot. And not nearly enough for you to get me to tell you where she is. And that's *not* a lie.'

'Okay, what we could do is . . .' His voice faded.

Brynn laughed. 'You were going to lie to me, weren't you?'

'Yeah, I was.' He grinned.

'Going to give me some hope, right?'

'That's right. But it felt wrong.' He reached into his pocket and pulled out a map. Opened it and spread it between them. He located the faint road where they were. Flicked on the overhead light. 'Where is she, Brynn?'

She noted the tiny blue dot that was the lake where Michelle waited. She said, 'I'm not telling you.'

He shook his head. 'Well, I won't hurt you. That's not digni-fied. And your family's safe.'

'I know that.'

He drew his gun. Glanced at it. 'But . . . you understand.'

He's reluctant to shoot, she thought, surprised. But shoot he would. In a curious way, though, she felt that she'd won this part of the game. And she felt too, with a deep pang, that she'd also lost. Not because of her death. But for a dozen reasons that hovered far outside this van, this forest, this park.

The silence was awkward, like that surrounding a couple near the end of their first date.

'Hart, this is your last chance.'

He laughed.

'Call nine-one-one. I meant what I said. I'll ask the D.A. to be lenient. No more lies between us, Hart. I mean it.'

His head was down, he was caressing the black gun absently.

'You going to surrender?' she persisted.

'You know I can't.'

They exchanged rueful smiles.

Then a faint frown crossed Hart's face as he glanced out the window. 'What—?'

The van was moving. It was easing downhill and picking up speed.

In the moments just before he'd climbed inside she'd shifted the transmission into neutral with her bound hands, disengaged the emergency foot brake and then sat back. As they'd been talking she'd kept her foot on the main brake pedal. Finally when it was clear she couldn't talk him into giving up she'd lifted her foot. The van, pointed downhill, surged forward. It now bounded over a railroad tie parking barrier in the lot and began careening down the steep hillside filled with brush and saplings.

'Christ,' Hart muttered. He grabbed for the wheel and transmission lever but Brynn slammed herself sideways, colliding with his bad arm. He shouted in pain.

The vehicle sped up, crashing into rocks, which made it veer to the left, then, going a good twenty miles an hour, rolled on its side, the passenger window exploding inward.

As Brynn pitched hard into Hart's chest, the van began to tumble madly down the endless hillside.

By the time Tom Dahl drove Graham Boyd back to the Feldmans' house, two State Police cars, lights flashing, were bounding up rough Lake View Drive. They made the turn fast, churning up dust, and hurried along the driveway. The six troopers climbed out.

Grahame shook Dahl's hand solemnly and wandered off to his truck, pulling his phone from his pocket. Dahl joined the WSP's night watch commander, Arlen Tanner, a big man with a mustache. He and the sheriff had worked together for years. Dahl briefed him and the other men.

Tanner said, 'Crime Scene'll be here in a half hour. So it's a search-and-rescue?'

'That's right, Arlen. We've got teams from Humboldt and a half-dozen troopers from Gardener coming. Barlow County'll send some too.'

'Woke up our two divers. They're on the way.'

'I'm not sure we'll need 'em. It's likely our officer got out of the car and hooked up with a friend of the victims. They're in the woods around here someplace. But we're pretty sure the two shooters're after them.'

Dahl received a phone call. The area code told him it

was coming in from the Kenosha area. He frowned. Take it or not.

Hell. Better.

'Sheriff Dahl here.'

A somber voice on the other end of the line said, 'Sheriff, this's Andrew Sheridan . . .' He said this as if Dahl ought to know.

Uncertainly the sheriff said, 'Yessir?'

'I worked with Emma Feldman. I just heard.'

Oh. That was it. After discovering the bodies, Dahl had called the law firm assistant and gotten the name of several partners Emma Feldman regularly worked with. He'd taken a deep breath and delivered the news. Word would travel fast, of course, in those circles.

'I'm sorry, sir. Sorry for your loss.'

'Thank you, Sheriff.'

They talked for a moment or two, Dahl giving away what he could, which wasn't much. Sheridan finally got down to business. 'Sheriff, this is a hard time for everybody. But I have to ask you something. About Emma's files. She had some with her, didn't she?'

'Yessir, she did.'

'Are you going to want them for evidence?'

'Yes, they'll have to be processed. It looks like somebody went through them.'

'What?' Sheridan's voice was alarmed. 'Who?'

Dahl lifted eyebrows apologetically to Arlen Tanner. 'Just be a minute,' he whispered. Then, into the phone: 'We aren't sure, sir.'

'So we can't have them back?'

'Not yet. No.'

'Do you know when we can?'

'I can't say at this time.'

'Then can I ask that you secure them somehow?'

'As evidence, they'll be locked up, sir.'

A hesitation. Sheridan finally said, 'Nothing critical but we worry about trade secrets and issues like that. You understand.'

No, he didn't. But he said, 'We'll make sure they'll be safe.'

'Well, thank you, Sheriff. If there's anything I can do, anything at all, just let me know.'

Yep, let me do my job.

They disconnected. Dahl was irritated but couldn't blame the man. The practicality of his call didn't mean he wasn't mourning. Like Dahl, Sheridan had a job to do.

The sheriff's radio crackled again. Then he heard: 'More company's coming, Sheriff.'

'Rescue team, tow truck?'

'No, private car.'

'Get the tag?'

'Wisconsin. All I saw.'

'Okay.'

The sedan slowed and turned toward 3 Lake View, the house lit up like the *Titanic* in her last hours, Dahl decided, having just seen the movie with his wife. He waved the car to a stop with his flashlight and asked the driver to get out. The businessman in his mid thirties or so, stared at the tableau, his face etched with concern. He climbed out. 'What's wrong? What's going on?'

Tanner deferred to Dahl, who said, 'Could I see some ID, sir? What's your name?'

'Ari Paskell.' He offered his driver's license the state police commander, who handed it to one of his troopers to check out.

'Please, what's going on?'

'What's your business here?'

'Business? I was coming to spend the weekend with Emma and Steve! What's going on? I've been calling them all night and can't get through.'

'How do you know them?'

'Steve and I are friends. We used to work together. He invited me to spend the weekend. Are they all right?'

Dahl glanced at Graham, who was staring into the woods. How I hate this, the sheriff thought. He then noticed the trooper in the front seat of his squad car. He nodded, meaning that the man's license and tag checked out. Dahl lowered his voice, 'I'm very sorry to have to tell you this, sir. But there's been a crime. The Feldmans were, well, they were the victims of a homicide tonight.'

'My God, no! But, no, you can't be right . . . I just talked to Steve this afternoon.'

'I'm afraid there's no doubt.'

'No,' he gasped. 'But . . . no. You're wrong!' His face went even paler than it had been.

Dahl wondered if he was going to slip into hysteria. It happened pretty frequently at times like this, even with the tough folks, which this fellow sure didn't seem to be.

'I'm sorry.'

'But it can't be.' The man's eyes were wide, hands shaking. 'I brought them their favorite beer. And I got fresh bratwurst. I mean, the kind we always have.' His voice cracked. 'I got them a few hours ago. I stopped in . . .' He lowered his head. In a defeated voice he said, 'Are you sure about this?'

'I'm sorry, sir.'

Paskell leaned against his car, saying nothing, just staring at the house. He'd be reliving memories, pleasant ones, of events that there'd be no repeat of.

Deputy Eric Munce joined them.

'What happened?' Paskell whispered. 'Who did it?'

'We don't know. Now, Mr Paskell—'

'But they're not rich. Who'd rob them?'

'Mr Paskell, do you know who the other houseguest is? All we know is she's a woman from Chicago used to work with Emma.'

He shook his head. 'No, they said somebody else'd be visiting. I don't know who.'

'I think you should head back home, sir. Or get a motel if you're too tired or upset to drive. There're some past Clausen on Six Eighty-two. There's nothing you can do here now.'

He didn't seem to hear. He was frowning.

Dahl paid a bit more attention and, like he always did with witnesses, gave him time to play the thought to the surface.

'This is probably crazy . . .' He cocked his head, recalling something. 'Just a thought.'

Usually civilians' thoughts *were* crazy. But sometimes they led to the killer's front door. Dahl said, 'Go on.'

'Steven was talking to me, this was last fall?'

'Yessir?'

'And he said he'd had a run-in with a man up here. At one of the stores. A big guy. A local fellow, Steve said. It was stupid incident, about nearly bumping cars in the lot. The guy went crazy. Followed him home, threatened him.'

'He give you any details?'

'No. Just he lived around here and he was pretty big. Three hundred pounds.'

Munce looked at Dahl, shaking his head. 'Doesn't seem like the perp. It was two of them, and nobody was that big, to judge from the footprints. Did he give you a name or description?'

'No, it was just one of those stories: This scary thing happened to me, you know. But he was shook up. No question. I mean, the big man came right up to his front door . . . If there were more than one person here tonight, maybe he brought a friend.'

If Dahl had a dollar for every conflict in a parking lot that could have turned violent but didn't, he'd be rich. He asked, 'Could you give me your number, Mr Paskell? We may want to ask you a few questions.'

Paskell was looking at the car, where the groceries bought specially for his friends sat, soon to be discarded. Would he throw them out in anger or despair? Despite his benign appearance, the man was, Dahl figured, a rager. 'Mr Paskell?'

He still wasn't listening. Then the sheriff asked again and the friend blinked. 'My number. Yeah, sure.' He recited it for Dahl.

Brawny Tanner, stroked his mustache and looked at the sheriff, his expression saying: It never gets any easier, does it?

'Are you all right to drive?' Dahl asked.

'A few minutes.' He was gazing at the house. 'Just a few minutes.'

'Sure. You take your time.'

The businessman, his face a mask, pulled out his phone. He rubbed it between thumb and finger, postponing the call to friends for as long as he could. Dahl left him to the agonizing task.

Prescott and Gibbs were putting up crime scene tape. Munce reported that the three deputies had gotten a 'ways' into the woods and had lost all trace of the women's trail.

'Whatta you think about that big local fellow?' Tanner asked Dahl.

'Doesn't set off fireworks for me, Arlen. But we'll keep it in mind. Get me a map. Anybody got a map? And spotlights?'

Map, yes; spots, no. So they walked up the steps to the front porch, whose overhead light was blazing and attracting the first few bugs of the season. One deputy produced the map and set it on a wooden café table on the porch, moved the chairs back. The houses here weren't depicted but Lake View Drive was, a narrow yellow line. Lake Mondac was on one side and on the other was a vast mass of green, Marquette State Park. Elevations and trails were shown, ranger stations, parking lots and a few of the scenic highlights: Natural Bridge, Devil's Deep, the Snake River Gorge.

Tens of thousands of acres.

Dahl looked at his battered Timex. 'Give it five, six hours since the murder. How far could Brynn and the girl get? In that brush, at night, not very.' His leg hurt like the dickens.

Prescott ambled up. 'Found something by the garage, Sheriff.'

The troopers eyed the deputy's bulk. He nodded at them, as confident as any twenty-seven-year-old could be.

'What's that?'

'Found a tarp, the sort you'd cover a canoe with. And drag marks leading to that stream. It runs into the lake.'

'Footprints?'

'Couldn't tell. It's grass and gravel. But the skids could be fresh. And I looked in the garage. There's only one life vest. No paddles. I'll bet they took the boat.'

Dahl looked over the map. 'No streams or rivers flowing out of the lake. They could get as far as the opposite shore but then they'd have to hoof it.'

'They have the boots for it,' Munce pointed out. 'Swapping footgear.'

Dahl noticed that Graham still hadn't left yet, but was hanging back, eyes on the dark woods.

'Graham, you help us out here?'

He joined them and accepted various measures of sympathy from the other law enforcers after introductions were made and they learned it was his wife who was missing.

Dahl explained about the canoe.

Graham shook his head. 'I don't think it was Brynn who took it.'

'Why not?'

'She hated boats. Hated water.'

'Well,' Commander Arlen Tanner pointed out, 'tonight was a pretty extreme situation. She might've made an exception.'

'Only if there was no other way to go.'

Dahl asked, 'Did Brynn know the state park good?'

'Some. And I saw her in the car before she left, looking over her map. She always does that. Prepares, you know. She and her ex came here a few times. She and I've never been.'

Munce said, 'Brynn and me were on a search-and-recovery here a while ago.' He was frowning and tense, as if there was something he'd been meaning to bring up. 'Gotta say, Tom. Don't know why you didn't have me come up here. I wasn't but twenty minutes away.'

'Thought you were busy. On that grand theft auto thing.'

'No, no. Didn't you hear? That was a mistake. I would've come.'

Dahl continued to examine at the map. 'We know she got dry clothes and she hooked up with that friend of the Feldmans. They came back to the house here, got boots and then took off. But which way?'

Tanner liked the canoe idea, despite what Graham'd said. 'Could've paddled across the lake and are hiding there. Or if they didn't take the boat they could be up there.' He gestured at the steep hill behind the house; it was covered with vegetation.

Another trooper shrugged. 'I'd vote for Six Eighty-two. They'd plan on flagging down a car or truck or getting to one of the houses along there. It'd take 'em a few hours but they could do it.'

Dahl felt the same.

Graham was shaking his head.

'What?' Dahl asked.

'I don't think she'd go that way, Tom. Not if those men were still around.'

'The highway's the closest to safety for them,' Dahl said. He was inclined to believe the men were in the area here and moving slowly toward the highway.

'Brynn wouldn't lead them to anybody's house. Not out

here. She wouldn't endanger anybody innocent. She'd keep running. And she wouldn't hide either.'

'Why not?' Tanner asked.

'Because she wouldn't.'

'I don't know, Graham,' Dahl said. 'Okay, she might not go to a house but she could flag down a car.'

'And how many did you see on the road when you drove up? I saw a hundred deer and one Chevrolet. She knows how deserted it is round here.'

'Well, whatta *you* think she did, Graham?' Munce asked.

'Headed into the park itself. Straight into the middle.'

'But she'd know none of the ranger stations're open this time of year.'

'But they have phones, don't they?'

'They're not working if they're closed for the season.'

'Well, pay phones.'

'Maybe. I don't know.'

Tapping the map. 'I'm not even sure she'd go for a ranger station. I think maybe she'd make for the interstate.' His finger tapped the Snake River Gorge Bridge.

Arlen Tanner was looking over the map. 'All respect, Mr Boyd, that's a lotta ground to cover. How'd they find their way? We've had people lost in this place for nearly a week. It's thousands and thousands of acres. And it's pretty rough, a lot of it. Caves, drop-offs, swamps.'

'That's exactly what she'd want.' Graham countered. 'The harder, the better. If those men are after them. Put her more in control.'

One of the troopers, looking like a big, buff soldier, offered, 'That's, what? Seven, eight miles from here. It's mostly off-trail. And the gorge is one of the most dangerous places in the park.'

'All respect,' Tanner announced, 'the odds are they're going to be hiding around here somewhere. Or hiking back to the highway. That's the logical approach.'

Dahl said, 'I agree with Arlen, Graham. I know her too but nobody'd strike out in that direction. She'd never find her way, even with GPS and a map and in daylight. I think for now we've got to concentrate around here. And Six Eighty-two.'

'At least send a few people into the park at the Snake River Gorge, Tom,' Graham insisted.

'We just don't have the manpower, Graham. I can't send volunteers, not with those men out there. Has to be armed troopers or deputies. Now go on home, Graham. Joey's going to be worried. He's got to know you're there for him. I'm talking as a father now. Not a cop . . . I promise, your number's the first one I call, we find anything.'

Eric Munce walked Graham back to his truck.

Dahl stood on the porch and looked out over the chaos of the front yard: the lights, the law enforcers, the police cars, an ambulance useful only as a taxi ride for two dead bodies. The victims' friend, Paskell, had joined Graham and Munce. They shook hands and seemed to be sharing mutual sympathy.

As he turned back to the map to organize the search parties, Dahl said a short prayer that ended with: And bring Brynn home to us, if you please.

Steam or smoke or both rose from the van. But even if it was burning it wouldn't blow up.

They never did.

Brynn McKenzie lay on her back, breathing hard, locating pain, and thinking: In the movies every car that crashes blows up. In real life they never do. She'd run probably a hundred highway accidents. Including four fires that wholly immolated the vehicles. The cars or trucks burned furiously but none of them had ever actually exploded.

Which hadn't stopped her from escaping as fast as she could through the gap where the windshield had been – moving like a caterpillar with her hands taped, scrunching along painfully over glass and rocks – and putting as much distance between herself and the shattered van as possible. She'd paused only to turn her back to Hart's map and grab it, then crumple it into a ball.

She was now about twenty feet from the vehicle, which lay on its side at the foot of the steep hill they'd tumbled down sideways – that orientation had probably saved her life. Had they kept going forward, over the drop, the airbags would have come and gone with first impact and the final drop would have fired them out through the windshield and underneath the tumbling vehicle.

As it was, ironically Hart might have saved her life. She recalled how he'd broken her fall as she'd slammed into him, smelling of aftershave, smoke and bleach.

She was hurting in various places but she tested the important appendages. They all seemed to work. It was odd not having the use of her hands, still taped behind her, to evaluate injuries. The wound in her cheek, and the gum where the tooth had been, still won the pain award. The throbbing had claimed everything north of her shoulders.

Where was Hart? She couldn't see him.

She looked to the top of the hill – it seemed very far away – where there was a faint light from the camper. She could hear Hart's partner calling him. He'd undoubtedly heard the crash but couldn't see the van, which had rolled through tall stands of brush.

They hadn't fallen all the way to the bottom of the ravine. The van was resting on a flat area about twenty feet wide, at the edge of which was another drop – about thirty feet down, she estimated, to a fast-moving stream.

She told herself: Your legs're working fine. Get up.

Only she couldn't. Not with her hands taped. She couldn't find any leverage.

'Fuck.' A word she'd said perhaps only a dozen times in her life.

Finally she tucked her knees up and managed to roll onto them, facedown, and then rose, staggering upright. She slipped the map into the back waistband of her sweats and looked around quickly for Hart.

And there he was. He'd been thrown free – which is usually the way she described the demise of a crash victim who wasn't wearing his seatbelt and had rag-dolled against a tree or signpost. He lay on his back on the other side of the van. His eyes were closed but his leg was moving, his head lolling slightly.

His black Glock lay about fifteen feet from him.

She decided she could kick the weapon forward like one of Joey's soccer balls until she was safely away then drop to her knees and pick it up, then crawl upright again.

But starting for the weapon, Brynn had heard a whimper. She spun around and saw Amy – the little blond girl, in her dirty white T-shirt and denim skirt, clutching her toy. She was running down the hill in a panic. Maybe Hart's partner had scared her and she'd fled from the camper.

Brynn was between her and Hart, who was coming to consciousness. His eyes were closed. But his fingers were clenching and unclenching. He moaned.

The girl was nearly at the foot of the hill, running blindly, sobbing. In ten seconds she'd be over the edge of the ravine.

'Amy! Stop!'

She couldn't hear or if she did she paid no attention.

A glance back toward Hart. He was trying to sit up, looking around, though he hadn't seen her yet.

The gun? Oh, how she wanted the gun!

But there was no choice. Brynn gave up on the weapon and began sprinting toward the girl. She intercepted her about three feet from the cliff edge, dropping to her knees painfully right in front of the child.

Startled, the child pulled up fast.

'It's okay, honey. Amy. Remember me? It's all right. Be careful. I don't want you to fall. Let's get back, over there, into those bushes.'

'Where's Mommy?'

'I'm not sure. But I'm here. You'll be okay.'

'I heard—'

'Come on with me.'

Brynn glanced back. Hart was struggling to get up. Still hadn't seen her.

'Hart!' The voice came from the top of the cliff. Brynn saw the silhouette of Hart's partner.

'Amy, let's go over there. I don't like that cliff.'

'Where's my *mommy*?' A raw edge to her voice.

'Come on.' Brynn hated herself for saying it but she had to: 'I'll help you find her.'

The hysteria faded. 'Okay.'

Brynn moved fast toward the base of the cliff and led the girl into a thick stand of brush and tall grass, out of sight from Hart.

'I'll help you find your mother but I can't do it with my hands this way. Can you help me? You know how you were taping those bags?'

She nodded.

'Well, I have tape on my hands.'

'Rudy did that.'

'That's right. It was like a joke.'

'I don't think it was a joke. He does lots of things like that.'

'It hurts my hands. Will you take it off?'

'I'll take it off. Okay. I don't like Rudy. He looks at me sometimes when he thinks I'm asleep.'

Brynn's heart thudded. 'You don't have to worry about Rudy anymore. I'm a policewoman.'

'You are? Like Charlie's Angels?'

'Like that, yeah, Amy.'

'You're older than them.'

Brynn nearly smiled.

Amy was slowly tugging at the tape. 'How did you know my name?'

'Your father told me.'

'He's not my father.'

'Charlie told me.'

After a number of false starts, she was unwinding the duct tape. 'Why did Rudy do that?'

'He was going to hurt me. But don't say anything, Amy. There are other people around. We don't want them to hear us.'

'I saw them. I think one of them hurt my mommy.'

'Don't worry; I won't let anybody hurt you. Just don't say anything now. We'll be quiet. Both of us.'

'Okay.'

At last her hands were free. Brynn rubbed them. She'd scraped an elbow but the parka had protected her pretty well and there was no other damage that hadn't been there before the tumble down the hill. She grabbed the precious map and put it in her ski parka.

'Your face is funny,' the girl said, looking at the black crust of the wound and the swelling.

'I know. Now, let's be quiet.' A smile. 'Okay?'

'Okay.'

Crouching, Brynn led her back quietly toward the clearing where the van lay. She peeked through the bushes.

Hart was gone.

So was the gun.

Graham Boyd drove fast, away from that place where two bodies lay in a fancy vacation house, his wife's clothing in another, and her car at the bottom of a black lake.

He tried to leave those images behind. But he couldn't.

He'd thought he'd be seeing Sandra, then stopping for a fast drink at JJ's – so he could honestly tell Brynn he'd been to the poker game.

But, man, had everything changed . . . He'd never experienced a night like this one.

Glancing up into the rear-view mirror, he saw the police car behind him, coming up close, real fast. Graham glanced at the speedometer. He was doing 85.

He drove a half mile farther, then pulled over. Leaned his head against the steering wheel, gripping the plastic compulsively with his strong hands.

A few minutes later a uniformed officer was standing beside the driver's side window. Graham took a deep breath and climbed out of the car. He stepped to the officer and shook Eric Munce's hand. 'Thanks. I really mean it. I knew you'd understand. Nobody else would.'

'Isn't the most regular thing in the world but I'll go on your word, Graham.'

Brynn's husband zipped his jacket up. He got his flashlight and a Buck knife from the tool carrier in the back of the truck. As he relocked the box, he said, 'I'm not sure I'm right. Not sure at all. But everything I know about her tells me that she'd head this way.'

'And the canoe?'

'If she used it, it was a trick. To fool those men. Shoved it in the lake and then took off on foot. Brynn hated the water. She'd never try to escape that way if she could help it.'

Lakes and oceans weren't her environment. He didn't explain to Munce about his wife's control issue.

'I sure hope you're right, Graham . . . I'd like a piece of those bastards,' Munce muttered, eyes gleaming. He had a round face, narrow light-colored eyes and short blond hair. He looked more like a Marine than a deputy and Graham wondered if he'd been in the military. He asked.

'Yessir, I was.' Then confessed: 'National Guard. Never saw the big show, though.' He shrugged with a stoic grin.

Munce then asked, 'But there was that ranger station on the map, you saw it? The one near Apex Lake. Why wouldn't she make for that?'

'Might have. I'm not saying I'm certain. But I think Brynn'll take the harder route, like I was saying. It'll equalize them, the women and those men after 'em. On a trail, the men can move faster. In the woods she'll have the advantage. And Brynn won't let anybody get an edge over her.'

'Woman must be hell to play cards with.'

'We don't play cards,' Graham said absently, staring at the map.

He then looked over the dark woods. One car whizzed past. The highway was otherwise empty.

'You'd be a good cop, Graham.'

'Me?' He laughed grimly. 'No, sir.' He tapped the map. 'Here's the Joliet Trail. She'll leave the path about there.' He touched a spot. 'Then make for the Snake River and follow it right up here to the interstate.'

Munce looked at the steep hill, vanishing below them into a morass of woods. 'That's a tough climb. You ever been here?'

'To the park? Yeah, but not here. Hiking when I was younger.' Graham recalled asking Joey to come with him several times in the past year. The boy had always declined, with a look on his face that said, And I'd want to do that *why*? Graham had regretted that he hadn't insisted. He believed he could've made Joey enjoy himself.

Thinking, Should've listened to my instincts.

Then: What does it matter?

Munce told him he was familiar with this area. He and Brynn had been involved in a search-and-recovery mission that had ended about a mile from here.

Graham noted the word 'recovery,' as in 'body recovery'. Not a successful rescue. The deputy continued, 'I remember some paths. Hikers and rock climbers made them. There're some level areas but we're going to see mostly drop-offs, twenty, thirty feet, some of them. Even more. You'll come on them real sudden. Watch where you walk.'

Graham nodded. He said, 'I'm guessing they'll stick close enough to hear the river, to guide them. That means they'll be somewhere in a strip fifty, a hundred yards wide, from the edge of the gorge. That's where we should make our way down. We can't call to 'em loud, give ourselves away . . . We'll just have to stop every so often and look around us. We could probably whisper. The sheriff said it's two men are after them, right?'

'Yeah, what the footprints show.'

Graham looked at the deputy's car, the shotgun locked in the front seat.

'I don't have a gun here, Eric.'

'I can't do that, Graham. That's a lose-your-job thing.'

'Ah.'

'Stay close. I scored second in the department shooting competition.'

'Well, maybe it wouldn't be a bad idea for you to have two at least.'

Munce considered this. He returned to the car, unlocked the shotgun, pocketed a half-dozen shells. He locked the car door and returned to Graham. Together they walked to the edge of the forest and peered down the slope of rocks and trees. To their left the river, a hundred feet down the sheer gorge walls, roared as it broke over boulders and tree trunks and a small dam, at the bottom of which was an eerie sink-hole where leaves and trash spiraled into a foul broth and disappeared.

'Looks like the waterway to hell.'

'Thanks for this, Eric. You going to get into trouble?'

'Sheriff sent us out to search. I said I was checking some roads north. I just didn't say how far I was going.'

'Tom's a good man but I have a feeling he's wrong on this one. I know my wife.'

For a few minutes they wound, or muscled, their way through stands of thick brush, then over a soft bed of pine needles, which was a pleasure after the ornery forsythia, vinca and other viney plants that seemed unnaturally attracted to their boots. The hussssh of the water from the Snake River grew louder.

'Time to get serious here.' Munce bent down, spat in the dirt and made mud. He smeared it on his face and cheek-bones. Graham hesitated, feeling foolish, then did the same.

'Okay. Well, let's do it.' Munce racked the shotgun, put the safety on and led the way. They started downward into an impossible tangle of trees and branches and rocks and shadow.

Graham whispered, 'Eric, curious. Was it Brynn who beat you?'

'Beat me?'

'In the shooting competition. You said you were second.'

'Oh, no, was Dobbie Masters. Boy come outa his momma's tummy with a pistol in his hand. But I will say this, Brynn may not be the best shot, but she empties the clip and reloads twice as fast as anybody on the force. In a firefight, that counts for more. Believe me.'

James Jasons finished his second hamburger, which was cold but he wanted the calories. He drove along the interstate, glancing from time to time at the screen on a small box stuck to the Lexus dashboard.

The indicator told him he was about one mile from his target, which had stopped moving and had been parked by the roadside for about ten minutes.

Jasons assessed his performance as the Feldman's grieving friend Ari Paskell, which was one of his four identities, complete with car registration and driver's license. When you work for somebody like Stanley Mankewitz the budget isn't quite unlimited but it's big enough that you can afford the tools to do your job with the union boss's favorite word – efficiency.

Back at the Feldman house, as he'd pretended to compose himself after learning the sad news, he'd learned plenty. He'd made up the story about a phone call from Steven to learn what the police actually suspected that there were two of them and they weren't physically large, thank you, Deputy Munce.

He'd also told the story to plant the seed that the killing was locally motivated; it didn't originate in Milwaukee. He couldn't tell if Dahl believed that or not.

Jasons had also overheard other snippets, giving him a good idea of what the police knew about the crime, while pretending to make a phone call – you're invisible when you're on your mobile; nobody thinks you're listening. The sheriff missed that completely but Jasons didn't put him down as a small-town rube. Brilliant people always look for the simplest, most logical explanation for a situation and Jasons had offered one: a grieving friend, a driver's license and a legitimate tag number on a nice car.

It helped too that Jasons had left soon after, as he'd been asked to, before the sheriff started to wonder about this continued presence.

In fact, he didn't need to stay. Because his next steps had nothing to do with how the police were handling the investigation. No, he had focused on the husband of that woman deputy who'd fled into the woods, escaping Emma Feldman's killers. Noting the conspiratorial conversation that Graham Boyd had had with Eric Munce, Jasons deduced that they were planning their own renegade search, independent of the sheriff's plan.

Dahl might've known his staff and he might've known logic, and human nature in general – all good cops did – but he hadn't known the sort of things you learn about a person by sharing a life and spending bedroom time with him. Jasons just had to look at his own relationship with Robert to know this was true.

So he put his money on the husband and Munce to lead him to the deputy – named Brynn – and to the Feldmans' friend, the witnesses to the murder.

The two women who were the moths drawing the men Jasons was trying to keep alive tonight.

He recalled, back at the Lake Mondac house, Graham shaking 'Paskell's' hand and giving his sympathies. Then Jasons had wished them luck with the search. Graham had then turned away and spoken to Munce, the deputy looking down as he considered the words. Munce then said something back and they'd both looked at their watches.

Might as well shout their intentions over a megaphone.

But, it turned out, everybody else was concentrating on the business at hand and the exchange had gone unnoticed. On the pretext of asking another officer directions, Jasons had passed by the husband's pickup truck and dropped what looked like a small chip of wood inside the bed, behind some potted plants. The wood chip contained a GPS tracker – originally designed for hunters to use to track their dogs should they get overly enthusiastic when going after a shot bird and vanish into the distance.

Jasons owned and had used lots of equipment from security services, some of it worthy of master spies. But these dog trackers, which sold for about five hundred dollars, were far superior to the security equipment that cost ten times as much (even more if the customer was the federal government, he'd learned).

Now, as he approached what a sign reported was the Snake River Bridge, the tracker was humming steadily. Then he saw the white pickup and a squad car parked off the road, half hidden in some bushes about two hundred yards this side of the bridge.

Jasons piloted his Lexus past them.

So this was where they believed Deputy McKenzie and the two killers were heading.

Jasons drove over the bridge, below which was an impressive moonlit gorge. Then as soon as the interstate was deserted he made a U over the flat, grassy median and crossed the bridge again going the other way. Then, about even with where the men had parked, on the other side, he nosed his car into a woody area off the shoulder and pulled to a stop.

He climbed out and stretched. He opened the trunk and

replaced his sports coat with a windbreaker and his dress shoes with boots. He took out a canvas bag, which he slung over his shoulder.

Waiting for a massive Peterbilt tractor-trailer to pass, swirling dust and grit in its wake, he crossed asphalt, the median and then more road and vanished into the woods.

At the pond, an oval far smaller but no less dark and eerie than Lake Mondac, Brynn touched her finger to her lips and glanced at Amy, smiling.

The little girl nodded. She was wearing Brynn's dark sweatshirt over her white T. Her legs were bare and pale but she didn't seem cold. She'd given up asking about her mommy and now walked dutifully beside Brynn, cuddling Chester, a stuffed creature of indeterminate species.

Surveying the pond, their rallying point, Brynn thought how happy she'd been when she'd first met Charlie Gandy. An ally, a weapon, a ride to safety.

Control.

And it had all been just a cruel joke. She didn't even have her spear anymore. She felt wholly depleted. She pulled the girl down beside her and continued to scan the pond carefully.

Motion. In the bushes. Brynn tensed and Amy looked at her warily.

Was it Hart and his partner?

Was it the wolf who'd attached himself to them?

No. Brynn exhaled long. It was Michelle.

The young woman was crouching, like a huntress. The

spear in one hand and something in the other – the knife, it seemed. Waiting for the killers, defiant, tense, as if daring them to try to hurt her.

Brynn and the girl started to make their way toward the woman. In a whisper Brynn called, 'Michelle! It's me.'

The woman froze. But then Brynn moved forward and stepped into a wash of azure-white light from the moon.

'Brynn!' Michelle cried, slipping the knife into her pocket and running forward. She stopped, seeing Amy standing bewildered behind Brynn's back.

The women embraced briefly and Michelle dropped to her knees, hugging the girl. 'Who's this?'

Amy eased free from the overly emotional embrace.

'This's Amy. She's going to come with us.' Brynn shook her head, foregoing for now the story of how she'd come by her young companion. Michelle was sensitive enough to ask no questions.

'You're adorable! And who's *this*?'

'Chester.'

'He's as cute as you are.'

The little girl remained somber, sensing the atmosphere of tragedy if not comprehending the actual events that had caused it. If she didn't know about her mother's fate, maybe she hadn't witnessed the other killings.

The moon was lower now and the darkness, deepening. Curiously, Amy was the only one among them who didn't seem uneasy at this. Maybe if you have parents like hers, fear of the dark doesn't figure much in your life.

The girl blinked at a flying squirrel as it sailed past. Brynn hoped she'd laugh, or show a bit of delight at the bizarre animal. Nothing. Her face was a mask.

'I heard some noises,' Michelle said. Meaning the gunshots. 'Our friends . . . ?'

'Still with us. One hurt a little more but mobile.'

'So they could be on the way here.'

'We have to get going. To the Snake River. We'll climb the gorge and be at the interstate in forty-five minutes. An hour, tops.'

'You said there was an easier way.'

'Easier but a lot longer. And Hart thinks we're going that way.'

Michelle blinked. 'You talked to him?'

'Yep.'

'You did?' the woman whispered in astonishment. 'How'd that happen?'

She told her briefly about her captivity in the van.

'Oh, my God. He nearly killed you.'

It was pretty close to mutual, Brynn reflected.

'And what'd he say?'

'Not much. But I told him we were making for the interstate, so he'll think we're going toward Point of Rocks.'

'Like reverse psychology.'

'Yep.' Brynn dug the map out of her pocket and opened it.

'Where'd you get that?'

'Stole it from him – our friend Mister Hart.'

Michelle gave an astonished laugh.

Brynn oriented herself and pointed out where they were. She didn't need a compass reading. The map was detailed and it was easy to tell from landmarks the best route. She pointed out the direction to head.

'I want my mommy.'

Brynn shook her head at Michelle and said to the girl, 'Honey, we have to get out of here before we can find her. And that means walking. Do you like to walk?'

'I guess.'

'And then we're going to climb a hill.'

'Like rock climbing? There's a climbing wall near my school. Charlie said he'd take me but he never did.'

'Well, this'll be like that. Only more adventurous.'

'Like Dora the Explorer,' Michelle said. 'And Boots . . .' When Amy looked at her blankly the young woman added, 'The monkey.'

'I know. I just, like, haven't seen that for years. That's not what Mom and Charlie watch.'

Not wishing to speculate on what was viewing material in that household, Brynn said cheerfully, 'Let's go.' Then to Michelle: 'You keep the spear. You can use it for a crutch. Let me have one of the knives.'

Michelle pulled a Chicago Cutlery out of her jacket and handed it to Brynn.

A bit of control. Not much. But better than nothing.

A faint laugh. Brynn turned to Michelle, who was studying her. 'Do I look as bad as you?' The young woman asked.

'Doubt it. I just experienced my second car wreck of the night. I win. But, yep, you're not so hot either. I wouldn't go out on the town without a makeover.'

Michelle squeezed her arm.

They started hiking.

The Snake River was closer than she'd estimated. They made it in a half hour and that included keeping to the thickest cover and pausing to look behind them frequently for the men.

Of whom there was no sign. This was reassuring but Brynn wouldn't allow herself the thought that Hart had fallen for her bluff and was in fact headed in the opposite direction along the riverbank.

They paused in a circle of tall grass and to look up and down the bank of the wide, shallow river punctuated with rocks, logs and small islands.

No one.

'Wait here.' Clutching the knife, Brynn eased forward. She knelt on the bank and immersed her face in the freezing water. Now she didn't mind the cold, which dulled the pain in her cheek and neck. Then she drank what must have been a quart. She hadn't realized she was dehydrated.

She studied the otherworldly landscape, saw no one else and motioned to Michelle and Amy to join her. They too drank.

Then Brynn gazed up the hill, in the direction of the interstate. It couldn't be more than a mile away.

Though a mile straight up.

'Jesus,' Michelle said, following Brynn's eyes. About fifty feet away the landscape went up at a steep angle – at least thirty degrees, though at points it seemed forty-five. There were also vertical faces. They couldn't climb those, of course, but Brynn knew, from the search-and-rescue a few years ago, that they wouldn't have to. It was possible to hike up if you picked your route carefully. There were also a number of wide plateaus that were more or less flat and filled with vegetation for cover.

They now walked to the beginning of the hill, the churning river on their right, where the gorge began.

Looking back, Michelle gestured at the muddy ground behind them. 'Wait, our footprints.'

'They don't look too obvious.'

'They will to somebody with a flashlight.'

'Good point.'

Michelle ran back to where they'd taken their drinks and broke some branches off an evergreen bush. Then backing toward the cliff, she swept the leaves over the mud, wielding the improvised broom furiously, obscuring their footprints. Brynn could hear her gasping hard. Michelle ignored her injured ankle, though the pain must have been significant.

Brynn was watching a woman very different from the rich dilettante of earlier in the evening, bragging about future stardom and whining about other people's shoes and thorn pricks. Brynn had known people who collapsed under the smallest stress and people who un-expectedly rose to meet impossible challenges. She'd been sure that Michelle fell into the first category.

She was wrong.

And she knew now she had an ally.

The young woman joined the others.

Amy yawned. 'I'm tired.'

'I know, honey,' Michelle said. 'We'll get you to sleep soon. Can I put Chester in my pocket?'

'Will you zip it up so he won't fall out?'

'You bet.'

'But don't close it all the way. So he can breathe.'

Acting so much younger than her years, Brynn reflected sadly.

Michelle slipped the stuffed animal into her pocket and they started to climb as in the distance, on the interstate, a truck's engine brake rattled harshly, beckoning them forward.

Graham and Munce were making their way carefully down the slope from the interstate.

A truck sped past behind them, the noise dampened by the foliage and confused by the wind as the driver downshifted and filled the night with the rattle of a Gatling gun.

Soon they were well into the trek, not talking, uttering only labored breathing – the effort to stay upright and not fall forward was as great as a climb upward would have been. They could hear the rush of the river, a hundred feet below, in the cellar of the gorge.

Graham made his living with flora and he was keenly aware of how different the vegetation around him now was from that at his company, plants sitting subdued in ceramic pots or lolling on bundled root balls. For years he'd changed the geography of residences and offices by plopping a few camellias or rhododendrons into planting beds primed with limey soil and tucking them away under a blanket of mulch. Here, plants weren't decorations; they were the infrastructure, population, society itself. Controlling all. He and Munce meant nothing, were less than insignificant, as were all the animals here. It seemed to Graham that the croaks and hisses and hoots were desperate pleas that the trees and plants blithely ignored. Indifferent.

And treacherous too. Once, they had to tightrope walk across a log above a thick sea of poison ivy, to which he was allergic. Had any touched his face, the rash and swelling would have blinded him. Even dead vegetation was dangerous. Munce stepped on a ledge covered with last year's leaves, which slid out from underneath him, starting a small avalanche of loam, gravel and dirt. He'd saved himself from a twenty-foot-fall down a steep rocky slope by grabbing a fortuitous overhanging branch.

And as they wound downward, looking for the safest route, Graham couldn't help thinking that the noise from stepping on a desiccated branch or kicking an unnoticed pile of crisp leaves might also alert the killers.

They found some paths, which summer hikers had worn, but the trails were sporadic and didn't run very far so the men were forced to make their own. Sometimes a path would vanish at the edge of a cliff and they had to climb down six, seven feet. When they did this Munce set the safety on the shotgun and handed it to Graham, who waited until the deputy was down, and then regretfully passed it back.

They were now a hundred yards from the interstate with the dangerous precipice above the gorge not far away on their left.

To maintain silence Munce would give hand commands. He'd indicate pause, go right or left, look at this or that. Graham thought it was as silly as the face paint but he'd talked Munce into this mission and if the young man wanted to play soldier, fine with him.

They paused, looking down a very steep hill. They'd have to use saplings and trees as handholds. Munce grimaced and started to reach out for one when Graham cried out in a whisper, 'No! Eric, no!'

The deputy turned back quickly, eyes wide, fumbling with the gun. He slipped on the incline and went down hard, sliding headfirst along the bed of pine needles, slippery as ice. Graham lunged forward and managed to seize the deputy's cuff.

'Jesus. What?' The deputy managed to turn around, grab Graham's hand and together they scrabbled to more level ground. 'You see something?'

'Sorry,' Graham said. 'Look.'

Eric, frowning, didn't get it at first. Then he saw that Graham was pointing to the thin tree trunk he'd almost grabbed. From it protruded needle-sharp thorns, each about two inches long.

'It's a honey locust. Most dangerous tree in the forest. They're illegal to plant in a lot of places. One of those thorns'd go right through your hand. People've died from infections.'

'Lord, I never looked. There more of 'em around here?'

'Oh, yeah, if there's one there's others. And over there? See that?' Graham pointed to a stubby trunk. 'Hercules'-club. Hard to see in the dark but they've got thorns too. And with the woods thinning that means more sun and more blackberry – you know, brambles – and wild roses. Blackberry thorns'll break off in your skin. And you don't get 'em out right away they'll get infected. In a big way.'

'Damn land mines,' Munce muttered. Then he froze. And, foregoing the cryptic hand signals, he whispered, 'Way down there. A flash. You see anything?'

Graham nodded – a faint dot of bluish light. Maybe a flash-light or a reflection of the moonlight on metal or glass. It was about three-quarters of a mile away.

Munce undid the thong that covered his black pistol and gestured to Graham to follow him.

Hart was looking down at the GPS, which had survived the van crash in better condition than he had. Nothing broken, just sore. But *everyplace* was sore and the bullet wound in his arm had started to bleed again.

Thank you, Michelle.

Thank you, Brynn.

A wave of anger seared him and for a moment he didn't give a damn about craftsmanship; he wanted to get even. He wanted to pay them both back in a big way. Sweet, bloody revenge . . .

Maybe Compton Lewis was on to something.

They were standing on the banks of the Snake River, which ambled out of the flatter forests, east, on their right, and flowed into the compressed gorge west.

He'd lost the map in the crash but they'd gotten here by using the GPS, which wasn't as detailed but was good enough. 'Way I figure it . . .' His voice faded as he glanced at Lewis. 'You okay?'

'Yeah.'

The other man was standing with his hands at his sides, holding the shotgun. Apart from his natural slump, he looked like a soldier on guard duty.

'Bothered you, killing that woman, right?'

'Didn't think it would. But . . . seeing her eyes, you know.'

'That's hard,' Hart said. Though thinking: Maybe the first one. Then you don't even notice it.

He was replaying the scene at the camper. Lewis starting the fire beneath the Winnebago, then returning to the other side. Two men had rushed out the front door, a fat one and a thinner one with a beard, carrying a fire extinguisher. A woman hurried out the back door, looking frantically around, screaming. Hart had shot the men quickly, before the fat one could even reach for his gun. Lewis, in the rear, had the shotgun trained on the woman. But he'd done nothing at first.

Hart was going to do Lewis a favor and shoot her too but he heard the bang as the shotgun went off, as if by itself. Lewis had seemed surprised. As the heavy woman stumbled backward, her chest and neck rippled, then started to bleed. She dropped to her knees and began to crawl toward Lewis. The second time, he actually aimed and fired. She fell backward, kicked some, then died.

'That was unpleasant,' Hart said.

Lewis nodded.

'I was telling you, they were tweakers. Probably slamming their own stuff. Nobody cooks meth without using it. Maybe not at first but they get addicted. It eats their souls.'

'Yeah,' Lewis said softly. Then he came back to earth, Hart could see in his eyes.

Hart continued, 'Way I figure it is this.' He showed him the GPS on the BlackBerry. 'It's nearly six miles to Point of Rocks, going that way, upstream.' He pointed right. Then he indicated the gorge, to their left. 'But that way, up that hill, they'll be at the interstate in forty minutes, an hour. And that's where they're going.'

'You're sure?'

'Pretty sure. She told me she was. When we were in the

van. But she's the Trickster, remember? She knew there was a chance I'd survive the crash. Which meant that she had to give me information that'd lead me in a different direction. She'd said the interstate, thinking I'd believe it was really Point of Rocks.'

'You think she was playing that game?'

Hart put away the BlackBerry and strode up and down the riverbank. 'Hey, Lewis, what's that look like to you?' He shone the flashlight on the ground.

'Like, I don't know. Somebody was sweeping, covering up footprints.'

'Yeah. It does.' He walked to the base of the steep hill. 'Okay. Here we go.' He found a broken branch. 'Here's her broom. They *did* come this way. And look at that . . .' He pointed out a tiny set of shoe prints. 'That little girl. In the camper. She must've got out.'

Lewis had gone quiet again, and he rubbed his tattoo – the cross on his neck – compulsively.

Hart said, 'I'm not inclined to kill children. We'll take care of the women but let the girl be.'

But, funny, Lewis was bothered by something else.

'One thing I want to say. I should've before. But . . .'

'Go on, Comp.'

'That robbery I told you about?'

'The robbery?'

'The bank.'

In the snow, Hart remembered. Where he'd traded shots with the bank guard who was a former cop. 'Yeah?'

'Wasn't quite honest with you.'

'That right?'

'Something's been eating at me, Hart.'

He was no longer the sarcastic 'my friend.' And hadn't been for hours. He said, 'Go ahead, Comp. What is it?'

'Truth is . . . we didn't get away with fifty thousand. Or

whatever I said. Was closer to . . . okay, it was closer to three. Really two and some change. And, okay, it wasn't a bank. Was a guard refilling the ATM outside . . . and I only fired to scare him. He dropped his gun. And peed his pants, I think. He didn't have any backup piece either . . . I boost things up sometimes, exaggerate, you know. Got into the habit around my brother. Kind of had to, growing up. Got disrespected a lot. So. There you have it.'

'That's it, the confession?'

'Guess so.'

'Hell, Comp, I wouldn't want to work with somebody didn't have a healthy ego. Way you can look at it, you made two thousand bucks for, what, two minutes' work?'

''Bout that.'

'That's about sixty thousand an hour. And he peed his pants? Hell, that made it worth it right there.' Hart laughed.

Lewis asked shyly, 'You still interested in doing a heist together, you and me?'

'You bet I am. Sooner we're done here, the sooner we can start planning some jobs that don't crash and burn. One hundred ten percent.'

Repressing a grin, Lewis tapped his cigarettes again, like a good Catholic blessing himself.

The trek was much harder than she'd anticipated.

The hillside was so steep in places that it couldn't be climbed, at least not with a ten-year-old in tow. Brynn frequently had to find alternative routes.

'How about there?'

Brynn glanced at the place where Michelle was pointing. It seemed to be a fairly level path between a rock ledge and a dense cluster of trees. Brynn considered it but that way would leave them completely exposed from below, with no escape routes. They had to bypass the path, taking precious minutes to find a way around. Brynn wasn't entirely confident that Hart had bought the ploy about Point of Rocks. She was beginning to feel an itching sensation on the back of her neck, as if the men were drawing close.

The women continued upward, looping around a formation of limestone, twenty feet high. Brynn could see that rock climbers had been here. Metal spikes had been pounded into the cracks. Tonight the hobby struck her as pure madness. Something Joey would try. But she put her son out of her head. Concentrate, she told herself.

A brief respite as they traversed a fairly level trail.

Then upward again, gasping for breath, all three of them.

The sound of the Snake running through the gorge on their right grew softer as they moved higher. Brynn guessed they were now sixty feet or so above the river.

'Oh, no,' Michelle whispered. Brynn too stopped. Their level plain suddenly ended in a sheer rock wall, a dead end. To the right, the ground extended to a steep drop-off into the gorge. Brynn walked toward it slowly. Their only route was a six-inch ledge. 'We can't go that way.'

She sighed in frustration. The men couldn't be more than a half mile from the interstate but the hike was taking forever. To go back and find a way around the wall would add another ten minutes.

Brynn looked back, then surveyed the wall. It was about twenty feet high and not completely vertical. The slope was probably seventy degrees in most places and the surface was cracked and craggy. She asked Michelle, 'Can you do it?'

'Damn right, I can.'

Brynn smiled, said to Amy, 'You and I'll climb together. You remember when you were little and played piggyback. You want to do that now?'

'I guess. Rudy wants me to play piggyback sometimes. I don't like it. He smells bad.'

Brynn shot a glance to Michelle, who grimaced in disgust. But Brynn smiled at Amy. 'Well, I probably don't smell too good either. But it'll be fun. Come on. Let's go.' Brynn turned around. She whispered to Michelle, 'I'll go up first. If something happens, I drop her, try to break her fall. Don't worry about me.'

Michelle nodded and boosted the girl up, whispering, 'Can you handle her?'

'No choice,' Brynn gasped.

The theme for the evening.

Though the burden wasn't as great as it could be. She was

thinking how thin the little girl was . . . and about the sad fate that had landed her squarely in such neglect.

They started up the cliff, a foot at a time. Heart slamming, legs burning, Brynn slowly climbed. About fifteen feet from the ground, the muscles in her legs began quivering. More from fear than from effort. How she hated heights . . . She paused frequently.

Amy, with her arms around Brynn's neck, was holding on tightly, making it hard for Brynn to breathe, but she'd rather the child kept a solid grip.

Her rubber legs propelled her another five feet, then ten, grasping handholds harder than she needed to; her fingers were cramping. Even her toes curled painfully, as if she were climbing barefoot.

Finally, an eternity, her head was over the edge, and she was looking at a flatter plain. In front of her was a huge tangle of forsythia. Not daring to look down, she grabbed all the vines within arm's length in her right hand, tested them and, with a deep breath, let go of the rock. She pulled herself halfway over the edge and then said, 'Amy, go over my head. Put your knees on my shoulders and climb. When you're on the top, stop. Just stand there.'

Brynn was about to offer more reassurance but the girl said quickly, 'Okay,' and climbed off. And stood motionless, at attention.

A child used to doing exactly as she was told.

Brynn then pulled herself the rest of the way over the top and sat down, breathing hard. She looked over the side – disappointingly, it seemed much less intimidating from this end, as if the effort and fear had been wasted. She beckoned Michelle up. The young woman climbed quickly, despite her bad ankle – thanks to youth and that fancy butt-firming health club of hers. Brynn helped her over the edge and the three sat together in a huddle, catching their breath.

Brynn oriented herself and, looking around, found what seemed to be a path that led upward. They started walking again.

Michelle eased close to Brynn, 'What'll happen to her?'

'If she doesn't have kin, a foster home.'

'That's sad. She should be with a family.'

'The system's pretty good in Kennesha. They check on the families real well.'

'Just nice if she could go to somebody who really wanted her. I'd love her.'

Maybe one of the problems between Michelle and her husband had to do with children. He might not have wanted any.

'Adoptions're possible. I don't know how that works.' Brynn touched her cheek. It hurt like hell. She saw Michelle's eyes focused on Amy. 'So you'd like kids?'

Breathlessly the young woman responded, 'Oh, they're the best. I just love them . . . The way you guide them, teach them things. And what they teach you. They're always a challenge. Children make you, I don't know, whole. You're not a complete person without them.'

'You sound like an expert. You'll be a good mother.'

Michelle gave a laugh. 'I intend to be.'

For the moment at least, thoughts of unfaithful husbands and marriages in shambles had faded and the woman seemed to be envisioning a brighter future.

And what about me? Brynn thought.

Keep going, she told herself. Keep going.

Lewis had made an improvised sling for the shotgun and was carrying the weapon on his back. The men were going straight up the slope as best they could, Hart figuring that the women would be taking an easier route because of the girl.

Hart thought of the professional couples and their kids he saw at the rock climbing walls at recreation areas and sports stores near where he lived. He'd wondered if any of the parents actually had jobs that required them to climb like this. But no, of course they didn't. They were paper pushers. They made ten times what he did, their lives were never endangered, they never felt the pain that Hart was experiencing. Yet he would never dream of swapping lives with them for any money.

They're nothing but dead bodies, Brynn. Sitting around, upset, angry about something they saw on TV doesn't mean a single thing to them personally. Going to their jobs, coming home, talking stuff they don't know or care about . . .

They came to a flat stretch and paused, looking around carefully. He wasn't going to forget that both women had attempted to kill them tonight and he had no reason to think they'd given up trying. Sure, they wanted to escape. But he couldn't get Brynn's eyes out of his mind. Both in the driveway of the Feldmans' house and then in the van just before she released the brake, risking her own death to stop him.

You have the right to remain silent. You have the right to an attorney . . .

Hart had to smile.

At that moment a faint scream sounded in the distance, ahead of them. A high squeal.

'The hell's that?' Lewis looked alarmed. 'Fucking *Blair Witch Project.*'

Hart laughed. 'That's the girl. The little girl.'

'She's as good as your GPS, Hart.'

And they broke into a run.

'An animal?' Munce asked in a whisper.

Graham cocked his head, listening to the keening howl somewhere nearby, to their left, it seemed, carried on the breeze. He'd seen an animal – a coyote or feral dog, maybe even a wolf – on a ridge, looking their way. Was that the source of the sound? He knew plants, he knew soil and silt and rock. He didn't know animals or their habits.

'Could be, I don't know.'

It hadn't sound like a woman's voice. It'd almost seemed like a child. But that couldn't be.

'Maybe the wind,' Munce offered.

Though there'd been a sense of urgency, an uneasiness about it. Fear more than pain.

Then silence.

Wind, bird, animal . . . Please. Let it be one of those.

'Down there,' Munce said. 'Right below us.'

Graham was frowning at the daunting sweep of trees that disappeared away from them. They'd come about a quarter mile, picking their way slowly through the dense woodland. It was a much longer trek than expected, owing to detours around brush thick as scouring pads and steep cliffs that couldn't be negotiated without rappelling gear – which Munce had announced he wished they'd had and Graham was grateful they didn't.

They started down the hillside, using trees as handholds once again. Then they found themselves stymied – in a funnel of rock. 'I think that's our only option,' Munce said, pointing down a chute descending away from them. It was about six feet wide and at a 45-degree slope, littered with shale and gravel and dirt. Slippery as ice. And if you fell you'd slide along the rugged stone surface for a good fifty feet to a precipice. They couldn't see what lay beyond. 'Or we go back and try to make our way around.'

Just then another wail filled the night. The men looked at each other, eyes wide.

There was no doubt the sound had come from a human throat.

'We go,' Graham said, torn between a frantic need to find the source of the screams and fear that, if they lost their footing here, they'd find themselves tumbling off a cliff – or sliding into a grove of deadly honey locust.

'Where's my mother?' Amy shrieked again.

'Please, honey,' Brynn said to the little girl. Held her finger to her lips. 'Please be quiet.'

Exhausted, emotionally drained, the little girl was losing it.

'No!' she wailed. Her face was bright red, eyes and nose streaming. 'Noooo!'

'Those men will hurt us, Amy. We have to be quiet.'

'Mommy!'

They were on a relatively flat stretch of ground in a thick forest, the trees only a yard or two apart. They'd been moving along well when suddenly Amy had become hysterical.

'Where's my *mother*? I want to go back to her!'

Forcing a smile onto her face, Brynn knelt down and took the girl by the shoulders. 'Please, honey, we have to be quiet. We're playing that game, remember? We need to be quiet.'

'I don't want to play any games! I want to go back! I want mommy!'

The girl's age was close to ten but once again Brynn thought she was acting more like a five- or six-year-old.

'Please!' she begged the child

'Nooo!' The volume of the accompanying squeal was astonishing.

'Let me try,' Michelle said, kneeling in front of Amy and setting down the spear. She handed the girl her stuffed toy. Amy flung it to the ground.

Brynn said, 'I'll check behind us. If they're nearby they had to've heard her.' She jogged back twenty feet and climbed a small hillock, gazed back.

The girl's screaming seemed like a siren.

Brynn squinted through the night.

Oh, no . . .

She was dismayed, but not surprised to see, two hundred yards away, the men making their way in this direction. They paused and looked around, trying to find the source of the commotion.

Thank goodness, though, just at that moment Amy fell silent.

The men continued to look around them for a moment and then started walking again. They vanished behind a stone wall.

Brynn returned to Michelle and Amy. The little girl, though still unhappy, had stopped crying and was clutching her toy once more.

'How'd you do that?'

Michelle shrugged, grimacing. Whispered: 'Wasn't such a great idea. I told her we were on our way to see her mommy. Couldn't think of what else to say.'

Well, it didn't matter. The girl would learn the truth sooner or later but for now they sure couldn't afford the screaming. Brynn whispered, 'They're back there.'

'What? Hart and his partner?'

A nod.

'How?'

Hart, of course. Brynn said, '*Reverse*-reverse psychology. Two hundred yards or so back. We've got to move.'

They headed toward the gorge, the ground being flatter, then north again toward the interstate. They knew the direction, because the river was on their right but, with the landscape more open as they rose higher, they were forced to zigzag – now seeking out brush and trees for cover. It was taking too long, Brynn reflected, feeling Hart's presence growing closer.

She led Michelle and Amy back into the thicker woods and they continued north. Suddenly faint light streaked from left to right, a truck or car on the interstate. A half mile, maybe less. Brynn and Michelle shared a smile and started forward again.

Which is when they heard a snap of a footstep, to their left, somewhere in a thick pine forest. The sound was close. Brynn looked at the little girl, whose gaunt face warned of another outburst.

Another snap. Closer. Footsteps, definitely.

Hart and his partner must have moved faster than Brynn had expected, closing the 200 yards in only fifteen minutes. They'd probably found a smooth trail the women had missed.

Brynn pointed to the ground. The three of them went prone behind a fallen tree. Amy started to cry again but Michelle pulled her close and worked her magic once more. Brynn picked up handfuls of leaves and, as quietly as she could, spread them on top of the other two. Then she also lay down and camouflaged herself.

The footsteps grew closer, then were lost in the rustling wind.

Then Brynn gasped. She believed she heard somebody whispering her name.

Her imagination, of course. It was just the breeze, which was blowing steadily, swirling leaves and hissing through branches.

But then she heard it again. Yes, definitely, 'Brynn', in a faint whisper.

Her jaw quivered in shock. Hart!

Eerie, as if he had a sixth sense she was nearby.

Again, though the name was indistinct, lost in the sounds of the forest.

In her exhaustion and pain she almost thought the voice sounded like Graham's. But that was impossible, of course. Her husband was home asleep now.

Or perhaps *not* home, and asleep.

'Brynn . . .'

She touched her finger to her lips. Michelle nodded, reaching into her jacket for the knife.

The steps began again, very close, it seemed, and heading directly toward the fallen tree they hid beneath.

Times hide too . . .

Thinking of the men with their loud, loud guns, that memory came back to her again: Her first husband, eyes wide in shock and agony, stumbling back under the nearly point blank impact of the slug, as Brynn's service weapon, a revolver at the time, clattered to their kitchen floor.

Was there some sort of justice at work here, a divine or spiritual payback?

Would her fate now be similar to Keith's?

The footsteps grew closer.

Silently Brynn sprinkled more leaves over the threesome. And closed her eyes, thinking that when he was younger Joey believed that doing this would make you disappear.

'Brynn,' Graham called again, as loud as he dared, but still in a whisper.

Listening. Nothing.

As they'd approached this portion of the woods, the screaming had stopped. And they'd seen no one. But as they continued their trek, Graham was convinced he'd heard a woman's voice, whispering, and some rustling of foliage very close by. He couldn't tell where, though, and risked saying his wife's name.

No response but he heard more rustling and they'd headed for the sound, Munce with his shotgun ready.

'Brynn?'

Now the men were next to the trunk of a large fallen oak, looking around in all directions. Graham frowned and touched his ear. Munce shook his head.

But then the deputy stiffened, pointing to a field of rocks and brush. Graham caught a glimpse of a figure about a hundred yards away, holding a rifle or shotgun, moving from right to left.

The killers. They *were* here!

Graham pointed down at the deputy's radio, which was

off. But Munce shook his head and pointed again to his own ear, meaning presumably that to turn it on would result in a telltale crackle.

Munce hurried along a path Graham hadn't seen before. He realized the deputy was going to flank the man with the gun.

He thought: What the hell am I doing here?

And lost himself entirely in this insane pursuit.

The footsteps receded from the oak tree.

Finally Brynn lifted her head, gingerly, worried about the noise the leaves would make.

But when she peered over the tree trunk she saw the shadowy forms moving away into the early-morning murkiness.

The men had been just a few feet away from where they'd hidden. If Amy had made a single whimper all three of them would be dead now. Brynn's hands were shivering.

The men vanished into a wall of trees.

'Come on,' she whispered. 'They're headed away from us. Looks like they're going back down the hill. Let's move fast. We're not far from the highway.'

They rose, shedding leaves, and started uphill again.

'That was close,' Michelle said. 'Why'd they go on past?'

'Maybe heard something. A deer.' Brynn wondered if their guardian angel, their wolf, had distracted the men. She looked at Amy. 'I'm proud of you, honey. You stayed quiet real nice.'

The girl clutched Chester and said nothing, remained sullen and red-eyed. Her expression echoed exactly how Brynn felt.

They wound their way up several long slopes. Michelle gave

a smile and pointed to the horizon. Brynn saw another flash of headlights.

The glow of heaven.

She assessed the last obstacle: a tall rocky hill, to the right of which was a hundred-foot drop into the gorge. To the left was a dense thicket of brambles that extended some distance to more tall, rocky outcroppings.

They couldn't climb the hill itself; the face was a sheer ascent that rose forty or fifty feet above their heads. But on the left side of the rise, above the brush, a narrow ledge ran upward and appeared to lead directly to a field and, beyond that, the interstate. The ledge was steep but could be hiked. It was apparently a popular starting point for rock climbers; the stone face above it, like the ones she'd seen earlier, was peppered with metal spikes.

Brynn was wary of the ledge for two reasons. It would completely expose them to the men for the five or so minutes it would take to traverse. Also, it was very narrow – they'd have to go single file – and a fall, though not far, would land them in a tangle of bushes that included barberries. She remembered these from Graham's nursery. They were popular with customers, having striking berries and brilliant color in the autumn, but evolution had armed them with thin, brittle needles. After the winter's dieback these beds were now barren of foliage and the needles, along the entire lengths of the branches, were vicious spikes.

But, she decided, they'd have to chance it. There wasn't time to look for alternative routes.

Besides, she recalled, after coming so close to the oak tree where the women had been hiding, Hart and his partner had turned the other way, moving back down the hillside.

'Time to go home,' Brynn murmured and they began to climb.

Graham and Munce, moving cautiously, in silence, were getting close to where they'd seen the man with the shotgun disappear into the bushes.

Munce motioned for them to stop. The deputy cocked his head and scanned the landscape, the muzzle of the scattergun following the course of his gaze.

Graham wished he'd insisted on a weapon. The Buck knife in his pocket seemed pointless. He thought about asking for the deputy's pistol. But he didn't dare make a sound now. Ahead, no more than thirty feet, came a rustle of branches and dry leaves as the invisible suspect pushed through brush.

A snap of a footstep. Another.

Graham's heart pounded. He forced himself to breathe quietly. His jaw was trembling. Munce, on the other hand, looked completely in his element. Confident, making economical movements. Like he'd done this a thousand times. He crouched and pointed to the crook of a large rock, meaning, Graham understood, to wait. The landscaper nodded. The deputy touched his pistol once, as if to orient himself as to its exact location, and gripping the shotgun in both hands, moved forward slowly, keeping his head up, looking around but sensing leaves and branches and avoiding them perfectly.

More footfalls on the other side of the bushes. Graham looked closely but could see no one. The sound was clear, though: the man was stalking through the woods, pausing occasionally.

Munce moved toward the killer in complete silence.

He paused, about twenty feet from the line of brush, cocked his head, listening.

They heard the footsteps again on the far side of the foliage, the men not trying to be silent; they were ignorant that they were no longer hunters but were themselves prey.

Munce stepped forward silently.

It was then that the man with the shotgun stepped out from behind a tree, no more than six feet behind Munce, and shot him in the back.

The deputy gave a cry as he was blown forward onto his belly, the weapon flying from his hand.

Graham, eyes wide in horror, gasped. Jesus, oh . . . Jesus.

The attacker hadn't said a word. No warning, no instruction, no shout to give up.

He'd just appeared and pulled the trigger!

Eric Munce lay on his stomach, his lower back shredded and black with blood. His feet danced a bit, one arm moved. A hand clenched and unclenched.

'Hart, I got him,' the shooter called to someone else, whispering.

Another man came running up from behind the hedge, breathing hard, holding a pistol. He looked down at the deputy, who was barely conscious, rolled him over. Graham realized that this other one – Hart, apparently – had been in the bushes, making the noise of footsteps to distract Munce.

Horrified, Graham eased back into the crevice of basalt, as far as he could go. He was only twenty feet from them, hidden by saplings and a dozen brown husks of last year's ferns. He looked out through the plants.

'Shit, Hart, it's another cop.' Looking around. 'There's gotta be more of them.'

'You see anybody else?'

'No. But we can ask him. I aimed low. Coulda killed him. But I shot low to keep him alive.'

'That was good thinking, Comp.'

Hart knelt beside Munce. 'Where are the others?'

Graham pressed against the rock, hard, as if it could swallow him up. His hands shaking, he could barely control his breathing. He thought he might be sick.

'Where are the others? . . . What?' Hart lowered his head. 'I can't hear you. Talk louder, tell me and we'll get you help.'

'What'd he say, Hart?'

'He said there weren't any. He came by here on his own to look for some women escaped from two burglars.'

'He telling the truth?'

'I don't know. Wait . . . he's saying something else.' Hart listened and stood. In an unemotional voice he said, 'Just, we can go fuck ourselves.'

The one called Comp said to Munce, 'Well, sir, you're pretty much the one fucked here.'

Hart paused. He knelt again. Then stood. 'He's gone.'

Graham stared at the limp form of the deputy. He wanted to sob.

Then he saw, ten feet away, Munce's shotgun, lying where it had landed when the deputy had flown to the ground. It was half covered with leaves.

Graham thought: Please, don't look that way. Leave it. I want that gun. I want it so bad I can taste it. He realized how easily he could kill right now. Shoot them both in the back. Give them the same chance they'd given the deputy.

Please . . .

While the man who'd killed Munce stood guard, his gun ready, Hart searched him and pulled the radio off the deputy's belt. He clicked it on. Graham heard staticky transmissions. Hart said to Comp, 'There's a search party but everybody's over at Six Eighty-two and Lake Mondac itself . . . I think maybe this boy was telling the truth. He must've come over here on a hunch.' Hart shone a flashlight on the front of the deputy's uniform, read his nametag, then stood up and spoke into the radio. 'This's Eric. Over.'

A clattery response Graham couldn't hear.

'Bad reception here. Over.'

More static.

'Real bad. I can't find any trace of anybody over here. You copy? Over.'

'Say again, Eric. Where are you?' a voice asked, carrying through the air to Graham's ears.

'Repeat, bad reception. Nobody's here. Over.'

'Where are you?'

Hart shrugged. 'I'm north. No sign of anybody. How's it looking at the lake?'

'Nothing around the lake so far. We're still looking. Divers haven't found any bodies.'

'That's good. I'll let you know if I find anything. Out.'

'Out.'

Graham was staring at the shotgun, as if he could will it to become invisible.

Hart said, 'Why isn't anybody over here, except him, though? I don't get it.'

'They're not as smart as you, Hart. That's why.'

'We better get a move on. Take his Glock, his extra clips.'

Graham shrank back against the rock.

Leave the shotgun. Please, leave the shotgun.

Footsteps sounded on the crinkly leaves.

Were they coming his way? Graham couldn't tell.

Then the footsteps stopped. The men were very close.

Hart asked, 'You want the cop's scattergun?'

'Naw, not really. Don't need two.'

'Don't want anybody else finding it. You want to pitch it into the river?'

'Sure thing.'

No!

More footsteps. Then a grunt of somebody throwing a heavy object. 'There she goes.'

After a delay Graham heard a clatter.

The men resumed walking. They were closer yet to where Graham huddled between earth and stone. If they went to their left, around the boulder, they'd miss him. To the right they'd trip over him.

He unfolded his knife. It clicked open. Graham recalled that last time he'd used it was to cut a graft for a rose bush.

At the sound of the gunshot – it was close – Michelle had gasped and spun around, letting go of Amy's hand.

The girl, panicked again, hurried back down the ledge, whimpering.

'No!' Brynn called, 'Amy!' She eased past Michelle, staring at the thorny bushes below, and then trotted after Amy. The girl saw her coming, though, and just as Brynn approached, she dropped to the ledge, squirming away. 'No!' she squealed. She dropped Chester, who tumbled over the side. The tiny child lunged for the toy . . . and went over the edge herself, tumbling toward the barberries. Brynn's hand shot out and caught Amy by the sweatshirt. Luckily she was facing downward. Had she been upright the skinny girl would have slipped out of the garment and fallen into the mass of thorns.

The girl screamed in fear and pain and for the loss of her toy.

'Quiet, please!' Brynn cried.

Michelle ran back, reached down, grabbed the girl's leg, and together the women wrestled her onto the ledge.

The girl was going to scream again but Michelle leaned close and whispered something, stroking her head. Amy once again fell silent.

Brynn thought, Why can't I do that?

'I promised her we'd come back and get Chester,' Michelle whispered as they started moving up the ledge again.

'Goddamn it, if we get out of here, I will personally wade through those thorns and get him,' Brynn said. 'Thanks.'

They had another two hundred feet to go on before they reached the top.

Please, let there be a truck when we get there. I'll get 'em to stop if I have to strip naked to do it.

'What was that shooting?' Michelle asked. 'Who was—'

'Oh, no,' Brynn muttered, looking back.

Hart and his partner were breaking from the same bushes where Brynn had paused to consider whether to climb the ledge five minutes ago.

They paused. Hart looked up and his eyes met Brynn's. He grabbed his partner's arm and pointed directly at the women on the ledge.

The partner worked the shotgun, ejecting one spent shell and chambering a new one and both men began to sprint forward.

'Take your shot,' Hart called to Lewis.

They were both breathless, gasping. His heart was pounding too hard to use the pistol but his partner might be able with the shotgun to hit the one who was last going up the rocky ledge, Michelle.

Good.

Kill the bitch.

Lewis stopped, took a deep breath and fired a round.

It was close – Hart could see from the dust on the rock – but the pellets missed. And just then the trio vanished as they leapt off the ledge at the top into what seemed to be a field.

'They'll be making straight for the highway – through the clearing and into the woods. They've got the kid. We can beat them if we move.'

The men were winded. But Lewis nodded gamely and they started up the ledge.

Graham Boyd flinched as the gunshot sounded, no more than a quarter mile away.

He was in a precarious position, perched on the edge of a cliff of sandstone, the Snake River churning past nearly a hundred feet below. He was staring down and in the dim light he believed he could see the shotgun that Eric Munce's murderer had flung over the edge. It was about fifteen feet below him on a jutting rock.

Oh, did he want that gun!

The men had passed by him, on the other side of the rock, and vanished into the tangle of the woods. When he could no longer hear them, Graham had risen and, crouching, made his way to the edge of the gorge.

Could he make the climb down and retrieve the weapon?

Well, goddamn it, he was sure going to try. He was burning with fury. He'd never wanted anything more in his life than to get his hands on that gun.

He squinted and, studying the rock face, found what seemed to be enough hand- and footholds to climb down to a ledge and from there grab the shotgun.

Hurry. Get going.

Breathing hard, he turned his back to the gorge and eased over the side. He began feeling his way down. Five feet, eight. Then ten. He moved as fast as he dared. If he fell he'd bounce off the outcropping and tumble down the steep incline of the gorge walls – vertical in places – into the rocky water far below; streaks of white foam trailing downstream were evidence that boulders were plentiful.

Twelve feet.

He glanced down.

Yes, there was the shotgun. It was balanced unsteadily right on the edge of the outcropping. He felt a panicked urgency to grab the gun fast before a gust of wind tipped it over the side. He continued down, getting as close as he could. Finally he was level with the weapon, though it was still four or five feet to his right. Graham had thought there was some way to ease sideways toward it but what seemed like the shadows of footholds were just dark rock.

Inhaling hard, pressing his face against a cold, smooth muddy rock. Go for it, he told himself angrily. You've come this far.

Gripping a thin sapling growing from a crack in the cliff, he reached for the gun. He came within eight inches of the barrel – the black disk of the muzzle was pointed directly at him.

Below the water raged, growling and hissing.

Graham sighed in frustration. Just a few inches more. Now!

He slid his hand further along the sapling and swung out with his right again, more forcefully.

Two inches from the gun.

Extending his grip once more, he tried a third time.

Yes! He got his fingers around the barrel.

Now, just—

The sapling snapped under his weight and he slipped sideways a foot or so, held in place only by a strand of slick wood and bark. Crying out, Graham tried to keep a grip on the shotgun. But it slipped from his sweat-slick fingers and tumbled over the side, striking another outcropping ten feet below and cartwheeling into the river, eighty feet below.

'No!' Heartsick, he watched as the weapon vanished into the black water.

But he had no time to mourn its fate. The sapling gave way completely, and Graham grabbed the outcropping, though he was able to keep his grip for merely ten seconds before his fingers slipped and he began to fall, almost in the same trajectory as the shotgun he'd so dearly desired.

But they'd never make it to the highway in time, Brynn realized.

She gasped in dismay. Just as the shotgun fired they'd leapt off the rocky shelf and into the field. But she'd misjudged the distance to the trees. The strip of forest next to the interstate was an easy three hundred yards away. The ground was flat, filled with reed canary grass, heather and a few saplings and scorched trunks. She recalled that this had been the site of a forest fire a year ago.

It would take them ten minutes to cross and the men would be here in far less time than that; they were probably already on the ledge.

Brynn looked at Amy, her terrified face ruddy with tears and streaked with dirt.

What can we possibly do?

It was Michelle, leaning against the spear, gasping, who supplied the answer.

'No more running. It's time to fight.'

Brynn held her eye. 'We're way outgunned here.'

'I don't care.'

'It's a long shot, you know.'

'My life's been nothing but sure things. Treadmills and lunch at the Ritz and nail salons. I'm sick of it.'

They shared a smile. Then Brynn looked around and saw that they could turn to the right and climb up a steep incline to the top of the cliff, which was above the ledge the men were on now. 'Up there. Come on.'

Brynn led the way, then Amy, then Michelle. They looked down to see the men moving cautiously along the trail, a third of the way into it. Hart was in the lead.

They assessed their pathetic weapons: the spear and the knife. But Brynn wanted to keep those for the last minute. She pointed to the rocks littering the area: some were too big to budge, but others could, with some difficulty, be rolled or lifted. Also, there were plenty of logs and thick branches.

Brynn growled, 'Let's send 'em into the thorns.'

Michelle nodded.

Then Brynn had an idea. She took the compass bottle from her pocket. With the knife she cut off a long strip of cloth from her ski parka and tied it around the bottle. She gripped the candle lighter.

Michelle pointed out, 'It's just water.'

'They don't know that. As far as they know it's full of alcohol. It'll stop 'em long enough for us to get some rocks down on them.'

Brynn peered down. The men were almost directly below them. She whispered, 'You ready?'

'You bet I am,' Michelle said. She lit the strip – the nylon burned bright and sizzling.

Brynn leaned over the edge, judged the distance and let the bottle fall from her hand. It landed on the ledge about five feet in front of Hart and bounced but stayed put.

'What—?' Hart gasped.

'Shit, it's alcohol!' the partner cried. 'It's going to blow, get back.'

'Where are they?'

'Up there. Someplace.'

The shotgun fired and a few pellets struck the rock face near the women. Amy, huddled nearby, began to scream. But Brynn didn't care. Somehow screaming and howling seemed just right under the circumstances. They weren't a deputy and a dilettante actress. They were Queens of the Jungle. She actually shivered and felt an urge to give another of her wolf cries.

Together they rolled the biggest rock they could – it must've weighed forty or fifty pounds – toward the edge of the cliff. They muscled it up and Brynn rolled it into space. Then looked down.

The aim was perfect but fate intervened. The rock wall wasn't completely vertical; the missile hit a small outcropping and bounced outward, missing Hart's head by inches. The rock did, however, crack apart the formation it struck and showered the men with fragments. They backed up ten feet along the ledge. The partner fired again but the pellets hissed past the women and upward.

'We can't stop,' Brynn called, gasping in a whisper. 'Hit them with everything we can pick up.'

They pitched a log, two boulders and a dozen smaller rocks.

They heard a cry. 'Hart, my hand. Broke my fucking hand.'

Brynn risked a peek. The partner had dropped his shotgun into the brambles.

Yes!

Hart was gazing upward. He saw Brynn and fired two shots from his Glock. One spattered the cliff nearby but she dodged before the shrapnel hit her.

She heard Hart call, 'Comp, the fuse's out. Look. Get that rubble off the path. Kick it off.'

'Hell, Hart, they're going to break our skulls.'

'Go ahead. I'll cover you.'

Brynn was nodding at a log, about five feet long and a foot in diameter, with several sharp spiky limbs a few inches long. 'That.'

'Yes!' Michelle smiled. Together the women got onto their knees and pushed the trunk parallel to the cliff's edge. Gasping from the effort, they collapsed against it.

Brynn held up a finger. 'When I tell you to, throw a rock behind them.'

Michelle nodded.

Brynn grabbed the spear.

She thought of Joey. She thought of Graham.

For some reason her first husband's image made an appearance.

Then she nodded. Michelle pitched a rock down the ledge.

Brynn stood. She saw Hart looking behind him, toward the clatter of the rock and, giving an otherworldly howl, she flung the spear at the partner's back as he bent down to muscle debris off the ledge.

'Comp!' Hart cried, looking up at just that moment.

The man spun around and danced back from the spear, which missed him by inches, digging into the stone at his feet with a burst of sparks. He slipped and rolled off the ledge. All that kept him from falling was his left-handed grip on a crack in the rock. His feet dangled above the vicious thorns.

Hurrying to him, Hart glanced up and fired. But Brynn was out of his line of sight and helping Michelle push the deadly log closer to the edge.

Brynn took another fast look – Hart was bent over, his back to her, gripping his partner by the jacket and struggling to pull him up. They were thirty feet below, in a direct line, and the rock face here was smooth. The impact of the log would shatter bones if not kill outright. One of them at least would be knocked into the sea of thorns.

No hesitation now.

Brynn got a good grip on her side of the log and Michelle on hers. 'Go!' Brynn whispered.

The log was twelve inches from the edge of the cliff.

'More!'

Six inches.

Which was when a sharp crack sounded on the cliff face only feet below Brynn and Michelle, and a shower of dust and stone chips blew into the night. A moment later the distant boom of a rifle shot filled the air.

The women dropped to their stomachs. Brynn crawled to Amy and pulled the hysterical girl to the ground, cradling her.

Another shot. More rock exploded.

'Who?' Michelle gasped. 'That wasn't from them. There's somebody else out there! Shooting at us!'

Brynn stared into the distant woods.

A muzzle flash from a long way off. 'Get down!' She ducked and another high-velocity rifle round slammed into the log they'd been pushing forward.

Brynn risked a fast look downward. Hart had pulled his partner back onto the ledge but they too were crouching, not sure of what was going on. It seemed the shooter was focusing on the women but the men were probably wondering if they themselves were the targets. The two men, completely exposed, apparently decided to retreat back down the ledge.

Brynn said, 'They're leaving. Let's get out of here.'

'Who the hell is it?' Michelle muttered. 'We almost had them!'

'Come on. Hurry.'

They couldn't return to the clearing, where they'd be easy targets for whoever was shooting, so they crawled closer to the gorge, away from the sniper. They were soon safe on the other side of the hill, though nearby was a sheer drop into the gorge; Brynn eyed it warily and kept as far away as she could. She asked Amy, 'Honey, did Rudy and your mommy have other friends who stayed with you? Somebody who wasn't at the camper tonight?'

'Sometimes.'

That was probably it; a partner of Gandy and Rudy who'd seen the carnage at the meth lab and had somehow trailed them here.

The silence was interrupted by the beckoning sound of a big tractor-trailer downshifting as it came to the bridge. Brynn looked along the edge of the gorge. They could walk that way to the interstate under pretty good cover.

The sky was now growing lighter – dawn couldn't be too far off – and they could easily pick their way through the paths toward the highway. Brynn hugged Michelle. 'We almost had 'em.'

Not smiling, Michelle said, 'Next time.'

Brynn hesitated. 'Well, let's hope there isn't one.'

Though it seemed from her fierce expression that the young woman wasn't hoping for that at all.

'Another cop?' Lewis asked, referring to the shooter.

He was flexing his hand. It wasn't broken but the rock had jammed his thumb. The man was mostly upset he'd lost his shotgun in the bramble patch. And his anger at the women had grown exponentially.

As they hunkered down behind a boulder at the foot of the ledge, Hart listened to the dead deputy's radio. Routine transmissions about search parties. Nobody had even heard the shots. Nothing about any other cops in the area.

'More meth people, I'll bet. On the way to the camper.' Hart turned on his GPS. He had to tame his anger. They were so close to their prey. But they couldn't go after them; the ledge was the only way and they'd be sitting ducks.

'We'll go around to the left, through the woods. It's longer but we'll have good cover right to the highway.'

'What time is it?' Lewis asked.

'What does it matter?'

'I just want to know how long we've been doing this shit.'

'Way too long,' Hart said.

James Jasons, holding the Bushmaster .223 rifle, looked at the rock face he'd just been firing at. He'd done the best he could, considering there was virtually no light and he was more than two hundred yards away from the target.

He waited, scanning the area with his night-vision binoculars but saw no signs of the men or the women. There would have been quite a story about how the cave-man confrontation – the two men dodging rocks and logs – had come about.

For ten minutes he scanned the field and forest around him. Where were they?

The men had fled back down the rocky ledge. Since they had apparently lost their car they'd be making for the interstate – to flag down a ride. But there were a lot of different routes they could take to get to the highway from the ledge. The odds were that they'd be coming in this general direction. It was wildly overgrown but possibly Jasons could find them. On the other hand, they might have gone around to the far side of the hill, after the women. It seemed like a much steeper climb and would have to be made without cover but, who knew? Maybe the men were pissed off about the attack and hell-bent on getting their prey.

Still, Jasons didn't want to do anything too quickly. He looked over the brush, scanning with the night-vision binoculars. Much of the vegetation moved but that seemed due to the breeze, not escaping humans.

He saw movement not far away. He blinked and gave a gasp as he focused his binoculars. He was looking at a wild animal of some kind, a coyote or wolf.

The night-vision system gave it a ghostly green-gray color. Its face was lean and the teeth white and perfect, visible through the slightly bared lips and jowls. He was glad the creature was some distance yards away. It was magnificent but fierce.

The animal lifted its head, sniffed, and in an instant was gone.

I'm a long, long way from home, James Jasons thought. He'd tell Robert an edited version of the story, in which the animal, though not the gunfire, would figure.

He continued to scan the nearby field and forest, but saw no sign of Emma Feldman's killers. They could easily have been here but it was impossible to tell with the dense vegetation.

And what about Graham and the deputy?

The gunshot he'd heard before the killers arrived at the rock ledge hinted at their fate. It was a shame but you can't get in over your head. Just can't do it.

Jasons waited another ten minutes and decided it was time to get back to the interstate. He slung the canvas bag over his shoulder and without disassembling the rifle melted into the forest.

They continued along the ridge of the gorge and toward the highway, the Snake River pounding over rocks far below.

Brynn didn't dare look to her right, where ten feet away the world ended, a sheer cliff. She held Amy's hand, and stared directly ahead at the path in front of them.

She paused once, looking back. Michelle was hobbling along well enough, though clearly exhausted. The little girl appeared almost catatonic.

The time was still very early and, from what they could hear, there wasn't much traffic on the road yet. But an occasional semi or sedan would cruise by. All they needed was one.

The bridge suddenly loomed ahead and to the right. They plunged into a band of trees and emerged into a strip of grass about thirty feet wide. Beyond that were the shoulder of the interstate and the beautiful strips of graying asphalt.

No cars or trucks in sight just yet and they'd come too far to make mistakes now.

They remained in the tall grass, like timid hitchhikers. Brynn found herself weaving a bit; this was about the first smooth, level ground she'd been on in close to nine or so hours and her inner ear's gyroscope was having trouble navigating.

Then she laughed, looking down the highway.

A car was heading around a curve toward them. It was a Kennesha County Sheriff's Department car, its lights flashing, moving slow. A driver had heard the shots and called 9-1-1 or the State Police's #77.

Brynn raised a hand to the car, thinking: she'd have to call in immediately about the shooter at the ledge.

The car slowed and swerved onto the shoulder and then eased to a stop between her and the highway.

The doors opened.

Hart climbed out of the driver's side, his partner from the other.

'No!' Michelle gasped.

Brynn exhaled a disgusted sigh. She glanced at the car. It was Eric Munce's. Her eyes went wide.

'Yeah, he didn't make it,' said the partner, the man she'd come close to shooting back in the Feldmans' dining room. 'Fell for the oldest trick in the book.'

She briefly closed her eyes in horror. Munce . . . the cowboy had come out to save her. And charged to his own death, outmatched.

Hart said nothing. He held his black pistol and gazed at the captives.

The partner continued. 'And how are you, *Michelle*?' Emphasizing the name. He pulled a woman's purse out of his pocket. Stuffed it back. 'Nice to make your acquaintance.'

The woman said nothing, just put her arms around the little girl protectively, pulled her close.

'You ladies have a nice stroll through the woods tonight? Good conversation? You stop for a tea party?'

Hart focused on Brynn. He nodded. She easily held his eye. He lowered the gun as a sedan on the far side of the divider cruised past. It didn't even slow. In the pale dawn light it might have been hard to see the drama unfolding in the grass on the other side of the road. Soon the car was gone and the highway was empty.

'Comp?' Hart asked, his eye on Brynn.

The skinny man glanced over, kneading his earlobe. 'Yeah?'

'Stay right in front of them.'

'Here?'

'Yeah.'

'You bet,' the partner, 'Comp' apparently, said. 'You want me to cover 'em?' He started to reach for the silver automatic pistol in his jacket.

'No, that's okay.' Hart stepped directly in front of the man, facing him.

Comp gave an uncertain smile. 'What is it, Hart?'

Only a moment's hesitation. Then Hart lifted the gun to his face.

Smiling uncertainly, Comp touched the blue-and-red tattoo of a cross on his neck, then kneaded an ear lobe. He shook his head. 'Hey, what're you—?'

Hart shot him twice in the head. The man collapsed on his back, left knee up.

Amy screamed. Brynn could only stare as Hart turned and, keeping his gun on the women and girl, stepped backwards to his partner's body.

Michelle's eyes went cold.

Hart bent down, and pulled Comp's SIG-Sauer 9mm from his waistband and wrapped the dead man's limp fingers around it.

So this was to be the scenario, Brynn understood. With the dead hand around the Sig, he'd shoot the women, leaving telltale gunshot residue on the partner's skin. He'd then stand over Brynn's body to do the same, putting a second gun in her hand – Munce's Glock, probably – and fire a couple of rounds into the trees.

The police would reason that the partner had killed the three of them and Brynn got off two final shots to take him out before she died.

And Hart would disappear forever.

A curious feeling, having only minutes to live. Her life wasn't replaying itself. But she was thinking of regrets. She gazed at the woods, the smooth edge of trees and brush severed by the shoulder and highway, tamed. She nearly expected their wolf friend to stick its head out and look their way before vanishing into the woods again.

Then Hart was twisting the dead partner's arm up and to the left, aiming at Brynn first with the SIG-Sauer.

Michelle pulled Amy even closer in front of her, and was reaching into her leather jacket, perhaps for their last Chicago Cutlery knife. She was going to fling it at Hart, it seemed.

A final, desperate gesture. And futile, of course.

Joey, Brynn thought, I—

Then came the shout, startling them all.

'Don't move! Drop it!'

Breathless and limping, Graham Boyd pushed from the woods behind Hart, holding a small revolver.

'Graham,' Brynn cried in astonishment. 'My God.'

'Drop it. Now! Put it down.' Her husband's clothes were streaked with mud – and blood too, she could now see – and torn in several places. His face was bruised and filthy too and through the mask his eyes shone with pure anger. She'd never seen him like this.

Hart hesitated. Graham fired a round into the dirt at his feet. The killer flinched, sighed. He set the gun on the ground.

Brynn recognized the pistol; it was Eric Munce's backup, which he kept strapped to his ankle. She remembered mentioning to Graham that he kept a second gun there. There were mysteries here but Brynn didn't waste time speculating about how her husband and Munce had come to be at the

Snake River Gorge. She stepped forward, took the pistol from her husband, verified that it was loaded still and motioned Hart out of the grass and onto the shoulder, where he'd be more visible. And a better target.

Control . . .

'Kneel down. Hands on the top of your head. If a hand comes off your head, you'll die.'

'Of course, Brynn.' Hart complied.

More vehicles were hissing past now, drivers off late shifts or hurrying to early ones. If anyone inside the cars or trucks saw the drama unfolding on the shoulder nobody was stopping

'Graham, get his Glock and the other gun.' Indicating the ostentatious silver SIG-Sauer that Comp had been carrying. 'There's one weapon unaccounted for. Eric's. Search him.' Keith had taught her always to count weapons at scenes.

Graham did and found the deputy's service Glock. He put Hart's black gun and Comp's silver one on the grass beside Brynn.

But he kept Munce's pistol. He looked at it closely. Then her husband fired a shot into the ground, presumably to make sure it was loaded and cocked.

Graham turned the square automatic on Hart, who gazed past the muzzle, his gray eyes calm. There are no safeties as such on Glocks. You just point and shoot. Graham knew this; Brynn had instructed him and Joey about how to load and fire hers. Just in case.

'Graham!'

He ignored his wife. In a low, threatening tone he asked Hart, 'Who'd I talk to when I called? The dead one or you?'

'It was me,' Hart said.

'Graham,' she whispered. 'Everything's going to be fine now. Help me, honey. I need some plastic hand restraints. Look in the glove compartment.'

Her husband continued to stare into Hart's eyes. The gun pointed unwaveringly at his head. The trigger poundage was very light. A twitch was enough to release a round.

'Graham? Honey? . . . Please.' There was desperation in her voice. If he fired it would be murder. 'Please.'

The big man took a deep breath. He lowered the gun. Finally he said, 'Where? The restraints?'

'Graham, please, give me the gun.'

'Where are they?' he snapped angrily. He kept the pistol. Brynn noticed Hart smiling at her.

She ignored it and answered her husband, 'The glove compartment.'

He stepped to the car. 'I don't see any.'

'Try the trunk. They'll be in a plastic bag. Maybe a box. But first, call it in. The radio's on the dash. Just push the button, say who you are, say ten-thirteen and then give the location. The engine doesn't have to be on.'

Staring at Hart, Graham picked up the microphone and made the call. Frantic responses came from a half-dozen deputies and troopers but, bless him, he said only what was necessary: location and the situation. He dropped the mike on the seat and popped the trunk.

Hart kept his eyes on Michelle, who stared back with pure hatred. He smiled. 'You came close, Michelle. Real close.'

She said nothing. Then he turned to Brynn and, in a voice that only she could hear, asked, 'At the camper back there, after you crashed the van?' He nodded at the vastness they'd just come through. 'When I was out of it, just lying there. You saw me, didn't you?'

'Yes.'

'My piece was nearby. Did you see that too?'

'Yes.'

'Why didn't you go for it?'

'The little girl was going to fall. I went after her instead.'

'One of those hard choices.' He nodded 'They do present themselves at the worst possible times, don't they?'

'If they didn't,' Brynn replied, 'they wouldn't be hard choices then, would they?'

He gave a faint laugh at this. 'Well, say the girl hadn't been there. Would you have taken my piece and killed me? Shot me while I was out?' He cocked his head and said softly, 'Tell the truth . . . No lies between us, Brynn. No lies. Would you have killed me?'

She hesitated.

'You thought about it, didn't you?' He smiled.

'I thought about it.'

'You should have. You should've killed me. I would've, it'd been you. And you and me . . . we're peas in a pod.'

Brynn glanced at Graham, who couldn't hear the exchange.

'There have to be a few differences between us, Hart.'

'But that's not one of 'em . . . You're saying you would just've arrested me?'

'You forget. I already had.'

Another smile, both his mouth and his gray eyes.

A truck roared past. An occasional car.

Then Graham called, 'I've got them.'

Which was all Hart needed. As Brynn glanced up he sprang to his feet. He wasn't close enough to get to her – Brynn had made sure of that. But that wasn't his intent. He jumped over the body of his partner and sprinted the twenty feet to the highway. Brynn's shot missed him by an inch. She couldn't fire again because of the oncoming cars. Not even looking, Hart sprinted into traffic, an act of pure faith. He could have been killed instantly.

He made it to the center lane, froze, then leapt aside as the driver of a Toyota SUV swerved in panic. The vehicle rolled onto its left side and, in a shower of sparks and a hideous screech, skidded along the shoulder and right lane, missing the women and the child by feet. They dove to the ground, pure instinct.

The SUV jettisoned bits of plastic and glass and metal and finally came to a rest, the horn wailing and airbag dust rising from the empty window frames.

A dozen other cars and trucks skidded to a stop. And before Brynn could draw another target on Hart, he'd run into the left lane, leapt over the hood of a stopped sedan, dragged out the driver – a man in a suit – and climbed in. He sped onto the median and accelerated past the stopped cars then into the lane again. Brynn aimed Munce's revolver but had only a brief clear target – between two good Samaritans climbing out of their vehicles – and she wouldn't risk injuring them.

She lowered the gun and ran to the Highlander to help the occupants.

A witness to the carnage, James Jasons crouched in fragrant bushes a hundred yards down the highway from where the SUV lay on its side.

Sirens sounded in the distance.

He believed he saw Graham Boyd helping some of the injured. The absence of the uniformed deputy, Munce, might explain the gunshot he'd heard earlier from deep within the forest.

The sirens grew closer as he dismantled his gun and put it in the canvas bag. The traffic on this side of the highway was at a standstill. On the other side the cars and trucks were still moving but slowly, as voyeurs strained to see what had happened.

As if there was an explanation for these bizarre events.

One of the killers lay dead – his body now covered by a tarp – and the other had escaped, but there seemed to be no other serious injuries.

Jasons had been partially successful. There was nothing to do but leave.

With his cap low over his eyes he walked through the stopped line of traffic and onto the median. It took a bit more dancing but the gawkers let him through three lanes without his even having to run. Though once on the other side he moved quickly into the woods to make sure none of the law enforcers noticed him. He sprinted to his Lexus.

Jasons started it up and eased out onto the shoulder then accelerated to the speed of traffic – it was only about thirty miles an hour – and merged. He pulled the satellite phone from the bag, which was now on the seat next to him, and scrolled through speed dial. He went past his partner's name, and then his mother's and pushed the third button on the list.

Even though it was very early in the morning, Stanley Mankewitz answered on the second ring.

'No ID.'

Brynn glanced up from the back step of the ambulance, where she sat next to Graham.

Tom Dahl was referring to Comp, the man shot and killed by Hart. His partner. Of all the horrors that night perhaps the worst was the look of betrayal in the young man's face just before Hart pulled the trigger.

'We got money, a couple boxes of ammo, cigarettes, gloves, Seiko watch. That's it.' They'd recovered Michelle's purse too, which might contain the men's fingerprints. Dahl would send officers to find Comp's shotgun in the brambles and Eric Munce's, which Graham explained was in the river.

Brynn's husband had told the story of how he'd tried to retrieve it but had fallen in the process. He'd landed on a shelf of rock, bruised and scraped but otherwise unhurt. He'd then climbed up the cliff face and was walking back past Eric Munce's body when he recalled that the man was wearing an ankle holster with a backup revolver in it. He'd taken the gun and hurried toward where he'd heard the gunshot.

'What was his name?' the sheriff asked, looking at the man's body, covered by a green tarp and lying nearby.

'Comp,' Brynn said. 'Something like that.'

A medical technician had daubed Brynn's cheek with brown Betadine and Lanocaine and was now easing a bulky bandage onto it. He was going to stitch it. She said no. A needle and thread would make a bigger scar and the thought of two facial deformities was too much for her.

He put a tight butterfly bandage on and told her to see a doctor later that day. 'Dentist too. That busted tooth'll start to bother your tongue pretty soon.'

Start to?

She told him she would.

Brynn was staring at Comp's body. She simply couldn't understand why Hart had killed him. This was the man Hart had risked his own life to save just a half hour earlier on the ledge – nearly getting crushed by a log, in fact, to pull the man to safety.

And Hart had told him to stand still, then shot him – casual as could be.

Brynn saw the circus of flashing lights. Heard the voices shouting, the crackle of radios.

In addition to Dahl, there were other deputies from the Kennesha County Sheriff's Department and a baker's dozen of state troopers. Two FBI agents too, who'd tossed off their suit jackets, were helping out however they could, including stringing crime scene tape. No egos were present. They'd show up later.

Head down, Michelle sat on the grass, her back against a tree, cradling sleeping Amy, both wrapped in blankets. The medics had looked them both over and neither was badly injured. Michelle's ankle turned out to be just a pulled muscle.

Somber, Michelle clutched the girl tightly, and Brynn supposed she was mourning for them both – two people who had lost someone close to them so violently on this terrible night, people who had left an innocence behind, dead or dying, in the tangled woods.

Brynn rose from the ambulance and stiffly walked over the grass to Michelle. 'Did you get through to them?' Brynn asked. Michelle was going to call her brother and his wife, who lived north of Chicago, to come pick her up.

'They're on their way.' Then her voice faded and she gave a stoic smile. 'Never got a message from my husband.'

'Did you call him?'

She shook her head. And her body language said she wanted to be alone. She brushed Amy's hair gently. The child was snoring softly.

Brynn tested her wounded face, wincing from the pain, despite the topical anesthetic cream, then joined Dahl and the FBI agents. She fought through her fuzzy mind – once the pursuit had stopped, disorientation had flooded into the vacuum with a smack – and gave them a synopsis of everything that had happened from her arrival at Lake Mondac, the escape, the portable meth lab, the surprise gunshots fired at them when they were on the rock ledge.

'One of Rudy Hamilton's people?' an FBI agent said, hearing Brynn's opinion as to the identity of the sniper by the ledge. 'I don't know.' He seemed doubtful.

'Rudy said somebody named Fletcher might be in the area.'

The agent nodded. 'Kevin Fletcher, sure. Meth and crack bigwig. But no evidence he operates around here. He sticks close to Green Bay. Makes ten times as much up there. No, I'm still betting the shooter was some muscle Mankewitz sent.'

'Drove down here to protect his hit men?'

'I'm guessing,' the other said.

Of course they were eager to pin anything on Mankewitz, short of the Kennedy assassination. Still, Brynn didn't disagree;

it would make sense. And the shooter *had* saved Hart and Comp from crushed skulls or a fall into the barbed wire thorns.

'You get a look at him?'

'Nope. Don't even know where he was.'

The agent looked out over the woods. 'That's not going to be an easy crime scene.'

And then they all grew silent as a recovery team carried Eric Munce's body from the woods. The bag was dark green. The men started to set it near the body of the other killer, but hesitated and, out of respect, set it farther away, on the grass, not the shoulder.

'I've seen those bags a dozen times,' Brynn said softly to Dahl. 'But never with one of ours inside.'

The driver of the SUV and his girlfriend were sitting dazed on the ground near the ambulance. Their seat belts had kept them from any damage but bruising. The man who'd been pulled from his car by Hart was uninjured but his fear or ego kept prompting him to mutter about lawsuits until somebody suggested he could sell his story to *People* or *Us*. It was meant sarcastically to shut him up. But he seemed to like the idea. And he did shut up.

Brynn walked up to her husband and he put his arm around her. She asked Dahl, 'Eric's wife?'

A sigh. 'I'm going by there now. In person, no calls.'

Graham looked at the body bag containing the deputy. 'Well,' he said, as if it hurt to take enough breath to speak. Brynn rested her head against his shoulder. She was still astonished that he'd driven all this way to try to find her. Dahl wasn't happy that he and Munce had tried an end run, particularly as it had resulted in the deputy's death. Still, if they hadn't, Brynn, Michelle and Amy would be dead now. And they wouldn't have stopped at least one of the killers and collected good evidence that might lead to Hart and ultimately the man who had hired them.

Deputies Pete Gibbs and big Howie Prescott, breathing hard, came out of the forest with several state troopers. They were carrying clear plastic bags. Inside were shell casings and an empty ammunition clip.

They placed Comp's personal effects into another bag. Michelle's purse and Hart's map went into others.

Brynn looked over the evidence, thinking: Hart, who the hell are you? 'Tom, did CS do a prelim dusting at the Lake Mondac house?'

'Sure. Found about five hundred prints. Mostly the Feldmans'. None of the others set off alarms. The stolen Ford had about sixty and they were negative too. Those boys wore gloves the whole time. Smarter'n our criminals 'round here.'

'What about the spent brass and shells?'

'Found a ton of it. Yours, theirs. Went over the whole place with a metal detector. Even fished some out of that creek beside the garage. But no prints on a single shell.'

'None?' Brynn asked, dismayed. 'They wore gloves loading their weapons?'

'Looks like it.'

Yep, smarter than our criminals . . .

Then she jabbed a finger at one of the evidence bags from this scene. 'Tom, this's our chance. Maybe there're no prints on the brass – Hart'd expect to leave that. But he's taken the weapon apart to clean and load it. There's a print on one of those clips, I guarantee it. And the map. And they were carting around Michelle's purse. They must've opened it. I'm taking the evidence up there myself – to the lab in Gardener.'

'You?' Dahl scoffed. 'Don't be nuts, Brynn. The state folk can handle that. Get some rest.'

'I'll get some sleep in the car on the way home. Grab a shower and head over there.'

Dahl nodded at the troopers. 'Half these boys're stationed in Gardener. They'll drop everything off at the lab.'

She whispered, 'And everything'll sit gathering dust for two weeks. I *want* him, Tom.' A nod up the highway, where, peering over the ribbed pistol barrel, she'd last seen Hart in the 'jacked car speeding away. 'I'm going to stand over the tech like a school teacher till I get some names from AIFIS. I want that man bad.'

Dahl looked at her grim, determined expression. 'All right.'

Brynn locked the bags in the glove compartment of Graham's truck, which he'd collected a quarter mile down the road. She noticed ripe green azaleas in the back bed. They were just starting to bud. Pink and white.

She leaned her head against her husband's shoulder again. 'Oh, honey. What a night.' He looked up. 'You came. You came to find me.'

'I did, yes.' He gave her a distracted smile. He was clearly shaken – who wouldn't be? – having seen and experienced what he had tonight.

'Let's get home. I called Anna but they'll want to see you. Joey didn't take this whole thing too well.' He was going to say something else, she sensed. But didn't.

Then another State Police car pulled up and a trooper and a short woman in a suit, Latina, climbed out. She was from Child Protective Services.

Brynn joined them, introduced herself and explained what had happened. The trooper, who was solid, square-jawed and looked like an ex-soldier, registered some shock at the news. The social worker, her face calm and observant, apparently had heard it all before. She nodded matter of factly and jotted some notes. 'My office has lined up an emergency foster couple. They're good people. I know them well. We'll stop by the doctor, get her checked out and I'll take her over there now.'

Brynn whispered, 'Can you imagine? Meth cookers for parents. *And* they had her helping them? And look at her neck.' She'd noticed sausage red marks from where her mother or

Gandy – or maybe that disgusting Rudy – had grabbed Amy by her throat, a threat or punishment. They didn't seem serious but Brynn still shivered with anger. And for a troubling moment felt a dark satisfaction that Hart had killed them.

They joined Michelle, whose face was as pale as the cloudy dawn sky overhead. She was clutching Amy possessively. The girl was now awake.

The social worker nodded at Michelle and then crouched down. 'Hi, Amy. I'm Consuela. You can call me Connie, if you want.'

The girl blinked.

'We're going to take you for a ride to see some nice people.'

'Where's Mommy?'

'These are some very nice people. You'll like them.'

'I don't like Mommy's friends.'

'No, they're not friends of hers.'

'Where's Chester?'

'We'll get Chester for you,' Brynn said. 'That's a promise.'

The social worker put her arm around Amy and helped her to her feet, then wrapped the blanket tighter around the girl. 'Let's go for a ride.'

The girl gazed absently at Michelle and nodded.

The young woman watched her go with such a look of affection that one might have thought she was the girl's mother.

There was silence for a moment.

'I know all you've been through. But I have something else to ask.'

Michelle glanced at her.

'It'll be a couple of hours before your brother gets here?'

'I guess.'

'I know this is hard. I know you don't want to. But will you come back to my house for a little while? We're not too far away. I can get you a change of clothes, something to eat and drink.'

'Brynn,' Graham said. He was shaking his head. 'No.'

She glanced his way but continued speaking to the young woman. 'I need you to tell me everything you can remember about Hart. Anything he mentioned or any mannerisms. Or anything Emma might've said about the case. While it's fresh in your mind.'

'Absolutely.'

'She needs rest,' Graham said, nodding at Michelle.

'She has to wait somewhere.'

'No, it's okay, really,' Michelle said to Graham. 'I don't want him to hurt anybody else. I'm not sure what I can do. But I'll help.' Her voice was firm.

The medical examiner's van headed off, the two bodies in the back. Brynn noted that it was her husband who seemed the most upset of any of them as they watched the departure of the boxy vehicle, sickly yellow-green. The sky was now light, the color of diluted egg yolk, and the traffic was thicker, easing through the one open lane, gawkers taking in the overturned SUV, the dark puddles on the highway.

Brynn explained to Tom Dahl about interviewing Michelle. 'She can wait at my house until her brother arrives. Anna'll look after her while I'm at the state lab.'

The sheriff nodded. Then said, 'And we'll need to talk to you, Graham, about what happened with Eric. Can you come down to the station?'

Graham looked at his watch. 'I should get Joey to his English tutor.'

Brynn said, 'He can stay home today. We'll both be too busy.'

'I think he should go.'

'Not today,' Brynn said.

Graham shrugged then turned to the sheriff and said that he'd call the station and arrange a time.

Dahl then extended his hand to her. She blinked at the

solemn gesture. She took it awkwardly. 'I owe you more than a half day, Brynn. A lot more.'

'Sure.' She took Michelle's arm and they followed Graham to his truck.

'Mom. Like, where were you? Shit. What happened to your face?'

'Just an accident. Watch your language.'

'My God!' Anna cried.

'It's all right.'

'It's not all right. It's all black and blue. And yellow. And I can't even see what's under the bandage.'

Brynn recalled that she'd have to make an appointment for a new molar. She touched the gap with her tongue. The pain had vanished. Her mouth just felt weird.

'What happened, Mom?' Joey was wide-eyed.

'I fell.' Brynn hugged her son. 'Tripped. You know how clumsy I am.'

Her mother eyed the bandage and said no more.

Michelle walked into the living room. The tape on her ankle – and the painkillers – had done the trick. She was no longer limping.

'Mom, this is Michelle,' Brynn said.

'Hello, dear.'

The young woman nodded politely.

'Joey, you go upstairs. I'll call your tutor. Graham and I'll be busy today. You're staying home.'

Graham said, 'Really. I can drop him off.'

'Please, honey, it'll be better.'

'You two are a mess,' Anna announced. 'What happened?'

Brynn glanced at the TV, off at the moment. Her mother would find out soon enough but she was glad the local news wasn't on. 'I'll tell you in a bit. Joey, you've had breakfast?'

'Yeah.'

'Upstairs. Work on your history project.'

'All right.'

The boy trooped off, with a glance back at Michelle. Graham went into the kitchen.

In her deputy voice, her calm voice, Brynn said, 'Mom, Michelle's friends were killed. That was the case I was on tonight.'

'Oh, no.' Shocked, Anna stepped close and took Michelle's hand. 'I'm so sorry, dear.'

'Thank you.'

'Her brother's on his way. She'll be here for a little while until he gets here.'

'You come over here and sit down.' Anna indicated the green couch in the family room, where Graham and Brynn sat together in the evenings if TV was on the agenda. It rested perpendicular to Anna's rocker.

Michelle said, 'I'd really like to take a shower, if I could.'

'Of course. There's a bathroom down that hall. There.' Brynn pointed. 'I'll bring you some clothes. Unless you'd rather not.' Thinking of the woman's earlier aversion to wearing Emma Feldman's boots.

Michelle was smiling. 'I'd love some. Thanks. Anything you've got.'

'I'll hang them on the door.' Brynn, thinking that at last she'd have a use for her skinny-girl jeans, which she hadn't worn in two years but hadn't quite been able to throw out.

Anna said, 'There're bath towels in the closet. I've got coffee. Do you want tea? I'll make you some food.'

'If it's not too much trouble.'

Brynn noted that the woman's last complaint about her blood sugar had been eons ago.

Anna led her to the bathroom and returned.

'I'll give you the details later, Mom. They tried to kill her too. She saw the bodies.'

'No!' Anna's hand went to her mouth. 'No . . . What's the poor thing going to do? Should I call Reverend Jack? He could be here in ten minutes.'

'Let's ask her. Might be a good idea. But I don't know. She's had so much coming at her. And one of our deputies was killed.'

'No! Who?'

'Eric.'

'That cute boy? With the brunette wife?'

Brynn sighed. She nodded. Reflecting: With the brunette wife and a young baby.

'Did you get shot?' Anna asked abruptly.

'Collateral injury. Like a ricochet.'

'But you were shot?'

She nodded.

'What on earth happened?'

Brynn's calm broke, like pond ice cracking. 'Some really bad things, Mom.'

Anna hugged her, and Brynn felt the woman's body, hung on frail bones, shaking, as was her own. 'I'm sorry, honey. I'm sorry. But everything's going to be fine now.' Her mother stepped away, turning quickly, wiping her eyes. 'I'll get breakfast going. And you too. You need something.'

A smile. 'Thanks, Mom.' Brynn was desperately hungry.

As Anna stepped into the kitchen, Brynn called, 'Where's Graham?'

'Was here. I don't know. Out back, I guess.'

Water began to flow in the front bathroom. The pipes squealed.

Brynn went upstairs to get some clothes for Michelle. In the bedroom she looked at her matted hair, the cuts and bruises, the white bandage with its aureole of yellow and purple.

She replayed Comp's horrific death: the look on his face as he gazed at Hart, revealing pure betrayal.

Then the image of Hart's face looking back at her as he sped away in the stolen sedan, the image frozen over the bead sight of the pistol she held firmly.

You should've killed me . . .

She wanted a shower badly but she'd get clothes for Michelle first. She'd interview the young woman, then call Tom Dahl and the State Police and FBI with any new information about Emma Feldman or Hart or his partner that Michelle could recall – something that might lead to Mankewitz. Then she'd speed up to Gardener and bully the evidence through the crime lab.

Brynn found a T-shirt, sweats, the jeans, socks and a pair of running shoes. She'd get a garbage bag for Michelle to put her dirty clothes in. She supposed the designer items would have to be dry cleaned. She whiffed, smelled her own sweat, powerful. Smelled rusty blood too, mixed with the perfume of antiseptic.

In the kitchen the tea kettle started whistling, then stopped.

Listening to the whining pipes in the first-floor bathroom, Brynn rested her forehead against the cool glass of the window, looking out at Graham's truck. She was thinking of the evidence in the glove compartment, wondering how long it would take to get answers from the State Police lab in Gardener. Fingerprints could be done quickly now thanks to the FBI's integrated identification system. Ballistics would take longer but Wisconsin had a good database that might be able to trace one of the slugs in Hart's or Comp's pistols to prior crimes. Which might in turn lead to a full identification . . . or at least to somebody who could be pressured to dime Hart out.

Not a single print on the brass . . . She sighed, shaking her head.

A thought occurred to her. Brynn sat down on the edge of the bed, absently poked her tummy, as she often did, and called Tom Dahl.

'How you doing?' he asked. 'Exhausted, betcha.'

'Not yet. Waiting for it to hit. Got a question.'

'Sure thing.'

'About the scene at Lake Mondac.'

'Go ahead.'

'You said Arlen's Crime Scene folks searched the house with a metal detector and all they recovered was brass, right?'

'Yep. Fancy thing. Not like what the tourists use looking for arrowheads.'

'And no firearms?'

'Just brass and spent shells.'

'You said they searched the streams?'

'Yep. Found some brass there too. It was everywhere. Place was a turkey shoot.'

As I well know. 'Now, Michelle said she picked up one of their guns. She shot Hart with it. And then the tires. She used up all the ammo and threw it in the stream.'

'Wonder why nobody found it. Maybe it was one of those other creeks.'

'I'd love to get my hands on it . . . And I don't like the idea of unaccounted-for firearms. Anybody over at the house still?'

'Pete Gibbs's there. And Arlen has a couple of his boys. Might be somebody from Crime Scene too.'

'Thanks, Tom.'

'Wish you'd get some rest.'

'All in good time.'

She hung up and pulled on sweats, then called Gibbs at the Feldman house.

'Pete. It's me.'

'Oh, hey, Brynn. How you doing?'

'Ugh.'

'I hear that.'

She asked if any Crime Scene people were still there.

'Yep. A couple of 'em.'

'Do me a favor. See if anybody's recovered any pistols.'

'Sure, hold on.'

After a moment he came back on the line and reported that all they'd found were a few more shell casings that'd been missed last night. No weapons.

She sighed again. 'Thanks. How you doing?' He sounded shaken. She assumed it was Munce's death, but there was another source.

'Kind of an unpleasant thing happened,' he said ruefully. 'I had to break the news to one of the Feldmans' friends. She hadn't heard. Man, I hate doing that. She broke down. Went totally bonkers.'

'A friend?'

'Yeah. Took her nearly a hour to calm down. Though she was one lucky lady, I'll tell you. She was supposed to come up last night but something happened at work. She couldn't get on the road till this morning. Imagine if that hadn't happened.'

'Where'd she drive up from?'

'Chicago.'

'You get her number?'

'No. Didn't think to. Should I have?'

'I'll call you back.'

Brynn sat back on the bed, considering this.

A *second* houseguest was coming to visit last night? Another woman, and also from Chicago?

Wasn't impossible. But why didn't Michelle mention her? And why wouldn't the two women drive up here together?

An absurd thought began unraveling . . .

Embarrassingly absurd.

Yet Brynn couldn't quite dismiss it. All right, she'd been assuming all night that Michelle was the Feldmans' house-guest. But, when she considered the question now, she realized that she had no evidence that she actually was.

What if she wasn't a friend of theirs at all?

Absurd . . .

But the idea wouldn't fade. Brynn considered: What if Michelle was a stranger who wanted to *pretend* she knew them? Which she could do pretty easily – considering that *I* gave her all the information she'd need to play the role. 'Are you their friend from Chicago?'

And I asked her, 'What's your name?' Which told her I didn't know anything about her. And: 'Did you practice law with Emma?'

But, no, this was crazy. What would her motive be for lying?

Brynn gasped as another thought occurred to her, answering that question with horrifying clarity. On the interstate – at the Snake River Bridge – she'd recovered handguns from the men: Hart's Glock and Comp's SIG-Sauer. With the weapon that Michelle claimed to have found that meant the two men had brought *three* semiauto pistols and a shotgun.

Even for professional hitmen that seemed excessive.

And why had Crime Scene found all that brass with the metal detector but not the missing pistol?

My Lord, what if the gun wasn't Hart's or Comp's, but Michelle's?

But why would she bring a gun with her?

One answer: because *she* had been hired by Stanley Mankewitz to kill Emma Feldman and had brought along Hart and Comp, intending to kill them at the scene.

And leave their bodies behind, the fall guys.

Then Brynn recalled Michelle reaching into her jacket at

the interstate. She wasn't reaching for the knife; she was going for the gun she'd been carrying with her all night.

Which meant she still had it.

On the first floor the pipes stopped squealing as Michelle shut off the water.

With a grimace toward the empty gun lock-box, Brynn ran into the hallway and stepped into Joey's room and took him by the shoulders.

'Mom, what's wrong?' His eyes were wide.

'Listen to me, honey. We have a problem. You know how I tell you never to lock your door?'

'Uh-huh.'

'Well, today's different. I want you to lock your door and not open it for any reason. Unless it's Graham or me.'

'Mom, you look funny. I'm scared.'

'It'll be okay. Just do what I tell you.'

'Sure. What—'

'Just do it.'

Brynn closed the door. She ran down the stairs as quietly as she could, intending to get to the only guns nearby: the ones in Graham's truck, sealed in evidence bags.

On the second-to-the-bottom step Brynn stopped. The bathroom door was open. Steam roiled out. No sign of Michelle.

Go for the truck or not?

'Tea'll be ready in just a moment,' Anna called.

Brynn stepped into the ground floor hall.

Just as Michelle walked through an archway four feet away. In her hand was a small black automatic pistol. It was known as a baby Glock.

Their eyes met.

As the killer spun toward her, Brynn snagged a picture off the wall, a large family photo and flung it at her. It missed but as she dodged, Brynn launched herself forward. The women collided hard, both grunting. Brynn fiercely gripped Michelle's right wrist, digging her short nails into the woman's skin as hard as she could.

Michelle cried out, striking Brynn's head with her free hand.

The gun discharged once, then, as Michelle lowered it toward the deputy's body, it fired three times more. All the slugs missed.

Anna screamed and called for Graham.

Brynn slammed a fist into Michelle's face. She blinked in pain and spit flew. Eyebrows narrowed, her mouth a taut grimace, Michelle kicked Brynn's groin and elbowed her in the belly. But Brynn wasn't letting go of the gun, nothing could make her do that. The anger of the terrible evening, fueled by this betrayal – and her own gullibility – burned within her. She flailed and kicked and growled her wolf's growl.

The women grappled, knocking over furniture. Michelle fought furiously – no longer the helpless dilettante in the thousand dollar boots. She was crazed, fighting for survival.

The gun fired again. Then several times more. Brynn was counting the rounds. Baby Glocks held ten bullets.

Another sharp crack – and the weapon was empty, the slide locking back automatically, awaiting a fresh clip of ammunition. The women went down on the floor, Brynn pounding the woman's head, aiming for her throat. Michelle fought back just as fiercely, though – muscles toned at a health club, if that story was true, and backed by pure desperation.

Still, there was no doubt in Brynn's mind that she was

going to stop this woman, kill her if she had to, no doubt whatsoever. Using hands and teeth and feet . . . She was pure rage, pure animal.

You should've killed me . . .

Well, this time I won't make the same mistake.

Her fingers found Michelle's throat.

'Jesus, Brynn!' A man ran through the door and for a tiny portion of a second Brynn thought it was Hart. But by the time she realized it was her husband the distraction had had its effect. Michelle broke free and slammed the gun into Brynn's wounded cheek. The pain was so intense her vision clouded and she retched.

Michelle hit the lock on the gun and the receiver snapped shut. Though the gun was empty it appeared loaded and ready to fire. She aimed at Graham. 'Keys. To your truck.'

'What are you—? What?'

'Emmy, Emmy,' Brynn muttered, clutching her face, clawing futilely at Michelle.

'I'll kill her.' Shoving the gun into Brynn's neck. 'The fucking keys!'

'No, no! Here, take them. Please! Just leave!'

'Emmy!'

Michelle grabbed the keys. And ran outside.

Graham dropped to his knees, pulling his cell phone out, and dialed 9-1-1. He cradled Brynn, who pulled away and climbed to her feet. She started to black out, swayed against the stair rail. 'Emmy . . .'

'Who's Emmy?'

She forced herself to speak clearly through the pain. 'Empty. The gun was empty.'

'Shit.' Graham ran to the door as his truck skidded down the street and vanished.

Brynn rose, then heard a soft voice from nearby: 'Could somebody—'

Both Brynn and Graham turned toward the kitchen door, where Anna stood, her hands covered with blood.

'Please, could somebody . . . Look. Look at this.'

And she spiraled to the floor.

Rows of orange plastic chairs, in the corner of the brightly lit room. Walls and tiles scuffed.

Graham sat across from Brynn, knees close but not touching. Their eyes were focused mostly on the linoleum and they looked up only from time to time when the double doors swung open. But the doctors and employees pushing through them were on missions unrelated to Anna McKenzie's life.

Twining her fingers together, Brynn stared at her untouched coffee.

Sick with horror, sick with exhaustion.

Her phone quivered. She looked at the screen and muted the ringer, because she didn't want to take the call, not because of the *No Cell Phone Use* sign nearby.

A patient walked from the admitting window into the waiting area, sat down. Squeezed his arm and winced. He glanced once at Brynn and returned to his waiting state of numb silence.

'Been an hour,' Graham said.

'Nearly.'

'Long time. But that's not necessarily bad.'

'No.'

Silence again, broken by cryptic announcements over the hospital PA. Then Brynn's phone was vibrating again. This call she took. 'Tom.'

'Brynn, how's your mother?'

'We don't know yet. What do you have?'

'Okay. Michelle got through the roadblocks somehow. They haven't found your husband's truck.'

Brynn hunched forward and pressed her injured cheek, as if the pain were payment for her misjudgment.

Dahl continued, 'You were right. We found that friend who drove up from Chicago this morning. She was the only one coming to visit. Michelle, we guess, is a hit man . . . Well, hit *woman*.'

'Hired by Mankewitz or one of his people.'

'What they're figuring,' Dahl said.

'So Hart and Comp were supposed to be the bodies left behind.'

'The what?'

'The bodies left behind . . . She was going to make it look like they were the only killers and they got into a fight between themselves after the Feldmans were dead. So we wouldn't bother to look further. But it went bad. Hart reacted too fast or her gun jammed, who knows? She had to run. Then I found her in the woods.' Brynn pinched the bridge of her nose. Her laugh was bitter. 'And rescued her.'

Another doctor came out, through the double doors. Brynn stopped talking. The physician, wearing blue scrubs, kept going.

Brynn was reflecting on the look that passed between Hart and the young woman at the interstate.

You came close, Michelle. Real close . . .

Hart's words to her by the highway had a whole different meaning, now that Brynn knew the truth.

And she recalled Michelle's shocked reaction when Brynn

told her about meeting Hart in the van beside the meth cookers' camper. The woman would have been terrified that Hart had mentioned Michelle's real identity.

'And somebody from Mankewitz's crew was probably going to come pick her up when it was over. Hell, that's who was taking shots at us when we were on that cliff.'

Brynn was aware that Graham was staring at her, taking in the conversation.

She continued to the sheriff, 'She needed the evidence I'd brought with me – the guns and clips, the map, the boxes of ammunition. Her purse. That's why she was so willing to come back with us to our house. Something probably had her prints on them. Or trace evidence that might lead us to her. She'd planned to collect it at Lake Mondac after she'd killed Hart and his friend . . . Wait, Tom. What about her shoes? A pair of women's shoes at the Feldmans' house? In the yard. Any prints?'

'Recovered them. But no prints.'

'None?'

'Looks like they were wiped off, like the Ford. Wiped off with Windex.'

A faint laugh. 'She did that when I went for the canoe . . . Brother, did she have me fooled.' Brynn rubbed a knuckle against a faint bump on her rebuilt jaw, as she often did when thoughtful or upset. The betrayal stung her deeply. And she said in a soft voice, 'I was supposed to be one too.'

'What?'

'A body left behind. She was using me as bait. She didn't have a sprained ankle at all. She was moving slow to draw the men close. And she tried to keep them following in our direction all night. She broke the Mercedes window to set off the alarm – probably as the men were heading toward the highway. And complained about putting on those boots, made a big deal of it. She was stalling, trying to get them closer to us.

And who knows what else? She had some crackers. I'll bet she dropped those.' Brynn laughed sourly, shaking her head. 'Once, she had this outburst, screamed like a banshee. It was to let them know where we were. She was waiting for them to catch up. Then she'd shoot them in the woods. Me too.'

'Well, Brynn, why didn't she, you know, just shoot you right up front?' Dahl asked.

'She needed me for insurance maybe, or to help her get out of the area . . . Most likely use me to help her kill them.'

Aware that Graham had fallen silent, his jaw set, large hands clasped together.

Brynn told Tom she'd better go and asked him to call her if they found anything at all.

They disconnected and she turned to her husband to give him a summary of what had happened. He closed his eyes and rocked back. 'That's okay,' he said, cutting her off. 'I got enough.'

She touched his leg. He didn't respond. After a few minutes, she lifted her fingers away and called the neighbor where Joey was staying. She talked to her son for some moments, telling him the truth – that they didn't know anything yet about his grandmother. She let him ramble on about a video game he'd been playing. Brynn told him she loved him and hung up.

Husband and wife sat in silence. Brynn looked at her husband once then shifted her gaze down at the floor. Finally, after an eternity, he rested his hand on her knee. They remained that way, motionless, for some minutes – until a doctor came out of the double doors. He looked at the man with the hurt arm and then walked directly toward Brynn and Graham.

Terry Hart got rid of the car he'd hijacked on the interstate.

He did this as efficiently as he knew how: He parked it in the Avenues West area of Milwaukee with the doors locked but the keys in the ignition. Some kids wouldn't notice and some would notice but think it was a sting and some – in the quickly redeveloping area – would notice but would do the right thing and pass the car by.

The car, however, would still be gone within one hour. And harvested for parts in twelve.

Head down, exhausted and in agony from the gunshot and the other trauma of the night, Hart walked quickly away from the vehicle. It was a cool morning, the sky clear. The smell of fires from construction site scrap teased his nose. His instincts were still running the show and were directing him underground as fast as possible.

Walking along the sparsely populated streets he found the Brewline Hotel, though it was nowhere near the Brewline. It was the sort of place that thrived on business by the hour or by the week but rarely by the day. He paid for one week in advance with a bonus for a private bath, and was given a remote control and a set of sheets. The overweight woman clerk took no notice of his physical condition or absence of luggage. He trooped up the two flights of stairs and into room 238. He locked the door, stripped and dumped his fetid clothes into a pile that reminded him very much of Brynn McKenzie's soaked uniform at the second house on Lake View Drive.

He pictured her stripping.

The image aroused him for a few minutes until the throbbing from his arm tipped him out of the mood.

He examined the wound closely. Hart had taken paramedic training courses – because his job often involved physical injuries. He now assessed the wound and concluded that he didn't need a doctor. He knew several medicos who'd lost their tickets and would stitch him up, no questions asked or gunshots reported, for a thousand bucks. But the bleeding had stopped, the bone was intact and, though his bruise was impressive, the infection was minor. He'd start on antibiotics later today.

Hart showered under a stuttering stream of water, doing his best to keep his arm dry.

He returned to the bed, naked, and lay down. He wanted to consider the evening, to try to make sense of it. He thought back several weeks to a Starbucks in Kenosha, where he was meeting with a guy he'd worked with a few times in Wisconsin. Gordon Potts was a big hulking man, not brilliant but decent and someone you could trust. And he could hook you up with dependable labor when you needed it. Potts had said he'd been approached by a woman in Milwaukee who was smart, tough and pretty. He vouched for her. (Hart now realized that Michelle had bought the credentials with a blow job or two.)

Hart was interested. He was between jobs and bored. There was a deal going down in Chicago but that wasn't until mid-May. He wanted something now, needed some action, adrenaline. The same way that the tweaker Hart had killed in the state park last night needed to slam meth.

Besides, the job was a lark, Potts told him.

A few days later Potts had hooked him up with 'Brenda' – the fake name Michelle had offered – in a coffee shop in the Broadway District of Green Bay. She'd shake his hand firmly then said, 'So, Hart. How you doing?'

'Good. You?'

'I'm okay. Listen, I'm interested in hiring somebody. You interested in some work?'

'I don't know. Maybe. So how do you know Gordon Potts? You go back a long ways?'

'Not so long.'

'How'd you meet him?'

'A mutual friend.'

'Who'd that be?'

'Freddy Lancaster.'

'Freddy, sure. How's his wife doing?'

Michelle had laughed. 'That'd be tough to find out, Hart. She died two years ago.'

And Hart had laughed too. 'Oh, that's right. Bad memory. How does Freddy like St Paul?'

'St Paul? He lives in Milwaukee.'

'This memory of mine.'

The Dance . . . .

After his first meeting with Brenda-Michelle, Hart had made phone calls to both Gordon Potts and Freddy Lancaster to verify times, dates and places down to the tenth decimal. A dozen other calls too. Brenda Jennings was a petty thief with no history of informing on her partners – and was also, Hart now knew, an identity that Michelle had stolen.

So he arranged another meeting to discuss the job itself.

Michelle had explained she'd heard that Steven Feldman had been making inquiries about swapping old bills, silver certificates, for newer Federal Reserve notes. She'd looked into the situation and learned about some meat-packing executive who'd hidden cash in his summer home in the 1950s. A million bucks. She gave Hart the details.

'That's a lot of money.'

'Yeah, it is, Hart. So you're interested?'

'Keep going.'

'Here's a map of the area. That's a private road. Lake View Drive. And there? That's a state park, all of it. Hardly any people around. Here's a diagram of the house.'

'Okay . . . This a dirt road or paved?'

'Dirt . . . Hart, they tell me you're good. Are you good? I hear you're a craftsman. That's what they say.'

As he'd studied the map he'd asked absently, 'Who's they?'

'People.'

'Well, yeah, I'm a craftsman.'

Hart had been aware of her studying him closely. He looked back into her eyes. She said, 'Can I ask you a question?'

A lifted eyebrow. 'Yeah.'

'I'm curious. Why're you in this line of work?'

'It suits me.'

Hart was somebody who didn't believe in psychoanalysis or spending too much time contemplating your soul. He believed you felt in harmony or you didn't and if you bucked that feeling you were making a big mistake.

'God, doesn't the boredom just kill them? It would me. I need more, Brynn. Don't you?'

Michelle had nodded, as if she understood exactly what he meant and had been hoping for just that answer. She said, 'It looks like it does.'

He got tired of talking about himself. 'Okay. What's the threat situation?'

'The what?'

'How risky's the job going to be? How many people up there, weapons, police nearby? It's a lake house – are the other houses on Lake View occupied?'

'It'll be a piece of cake, Hart. Hardly any risk at all. The other places'll be vacant. And only the two of them up there, the Feldmans. And no rangers in the park or cops around for miles.'

'They have weapons?'

'Are you kidding? They're city people. She's a lawyer, he's a social worker.'

'Just the Feldmans, nobody else? It'll make a big difference.'

'That's my information. And it's solid. Just the two of them.'

'And nobody gets hurt?'

'Absolutely not,' she had said. 'I wouldn't do this if there was a chance anybody'd get hurt.' Brenda-Michelle had smiled reassuringly.

Lots of money, nobody hurt. Sounded good. Still, he'd said, 'I'll get back to you.'

Hart had driven home and researched what she'd told him. Sitting at his computer, he'd laughed out loud. Sure enough, it was all true. And he was confident that no cops in the world would come up with a sting like this. They offered drugs, perped merchandise, funny-money, but they didn't suggest a caper out of a Nicholas Cage movie.

Then came the big day. They'd driven up to Lake Mondac in the stolen Ford together. He, Compton Lewis and Michelle. The two men had broken in and, while they held the Feldmans at gunpoint, Michelle was supposed to come into the kitchen, tape their hands and start interrogating them about the money.

Instead of the duct tape, though, she was carrying a 9mm subcompact 'baby' Glock. She'd walked past Hart and simply shot the couple point blank.

In the ringing silence that followed she turned around and walked into the living room like nothing had happened.

Hart had stared at her, trying to figure it out.

'The fuck did you do?' gasped Lewis, who'd been poking around in the fridge for food, rather than where he should've been – watching the front of the house.

'Don't worry. I know what I'm doing.' She'd started going through the briefcase and backpack.

The men had been staring in shock at the bodies, while – they'd assumed – she'd was looking for a key to a secret room or lock-box or something. Hart himself had been frantically tallying up the offenses they'd just bought into. Felony murder being number one.

Then he saw her reflection: She was coming up behind him, lifting the gun.

He leapt sideways, instinctively.

Crack . . .

The tug on his arm.

Then returning fire as she escaped.

Lying in the spongy bed now, Hart knew exactly what had happened. There was no hidden treasure. Michelle had been hired to kill the Feldmans – Brynn had hinted at this as they'd sat in the van beside the meth cookers' camper.

Her plan was to leave Hart and Lewis in the Feldman's house, the fall guys.

And Hart couldn't help but laugh now. He'd hired Compton Lewis for exactly the same reason Michelle had hired Hart: an insurance policy, a fall guy. In case the robbery went bad and people ended up dead, Hart had been going to kill Lewis and set him up to look like the sole perp. That was why he'd gotten a loser he'd had no previous connection with. That scenario had nearly played out on the interstate. With Michelle, Brynn and the little girl together – and Hart had the squad car to escape by – it was time to conclude the evening. He killed Lewis and was about to kill the others with the SIG when who shows up but Brynn's husband?

I was thinking with my contacts, guys in my crew, and your, you know, the way you plan things and think, we'd be a good team.

Oh, you sad bastard, Hart thought. You really did believe that, didn't you? And here you were, fifty percent dead from the first time we sat down together, you tugging your green earring and scoffing about why were we in a faggot place like this that only sold coffee and not a real bar?

With sleep closing in, he pictured Michelle. Of all the people he'd worked with and for – dangerous Jamaican drug lords, South Side gangstas and OC bosses throughout the Midwest – that the petite, young redhead woman was the most deadly.

The cloak of sweet, the cloak of helpless, the cloak of harmless – hiding a scorpion.

He speculated about the two women together last night. What on earth had they talked about? Brynn McKenzie was not a woman easily fooled, and yet Michelle had been the consummate actress. He thought of those surreal moments in the van with Brynn.

So, Michelle was a friend of the family? Is that how she got mixed up in this whole thing? Wrong time and wrong place, you might say. A lot of that going around tonight . . .

The Trickster.

In the Feldmans' house he'd glanced quickly at a credit card in her purse and gotten her name. Michelle S. Kepler, he believed. Maybe Michelle A. There'd probably been a driver's license but he hadn't bothered to look for it then. He'd have to find her – before the police did, of course. She'd give him up in a minute. Oh, he had some work to do in the next few days.

But then, like Compton Lewis, Michelle faded from his

thoughts and he fell asleep with only one image in his mind: the calm, confident eyes of Deputy Brynn McKenzie, sitting beside him in the front seat of the van.

You have the right to remain silent . . .

They returned from the hospital at eight p.m.

Brynn and Graham picked up Joey from the neighbor's house and they drove home. Brynn got out of the car first and went up to the deputy, Jimmy Barnes, the one whose birthday was today. The balding, ruddy-faced man was parked on the shoulder in front of their house, all grim and quiet – the way everybody was in the Kennesha County Sheriff's Department, because of Munce.

In fact, the way a lot of people throughout the town of Humboldt were.

'Nobody's come by, Brynn.' He waved to Graham. 'Made the rounds a few times.'

'Thanks.'

She suspected that Michelle, whoever she was, would be long gone but the woman seemed frighteningly obsessed.

And, she reflected, Hart too knew her last name.

'Crime Scene's got what they need. I locked up after.'

'They say anything?'

'Nope. You know the state boys.'

It'd be against the laws of nature for the brass and the slugs from Lake Mondac not to match those collected in her house.

Barnes asked, 'Wasn't her friends? She was making all that up?'

'That's right.'

'And your mom. Heard she'll be okay?'

'She'll live.'

'Where'd she get hit?'

'The leg. Hospital another day or two. Therapy.'

'Sorry about that.'

Brynn shrugged. 'Lot of people don't make it 'round to see therapy.'

'Lucky.'

If your daughter bringing an armed killer into your house is luck, then I guess.

'Night now. Somebody'll make the rounds off and on.'

'Thanks, Jimmy. I'll see you tomorrow.'

'You'll be in?'

'Yep. You have a package for me?'

'Oh, yeah.' Barnes reached into the back and handed her a paper bag. She looked inside at a well-worn department Glock and two extra clips, along with a box of Winchester 9mm hollow points.

He then lifted a clipboard. She signed for the weapon.

'You got a clip loaded. Thirteen. None in the bedroom.'

'Thanks.'

'Get some rest, Brynn.'

'Night. Oh, and happy birthday.'

As he drove off she checked the clip anyway and chambered a round.

The family walked inside the house.

Upstairs she put the gun in the lock-box and returned to the kitchen.

Joey had eaten pizza at the neighbors. He walked around, staring at the bullet holes in the walls until Brynn told him not to.

Brynn took a long shower, the water hot as she could stand, and tied her hair back after towel-drying it. Didn't want the noise of the drier. She changed the bandage on her face, threw on sweats and went downstairs, where Graham was heating up spaghetti from last night. She wasn't hungry but felt she'd abused her system enough in the past twenty-four hours and was expecting it to go on strike if she didn't start to pamper soon.

They went into the dining room and ate for a while in silence. She sat back, looked at the label on her beer. She wondered what exactly hops were.

Then she asked Graham, 'What is it?'

'Hmm?'

'There was something you wanted to say at the hospital.'

'Don't remember.'

'You sure? I think you might.'

'Maybe something. But not now. It's late.'

'I think now is good.' She was chiding but serious too.

Joey came downstairs and was channel surfing in the family room, sitting on the green couch while he flipped through a schoolbook.

Graham stuck his head in the door. 'Joey, go upstairs. No TV.'

'Just ten min—'

Brynn started to speak. Graham continued into the family room. He said something that Brynn couldn't hear.

The TV shut off and she caught a glimpse of her sullen son climbing the stairs.

What was that about?

Her husband sat down at the table.

'Come on, Graham.' They rarely used each other's names. 'What is it? Tell me?'

Her husband sat forward, and she saw he was lost in debate.

'Do you know how Joey hurt himself yesterday?'

'The skateboard? At school?'

'It wasn't at school. And it wasn't just three steps in the parking lot. He was 'phalting. You know what that is?'

'I know 'phalting. Sure. But Joey wouldn't do that.'

'Why? Why do you say that? You don't have any idea.'

She blinked.

'He *was* 'phalting. He was doing close to forty or fifty on the back of a truck down Elden Street.'

'The highway?'

'Yes. And he'd been doing it all day.'

'Impossible.'

'Why do you say that? A teacher saw him. His section teacher called, Mr Raditzky. Joey skipped school. And he forged your name to a note.'

With yesterday's horror less immediate, this news was numbing, if not shocking. 'Forged?'

'Went in in the morning. Left and never came back.'

She sat back, eyes straying to the ceiling. A black dot of bullet hole was in the corner. Small as a fly. The slug had come all the way through here. 'No . . . I had no idea. I'll talk to him.'

'I tried. He wouldn't listen.'

'He gets that way.'

In a harsh voice Graham said, 'But he *can't* get that way. That's not an excuse. He kept lying to me and I told him no skateboarding until he tells the truth.'

'Are you sure—' Her initial reaction was to defend her son, to question Mr Raditzky's credibility, to ask who the witness was, to cross examine. She fell silent.

Graham was tense, shoulders forward.

More was coming.

But, fair enough. She'd asked for this.

'And the fight, Brynn. Last year? You told me it was a pushing match. Mr Raditzky seems to think that Joey beat him up.'

'He was a bully. He—'

'—was just taunting Joey. Talking to him is all. And Joey hurt him bad. We almost got sued. You never told me that.'

She fell silent. Then said, 'I didn't want word to get around. I pulled some strings. It wasn't all on the up-and-up. But I had to do it. I wanted to protect him.'

'He's not going to break, Brynn. You spoil him. His bedroom looks like a Best Buy.'

'I pay for everything I bought him myself.' She instantly regretted the barbed words, seeing the grimace on Graham's face. What he was saying to her now had nothing to do with money, of course.

Her husband continued, 'It's not good for him. All the indulgence. You don't have to be cruel . . . but you have to say no sometimes. And punish him if he doesn't listen to you.'

'I do.'

'No, you don't. You're a great cop, Brynn. But you're afraid of your own son. It's like you owe him, like you're guilty about something and paying back this debt. What's it all about, Brynn?'

'You're making it into something more than it is. Way more.' She gave a faint laugh, though she felt her heart chill – the way her skin had when the cold, black water rushed into her car at Lake Mondac. 'His fight at school . . . it was just something between Joey and me.'

'Oh, Brynn, that's the problem. See? That's what this is all about. It's *never* been "us". It's always you and Joey. I'm along for the ride.'

'That's not true.'

'Isn't it? What's this all about?' He waved his hand around the house. 'Is it about us, the three of us, a family? Or is it about you? You and your son?'

'It's about us, Graham, really.' She tried holding his eye but couldn't.

No lies between us, Brynn . . .

But that was Hart. And it was Keith . . . Graham was different. This is so wrong, she thought, being honest with bad men, while the good ones get lied to and neglected.

He stretched. She noticed that both their beers were exactly half full. He said, 'Forget it. Let's go to bed. We need sleep.'

She asked, 'When?'

'When what?'

'Are you leaving?'

'Brynn. This is enough for tonight.' A laugh. 'We *never* talk, not about anything serious. And now we can't stop. Tonight of all nights. We're exhausted. Let's just get some rest.'

'When?' she repeated.

He rubbed his eyes, first one, then both. He lowered his hands, looked at a deep scratch, inflicted at some point last night in the woods. A tear in the skin from a thorn or rock. He seemed surprised. He said, 'I don't know. A month. A week. I don't know.'

She sighed. 'I've seen it coming.'

He looked perplexed. 'Seen it coming? How? *I* didn't know it till tonight.'

What did he mean by that? She asked, 'Who is she?'

'"She"?'

'You know who. That woman you're seeing.'

'I'm not seeing anybody.' He sounded put off, as if she'd delivered a cheap insult.

She debated but kept to the course. She said harshly, 'JJ's poker games. Sometimes you go. Sometimes you don't.'

'You've been spying on me.'

'You lied to me. I could tell. I do this for a living, remember.'

He's no good at deception.

Unlike me.

Anger now. But more troubling, he sounded disgusted. 'What'd you do? Put a bug in the car? Have somebody from the department tail me?'

'I saw you once. By coincidence. Outside the motel on Albemarle. And, yeah, I followed you later. You said you were going to the game. But went there again . . .' She snapped, 'Why are you laughing? It broke my heart, Graham!'

'To break somebody's heart, you need to own a bit of it. And I don't. I don't have an ounce of yours. I don't think I ever did.'

'That's not true! There's no excuse for cheating.'

He was nodding slowly. 'Cheating, ah . . . Did you ask me about it? Did you sit down and say, "Honey, we have a problem, I'm concerned, let's talk about it? Get it worked out"?'

'I—'

'You know your mother told me about what Keith did. About your face. You know my first reaction? Oh, my God, that explains so much. How could I be mad at you? But then I realized that, hell, yes, I could be mad. I *should* be mad. And you should have told me. I deserved to be told.'

Brynn had considered telling him a hundred times. Yet she'd made up a bullshit story about a car crash. She thought now: But how could I tell him? That somebody flew into a rage and hit me? That I cried off and on for months afterward. That I cringed at the sound of his voice. That I broke into a hundred pieces like a child. I was ashamed that I didn't leave him, just bundle Joey up and walk out the door.

That I was afraid. That I was weak.

And that my delaying would have even more horrific consequences.

Keith . . .

But even now she couldn't tell him exactly what had happened.

And here, she understood, was a clue to the crime she'd committed against Graham, against the two of them: her silence, this inability to talk. Yet she felt that whatever the clue led to, even if she managed to figure it out, the solution would come too late. It was like finding conclusive evidence as to a killer's identity, only to discover that the perp had already died of natural causes.

'I'm sorry,' she said. 'But you still . . . ' Her voice faded as she watched him pulling his wallet from his slacks, fishing in it. She watched, obsessively touching the bandage on her cheek.

Jesus. Was it his lover's picture? she wondered.

He handed her a small white card.

Brynn squinted; the cheek wound made reading difficult out of her right, her stronger, eye.

She stared at the raised type: *Sandra Weinstein, M.D., LLC. 2942 Albemarle Avenue, Ste. 302, Humboldt, Wisconsin.* Hand-written at the bottom was: *Friday 7:30, April 17.* Brynn began, 'She's a . . .'

'Therapist. Psychiatrist . . . Shrink.'

'You—'

'You saw us *near* the motel,' Brynn, but not *at* the motel. She's in the professional building next door. I'm usually her last patient at night. Sometimes we leave the office at the same time. That's probably when you saw us.'

Brynn flicked the card.

'Call her. Go see her. I'll give her permission to tell you all about it. Please, go talk to her. Help me figure out why you love the job more than me. Why you'd rather be in your squad car than at home. Help me figure out how to be a father to a son you won't let me near. Why you got married to me in the first place. Maybe you two can figure it out. I sure can't.'

Brynn offered lamely, 'But why didn't you tell me? Ask me to go with you? To counseling? I would have!' She meant this.

He lowered his head. And she realized she'd touched a painful spot – like her tongue probing the gum where her tooth had once been.

'I should have. Sandra keeps suggesting it. I almost asked you a dozen times. I couldn't.'

'But why?'

'Afraid of what you'd do. Give up on us, think I was being too demanding, walk out the door. Or take control and I'd get lost in the shuffle . . . Make it seem like there was no problem at all.' He shrugged. 'I should have asked you. I couldn't. But look, Brynn, the time for that has passed. You're you, I'm me. Apples and oranges. We're so different. It's best for both of us.'

'But it's not too late. Don't judge by last night. This was . . . this was a nightmare.'

Then, astonishing her, he snapped. He shoved the chair back and leapt to his feet. The beer bottle fell, spewing foam over the plates. The easy-going man was now enraged. Brynn froze inside, replaying those nights with Keith. Her hand rose to her jaw. She knew that Graham wouldn't hurt her. Still, she couldn't help the defensive gesture. She blinked up at him and saw the wolf hovering nearby in the state park.

Yet, she realized the rage wasn't at her. It was, she believed, directed purely at himself. 'But I *have* to judge by tonight. That's what did it, Brynn. Tonight . . .'

What he'd said before. He wasn't planning on leaving until tonight. What did he mean? 'I don't understand.'

He inhaled deeply. 'Eric.'

'Eric Munce?'

'He's dead because of me.'

'You? No, no, we all knew he was reckless. Whatever happened didn't have anything to do with you.'

'Yes, it did! It had everything to do with me.'

'What're you talking about?'

'I used him!' His own jaw, square and perfect, was trembling. 'I know you all thought he was a cowboy. Last night nobody was going to look for you at the interstate. But I knew you'd go that way. So I told Eric if he wanted to see some action he ought to come with me. That's where the killers were headed.' Graham shook his head. 'I threw that out like it was a hunting dog's favorite treat . . . And he's dead because of me. Because I went someplace I had no business going. And I have to live with that forever.'

She leaned forward. He recoiled from her hand. She sat back and asked, 'Why, Graham? Why did you come, then?'

He gave a cold laugh. 'Oh, Brynn. I plant trees and flowers for a living. You carry a gun and do high-speed chases. I want to watch TV at night; you want to study the latest drug-testing kits. I can't compete with your life. I sure can't in Joey's eyes . . . Last night I don't know what the hell I was thinking. Maybe that there was some gunfighter deep inside me. I could prove myself. But that was a joke. All I did was get another human being killed . . . No goddamn business going out there. And I have no business here. You don't want me, Brynn. You sure don't need me.'

'No, honey, no . . .'

'Yes,' he whispered. Then held up a hand. The gesture meant: enough, no more.

He gripped her arm and squeezed softly. 'Let's get some sleep.'

As Graham went upstairs Brynn absently daubed at the spilled beer until the paper napkins disintegrated. She got a dishtowel and finished the job. With another, she tried to stanch the tears.

She heard his footsteps coming downstairs again. He was carrying a pillow and blanket. Without a glance her way, he walked to the green couch, made up a bed and closed the family room door.

'All done, ma'am.'

Brynn looked over at the painter, who was gesturing toward the living room and its repaired ceiling and walls.

'What do I owe you?' She peered around the house as if a checkbook floated nearby.

'Sam'll send you a bill. You're good for it. We trust you.' He gestured at her uniform. Smiled then stopped. 'The funeral's tomorrow? Deputy Munce?'

'That's right.'

'I'm sorry about what happened. My son painted his garage. The deputy was very civil to him. Some people aren't. They gave him an iced tea . . . I'm sorry.'

A nod.

After the painter left she continued to stare at the blank walls. No trace of the 9mm holes remained. She thought she should put up the pictures once more. But she didn't have the energy. The house was completely silent.

She looked over a list of things she had to do – calls to return, evidence to follow up on, interviews to conduct. Someone named Andrew Sheridan had called twice – he had some business connection with Emma Feldman and was asking about the files recovered from the house in Lake Mondac. She wondered what that was about. And somebody from the state's attorney's office had heard from the couple injured when their SUV overturned on the interstate. They were suing. The owner of the house at 2 Lake View had made a claim too. The ammonia had ruined the floor. Bullet holes too, of course. She needed to file a report. She'd delay that as long as she could.

She heard footsteps on the front porch.

Graham's?

A knock on the wooden frame. She rose.

'The bell's out, I think,' Tom Dahl said.

She swung the door open. 'Tom. Come on in.'

The sheriff walked inside. He noticed the repaired walls. Didn't comment on them. 'How's your mother doing?'

'She'll be okay. Feisty, you know.' She tilted her head toward the closed family room door. 'We made her up a bedroom downstairs. She's sleeping now.'

'Oh, I'll keep my voice down.'

'With the meds she's on, she'd sleep through a party.'

The sheriff sat and massaged his leg. 'I liked the way you phrased it. About those two killers: the bodies left behind. Described it pretty good.'

'Anything at all, Tom?'

'I'll tell you up front there's not much. That fellow got himself shot was Compton Lewis. Lived in Milwaukee.'

'Compton was his first name?'

'Ask his mother or father. Fellow was just a punk, a wannabe. Did construction around the lakefront and ran some petty scams, smash and grab at gas stations and convenience stores. Biggest thing was he and some folks tried to rob a guard refilling an ATM outside of Madison last year. They think Lewis was supposedly the getaway driver but he dropped his keys in the snow. His buddies ran off and he got busted. Did six months.' Dahl shook his head. 'Only kin I could track down was Lewis's older brother. The only one still in the state. The man took the news hard, I'll tell you. Started crying like a baby. Had to hang up and called me back a half hour later . . . Didn't have much to say, but here's his number if you want to talk to him.' He handed her a Post-it note.

'How about Hart?' She'd checked every criminal database in five states, all the nicknames, all the mug shots for every-body named Hart, Heart, Harte, Hartman, Harting . . . Nothing.

'No leads at all. That man . . . he's good. Look at the finger-prints. Didn't leave a single one anywhere. And digging the bullet with his DNA out of the woodwork? He knows what he's doing.'

'And Michelle? She would've given Hart and Comp a fake name but I'd guess Michelle is real; Hart and Lewis found her purse and probably looked through it. And she'd've told the truth to me – because I'd be dead by morning.'

'Dahl said, 'They're more concerned about *her*—'cause the FBI's sure it's Mankewitz who hired her and they want to prove him or one of his people hired her. But so far the snitches haven't come up with anything concrete yet.'

'Are they taking the composite picture of her I did to acting schools and health clubs?' Brynn was pretty sure the biography she'd told that night was a lie, its purpose to elicit sympathy from Brynn, but the young woman had been so credible it was worth checking out.

'I think they're working from the top down more, going for a Mankewitz connection first.'

He went on to say that he'd opened files on the four meth cookers killed by Hart and Lewis. They were murder charges; like 'em or not, drug dealers have a right not to be killed too.

If the mysterious shooter near the ledge in Marquette State

Park in the early hours of April 18 had any connection to the methamphetamine industry in Wisconsin or to Mankewitz, nobody'd been able to find it. The State Police had found the probable location of the shooter's nest but they'd recovered no physical evidence whatsoever. He'd collected all his brass and obscured his shoeprints. 'Everybody's a damn pro,' Dahl muttered. Then asked, 'How's that little girl doing?'

'Amy? No other family that Child Protective Services can find.'

'Sad.'

'Not really, Tom. At least she'll have a chance for a decent life now. She wouldn't've survived there with Gandy and his wife. . . . And I have to say she's looking okay. Pretty happy.'

'You saw her?'

'This morning. I bought her a new Chester and took it up.'

'A new . . . ?'

'Toy. I don't know what. Donkey-monkey or something. I was planning on going back to the park and getting the original. Just didn't have the heart.'

'That'd be above and beyond, Brynn. Physically, she's okay?'

'Well, nobody'd gone south.'

'Thank God for that.'

'But the marks on her neck?' Brynn grimaced angrily. 'The doctor who looked her over that night said they'd been made in the past few hours.'

'Few hours? You mean, it was Michelle did that?'

'Yep.' Brynn sighed. 'Amy was making some noise, and Hart and Lewis were nearby. Michelle pulled her aside to talk to her. And she was quiet after that. Half strangled the poor kid, I've got a feeling.'

'Lord, what a witch.'

'And Amy was terrified for the rest of the night. I never connected it.'

'Poor thing. Good you went to see her.'

She asked, 'That FBI fellow who's checking on Mankewitz? He'll call us? Or are they thinking we're bumpkins?'

'Never knew where that word came from.'

Brynn lifted an eyebrow.

'They think we're bumpkins but they said they'd let us know,' Dahl said.

'Still, give me his number. I'll call just to say hello.'

Snickering, Dahl dug through his wallet and found a card. Showed it to Brynn and she wrote down the information.

'You look tired. I owe you that time off. And I'm insisting you take it. That's from your boss. Kick back. Let Graham take care of things for a while. A man oughta know his way around the kitchen and grocery store and laundry. Lord knows, I do. Carole's whipped me into shape.'

Brynn laughed and Dahl missed the mournful tone. 'Well, I will. Promise. But not just yet. We've got open homicides and even if Mankewitz is behind it and the U.S. attorney comes in on RICO or conspiracy counts, it's still a state crime happened in our county.'

'What're you planning to do?' Dahl asked.

'Go where the leads take me. Here, Milwaukee, wherever.' She at least would follow up on some of the acting school and health club connections, anything else she could think of. Maybe gun clubs. The woman certainly knew how to use a firearm.

'And it won't do any good saying no?'

'You can fire me.'

He chuckled.

Brynn sighed. 'And this all ended up in our lap.'

'Usually, you know, you can't pick the bullet that hits you. Usually you can't even hear it coming.'

'What're you and Carole doing this weekend?'

'Maybe a movie. Only if her mother comes to baby-sit. These teenagers? They charge you ten dollars an hour and you have to feed them. I mean, something hot. What do you pay?'

'Graham and I don't go out much.'

'Better that way. Stay home, have dinner. No need to go out. Especially with cable. Best be going.'

'Say hi to Carole for me.'

'Will do. And regards to your mom. Wish her well.'

She watched him go and she stood, looking over the first item on her list.

II
MAY

Sitting in a diner in downtown Milwaukee, big, broad Stanley Mankewitz noted his reflection in the glass, intensified because of the dark gray afternoon light. The date was May 1 but the weather had been borrowed from March.

This was an important date in Mankewitz's life. International Workers' Day, picked by worldwide labor movements in the late 1880s to honor common workers. That particular date was selected largely to commemorate the martyrs of the Haymarket Massacre, in which both police and workers were killed in May 1886 in Chicago, following rallies by the Federation of Organized Trade and Labor Unions in support of an eight-hour workday.

May Day meant two things to Mankewitz. One, it honored working people – which he had been and which he now represented with all his heart, along with their brothers and sisters throughout the world.

Two, it stood as a testament to the fact that sacrifices sometimes had to be made for the greater good.

He had above his desk a quotation: the final words of one of the men sentenced to hang for his role in the Haymarket Massacre, August Spies (who, like all the defendants, scholars believed, was probably innocent). Spies had said, 'The time will come when our silence will be more powerful than the voices you strangle today.'

Sacrifices . . .

Reflecting now on that momentous day, Mankewitz gazed at his image, observing not his rotund physique, which pestered him occasionally, but his exhausted demeanor. He deduced this from his posture, since he couldn't see his facial features clearly, though they surely would have added to the overall profile.

He took a bite of his club sandwich, noted the American instead of the Swiss cheese, which he'd ordered. And too much mayo in the coleslaw. They always do that. Why the fuck do I eat here?

The Hobbit detective had been proving scarce lately, which Mankewitz cleverly punned to James Jasons really meant he was proving 'scared'.

Life had turned into a nightmare after the death of Emma Feldman. He'd been 'invited' to the Bureau and the state's attorney's office. He went with his lawyer, answered some questions, not others, and they left without receiving anything other than a chilly good-bye. His lawyer hadn't been able to read the signs.

Then he'd heard that the law firm where the Feldman woman worked was considering a suit against him for wrongful death — and their loss of earnings. His lawyer told him this was bullshit, since there was no legally recognized cause of action for that sort of thing.

More harassment . . .

Mankewitz snapped. 'Maybe it's also bullshit because nobody's proved I killed her.'

'Yeah, of course, Stan. That goes without saying.'

Without saying.

He looked up from his lopsided sandwich and saw James

Jasons approach. The thin man sat down. When the waitress arrived he asked for a Diet Coke.

'You don't eat,' Mankewitz said.

'Depends.'

Which means what? Mankewitz wondered.

'I've got some updates.'

'Go on.'

'First, I called the sheriff up there, Tom Dahl. Well, I called as the friend of the Feldmans – the aggrieved friend. Ari Paskell. I put on the pressure: How come you haven't found the killers, yet? Et cetera.'

'Okay.'

'I'm convinced he believed I'm who I said I was.'

'What'd he say about the case?'

Jasons blinked. 'Well, nothing. But he wouldn't. I was just making sure he wasn't suspicious about my trip up there. I'm checking on the case through other sources.'

Mankewitz nodded, trusting the man's judgment. 'What's up with our girlfriend?'

Referring to the deputy, Kristen Brynn McKenzie. Right after the events of April 17 and 18, Jasons had looked into who was leading the investigation into the deaths of the Feldmans. There was that prick of an FBI agent, Brindle, and a couple of Milwaukee cops, but it was the small-town woman who was really pushing the case.

'She's unstoppable. She's running with it like a bulldog.'

Mankewitz didn't think bulldogs ran much but he didn't say anything.

'She's better than the Bureau and Milwaukee PD combined.'

'I doubt that.'

'Well, she's working harder than they are. She's been to Milwaukee four times since the murders, following up on leads.'

'She have jurisdiction?'

'I don't think that's an issue anybody's worried about. What with all the shit that went down in Kennesha County. And the dead lawyer.'

'Why do I end up in the crock-pot?'

Slight James Jasons had no response to that, nor should he offer one, the union boss reflected. Besides, the answer was obvious: Because I think immigrants who work hard ought to be let into the country to take the jobs of people who're too lazy to work.

Oh, and because I say it in public.

'So, Ms. McKenzie's not going to stop until she gets to the bottom of what happened up there.'

'She's not going to stop,' Jasons echoed.

'Out to make a name for herself?'

His man considered this, frowning. 'It's not like she wants a notch in her gun or career advancement, anything like that.'

'What's her point then?'

'Putting bad people in jail.'

Jasons reminded Mankewitz again about being in the forest that night in April – an unarmed Brynn McKenzie on top of a cliff, launching rocks and logs down onto the men pursuing her, while they fired back with a shotgun and automatic pistol. She had only backed off when Jasons himself began firing with the Bushmaster.

Mankewitz knew without a doubt he wouldn't like Deputy McKenzie. But he had to respect her.

'What's she found exactly?'

'I don't know. She's been on the lakefront, Avenues West, the Brewline, over to Madison, down to Kenosha. Went to Minneapolis for the day. She's not stopping.'

The running bulldog.

'Anything I can use? Anything at all?'

Speaking from memory – he never seemed to need notes – Jasons said, 'There is one thing.'

'Go ahead.'

'She's got a secret.'

'Give me the gist.'

'Okay, six, seven years ago – married to her first husband. He was a state trooper, decorated, popular guy. Also, had a temper. Had hit her in the past.'

'Prick, hitting women.'

'Well, turns out he gets shot.'

'Shot?'

'In his own kitchen. There's an inquest. Accidental discharge. Unfortunate accident.'

'Okay. Where's this going?'

'It wasn't an accident at all. Intentional shooting. There was a cover-up. Might've gone all the way to Madison.'

'The kind of cover-up where people'll lose their jobs, if it comes to light?'

'Lose their jobs and probably go to jail.'

'This just rumors?'

Jasons opened his briefcase. He removed at limp file folder. 'Proof.'

For a little runt, the man sure did produce.

'Hope it's helpful.'

Mankewitz opened the folder. He read, lifting an eyebrow. 'I think it's very helpful.' He looked up and said sincerely, 'Thanks. Oh, and by the way, Happy May Day.'

He liked this town.

At least he liked it well enough as a temporary home.

Green Bay was flatter than the state park around Lake Mondac, less picturesque in that sense but the bay itself was idyllic, and the Fox River impressive in that hard, industrial way that had always appealed to Terry Hart. His father used to take him to the steel mill where the man worked in the payroll office, and the boy was always excited beyond words to don a hardhat and walk around on the floor, which stank of smoke and coal and liquid metal and rubber.

His rental house here was on one of the numbered streets, also working-class, not so great. But functional and cheap. His big problem was that he was bored.

Biding time never worked for Hart but biding time was what he had to do. No choice there, none at all.

If he got too bored, he'd go for a drive to the forest preserve, which he found comforting, especially since to get there he'd take Lakeview Drive – the name similar to the private road at Lake Mondac. He would go for walks or sometimes just sit in the car and work. Hart had several prepaid mobile phones and would make calls about forthcoming jobs.

Today, in fact, he was just finishing one of these walks, and noticed a maypole set up in one of the clearings. The children were running in a circle, making a barber pole. Then they sat down to their picnic lunch. A school bus was nearby, a yellow stain on the otherwise pretty green.

Hart returned to his rental house, drove around the block, just to be sure, then went inside. He checked messages and made some calls on a new prepaid mobile. Then he went into the garage, where he'd set up a small woodworking shop, a tiny one, of the residence. He'd been working on a project of his own design. It started out being just an hour or two a day. Now he was up to about four hours. Nothing relaxed him like working with wood.

As he sanded by hand, he thought back to that night in the woods, recalling all the trees there – oak, ash, maple, walnut, all the hardwoods that made up the medium for his craft. What he purchased as smooth, precisely cut lumber, with perfect angles at the corners, had begun as a huge, imposing, even forbidding creature, towering a hundred or so feet in the air. In one way it troubled him that the trees were cut down. In another, though, he believed he was honoring the wood by transforming it into something else, something to be appreciated.

He now looked over the project he'd been working on: an inlaid box. He was pleased with the progress. It might be a present for someone. He wasn't sure yet.

At eight that night he drove to downtown Green Bay, to a woody, dark bar that served pretty good chili and had a bowl and a beer, sitting at the bar. He got another beer when he finished the first and went into the backroom, where there was a basketball game on. He watched it, sipping the beer. It was a West Coast game and the hour was later here. Pretty soon the other patrons began to check their watches, then stand and head home. The score was 92-60 well into the second half and whatever interest had existed before the halftime show had evaporated.

Anyway, it was just basketball. Not the Packers.

He glanced at the walls. They were covered with old signs from Wisconsin's breweries of the past, famous ones he supposed, though he'd never heard of them. Loaf & Stein, Heileman, Foxhead. An ominous tusked boar stared at him from a Hibernia Brewing logo. A picture of a TV screen on which two women looked out at the audience. Penned below it was, *Hey there, from Laverne and Shirley.*

Hart asked for his check as the waitress passed by. She was polite but cool, having given up flirting with him when it wasn't reciprocated the first time, a week or so ago. In bars like this one, once is enough. He paid, left and drove to another bar not far away, in the Broadway District. He stepped out of the car and into the shadows of a nearby alley.

When the man came out of the bar at one a.m., which he'd done virtually every night for the past week, Hart grabbed him, pushed a pistol into his back and dragged him into the alley.

It took Freddy Lancaster about fifteen seconds to decide that the impending threat from Hart was worse than the equally dangerous but less-immediate threat of Michelle Kepler. He told Hart everything he knew about her.

One glance out of the alley and one single muted gunshot later, Hart returned to his car.

He drove back to his house, thinking about his next steps. He had believed Freddy when he'd said that neither he nor Gordon Potts knew exactly where Michelle lived but the man had disgorged enough information to allow Hart to start closing in on her.

Which he'd do soon.

But for now he'd do what he'd been obsessing about for the past several weeks. He yawned and reflected that at least he could get a good night's sleep. He wouldn't need an early start. Humboldt, Wisconsin, was only a three-hour drive away

At 2:30 p.m. on Monday, May 4, Kristen Brynn McKenzie
was in the bar area of a restaurant in Milwaukee, having
chicken soup and a diet soda. She'd just left appointments
with an MPD detective and an FBI agent, where they'd
compared notes about their respective investigations into the
killings of the Feldmans and the meth dealers in Kennesha
County in April.

The meetings had proven to be unhelpful. The goal of the
city and the federal investigations, it seemed, was to find a
link to Mankewitz, rather than capture those individuals who
had slaughtered an innocent husband and wife and left their
bodies ignominiously on a cold kitchen floor.

A fact that Brynn pointed out to both the detective and
the Feebie, neither of whom was moved by her assessment
to do more than curl his lips sympathetically. And with some
irritation.

She'd left the second appointment in a bad mood and
decided to grab some belated lunch and head home.

In the past few weeks Brynn McKenzie had logged 2300
miles in her own investigation. She was now driving a used
Camry – very used. The waterlogged Honda had died in the

line of duty, according to the insurance company, thus excluding it from her personal auto policy. She'd paid for the car herself, from her savings, which hurt, particularly since she wasn't sure about her financial future.

Graham had moved out.

They'd discussed the situation several times again after April 18. But Graham remained badly shaken by Eric Munce's death, for which he still blamed himself – though not Brynn, not at all (what a difference between him and Keith).

Graham had been gone only a few days, moving into a rental unit twenty minutes away. She found herself sad and troubled . . . but in some way relieved. There was also a large numbness factor. Of course, domestics were her specialty, and she knew it was far too early to say for certain where their lives were headed.

He was still paying his share of the bills – more than his share, actually, picking up all of Anna's medical expenses that the insurance company wasn't. But their lifestyle had been based on two incomes and Brynn was suddenly much more conscious of finances.

She ate a bit more of the cooling soup. Her phone buzzed. Joey was calling and she picked up immediately. It was just a check-in and she made cheerful comments as he told her a few things about gym class and Science, then hung up to hurry off to his final class.

After allowing that Graham might have been accurate in his comments about the boy – and about her rearing of him – she'd done some investigating (and interrogating) and learned that the reports of Joey's 'phalting were true; he'd hitched rides on trucks a number of times. Only by the grace of God had he been saved from serious injury. The class cutting, too, had occurred. Far more often than she'd expected. He was apparently a good forger of her signature.

She'd had several difficult talks with the boy, prodded, and coached, by her mother, who was reasonable but firm. (For once Brynn was pleased with a return a mother daughter relationship from the past.)

Brynn had swooped into her son's life like a tactical officer from a helicopter. He was only allowed to board at a local free-style course, when she was there with him. And he had to wear his helmet, no knit hip-hop hats.

'Mom, like, come on. Are you kidding?'

'That's your only option. And I keep your board locked up in my room.'

He'd sighed, exaggeratedly. But agreed.

She also required him to call in regularly and to be home within twenty minutes of the end of school. She was amused to see his reaction when she reminded him that the police have an arrangement with the local phone company that allows them to track the whereabouts of cell phones, even when they're not in use. (This was true, though what she didn't share was that it would be illegal for her to use the system to electronically check up on him.)

But if she was getting the rebellious behavior under control, there seemed to be nothing she could do with his moods about Graham's departure. Although her husband stayed in regular touch with his stepson, Joey wasn't happy at the breakup and she didn't know how to do anything about that. After all, she wasn't the one who'd walked out the door. She'd fix it, though she didn't have a clue how.

She pushed the soup away, reflecting that so much had changed since that night.

'That night'. The phrase had become an icon in her life. It meant a lot more than a chronological reference.

She was single again, had an injured mother in her care and a troubled son to keep an eye on. Still, nothing in the world would stop her from finding Michelle and Hart and bringing them in.

She was, in fact, wondering if there was anything she could salvage from the meetings she'd just had with the detective and FBI agent when she realized the bar was deathly quiet.

Empty. The waiter, bus boy and bartender were gone.

And then she had a memory: seeing a slight man walking behind her on the way from the police station here. She hadn't thought anything of it, but now realized that she'd stopped at one point to look in a store window; he'd stopped as well, to make a phone call. Or to pretend to.

Alarmed, she started to rise but felt the breeze of a door opening and sensed people behind her, at least two, it seemed.

She froze. Her gun was under her suit jacket and a raincoat. She'd be dead before she undid two buttons.

There was nothing to do but turn around.

She did so, half expecting to see Hart's gray eyes as he steadied the gun to kill her.

The heavier of the two, a man in his sixties, said, 'Detective, I'm Stanley Mankewitz.'

She nodded. 'It's *Deputy*.'

The other man, skinny and boyish, was the one she'd seen earlier, following her. He had a faint smile but humor was not its source. He remained silent.

Mankewitz sat on the stool next to hers. 'May I?'

'You're bordering on kidnapping here.'

He seemed surprised. 'Oh, you're free to leave any time, Deputy McKenzie. Kidnapping?'

He nodded to his associate, who went to a nearby table.

The bartender had returned. He looked at Mankewitz.

'Just coffee. A Diet Coke for my friend.' He nodded at the table.

The bartender delivered the coffee to the bar and the soda to Mankewitz's associate. 'Anything else?' he asked Brynn, as if saying, Want some cheesecake for your last meal?

She shook her head. 'Just the check.'

Mankewitz prepared the coffee carefully, just the right amount of cream, a sugar packet and a Splenda. He said, 'I heard you had quite an evening a few weeks ago.'

That night . . .

'And how would you know that?'

'I watch the news.' He gave off an aura of confidence that she found reassuring in one sense – that she was in no physical danger at the moment – but also troubling. As if he had another weapon, like knowing something that could destroy her life without resorting to violence. He seemed completely in control.

In this way he reminded her of Hart.

The union boss continued, 'Very important to be informed. When I was growing up, before your time, we had an hour of local news – five p.m. – and then national and international. Walter Cronkite, Huntley and Brinkley . . . Just a half hour. Me, that wasn't enough. I like all the information I can get. CNN. I love it. It's the home page on my BlackBerry.'

'That doesn't answer the question of how you happen to be here, when I just decided to come in on a whim . . . Unless you'd somehow found out I had an appointment at Milwaukee PD.'

He hesitated only a moment – she'd obviously touched something close to home. He said, 'Or maybe I've just been shadowing you.'

'I know *he* has,' she snapped, nodding at his slim associate.

Mankewitz smiled, sipped the coffee and looked with regret at the rotating dessert display. 'We have a mutual interest here, Deputy.'

'And what would that be?'

'Finding Emma Feldman's killer.'

'I'm not watching him drink very bad coffee two feet away from me right now?'

'It *is* bad coffee. How'd you know?'

'Smell.'

He nodded at the can of soda by her plate. 'You and my friend and that diet pop. That's not good for you, you know. And, no, you're not in the company of her killer.'

She looked behind her. The other fellow was sipping his soda while he looked over his own BlackBerry.

What was *his* home page?

'Don't imagine you work many murders in Kennesha County,' Mankewitz said. 'Not like this one.'

'Not like *these*,' she corrected. 'Several people were killed.' Now that she was alive and the bartender was a witness, even a bribable one, she'd started feeling cocky, if not ornery.

'Of course.' He nodded.

Brynn mused, 'What kind of cases do we run? Domestic knifings. A gun goes off accidental during a 7-Eleven or gas station heist. A meth deal goes bad.'

'Bad stuff, that drug. Real bad.'

Tell me about it. She said, 'If you've seen *COPS*, you know what we do.'

'April Seventeenth was a whole different ball game.' He sipped the bad coffee anyway. 'You in a union? A police union?'

'No, not in Kennesha.'

'I believe in unions, ma'am. I believe in working and I believe in giving everybody a fair shake to climb up the ladder. Like education. School's an equalizer; a union's the same. You're in a union, we give you the basics. You might be happy with that, take your hourly wage and God bless. But you can use it like a diving board, you want to go higher in life.'

'Diving board?'

'Maybe that's a bad choice. I'm not so creative. You know what I'm accused of?'

'Not the details. A scam involving illegal immigrants.'

'What I'm accused of is giving people forged documentation that's better than what they can buy on the street. They get jobs in open shops and vote to go union.'

'Is that true?'

'No.' He smiled. 'Those're the accusations. Now, you know how the authorities tipped to my alleged crimes? That lawyer, Emma Feldman, was doing some business deal for a client and she found a large number of *legal* immigrants were union members – proportionately a lot higher than in most locals around the country. From that, somebody started the rumor that I was selling them forged papers. All their green cards, though, were legit. Issued by the U.S. government.'

Brynn considered this. He seemed credible. But who knew? 'Why?'

'To break the union, that's why, pure and simple. The rumors start going around that I'm corrupt. That Local Four-oh-eight is a front for terrorists. That I'm encouraging foreigners to take our jobs . . . Bang, everybody votes to drop out and go open shop.' He was worked up. 'Let me explain exactly why I'm being persecuted here. Why people want Stanley Mankewitz out of the picture. Because I don't hate immigrants. I am all in favor of them. I'd rather employ a dozen Mexicans or Chinese or Bulgarians who come to this country – legally, I'll add – to work hard, than a hundred lazy born-here citizens any day. So I'm caught right in the middle. The employers hate me because I'm union. My own membership hates me because I promote people who aren't *Amurican*.' He drawled the last word, a good ole boy. 'So there's a conspiracy to set me up.'

Brynn sighed, having lost all interest in her soup and the soda, which had been flat to start with, probably as bad as the coffee, though it didn't stink.

Mankewitz lowered his voice. 'Did you know I saved your life on April 17?'

Her attention swung fully to him now. A frown. She didn't want to show any emotion but couldn't help herself.

Mankewitz said, 'I sent Mr Jasons there to protect my interest. I knew I didn't kill Emma Feldman and her husband.

I wanted to find out who really did. That could lead me to who was trying to set me up.'

'Please . . .' she said, giving him a skeptical glance. Her cheek stung and she rearranged her expression until the pain stopped.

Mankewitz looked over her shoulder. 'James?'

Jasons joined them at the bar, toting a briefcase. He said, 'I was in the forest, near that ledge you and that woman and little girl were on. I had a Bushmaster rifle. You were throwing rocks and logs down on those men.'

She asked in a whisper, 'That was you?' Jasons didn't look like he could even hold a gun. 'Shooting at us?'

'*Near* you. Not at. Only to break up the fighting.' Another sip of soda. 'I drove to the house at the lake. I said I was a friend of Steve Feldman. I followed your husband and that other deputy into the woods. I wasn't there to kill anybody. Just the opposite. My orders were to keep everyone alive. Find out who they were. I broke up the fight but I couldn't track them down to interrogate them.'

Mankewitz said, 'We have reason to believe that the rumors about my alleged illegal involvement came from someone in a company called Great Lakes Containers. Mr Jasons here managed to find some documents—'

'Find?'

'—some documents that suggest that the president of the company was in bad financial shape and trying desperately to kick out the union so he could cut wages and benefits. The head lawyer of Great Lakes provided us with some documents that prove the president was behind the rumors.'

'Did you tell the prosecutor?'

'Unfortunately, this documentation . . .'

'It was stolen.'

'Well, let's say it isn't discoverable under the Federal Rules of Evidence. Now, here's the situation. Since I have never sold any illegal papers, nobody can prove that I did. So eventually the charges will be dismissed. But rumors can cause as much damage as convictions. That's what the Great Lakes Containers and the other union shops are hoping for – to ruin me by destroying my reputation and break the union. So I need to stop as many of those rumors as I can. And my number one priority is convincing you that I didn't kill Emma Feldman.'

'In police school they teach us not to give up when a suspect says, "Really, I didn't do it."'

Mankewitz pushed the coffee away. 'Deputy McKenzie. I know about the shooting seven years ago.'

Brynn froze.

'Your husband.' He looked at Jasons, who said, 'Keith Marshall.'

Mankewitz continued, 'The official report was accidental discharge, but everybody believed you shot him because he attacked you again. Like he did when he broke your jaw. But since he was wearing his body armor and survived, he could testify that it was accidental.'

'Look—'

'But I know the truth. I know it was your son, not you, who shot Keith, trying to save you.'

No, no . . . Brynn's hands were shaking.

Another nod toward Jasons. A file appeared. It was old, limp. She looked at it. Kennesha County Board of Education Archives.

'What's this?' she gasped.

Mankewitz pointed to a name on the folder. *Dr R. Germain.*

It took her a moment to recognize it. He was Joey's counselor in the third grade. Joey'd been having trouble in school, aggression, refusing to do homework, and had seen the man several times a week. The boy had been further traumatized when the counselor had died of a massive heart attack the night after a session.

'Where did you get it?' Without waiting for an answer she ripped it open with sweating hands.

Oh, my God . . .

They'd assumed Joey, just five at the time of the shooting, had forgotten, or blocked out, that terrible night when his parents had fought, grappling on the kitchen floor. The boy had run to his parents, screaming. Keith had pushed him away and gone to hit Brynn in the face again.

Joey had pulled her weapon from the holster on her hip and shot his father in the chest, dead center.

They'd pulled in every favor they could and Brynn took the hit for an accidental discharge, which alone nearly ended her career. Everybody figured that she'd shot Keith on purpose – he was known for his temper – but no one suspected Joey.

As she now learned from the report, the boy had given Dr Germain a coherent and detailed account of what happened that night. Brynn had no idea that Joey recalled the event with such clarity. Apparently, she realized now, the only thing that had saved him from going into foster care – and, if a witch hunt had ensued, having Brynn and Keith criminally investigated for endangering a child, because of the weapon – was Germain's death and the file vanishing, unread, into the school archives.

Mankewitz added, 'The FBI and Milwaukee PD were close to finding this.'

'What? Why?'

'Because they want you off the case. Their investigation is meant to nail me. Yours is to find out what really happened at Lake Mondac.'

The assistant added, 'They've been looking into every aspect of your life. They'd use this for leverage to discredit you.' A glance at the file. 'Maybe even get you prosecuted and anybody who helped in the cover-up about Keith's shooting.'

Her jaw trembled as badly as on that night when she'd climbed from the pungent waters of Lake Mondac.

They'd take her son away from her . . . Her career would be over. Tom Dahl would be investigated too, for abetting the cover-up. People at the State Police would also come under investigation.

Mankewitz looked into her eyes, now swimming with tears. 'Hey, relax.'

She glanced at him. He tapped the file with a thick finger. 'Mr Jasons here assures me that this is the only file. There were no copies made. Nobody except you, Keith and your son knows what happened that night.'

'You do now,' she muttered.

'The only thing I'm doing with that file is giving it to you.'

'What?'

'Shred it. No. Do what I do. Shred it, then *burn* it.'

'You're not . . .'

'Deputy McKenzie, I'm not here to blackmail, I'm not here to leverage you into dropping the investigation. I'm giving this to you as a show of good faith. I'm innocent. I don't want you off the case. I want you to keep investigating until you find out who really did kill those people up there.'

Brynn clutched the file. It seemed to give off radiation. She slipped it into her backpack. 'Thank you.' With a trembling hand she drank some soda. She considered what he'd told her. 'But then who wanted Emma Feldman dead? What would the motive be? Nobody else seems to have one.'

'Has anybody *looked* for one?'

True, she admitted. Everybody'd been assuming all along that Mankewitz was behind the crimes.

The union boss looked away. His shoulders slumped. 'We've drawn a blank too, though there were some other cases Emma was working on that might have been sensitive enough to motivate somebody to kill her. One was a trust and estate matter for a state representative, the one who killed himself.'

Brynn remembered the story. The man had tried to cut his wife and children out of his will and leave all his money to a twenty-two-year-old gay prostitute. The media had broken the story and the politician killed himself.

'Then,' the labor boss continued, 'she had another case that was curious.' A glance at Jasons, the king of information and sources, apparently.

He said, 'A products liability case involving a new hybrid car. A driver was electrocuted. The man's family sued Emma Feldman's client, a company in Kenosha. They made the generator or electrical system or something. She was hard at work on the case but then all the files were pulled and nobody heard anything more about it.'

A dangerously defective hybrid? That was a possibility you didn't hear about much. In fact, never. There'd certainly be big money involved. She'd found something she shouldn't've?

Maybe.

And Kenosha rang a bell . . . She'd have to look at her notes from the past few weeks. A call to be returned. Somebody was interested in some of Emma Feldman's files. Somebody named Sheridan.

Mankewitz continued, 'But we couldn't come up with any particular leads. You're on your own now.' He waved for the check, paid, nodding at Brynn's unfinished soup. 'I didn't pay for that. Appearance of impropriety, you know.' He pulled his coat on.

The associate remained sitting but he fished a business card from his pocket. It contained only a name and phone number. She wondered if the name was real. He said, 'If you need me for anything, if I can be of any more help, please call. It's a voice mail only. But I'll get right back to you.'

Brynn nodded. 'Thank you,' she said again to both men, tapping her backpack.

'Think about what I told you,' Mankewitz said. 'Seems like

you and the FBI and everybody else's been looking in the wrong place.'

'Or,' said the skinny man said, sipping from his glass as if the soda were a vintage wine, 'looking for the wrong who.'

The police line bunting on the front porch had come undone; it wagged like a bony yellow finger in the breeze.

Brynn hadn't been back to the Feldmans' vacation house on Lake View Drive since that night, now almost three weeks ago. Oddly, in the afternoon daylight, the house looked starker than it had then. The paint was uneven and peeling in many places. The angles sharp. The shutters and trim unpleasing black.

She walked to the place where she'd stood beside her car, nearly hyperventilating with terror, in a shooting stance, waiting for Hart to rise from the bushes and present a target.

From that memory, her thoughts slipped naturally back to the school counselor's report that Mankewitz had given her, now indeed both shredded and burned in the backyard barbecue. The counselor had transcribed the incident pretty much the way it happened.

The night was also in April, curiously. She pictured herself blinking in horror as Keith, just home from a long, exhausting day on patrol, sat at the kitchen table and his anger slowly unraveled. She didn't know what had sparked the outburst; often, she couldn't remember. Something about their taxes and money. Maybe she'd misplaced some receipts.

Small. It was usually something small.

But the incident had escalated fast. Keith, getting that crazed look in his eyes, so terrifying. Possessed. His voice was low at first, then cracking, rising to a scream. Brynn had then said the worst thing she could: 'Calm down! It's no big deal.'

'I'm the one who's been working on it all day! Where've you been? Handing out parking tickets?'

'Calm down,' she'd snapped back, even as her heart stuttered and she found her hand protecting her jaw.

Then he'd snapped. He'd leapt up, kicking the table over, tax forms and receipts flying through the air, and charged her, beer bottle in hand. She'd pushed him away, hard, and he'd grabbed her by the hair and muscled her to the floor. They'd grappled, knocking chairs aside. He'd dragged her toward him, balling his fist up.

Screaming, crying, 'No, no, no.' Seeing his massive hand rearing back.

And then Joey was charging into them, sobbing himself.

'Joey! Get back,' Keith raged, intoxicated – though, as usual, not from alcohol but anger. He was completely out of control, drawing back his huge fist.

She tried to twist away, so the terrible blow wouldn't shatter her jaw again. Trying to protect Joey, who was stuck in the middle, screaming right along with his mother.

'Don't hurt Mommy!'

Then: *Crack.*

The bullet struck Keith directly in the center of the chest.

And the boy began screaming once again. The five-year-old had slipped his mother's Glock from her holster, probably meaning just to threaten. But the weapon has no traditional safety catch; just gripping the trigger could cause it to go off.

The gun spun to the floor as mother, father, son were frozen in a horrible tableau.

Keith, blinking, had stumbled back. Then dropped to his knees and vomited. He passed out. Brynn had gasped, sped to him and ripped his shirt open, seeing the disk of hot copper and lead fall from the Kevlar vest.

Ambulances and statements and negotiations . . .

And of course the indelible horror of the incident itself.

Yet Mankewitz and that skinny fellow Jasons didn't know the worst part. The part that she regretted every minute of her life.

After that night, life got better. In fact, it became perfect.

Keith found a good psychiatrist and went into anger-management and twelve-step programs. They went to couple's therapy. Joey too went into counseling.

And never again was there a harsh word between them, let alone a touch not motivated by affection or passion. They became the most normal of couples. Attending Joey's events and church. Anna and her husband warily returned to their daughter's life, having distanced themselves because of Keith.

No more big blowups, no harsh words. He became a model husband.

And nine months later she asked him for a divorce, and he had reluctantly agreed.

Why had she asked for one?

She'd spent hours, days wondering. Was it the aftershock of that terrible night? The accumulation of the man's moods? Or that she wasn't programmed to live a calm, a normal life?

I wouldn't trade the life I lead for anything. Look at most of the rest of the world – the walking dead. They're nothing but dead bodies, Brynn. Sitting around, upset, angry about something they saw on TV doesn't mean a single thing to them personally . . .

She thought back to that night after she and Graham had returned from the hospital after Anna had been shot. What he'd said to her.

Oh, Graham, you're right. So right. But I *do* owe my son.

I owe him big. I put him in a situation where he actually used a weapon to try to save his mother, when I should have taken him out of that household years before.

And then I left after everything got better, I took Joey away from a man who moved heaven and earth to turn his life around.

How can I help but spoil the boy, protect him? And hope for his forgiveness?

Touching her jaw, she now climbed onto the porch of the Feldmans' house. The scene had been released but a State Police lock-box was still on the door. She worked the combination, took the key and stepped inside. The place smelled of sweet cleanser and fireplace smoke, lured out by the damp air.

She saw bullet holes – from Hart's, from Lewis's shotgun, from Michelle's, from Brynn's own weapon as well. In the kitchen the floor had been scrubbed clean. Not a trace of blood remained. There were companies that did this, cleaning up after crimes and accidental deaths. Brynn had always thought that would be a good murder mystery novel: a killer who works for one of those companies and cleans the scene so completely the police can't find any clues.

In the kitchen she saw a half-dozen battered cookbooks, several of which she herself owned. She pulled down an old *Joy of Cooking*. She opened it up to the page where the red ribbon marked a recipe. Chicken fricassee. She laughed. She'd made this very dish. In the corner was written in pencil, *2 hours*. And the words *Vermouth instead*.

Brynn put the book back.

She wondered what would happen to the house now.

Abandoned for another generation, she supposed. Who'd want to be up here anyway? Imposing, harsh woods, no grocery stores or restaurants nearby and that lake cold and dark, like an old bullet hole in the county.

But then she cut all of these reflections loose, pushed them away, just like she and Michelle had shoved the canoe into the black stream last April and gone on their urgent way.

With a glance at where the bodies had lain – where she had almost joined them in death – Brynn returned to the living room.

'We have to leave.'

'Okay,' Joey replied to his mother and trooped down the stairs, wearing an Old West costume that Anna had made. Man, that woman knew her way around Singer sewing machines, Brynn thought. Always had. Some people are born to the skill.

Brynn had spent the past several days in Milwaukee and Kenosha, running down leads, some successful and some not. But she'd made a point of returning in time that evening to get to Joey's pageant.

Brynn called, 'Mom, are you okay in there?'

From the family room Anna said, 'I'm fine. Joey, I wish I could come. But I'll come to your party when school's over. I'll be fine by then. Who're you playing?'

'I'm this frontier scout. I lead people over the mountains.'

'It's not about the Donner party, is it?' Anna asked.

'What's that?' Joey wondered aloud. 'Like the Democrats?'

'In a way.'

'Mother,' Brynn scoffed.

Hobbling into the doorway Anna said, 'Turn around . . . My look at that. You look like Alan Ladd.'

'Who?'

'A famous actor.'

'Like Johnny Depp?' the boy asked.

'Heaven help us.'

Joey wrinkled his face. 'I don't want to put that makeup on. It's all greasy.'

Brynn said, 'You have to wear it onstage. People can see you better. Besides, it makes you look so handsome.'

He gave an exaggerated sigh.

Anna asked, 'Honey, I think Graham might like to go.'

'Yeah,' the boy said fast. 'Mom, can he?'

'I don't know,' Brynn said uncertainly, angry that her mother had – tactically, it seemed – asked this in front of Joey.

Her mother held her eye and gave her one of her patented ironclad smiles. 'Oh, give him a call. What can it hurt?'

Brynn didn't know the answer to that. And therefore she didn't want to ask him.

'He'd like the show, Mom. Come on.'

'It's short notice.'

'In which case he'll say he has other plans, thank you very much for the invitation. Or he'll say yes.'

She glanced back. Anna had been supportive emotionally after the breakup, but hadn't offered any opinion about it. Brynn assumed she was being her typical uninvolved self. But she wondered now if the pleasant smile – the smile of a spokeswoman for AARP on a television ad – hid a carefully planned strategy about her daughter's life.

'I'd rather not,' Brynn said evenly.

'Ah.' The smile faltered.

'Mom,' Joey said. He was angry.

Her mother's eyes slipped, for a split second, to her grandson. And she said nothing else.

Joey muttered, 'I don't know why he moved out. All the way over to Hendricks Hills.'

'How'd you know he was there?' Graham had just moved into a new rental yesterday.

'He told me.'

'You talked to him?'

'He called.'

'You didn't tell me.'

'He called *me*,' the boy said defiantly. 'To say hi, you know.'

Brynn wasn't sure how to react to this. 'He didn't leave a message?'

'Naw.' He tugged at his costume. 'Why'd he move there?'

'It's a nice neighborhood.'

'I mean why'd he move at all?'

'I told you. We had a different way of seeing things.'

Joey obviously didn't know what that meant but then neither did Brynn.

'Well, can't he come to the play?'

'No, honey.' She smiled. 'Not this time. Maybe later.'

The boy walked to the window and gazed outside. He seemed disappointed. Brynn frowned. 'What's that?'

'I thought maybe he was here.'

'Why?'

'You know, he comes by sometimes.'

'He does? To see you?'

'No. He just sits outside for a while then drives off. I saw him at school too. He was parked outside after class.'

Brynn kept her voice steady as she asked, 'You're sure it was Graham?'

'I guess. I couldn't see him real good. He had sunglasses on. But it had to be him. Who else would it be?'

Looking at her mother, who was clearly surprised at this news. Brynn said, 'But it might not have been him. You're not sure.'

Joey shrugged. 'He had dark hair. And it was like he was big like Graham.'

'Was it his car?'

'I guess it was. Something kind of blue. Looked neat. Like a sports car. Dark blue. I couldn't see too good. When he called he told me they never found his truck so he got a new one. I figured that was it. What's wrong, Mom?'

'Nothing.' She smiled.

'Come on. Can't you call him?'

'Not today, honey. I'll call him later.' Brynn scanned the empty road for a moment. Then turned and, smiling again – one of her mother's stoic smiles – said, 'Hey, Mom, you *are* looking better. Maybe you should come to the play after all.'

Anna was going to scold – she'd been after Brynn to let her come to the play all along – but she caught on. 'Love to.'

Brynn continued, 'We'll go to T.G.I. Friday's after. I'll help you throw something on. I'll be there in a minute.' She walked to the front door, locked it and went upstairs.

She opened the lock-box and clipped her holster containing the Glock to the back of her skirt waistband, pulled on a concealing jacket.

Staring out the window at the empty road in front of the house, she called Tom Dahl.

'Need a favor. Fast.'

'Sure, Brynn. You okay?'

'I don't know.'

'Go on.'

'Graham. I need to know what cars are registered in his name. Everything. Even the company cars.'

'He causing you trouble?'

'No, no. It's not him I'm worried about.'

'Just hold on a minute. I'll get into the DMV database.'

Less than sixty seconds later the sheriff's easy voice came back on the line. 'Rolling Hills Landscaping's got three forty-foot flatbeds, two F150 pickups and an F250. Graham himself has a Taurus he's leasing through his insurance company – 'causa that woman stealing his pickup last month, I'd imagine.'

'The Taurus? It's dark blue?'

'White.'

'Okay . . .'

She was thinking back to that night.

You should have . . . You should've killed me.

'Tom, I need somebody to watch the house again.'

'What's going on, Brynn?'

'Somebody was outside, parked. Checking out the place. Joey saw him. You know kids, might've been nothing. But I don't want to take any chances.'

'Sure we can do that, Brynn. Anything.'

On Thursday, May 7, Brynn was sitting in her cubicle clutching a cup of hot chocolate, really hot. This had become a recent addiction, though she'd given up her much-loved saltines and Brie sandwiches in compensation. She could drink three cups of cocoa a day. She wondered if this was because she'd been so chilled on that night. Probably not. Swiss Miss made a really good product.

She reflected that she and Graham had sipped hot chocolate at the Humboldt Diner at the end of their first date. The beverages had started out near 212 degrees when they'd begun talking, and the cups had been cold when they'd finished.

She was reading through her notes – hundreds of jottings, setting out the conversations she'd had after her meeting with Stanley Mankewitz. She'd never worked so hard in her life.

Looking for the wrong who . . .

Her office phone rang. She took a last sip and set the cup down. 'Deputy McKenzie.'

'Hello?' asked a Latina voice with the reserve most people displayed when calling the police. The caller explained she was the manager of the Harborside Inn in Milwaukee.

'How can I help you?' Hearing 'Milwaukee', Brynn sat

forward quickly, tense. The most likely reason for someone from that city to call was the Feldman murder case.

That was indeed the purpose and Brynn grew more and more interested as she listened.

The hotel manager said she'd seen on TV a composite picture of the man wanted in connection with the killings at Lake Mondac, a man possibly going by the name or nickname of Hart or Harte. Someone looking very similar had checked into the inn there on April 16. The manager had called the local police and they referred her to the Kennesha County Sheriff's Department.

The name of the guest was William Harding.

Harding . . . Hart . . .

'Is it true he's a killer?' the woman asked uneasily.

'That's our understanding . . . What was the address on the register?' Brynn snapped her fingers at Todd Jackson, who appeared instantly at her cubicle.

As the manager recited an address in Minneapolis, Brynn transcribed it and told the young deputy, 'Check this out. Fast.'

Asked about phone calls and visitors, the woman said there were no outgoing calls but the guest, Harding, met in the coffee shop with a skinny man with a crew cut, who the manager thought was rude, and a pretty woman in her twenties with short red hair. She looked a bit like the woman in the other composite picture the manager had seen.

Getting better and better . . .

Then the woman added, 'The thing is, he never checked out.'

'He's still there?' she asked.

'No, officer. He checked in for three days, went out the afternoon of the seventeenth and then never came back. I tried to call but directory assistance doesn't have anybody listed in Minneapolis, or St Paul, by that name at that address.'

She wasn't surprised when Jackson slipped her a piece of

paper that read: *Fake. A parking lot. No name in MN, WI, NCIC or VICAP.*

She nodded, whispering, 'Tell Tom we've got something here.'

Jackson disappeared as Brynn was scanning through her notes, flipping pages. 'What about a credit card?' she asked the manager.

'Paid cash. But the reason I called: He left a suitcase here. If you want to pick it up, it's yours.'

'Really? I'll tell you, I'd like to drive down there and look through it. Let me rearrange a few things and give you a call back.'

After they disconnected Brynn slouched back in her chair.

'You okay?' Tom Dahl asked, stepping into her cubicle, looking cautiously at her eyes, which she supposed reflected a certain gleam.

'I'm more than okay. We've got ourselves a lead.'

Michelle Alison Kepler – now brunette and severely collagened – sat in the bedroom of a ritzy house in a ritzy neighborhood of Milwaukee. She was painting her nails dark plum, their color on that terrible night in April.

She was reflecting on a truth that she'd learned over the years: that people heard what they wanted to hear, saw what they wanted, believed what they wanted. But to exploit that weakness you had to be sharp, had to recognize their desires and expectations then subtly and cleverly feed them enough crumbs to make them think they were satisfied. Hard to do. But for people like Michelle it was necessary, a survival skill.

Michelle was thinking in particular of her companion that night: Deputy Brynn McKenzie.

You're their friend? . . . From Chicago? . . . I heard you and Emma worked together . . . Are you a lawyer too?

My God, what a straightman you were, Brynn.

Michelle had found herself in a tough situation back there at the house. The Feldmans were dead. She'd found the files she'd been after and destroyed them, which meant she no longer needed Hart and Lewis. But then Hart had reacted like a cat . . . and the evening went to hell.

The escape into the woods . . .

Then finding Deputy Brynn McKenzie. She knew instinct-ively just what role to play, a role that the country hick deputy could understand: rich, spoiled girl, not very likeable but with just the right touch of self-questioning doubt, a woman who'd been dumped by her husband for being exactly who that husband encouraged her to be.

Brynn would be irritated at first, but sympathetic, which is just how we feel about most people we meet under difficult circumstances. We never like victims – until we get to know them and recognize something of them within us.

Besides, the role would keep Brynn from wondering why she didn't quite seem like your typical houseguest mourning the deaths of her host and hostess, murders she'd just committed.

I wasn't lying when I said I was an actress, Brynn. I just don't act on stage or in front of the camera.

But now it was three weeks later. And things were turning around. About time. She sure deserved a break. After all the outrageous, unfair crap she'd been through on April 17 and afterward, she'd earned some good luck.

Stuffing cotton balls between the toes of her left foot, she continued the nail painting.

Yep, God or fate was back on her side. She'd finally managed to track down Hart's full name and address – he lived in Chicago, as it turned out. She'd learned, though, that he wasn't spending a lot of time there lately; he was frequently in Wisconsin, which was sobering, but expected, of course. He was looking for her as diligently as she was looking for him.

He was looking for a few other people too, and apparently he'd found one. Freddy Lancaster had stopped returning phone calls and text messages. Gordon Potts would also be on Hart's list, though he was hiding way out in Eau Claire.

Michelle was cautious but not panicked. She'd cut nearly all ties between herself and the events of April 17. Hart knew used her real name – he knew it from looking through her purse that night, of course – but locating Michelle Kepler wouldn't be easy; she always made sure of that.

Ever since her teens Michelle had been an expert at working her way into other people's lives, finagling them into taking care of her. Playing helpless, playing lost, playing sexy (with men mostly, but with women too when necessary). She was presently living with Sam Rolfe, a rich businessman in Milwaukee (nobody saw, heard or believed what he wanted to better than Sam). Her driver's license listed an old address and her mail went to a post-office box, which she'd changed first thing on April 18, no forwarding.

As for the evidence implicating her in the Lake Mondac crimes – well, there wasn't much. She'd stolen from poor Graham's truck everything that contained her fingerprints – the map she'd given Hart and her purse. And when she'd swapped boots with her poor dead 'friend,' Michelle had wiped down her Ferragamos with glass cleaner (Brynn, leaving $1700 Italian leather? God, I hate you).

Now, the evidence from Lake Mondac was no longer a threat. But one very real risk remained. It needed to be disposed of.

And that would happen today.

Michelle dried her toenails with a hair dryer, pleased with the results, though irritated that she hadn't been able to get to the salon; with Hart loose she had to limit her trips out.

She left the luxurious bedroom and stepped into the living room where Rolfe sat on the couch with her daughter, Tory, five, and her son, Bradford, a skinny boy of seven, who didn't smile much but had a wad of blond hair you just could not resist ruffling. She couldn't look at her children without her heart swelling with a mother's love.

Rolfe had a pleasant face and lips that weren't too disgusting. On the negative side, he needed to lose about forty pounds and his hair smelled of lilac, which was so gross. She also hated his tattoo. Michelle had nothing against tats in general but he had a star on his groin. A big star. The pubic hair grew through part of it and his belly covered up another part depending on how he sat.

Oh please . . .

But Michelle was no complainer if the script didn't call for complaining. Rolfe had plenty of money from his trucking company and she could put up with making her sculpted body frequently available to him in exchange for . . . well, just about anything she wanted.

Michelle was an expert at spotting the Sam Rolfes of the world – men who heard, saw and believed. If God gives you a lazy streak, a slow mind for school or a trade, expensive tastes, a pretty face and better body, then you damn well better be able to sniff out men like that the way a snake senses a confused mouse.

Of course, you had to be watchful. Always.

Now, seeing her son and Rolfe laugh at something the TV judge was saying, looking like father and son, Michelle was enraged with jealousy. She had a momentary urge to tell Rolfe to go fuck himself and to walk out the door with her children.

But she pulled back. However angry she became, which was usually red-hot angry, she was usually able to control it. Survival. She did this now and smiled, though she also thought, with some glee, No blow jobs tonight, dear.

She wondered if he'd been talking about her to the children. She sensed he had been. She'd interrogate the boy later.

'Something wrong?' he asked.

'Nothing,' she said and ushered her son off the couch and ordered him to get her a soda from the kitchen.

She watched Brad wander off. And the jealousy switched, finger snap, to overwhelming love.

Unable to have children, despite trying since she was

sixteen, Michelle Kepler had been lucky enough to befriend a single mother in Milwaukee's netherworld, on the pretext of volunteering with a nonprofit organization to help the disadvantaged.

HIV-positive from sex or drugs or both, Blanche was often sick and would leave her son and daughter in Michelle's care. Despite her prescription drug cocktails to keep AIDS at bay, the poor woman's condition worsened fast – but she could take some solace in her written agreement to name Michelle as the custodian of the children if anything happened to her.

Which was fortunate because the woman died much sooner than expected.

A sad event.

Not long after which Michelle spent some time flushing down the toilet the six months' worth of prescription AIDS medicines she'd withheld from Blanche, substituting Tylenol, Prylosec and children's vitamins (which, thriftily, she also gave to the kids).

Now these two children were hers. She loved them with all her being. Doing what they were told, adoring her, and – as the therapist told her in a court-ordered session years ago – validating an otherwise unremarkable life. But fuck the therapists; Michelle knew what she wanted. Always had.

In fact, one of the tragedies of that night in April – thanks to the unexpected appearance of Brynn's husband with a gun – was Michelle's loss of Amy, another girl she could have brought into her family. After killing Brynn and Hart (Lewis too, if Hart hadn't done that for her), she'd have slipped away with her new daughter.

But that hadn't worked out.

Add one more offense to Brynn McKenzie's charge sheet.

Michelle now glanced at Tory, who was showing a picture she'd drawn to Rolfe. Brynn thought: The fat pig's not your daddy. Don't you dare ever think he is.

It was then that her phone rang. She noted caller ID, said to Rolfe, 'I better get this.'

He nodded complacently, complimented the little girl on the picture and turned back to the TV.

Brad brought the soda for his mother. He held it out.

'Do I look like I'm on the phone?' Michelle snapped, then stepped into the bedroom. In a Latina accent she answered, 'Harborside Inn. Can I help you?'

'Hi, yes. This's Deputy McKenzie. From Kennesha County. You called about a half hour ago?'

'Oh, sure deputy. About that guest. The one with the suit-case.'

'Right. I've checked my schedule. I can be in Milwaukee about five.'

'Let's see . . . could we make it five-thirty? We have a staff meeting at five.' Michelle was pleased at her performance.

I'm really an actress . . .

'Sure. I can do that.'

She gave Brynn the address.

'I'll see you then.'

Michelle hung up. Closed her eyes. God or Fate . . . thank you.

She walked to the closet and took out a locked suitcase. Opened it. She removed her compact Glock, put it in her Coach purse. She stared out the window for a moment, feeling both nervous and exhilarated. Then she returned to the living room. She said to Rolfe, 'That was the nursing home. My aunt's taken a bad turn.' She shook her head. 'God, that poor woman. It hurts me to the bone what she's going through.'

'I'm so sorry, sweetie,' he said, looking at her tormented face.

Michelle hated the endearment. She winced. And said, 'I have to go see her.'

'You betcha . . .' He frowned. 'Who is she again?'

Cool eyes turned his way. Meaning: Are you accusing me of something, or have you forgotten my relatives? Either way, you lose.

'Sorry,' he said fast, obviously reading her expression. 'Haddie, right? That's her name. Hey, I'll drive you.'

Michelle smiled. 'That's okay. I'd rather it was Brad and me. I've got to deal with it with family, you understand.'

'Well, you betcha. It's okay for Brad to see her, you think?'

She looked at the boy. 'You want to see your auntie, don't you?' He damn well better not say that he didn't have an auntie. She held his eyes as she took the soda from his tiny hand and sipped it.

He nodded.

'I thought you did. Good.'

Brynn McKenzie gathered up her backpack and pitched out her second cocoa cup of the day.

Thought again about Graham and their first date. Then about the last time they'd been out together alone – at a woodsy club on Route 32, dancing until midnight. It was one week before she'd found out he was 'cheating'.

Why didn't you ask me to go with you? . . .

And why hadn't he asked her to a therapy session?

'Hey, B?' a woman's voice interrupted. 'How 'bout Bennigan's later?' Jane Styles, another senior deputy, continued. 'I'm meeting Reggie. Oh, and that cute guy from State Farm's going to be there. One I told you about.'

Brynn whispered, 'I'm not divorced, Jane.'

The words 'not yet' tagged along at the end of that sentence.

'I just said he was cute. That's only information. I'm not calling the caterer.'

'He sells insurance.'

'We need insurance. Nothing wrong with that.'

'Thanks, but I've got something going on. Buy a policy for me.'

'Funny.'

Thinking of Hart, thinking of the Harborside Inn in Milwaukee, Brynn McKenzie walked down a corridor she'd been up and down so often that she tended not even to see it. On the walls were pictures of deputies killed in the line of duty. There were four over the past eighty-seven years, though Eric Munce's portrait wasn't up yet. The county had the photos mounted in expensive frames. The first fatality was a deputy with a handlebar mustache. He'd been shot by a man involved in the Northfield, Minnesota, train robbery.

She passed a map of the county too, a big one, pausing and glancing at the azure blemish of Lake Mondac. She asked herself, So, is what I'm about to do now a good idea, or a bad idea?

Then she laughed. Why bother to ask the question? It doesn't matter. I've already made the decision.

She fished the keys out of her pocket and pushed outside into a beautiful, clear afternoon.

Is it true he's a killer?

That's our understanding.

Driving through a gritty neighborhood of Milwaukee toward Lake Michigan, Michelle Kepler was saying to her son, 'What you're going to do is go up to this woman and say you're lost. She'll be parked and when she gets out of her car you go up to her and say, "I'm lost." Say it.'

'I'm lost.'

'Good. I'll point her out to you. And make sure you look, you know, upset. Can you do that? You know how to look upset?'

'Uh-huh,' said Brad.

She snapped, 'Don't say you know something when you don't. Now, do you know how to look upset?'

'No.'

'Upset is what I look like when you've done something wrong and you disappoint me. You understand?'

He nodded quickly. This, he got.

'Good.' She smiled.

In downtown Milwaukee, Michelle drove past the Harborside Inn then around the block. Returned to the hotel. The parking lot was half full. It was five p.m. Brynn McKenzie wasn't due here for another half hour.

'Better work.'

'What, Mommy?'

'Shhh.'

She circled once more, then pulled into a space on the street, twenty feet from the parking lot. 'What we're going to do is when that woman drives in, she'll park somewhere there. See? . . . Good. And then you and me both get out. I'm going to go around that way, behind. You go up to her and knock on the window closest to her. Tell her you're lost. And scared. She'll get out of the car. What are you going to tell her?'

'I'm lost.'

'And?'

'Scared.'

'And what do you look like?'

'Upset.'

'Good.' She rewarded him with another big smile, tousling his hair. 'Then Mommy's going to come up and . . . talk to her for a minute, then we both run back to the car and drive home and see Sam. Do you like Sam?'

'Yeah, he's fun.'

'You like him more than you like Mommy?'

The hesitation was like a hot iron against her skin. 'No.'

She pushed the jealousy away as best she could. Time to concentrate.

Michelle studied the area. Cars passed occasionally, a customer would come out of a tavern across the street or an elderly local would amble along the sidewalk. But other than that the neighborhood was deserted.

'Now. Be quiet. And shut the radio off.'

Her phone buzzed. She read the text message, frowned. It was from a friend in Milwaukee. The words were sobering. The man had just heard, about twenty minutes ago, that Gordon Potts had been killed in Eau Claire.

freek accd't, it reported.

Michelle's face tightened. Bullshit about the accident. It was Hart's work. But it was good news for Michelle. She'd been uneasy being out in public here in Milwaukee with Hart still loose. Now at least she knew he wasn't in town at the moment.

God or Fate, smiling on her.

Then right on the dot she saw the Kennesha County Sheriff's Department car pull into the parking lot of the Harborside Inn. Her palms began sweating.

God or Fate . . .

'Okay, Brad.' Michelle popped the locks and stepped out. Her son got out of the other side. 'Mommy's going to go around there,' she whispered. 'And I'll walk up behind that woman. Don't look at me. Pretend I'm not there. You understand that?'

He nodded.

'Do not look at me when I come up to the car. Say it.'

'I won't look at you.'

'Because if you look at me, that woman will take you away and put you in jail. She's that kind of woman. I love you so much that I don't want that to happen. That's why I'm doing this for you. You know all the trouble I go to for you and your sister?'

'Yes.'

She hugged him. 'Okay, now go tell her what I said. And remember "upset".'

As the boy walked toward the car, Michelle, crouching, slipped around a row of parked cars. She pulled the Glock from the pocket of her leather jacket, a new one, bought by Sam Rolfe to replace her favorite, a really beautiful number from Neiman-Marcus, which had been totally ruined on their walk through the woods that cold night in April.

As he drove along the road in Humboldt, toward Brynn McKenzie's house, Sheriff Tom Dahl was thinking about his deputy's years in the department.

The job had been tough on Brynn, especially taking on the worst assignments, the hurt kids, the hurt wives and girlfriends – men too sometimes. Another thing had been tough too: her fellow deputies' attitudes, because she was the over-achiever, always had been. The girl in the front row, raising her hand because she knew every answer. Nobody liked that.

But, hell, she got results. Look at what she'd done that night at Lake Mondac. He didn't know another deputy who would've pushed as hard as she had.

He didn't know another deputy who would have survived.

Dahl massaged his game leg.

He parked in front of the small house; they all were on Kendall Road. It was a neat place, trim and well kept up. And, thanks to Graham, it had the hell landscaped out of it. A lot different from the others here.

He got out of the car. Stood and stretched. A joint snapped somewhere. He'd given up worrying where such sounds originated.

Tugging on his hat, a habit, Dahl walked slowly through the gate and then up the serpentine sidewalk, bordered by more kinds of plants than he knew existed.

At the door he hesitated only a moment and then rang the bell. A double chime sounded.

The door opened.

'Hey, Sheriff.'

Brynn's son stood there. Seemed he'd grown another eight inches since they'd been together last, a department Christmas party.

'Hi, Joey.' Beyond him, in the living room, Anna McKenzie was moving toward the kitchen with a cane. 'Anna.'

'Tom.'

And behind her, in the kitchen, Brynn was taking the temperature of a roasting chicken as she stood beside the stove. He hadn't thought she cooked. Even knew how. The chicken looked pretty good.

She turned and lifted an eyebrow.

'We got her, Brynn. We got her.'

They sat in the family room, sheriff and deputy.

Iced tea, courtesy of Anna, sat between them.

Brynn said, 'Took longer than I thought. Been on pins and needles.'

Which didn't begin to describe her anxiety, waiting for the news.

Sheriff Dahl explained, 'There was a complication. The teams were in place around Rolfe's house. But when she came outside she had her son with her. She took her boy to the Harborside Inn.'

'She *what*?'

'She even sent him up to the car the decoy was in while she moved around back to shoot you, well, *her*, from behind.'

'Oh, my God.'

'The tactical team didn't want to move in while Michelle and kid were together. They were afraid she'd use him as a hostage. They waited till they separated at the parking lot. The boy's fine. He's in CPS with his sister.'

Thank you, Brynn prayed silently. Thank you. 'She was going to use her own child as a diversion and then shoot me right in front of him?' Brynn could hardly believe it.

'Looks that way.'

'What's the boyfriend's story?'

'Rolfe? They're questioning him now but looks like he was in the dark. If he should be arrested for anything it's bad judgment in women.' His cell phone rang. He looked at the caller ID. 'Better take this. S'the mayor. We're holding a press conference about the whole thing. Gotta get some notes.'

He rose and stepped outside, walking stiffly to his car.

Brynn sat back in the couch, staring at the ceiling, silently thanking Stanley Mankewitz and his narrow assistant – James Jasons, she'd learned – for leading her to Michelle Kepler.

Maybe you're looking for the wrong who.

After their get-together in the bad-coffee restaurant, Brynn had looked into other motives for murdering Emma Feldman, specifically the ones suggested by Mankewitz: suicidal state politicians and the Kenosha company making dangerous hybrid car parts. Some of her other cases too. But none of them had panned out.

She then considered Jasons's comment and wondered: What if 'the wrong who' might mean not who wanted to kill her.

But who was the intended *victim*?

As soon as Brynn began to consider that Michelle had wanted *Steven* Feldman dead, not Emma, the case fell into place. Feldman was a caseworker for the city's Social Services Department, part of whose job function was checking out child abuse complaints and, in extreme cases, placing victims in foster homes.

Recalling how the young woman had silenced poor Amy that night in Marquette State Park, Brynn had wondered if he'd been investigating Michelle, with an eye toward placing children she might have.

There was no record of a file involving anyone named Michelle but Brynn had recalled that at the lake house that night Steven's backpack was empty, while a number of Emma's files were scattered on the floor. Had Michelle thrown his files, including the one about her own children, into the fireplace?

When she'd returned to Lake Mondac, Brynn had taken samples of ash from the fireplace. She intimidated the state lab in Gardener into analyzing it ASAP and learned that it was identical to ash produced by burning the manila folders issued to city workers. She also found the coiled bindings of steno pads, which Feldman had used to take notes during field interviews.

Eventually, by talking to his colleagues and friends and reviewing scraps of notes and logs of phone calls, Brynn had discovered that some neighbors of a businessman named Samuel Rolfe had complained about his new girlfriend's treatment of her young children.

The girlfriend's name was Michelle Kepler.

Bingo.

The Milwaukee police had set up surveillance around Rolfe's house but before they could get a warrant to move in, Brynn had gotten the phone call from the purported manager of the Harborside Inn. It struck her as suspicious and, after hanging up, she'd checked the incoming number. A prepaid mobile.

She was sure the 'clerk' was Michelle, setting her up to be shot.

Tom Dahl called Milwaukee PD and they put together a tactical team to collar the woman as soon as she left Rolfe's elegant house.

Only one question remained. Did Brynn want to arrest Michelle in person?

The debate raged – oh, how badly she wanted to. But she finally decided no.

A detective from the Milwaukee Police Department dressed in a Kennesha County Sheriff's Department uniform and using a department squad car drove to the rendezvous at the Harborside Inn.

Brynn McKenzie went home.

The bell rang again – Tom Dahl, ever proper – and Joey let the sheriff back into the house. He was grinning as he stood in the doorway to the family room. 'Get this. They've got reporters everywhere!' He laughed. 'Fox, CBS, and I'm not talking the local affiliates. Oh, and CNN – the mayor's wondering if everybody who works there's blond.'

Brynn laughed. 'That's the way they grow 'em in Atlanta.'

The sheriff continued, 'Michelle's being transported to our lockup tonight. You'll want to interview her, I assume.'

'You bet. But not tonight. I told you. I have plans.'

So, is what I'm about to do now a good idea, or a bad idea? . . . Why even bother to ask the question? It doesn't matter. I've already made the decision.

She'd done what she needed to capture the Feldmans' killer; now it was time to begin reassembling her life. Or trying to.

She rose and walked him to the front door. Stepping outside, he said, 'So what's going on that's so important?'

'I'm making dinner for Anna and Joey. And then we're watching *American Idol*.'

Dahl chuckled. 'It's a rerun. I can tell you who wins.'

"Night, Tom. See you in the office bright and early.'

At nine a.m. on a stormy Friday, Michelle Alison Kepler sat in one of the two interrogation rooms in the Kennesha County Sheriff's Office. Originally for storage, the rooms had been stripped of shelves and boxes and set up with fiberboard tables and plastic chairs, along with a Sony video recorder from Best Buy. One of the deputies had installed a mirror he'd bought at Home Depot but it was for effect only. Any experienced perp could see it wasn't two-way. But in Kennesha County pinching pennies was part of law enforcing.

Minus her gun, armed only with pen and paper, Brynn sat down across from Michelle. She looked over at the woman who had lied to her so ruthlessly. Yet Brynn was oddly calm. Sure, she'd felt some sting of betrayal at the deception, thinking that they'd begun that night as survivors, then become allies, and finally friends.

But Kristen Brynn McKenzie was a cop, of course. She was used to being lied to. She had a goal here, information to gather, and it was time to get to work.

Michelle, confident as ever, demanded, 'Where's my son and daughter?'

'They're being well taken care of.'

'Brynn, please . . . They need me. They'll go crazy without me. Really, this is a problem.'

'You took your son to Milwaukee to help kill me?' Brynn's voice couldn't quite hide astonishment.

Michelle's face blossomed in horror. 'No, no. We were just going to talk to you. I wanted to apologize.'

'He's seven. And you took him with you. With a gun.'

'It's for protection. Milwaukee's a dangerous town. I have a permit but I lost it.'

Brynn nodded, her face neutral. 'Okay.'

'Can I see Brad? He's miserable without me. He could get sick. He inherited my low blood sugar.'

'Wasn't he adopted?'

Michelle blinked. Then said, 'He needs me.'

'He's being well taken care of. He's fine . . . Now, you've been arrested for murder and attempted murder and assault. You've been advised of your rights. You can withdraw from this interview at any time and speak to an attorney. Do you understand what I'm saying?'

Michelle glanced at the red light on the video recorder and said, 'Yes.'

'Do you wish to have an attorney present?'

'No, I'll talk to you, Brynn.' She gave a laugh. 'After all we've been through . . . why, we're sisters, don't you feel that? I shared with you, you told me about your problems at home.' She glanced at the camera with a sympathetic wince. 'Your son, your husband . . . We're like soul mates. That's pretty rare, Brynn. Really.'

'So, you're waiving your right to an attorney?'

'Absolutely. This is all a misunderstanding. I can explain everything.' Her voice was soft, reflecting the burden of the injustice that had befallen her.

'Now, why we're here,' Brynn began. 'We'd like a statement

from you, telling the truth about what happened that night. It'll be much easier on you, on your family—'

'What *about* my family?' she snapped. 'You didn't talk to them, did you? My parents?'

'Yes.'

'You didn't have any right to do that.' Then she calmed and gave a hurt smile. 'Why'd you do that? They hate me. They lied to you, whatever they said. They're jealous of me. I was on my own from day one. I made a success of my life. They're losers.'

Brynn's research had revealed that this was a woman whose background appeared normal and stable but whose personality was not. She'd grown up in a middle-class family in Madison, Wisconsin. Her parents still lived there, mother fifty-seven, father ten years older. According to them, they'd tried hard but had thrown up their hands at what Michelle's mother called the 'vindictive little thing'. Her father called her 'dangerous'.

The couple, horrified at what their daughter was accused of, though not completely surprised, explained how Michelle had made a career out of jumping from man to man – and in two cases a woman – living off them, then picking fights and scaring the hell out of her lovers with her enraged, vengeful behavior; ultimately they were grateful to see her go. Then she'd be on to someone else – but only if she had that someone else all lined up ahead of time. She'd been arrested for assault twice – attacking boyfriends who'd dumped her. She'd stalked several men and had three restraining orders in force.

Michelle now said, 'You can't trust anything my family says. I was abused, you know.'

'There's no record of that.'

'How's there going to be a record? You think my father would admit it? And they threw out my complaint. My father and the local police chief, they were in on it together. All I could do was get away. I had to fend for myself. It was hard for me, so hard. Nobody ever helped me.'

'It'll be easier,' Brynn continued, deflecting the woman's sob story, 'if you cooperate. There're still a few things we'd like to know.'

'I wasn't going to hurt you,' she whined. 'I just wanted to talk.'

'You pretended to be the hotel clerk. You changed your voice to sound Hispanic.'

'Because you wouldn't understand. Nobody understands me. If I'd been me, somebody would have arrested me and I'd never have the chance to explain. I need you to understand, Brynn. It's important to me.'

'You had a weapon.'

'Those men at the house . . . they tried to kill me! I was scared. I've been the victim of attacks before. My father, a couple of boyfriends. I have restraining orders out.'

She'd filed complaints against several lovers for domestic assault but the magistrates had rejected them when the police determined that the men had solid alibis, and concluded that Michelle had filed out of spite.

'You have three orders against *you*.'

She smiled. 'That's how the system works. They believe the abuser. They don't believe the victim.'

'Let's talk about the night of April seventeenth.'

'Oh, I can explain that.'

'Go ahead.'

'I was scheduled to have a meeting with Steven Feldman, the caseworker. I suspected Brad had been abused by one of his teachers.'

'Okay. Was this reported anywhere?'

'That's what I was going to meet with Mr Feldman about. I took the afternoon off work and went to see him but there was a problem with the buses and by the time I got to his office he'd left for the night. I knew it was important and I found out he was going to his place in Lake Mondac. He told me to come see him anytime to talk about Brad. He gave me his address. So I asked this guy I knew, Hart, to drive me up there. That was my mistake.' She shook her head.

'What's his full name?'

'That's it. He only goes by Hart. Anyway, he brought his friend along, Compton Lewis. Disgusting . . . gross. I should've said no right there. But I really wanted to see to Steve. So we all drove up to the house together. I was going to talk to Steven and then we were going to leave. But as we're driving up there, they start getting weirder and weirder. They're like, "Bet there's some nice shit in these houses." And, "Gotta be some rich people here." Next thing I know they see the Mercedes and they pull out guns, and I'm like, shit, oh, no. They go inside and start shooting. I tried to stop them. I grabbed this gun—'

'That compact Glock in your possession was stolen from a gun show a half mile from where you lived with Sam Rolfe.'

'It was *their* gun!' Michelle lowered her hands to her face, crying or pretending to.

'Would you like some coffee? A soda?'

Some crackers for your low blood sugar . . . like the one you scattered behind to lead Hart and his partner after us? Brynn kept a completely neutral face.

Michelle looked up. Eyes red, face dry. It reminded Brynn of how she'd looked throughout much of that April night.

I'm an actress . . .

Brother, what I bought into.

Michelle continued, 'I was devastated. I couldn't breathe I felt so terrible. Here it was, my fault. I'd brought those men up there. I can't tell you how bad I felt . . . I panicked. Sure, I lied a little. But who wouldn't? I was scared. And then I see you in the wilderness. Sure, I had the gun. But I didn't know who you were. Maybe you were with them. You had your uniform on. But you could have been part of it. I didn't know what was going on. I was just scared. I had to lie. My life has always been about survival.

'And what I feel worst about – I couldn't believe I did it: at your house. I had a panic attack. I was so scared . . . It was post-traumatic stress. I've always suffered from that. I thought Hart had gotten into your house . . . You came downstairs and scared me. The gun went off. It was an accident! I'll live with that forever. Hurting your mother by accident.'

Brynn crossed her legs and looked at the waifish, beautiful woman, whose eyes now filled with tears.

An Academy Award performance . . .

'The evidence and witnesses tell a little different story, Michelle.' And she gave the woman a synopsis of how they'd come to learn her identity and what they knew of her plan. The ballistics, the ash in the fireplace, Steven Feldman's phone records, the reports of her children being abused.

'I talked to Social Services myself, Michelle. Steven Feldman's supervisor. And to the witnesses and your son's teacher. Brad regularly had bruises on his arms and legs. Your daughter, Tory, had marks too.'

'Oh, they have an accident or two. You take a child into the emergency room and right away you're an abusive parent. I've never beaten him . . . Oh, what a politically correct world this is,' she snapped. 'Everybody swats their kids. Don't you?'

'No.'

'Well, you should.' She was smiling cruelly. 'Maybe you wouldn't be having so much trouble with Joey, like you were telling me. And you let him get away with it. *My* son won't get run over by a car or break his neck skateboarding . . . Children need direction. They don't respect you if you're not firm. And they want to respect their parents.'

Brynn now said, 'Michelle, let me run through the case

that we've got against you.' She rattled off summaries of expert testimony, witness statements and forensic evidence. It was overwhelming.'

The woman began to cry. 'It's not my fault! It isn't!'

Brynn reached over and shut off the camera.

The woman looked up cautiously. She dried her eyes.

'Michelle,' Brynn said softly, 'here's the situation. You heard the case against you. You will be convicted. There is no doubt in anyone's mind about that. If you don't cooperate you'll go into a ten-by-four cell, solitary confinement, forever. But if you do cooperate you'll stay out of a super prison, probably go to medium security. You may have the chance to see life outside before you're too old to appreciate it.'

'Can I see my children? I'll agree if I can see my children.'

'No,' Brynn said firmly. 'That's not in their interest.'

This troubled Michelle for a moment but then she asked brightly, 'A nicer cell? I'll get a nicer cell?'

'Yes.'

'And all I have to do is confess?'

'Well, that's part of it,' replied Brynn, as Michelle stared at the place on the camera where the glowing red eye had been.

Brynn McKenzie sat in the lunchroom of the Kennesha County Sheriff's Department, opposite Tom Dahl, who was reading through the transcript of the interview. The chairs were small, almost like the chairs at Joey's school. Dahl's body overhung his considerably. Brynn's did not. Her issue was tummy, not thigh.

Brynn was looking over her upside-down notes and the transcript.

Dahl startled her by slapping the transcript and looking up. 'Well, you got yourself a confession. Good job. And won't cost us much in terms of a plea. She'll go into Sanford? Medium-sec?'

'No furloughs, though. She sees the kids only if the social worker okays it.'

'And twenty-five minimum, no parole.'

Dahl ate some macaroni. 'You're not hungry?'

'No.'

'What about Hart? She say anything about him?'

'Hardly a word.'

'Maybe he's just gone away.'

She laughed. 'I don't think people like him do that. They

may hide out for a while but they don't beam themselves off the planet, like *Star Wars*.'

'That was *Star Trek*. TV show. Before your time.'

Brynn said, 'Well, too bad he can't. Somebody better find him fast, the FBI or Minneapolis PD or somebody. For his own sake.'

'Why's that?'

'Apparently he's on a few lists. He's done work for a lot of people who don't want him caught – professional hits and robberies, extortion. Now that word's out that he might get collared for the Lake Mondac thing, they're afraid he'll roll over. And Compton Lewis's family aren't real happy either about what happened to their kin.'

Dahl looked at her notes. She studied his baby skin. His face looks younger than mine, even subtracting the broken jaw and the buckshot wound.

Where's the justice in life?

'Why'd a pro like Hart get involved in something small like this, with the Kepler woman?' Dahl asked. 'Money? Sex? That woman wasn't ugly.'

'You don't think so?'

The sheriff laughed.

Brynn said, 'Don't think either of those would've swayed him. You want my opinion? He was bored.'

'Bored?'

'He was between jobs. It came along. He wanted a rush.'

Dahl nodded and wasn't smiling when he said, 'You,' pointing a dramatic finger at her.

She blinked. 'Me?'

'Just like you.' The sheriff waved his arm around the department. 'Well, you don't exactly do this for the money. You like the excitement, don'tcha?'

'I do it 'cause I love my boss.'

'Heh. So what's next? You're going after Hart, I assume. I need to beg the county supervisor for a budget increase?'

'Nope. I'm leaving the whole thing to the state police to follow up on.'

Dahl stopped the massage. 'You are?'

'We've got enough going on here.'

'Am I hearing this right?'

'They find Hart. I'll interview him, you bet I will. But I've done my bit. Anyway, you need somebody on the ground in the perp's turf. It's local contacts that solve cases.'

'You just wanted to say that. "On the ground." Okay, ship everything to the state boys. You're sure about this?'

'I am.'

A deputy stuck his head into the lunchroom. 'Hey, Brynn. Sorry to bother your lunch.'

'Yeah?'

'We just brought that guy in, the one hanging around the schools. You want to talk to him? You said you did.'

'Sure. What'd you get him for?'

'Fly was undone.'

'He waive his rights?'

'Yep. He has an explanation.'

Dahl guffawed. 'Sure he's got an explanation – he's a goddamn pervert.'

Brynn told him, 'I'll be right there.'

The tall man with broad shoulders and a crew cut was standing on the ladder leaning against the old but well-maintained colonial house in a pretty neighborhood south of Humboldt. It was a clear, cool Saturday morning and tasks like this were being replayed at thousands and thousands of homes around the country.

The man was painting the shutters dark green. Funny, Brynn reflected, in her ten years of living here, she'd always thought that green would be a pleasant color for the trim, but never wondered why. Now she understood. The house was set against a verdant pine forest, a shining example of the word 'evergreen'. She'd seen the trees every day but had never really been aware of them.

Glancing over his shoulder as the Camry approached, he hesitated, caught in mid-brushstroke, then slowly climbed down off the ladder. He set the paint bucket on the work table he had set up and wrapped the brush in plastic, so the latex enamel wouldn't dry on the bristles. Keith Marshall was forever meticulous.

Brynn braked to a stop in front of the garage. Joey climbed out and grabbed his suitcase from the backseat.

'Hi, Dad!'

Keith hugged his son, who tolerated the gesture and charged into the house. 'Bye, Mom!'

'I'll pick you up after school on Monday!'

'Don't forget the cookies!'

Her ex-husband started to say something but seemed to forget what it was, as Brynn shut the engine off and climbed out. In the past two years she'd never spent more than sixty seconds here when dropping Joey off for a visit with his father.

'Hello,' she said.

Keith nodded. His hair was flecked with a bit of gray but he hadn't gained a pound in the past ten years. What a metabolism that man had. Well, there was the sports too.

He strode over to her, gave her a brief hug. Not too hard, not too soft. And she was reminded of his good side, of which there was much. He was a cowboy, of course, but in the classic sense of a movie hero, not like poor Eric Munce, whose idea of policing wasn't confidence and quiet, but hardware and drama.

'So. How've you been?' she asked.

'Not bad. Busy. Get you anything?'

She shook her head. Looked up at the side of the house. 'Good color.'

'Had a sale at Home Depot.'

'What're you two up to this weekend?'

'Fishing. Then we're going over to the Bogles' barbecue tonight. Joey likes Clay.'

'He's a good boy.'

'Yeah, he is. His father's got some lacrosse gear. We're going to try it out.'

'Is there a sport that boy doesn't like?' Brynn smiled. 'You playing too?'

'Thought I might try it.'

'I'm riding again.'

'Are you?'

'When I can. Once a week or so.'

She and Keith had gone to a nearby stable a few times. He wasn't, though, a natural equestrian.

'I took Joey last time. He was good. Hates the helmet.'

'That's Joey. I'll make sure he wears one – and the face guard – at lacrosse.' Keith then looked away. 'We're just going on our own, us two boys.'

After all these years, divorced and the past buried if not wholly dust, Keith still seemed guilty about dating. She found this amusing. And charming.

'How's the State Police?'

'Same old same old. I heard they got that woman. The one you saved that night.'

The one I saved . . . 'That's one way to put it. She took a plea.'

'Was it as bad as the rumors?'

As soon as he'd heard about the events at Lake Mondac, Keith had called to find out if Brynn was all right. Graham had answered – she was out – and, though the men were always civil to each other, Keith had kept the conversation short, content to learn that she was safe. The rest of the information he would have gotten from the news and his law enforcement connections.

As they leaned against the front porch railing she now gave him the details. Some of them at least. He lifted an eyebrow. He was most interested, curiously, not in the gunplay, the bolos or the spear but in the compass. 'You made that?'

'Yep.'

He gave one of his rare smiles and wanted to know the details.

There was silence for a time, heavy and hot. When it was obvious she wasn't getting into the car and leaving, as usual, Keith said, 'I put a new deck on.'

'Joey told me.'

'Want to see it?'

'Sure.'

He led her around to the back of the house.

The last weekend of May, Terry Hart walked into a tavern in Old Town, in Chicago, near North Avenue, on Wells. The neighborhood was different from when he'd first moved here, in the seventies. Safer but a lot less atmospheric. Professionals had pushed out the old-time locals, the transient hotel dwellers, the folk singers and jazz musicians, drunks and prostitutes. Fancy wine and cheese shops and organic groceries had replaced the IGA and package stores. The Earl of Old Town, the great folk club, was gone, though the comedy venue Second City was still here, and probably would be forever.

The bar Hart was now striding into was born after the folk era but was still antique, dating to the disco craze. The time was just past 2:30, Saturday afternoon, and there were five people inside, three at the bar with one stool between them. Protocol among drinking strangers. The other two were at a table, a couple in their sixties. The wife wore a brimmed red hat and was missing a front tooth.

Living underground for a month and a half, Hart had grown lonely for his neighborhood and his city. He also missed working. But now that Michelle Kepler was in jail and his contact told him she'd given up trying to have him killed, he was comfortable surfacing and getting back to his life. Apparently, to his shock, she hadn't dimed him out during her interrogations.

Hart dropped down heavily on a stool.

'My God, Terry.' The round bartender shook his hand. 'Been a month of Sundays since you been in here.'

'Away on some work.'

'Whereabouts? What do you want?'

'Smirnie and grapefruit. And a burger, medium. No fries.'

'You got it. So where?'

'New England. Then a while in Florida.'

The bartender got the drink and carried the square of greasy green paper with Hart's order on it to a window into the kitchen, hung it up and rang a bell. A dark brown hand appeared, grabbed the slip then vanished. The bartender returned.

'Florida. Last time I was there, the wife and I went, we sat on the deck all day long. Didn't go to the beach till the last day. I liked the deck better. We went out to eat a lot. Crab. Love those crabs. Where were you?'

'Some place. You know, near Miami.'

'Us too. Miami Beach. You didn't get much of a tan, Terry.'

'Never do that. Not good for you.' He drained the liquor.

'Right you are.'

'I'll have another.' He pushed the glass toward the bartender. Looked around the place. He sipped the new drink. It was strong. Afternoon pours were big. A few minutes later the bell rang again and his burger appeared. He ate part of it slowly. 'So, Ben, everything good around town?'

'Yeah, I guess.'

'Anybody come in here asking about me?'

'Ha.'

'What, ha?'

'Like a line out of some movie. James Garner. Or some detective, you know. A P.I.'

Hart smiled, sipped his drink. Then ate more, with his left hand. He was using that arm, the shot one, for everything he could. The muscle had atrophied but was coming back. Just that day he'd finished with triple-0 steel wool on the box he'd started up in Wisconsin, using his left hand for most of the work. It was really beautiful. He was proud of the thing.

The bartender said, 'Nobody while I was here. Expecting somebody?'

'I never know what to expect.' A grin. 'How's that for a P.I. line?'

'You got a haircut.'

It was much shorter. A businessman's trim.

'Looks good.'

Hart grunted.

The man went off to refill somebody else's drink. Hart was thinking: If people drink liquor during the day it's usually vodka. And mixed with something else. Sweet or sour. Nobody drinks martinis in the afternoon. Why was that?

He wondered if Brynn McKenzie was eating lunch at that moment. Did she generally? Or did she skimp during the day and plan a big family dinner?

Which put him in mind of her husband. Graham Boyd.

Hart wondered if they'd talked about getting back together. He doubted it. Graham's place, a nice town house about four miles from Brynn's, didn't look very temporary. Not like Hart's apartment, when he'd broken up with his wife. He'd just crashed and hadn't gotten around to fixing up the place for months. He thought back to being with Brynn in that van, next to the meth cooker's camper. He'd never answered her question, the implicit one when she'd glanced at his hand: Are you married? Never answered it directly. Felt bad, in a funny way.

No lies between us . . .

The bartender'd said something.

'What?'

'That okay, Terry? Done right?'

'Yeah, thanks.'

'No problem.'

ESPN was on the tube. Sports highlights. Hart finished his lunch.

The bartender collected the plate and silverware. 'So you seeing anybody, Terry?' he asked, making bartender conversation.

Looking at the TV, Hart said, 'Yeah, I have been.' Surprising himself.

'No, shit. Who?'

'This woman I met in April.' He didn't know why he was saying this. He supposed because it made him feel good.

'Bring her in here sometime.'

'Ah, think we're breaking up.'

'How come?'

'She doesn't live around here.'

The bartender grimaced. 'Yeah, I hear that. Long distance. I had a stint in the reserves and Ellie and me were apart for six months. That was tough. We'd just started going out. And the fucking governor calls me up. When you're married it's one thing, you can be away. But just going out with somebody. . . . it sucks to commute.'

'Sure does.'

'Where is she?'

'Wisconsin.'

The bartender paused, sensing a joke. 'For real?'

A nod.

'I mean, it's not like we're talking L.A. or Samoa, Terry.'

'There're other problems.'

'Man and woman, there're always other problems.'

Hart was thinking, Why do so many bartenders say things in a way that sounds like it's the final word on a subject?

'We're like Romeo and Juliet.'

The bartender lowered his voice. He understood. 'She's Jewish, huh?'

Hart laughed. 'No. Not religion. It's her job more.'

'Keeps her too busy, right? Never gets home? You ask me, that's bullshit. Women oughta stay home. I'm not saying after the kids are grown, she can't go back part time. But it's the way God meant it to be.'

'Yeah,' Hart said, thinking how Brynn McKenzie would respond to that.

'So. That's it between you guys?'

His chest thudded. 'Probably. Yeah.'

The bartender looked away, as if he'd seen something troubling in Hart's eyes – either scary or sad. Hart wondered which. 'Well, you'll meet somebody else, Terry.' The man lifted his soda, which had some rum 'accidentally' spilled into it.

Hart offered his own bartenderism, 'One way or the other, life goes on, doesn't it?'

'I—'

'There's no answer, Ben. I'm just talking.' Hart gave a grin. 'Gotta finish packing. What's the damage here?'

The bartender tallied it up. Hart paid. 'Anybody comes around asking for me, let me know. Here's a number.'

He jotted down a prepaid mobile he used for voice mail only.

Pocketing the twenty-dollar tip, Ben said, 'P.I.'s, huh?'

Hart smiled again. He looked around the place and then headed out.

The door eased shut behind him as he stepped onto the sidewalk, the late May brilliant. The wind usually didn't blow in from Lake Michigan but Hart thought he could smell the ripe scent of water on the cool breeze.

He pulled on sunglasses, thinking back to that night in April, thinking about the absence of light in Marquette State Park. There was no such thing as a single darkness, he'd learned there. There were hundreds of different shades – and textures and shapes too. Grays and blacks there weren't even words to describe. Darkness as plentiful as types of woods, and with as many different grains. He supposed that if –

The first bullet struck him in his back, high and right. It exited, spattering his cheek with blood and tissue. He gasped, more startled than hurt, and looked down at the mess of the wound in his chest. The second entered the back of his head. The third sailed inches over him, as he dropped, and cracked obliquely into the window of the tavern. The glass began to cascade toward the ground.

Limp, Hart collided hard but silently with the sidewalk. Window shards flowed around him. One of the bigger sheets cut his ear nearly off. Another sliced through his neck and the blood began to flow in earnest.

'Morning,' Tom Dahl said.

He was standing in Brynn's cubicle, holding his coffee mug in one hand and two donuts in the other. Cheryl from reception had brought them. They rotated the duty. Every Monday, somebody brought pastry. To take the sting out of coming back to work maybe. Or maybe it was one of those traditions that had started for no reason and kept going because there was no reason to stop it.

She nodded.

'How was your weekend?' the sheriff asked.

'Good,' she said. 'Joey was with his dad. Mom and I met Rita and Megan for brunch after church. We went to Brighton's.'

'The buffet?'

'Yep.'

'They do a good spread there,' Dahl said reverently.

'Was nice.'

'So's the one at the Marriott. They have an ice statue swan. Gotta get there early. It melts down to a duck by two.'

'I'll keep that in mind,' Brynn said. 'You guys do anything fun?'

'Not really. In-laws over. That father of hers . . . man is skinny as your pencil. Had three helpings of chicken and before we were done he was dunking his bread in the mushroom soup at the bottom of Carole's green bean casserole. I mean, for pity's sake.'

'That's a good casserole,' said Brynn, who'd had it several times.

'God made serving spoons for a reason.' Dahl glanced down at the donut balancing on a paper plate atop his coffee mug. 'Krispy Kreme today. I myself am partial to the ones you bring.'

'Dunkin Donuts.'

'Right. They don't make 'em with that little knob anymore, do they?'

'I don't know, Tom. I just ask for three dozen. They mix 'em up for me.'

She kept waiting.

He said, 'So. You heard, didn't you?'

'Heard?'

He frowned. 'Milwaukee PD called. That detective working on the Lake Mondac case?'

'Nobody called me.' She lifted an eyebrow.

'Hart was killed.'

'What?'

'Looked gangland. Shot in the back of the head. North side of Chicago. That's where he lived, it turned out.'

'Well. How 'bout that.' Brynn sat back, eyed her own coffee. She'd seen the donuts but hadn't given in.

'You were right. Man had some enemy or another.'

'Any leads?'

'Not many.'

'They find out anything about him?'

Dahl told her what Chicago PD had relayed to Milwaukee: Terrance Hart was a security consultant, with an office in Chicago. He made $93,043 last year. He would provide risk assessments to warehouse and manufacturing companies and arrange for security guards. Never been arrested, never been the subject of any criminal investigation, paid his taxes on time.

'Man traveled a lot, though. A lot.' The sheriff said this as if that alone was a cause for suspicion.

Dahl added that he'd been married briefly, no kids.

Marriage doesn't suit me. Does it suit you, Brynn?

His parents lived in Pennsylvania. He had one younger sibling, a brother who was now a doctor.

'A doctor?' Brynn frowned.

'Yeah. The family was pretty normal. Which you wouldn't expect. But Hart himself was always living on the edge. In trouble at school a lot. But, like I said, no arrests. Kept up a good front. His company's done okay. And, get this, he was a woodworker. I mean, high-class stuff. Furniture, not just the bookshelves I hammer together. Had this sign above his work-bench, what a teacher of mine told me: "Measure twice, cut once." Not your typical hit man.'

'What was the story with the shooting?'

'Pretty simple. He'd moved back to his town house from Green Bay, where he'd been hiding out. But with Michelle away there was no reason not to go home. He went to one of his old hangouts for lunch on Saturday afternoon. Walked out and somebody got him from behind.'

'Any witnesses?'

'Not really. Everybody in the bar hit the deck as soon as the gunplay started. Chicago, after all. Nobody could tell the cops anything concrete. Street was deserted. A few cars took off fast. No tag or IDs.' He paused. 'There's a connection here.'

'Here?' Brynn asked, watching him take a bite of the fried dough, as crumbs parachuted to the faded carpet.

'Well, Wisconsin. The ballistics on the slugs match a weapon might've been used in a shooting in that gas station thing over in Smith about six months ago? Exxon. The clerk nearly got killed.'

'I don't remember.'

'The State Police handled it. Nobody here was involved.'

'The same gun?'

'They think. But who knows? That ballistics' stuff. Not as easy as *CSI* makes it look.'

Brynn said, 'So the perp here ditched the gun and somebody found it and it got sold on the street.'

'Guess so.'

'Recycling at its worst.'

'Amen.'

Brynn sat back, made a bridge across the top of her coffee mug with a skinny wood stirrer. 'What else, Tom? Looks like there's more.'

Dahl hesitated. 'Guess I should say. Hart had your name in a notebook in his pocket. And your address too. And in the apartment they found some other things. Pictures.'

'Pictures?'

'Digital ones he'd printed out. Of the outside of the house. Taken recent. You could see the spring buds. The pictures were in this wooden box – a fancy one. Looks like he made it himself.'

'Well.'

A long sigh. 'And I have to say, there were some of Joey's school too.'

'No. Of Joey?'

'Just the school. I was thinking he might've been staking it out to get a feel for your schedule . . . In his apartment he had a suitcase being packed. Inside was a weapon and a sound suppressor. I've never see one of those. Except in the movies. I thought they were called silencers but the detective called them a suppressor.'

She was nodding slowly. Kept stirring coffee that didn't need it.

'We'll take your house off the special patrol route, if you're comfortable with that.'

'Sure. Sounds like everything's accounted for, Tom.'

'It is. Case closed. I don't think I ever said that, not in fourteen years.' Clutching his breakfast he wandered back to his office.

Chestnut hair pinned up, a concession to a surprise Wisconsin heat wave, Kristen Brynn McKenzie was walking past a dozen pines, round and richly green. Sweat blossomed under the arms of her tan uniform blouse and trickled down her spine. She was looking at the plants, studying them closely. They weren't much taller than she was. As she moved along she lowered her hand and let it drag across the three-inch needles. They yielded without prickling.

She paused and looked at them.

Recalling, of course, April. She'd been thinking a lot about those twelve hours in Marquette State Park, remembering with odd clarity the sights and smells and feel of the trees and plants that had saved her life. And that had nearly ended it.

Why, she wondered, gazing at pines, would they have evolved this way, these shapes and shades, some the color of green Jell-O, some the shade of Home Depot shutters? Why were these needles long and soft, and why had barberry brambles, where Amy's toy, Chester, was entombed, developed those terrible thorns?

Thinking of the foliage, the trees, the leaves. Wood alive and wood dead and decaying.

Brynn continued on, found herself next to several huge camellias, the blossoms widely unfolded from their tight pods, cradled in waxy green leaves. The petals were red, the color of bright blood, and her heart tapped a bit at that. She kept walking. Now past azaleas and ligustrum and crape myrtle, ferns, hibiscus, wisteria.

Then she turned the corner and a short, dark-complexioned man holding a hose blinked in surprise and said, 'Buenos dias, Mrs McKenzie.'

'Morning, Juan. Where is he? I saw his truck.'

'In the shed.'

She walked past several piles of mulch, fifteen feet high. A worker in a Bobcat was stirring it, to prevent spontaneous combustion. It could actually smolder up a storm of smoke if you didn't. The rich smell surrounded her. She continued on to the shed, really a small barn, and walked through the open door.

'I'll be with you in a second,' Graham Boyd said, looking up from a workbench. He was wearing safety goggles and, she realized, seeing only her silhouette. He'd be thinking she was a customer. He returned to his task. She noted that the carpentry was part of an expansion project and he seemed to be doing the work himself. That was Graham. Even after he'd moved the last of his things out of their house he'd returned to finish the kitchen tiling. And had done a damn good job of it.

Then he was looking up again. Realizing who she was. He set the board down and took the goggles off. 'Hi.'

She nodded.

He frowned. 'Everything okay with Joey?'

'Oh, sure fine.'

He joined her. They didn't embrace. He squinted, looking at her cheek.

'You had that surgery?'

'Vanity.'

'You can't see a thing. How's it feel?'

'Inside's tender. Have to watch what I eat.' She looked around the building. 'You're expanding.'

'Just doing what should've been done a long time ago. Anna says she's doing better. I called.'

'She said. More house-ridden than she needs to be. The doctors want her to walk more. I want her out more too.' She laughed.

'And Joey's been off skateboards, unless law enforcement's present, hmm? Grandma gave me a report.'

'That's a capital crime in the house now. And I've got spies. They tell me he's clean. He's really into lacrosse now.'

'I saw that special. About Michelle Kepler and the murders.'

'On WKSP. That's right.'

'There were some cops from Milwaukee. They said *they*'d arrested her. You didn't even get mentioned. Not by name.'

'I didn't go along for the party. I was off that night.'

'You?'

She nodded.

'Didn't they interview you, at least? The reporters?'

'What do I need publicity for?' Brynn was suddenly awkward, her face burned like that of a middle-school girl alone at a dance. She thought back to her very first traffic stop. She'd been so nervous she'd returned to her squad car without handing the driver his copy of the ticket. He'd politely called her back and asked for it.

Nervous now, nervous all last night – after her mother had said she'd 'run into' Graham at the senior center, and Brynn had stopped her cold.

'*So, come on, Mom. What is this, a campaign to get us back together?*'

'*Hell, yes, and it's one I aim to win.*'

'*It's not that easy. Not that simple.*'

'When've you ever wanted easy? Your brother and sister, yes. Not you.'

'Okay, I was thinking about going to see him.'

'Tomorrow.'

'I'm not ready.'

'Tomorrow.'

A worker stuck his head in and asked Graham a question. He answered, speaking in Spanish. All Brynn caught were the words for 'in the middle.'

He turned back, said nothing.

Okay. Now.

'Just wondering,' she said. 'I'm on break. You've been up since six, I'll bet. And I've been up since six. Just wondered if you wanted to get coffee. Or something.'

And, she was thinking, to spend some time talking.

Telling him more about what happened that night in April.

And telling him a lot of other things too. Whatever he'd listen to, she'd tell him.

Just like a few weeks ago when she'd sat in the backyard with Keith and done the same. Part confession, part apology, part just plain talking. Her ex, though cautious at first, had been pleased to listen. She wondered if her present husband would. She surely hoped he would.

Several heartbeats of pause. 'Sure,' he said. 'Let me finish this board. Okay. I'll be at the diner.'

Graham turned away. And then stopped. He looked back at her, shook his head, frowning.

Brynn McKenzie found herself nodding. She understood. Understood completely.

Graham Boyd had been flustered at first, seeing her just appear like this. He'd agreed impulsively, not knowing what to make of her invitation. Now, reality had returned. He was recalling his own anger and pain from that night in April. And from the months leading up to it.

He had no interest in whatever she was up to here.

Ah, well, she couldn't blame him one bit. The moment for conversations of the sort she had planned had come and gone long ago.

Flawed jaw set and fixed cheek taut, Brynn gave a wan smile. But before she could say, 'That's okay,' Graham was explaining, 'I'm not really into the diner much anymore. There's a new place in the mall opened up. Coffee's a lot better. Pretty good hot chocolate too.'

She blinked. 'Where is it?'

'Downstairs, next to Sears. I'll be ten minutes.'

About the Author

A former journalist, folksinger and attorney, Jeffery Deaver is an international number-one bestselling author. His novels have appeared on a number of bestseller lists around the world, including *The New York Times, The Times* of London and *The Los Angeles Times*. His books are sold in 150 countries and translated into 25 languages. The author of twenty-five novels and two collections of short stories, he's been awarded the Steel Dagger and Short Story Dagger from the British Crime Writers' Association, is a three-time recipient of the Ellery Queen Reader's Award for Best Short Story of the Year and is a winner of the British Thumping Good Read Award. His thriller *The Cold Moon* won a Grand prix from the Japanese Adventure Fiction Association and was named Book of the Year by the Mystery Writers Association of Japan.

He's been nominated for six Edgar Awards from the Mystery Writers of America, an Anthony Award and a Gumshoe Award. His book *A Maiden's Grave* was made into an HBO movie starring James Garner and Marlee Matlin, and his novel *The Bone Collector* was a feature release from Universal Pictures, starring Denzel Washington and Angelina Jolie. His most recent books are *The Broken Window, The Sleeping Doll, The Cold*

Moon, *The Twelfth Card* and *More Twisted: Collected Stories, Volume II*. And, yes, the rumors are true, he did appear as a corrupt reporter on his favorite soap opera, *As the World Turns*.

Roadside Crosses, the second in the series featuring Kathryn Dance, who had her book-length debut in last year's *The Sleeping Doll*, publishes in July 2009 and the next Lincoln Rhyme novel in 2010.

Readers can visit Jeffery Deaver's website at www.jefferydeaver.com.

The new Lincoln Rhyme thriller

The
BROKEN WINDOW

Jeffery
DEAVER

He is watching you.

He knows you, better than you know yourself.
And he is using his knowledge to plan your death.

But you are not his only victim.
He is also watching your killer.

He is about to get away with the perfect murder . . .

Out now

HODDER

The new Kathryn Dance thriller

ROADSIDE CROSSES

Jeffery
DEAVER

A highway patrol trooper notices something strange on the side of
the road: a homemade cross, fashioned as a memorial. Except the
date being 'remembered' is the following day – the day the police
find a kidnapped teenage girl in the trunk of a car, left for dead.

Special Agent Kathryn Dance, the kinesics expert with the
California Bureau of Investigation, is on the case. The teenage
victim points her to an online community where bullying is rife.
It looks as though one teen has finally snapped.

Then further crosses appear. Now Dance must race against the
clock to find the attacker before he can carry out his deadly plans
for revenge . . . in the cyber world and the real.

Out now

HODDER &
STOUGHTON